By Carole Nelson Douglas from Tom Doherty Associates

MYSTERY

MIDNIGHT LOUIE MYSTERIES

Catnap
Pussyfoot
Cat on a Blue Monday
Cat in a Crimson Haze
Cat in a Diamond Dazzle
Cat with an Emerald Eye
Cat in a Flamingo Fedora
Cat in a Golden Garland
Cat on a Hyacinth Hunt
Cat in an Indigo Mood
Cat in a Jeweled Jumpsuit
Cat in a Kiwi Con
Cat in a Leopard Spot
Cat in a Midnight Choir
Cat in a Neon Nightmare
Cat in an Orange Twist
Cat in a Hot Pink Pursuit
Cat in a Quicksilver Caper
Cat in a Red Hot Rage
Cat in a Sapphire Slipper
Cat in a Topaz Tango
Cat in an Ultramarine Scheme
Cat in a Vegas Gold Vendetta
Cat in a White Tie and Tails
Cat in an Alien X-Ray
Midnight Louie's Pet
    Detectives (anthology)

IRENE ADLER ADVENTURES

Good Night, Mr. Holmes
The Adventuress* (Good
    Morning, Irene)
A Soul of Steel* (Irene at
    Large)
Another Scandal in
    Bohemia*(Irene's Last
    Waltz)
Chapel Noir
Castle Rouge
Femme Fatale
Spider Dance

Marilyn: Shades of Blonde
    (anthology)

HISTORICAL ROMANCE

Amberleigh†
Lady Rogue†
Fair Wind, Fiery Star

SCIENCE FICTION

Probe†
Counterprobe†

FANTASY

TALISWOMAN

Cup of Clay
Seed Upon the Wind

SWORD & CIRCLET

Six of Swords
Exiles of the Rynth
Keepers of Edanvant
Heir of Rengarth
Seven of Swords

* These are the reissued editions
† Also mystery

Cat in an Alien X-Ray

A MIDNIGHT LOUIE MYSTERY

Carole Nelson Douglas

A TOM DOHERTY ASSOCIATES BOOK
NEW YORK

This is a work of fiction. All of the characters, organizations, and events portrayed in this novel are either products of the author's imagination or are used fictitiously.

CAT IN AN ALIEN X-RAY

Copyright © 2013 by Carole Nelson Douglas

All rights reserved.

A Forge Book
Published by Tom Doherty Associates, LLC
175 Fifth Avenue
New York, NY 10010

www.tor-forge.com

Forge® is a registered trademark of Tom Doherty Associates, LLC.

ISBN 978-0-7653-6594-1

Forge books may be purchased for educational, business, or promotional use. For information on bulk purchases, please contact Macmillan Corporate and Premium Sales Department at 1-800-221-7945, extension 5442, or write specialmarkets@macmillan.com.

First Edition: August 2013
First Mass Market Edition: July 2014

Printed in the United States of America

0 9 8 7 6 5 4 3 2 1

*For all those who bring
these wise and "ancient aliens" called cats
into their homes and hearts,
nine dimensions are not enough.*

Contents

viii • Contents

Contents • ix

Cat in an
Alien X-Ray

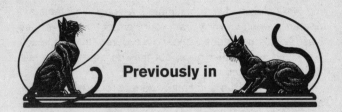

Midnight Louie's Lives and Times . . .

Las Vegas is my beat.

I love this rambling, gambling entertainment capital with its super-sized dose of lights, action, and cameras—security or otherwise.

The lights . . . the security and tourist cameras . . . and the action remain as bright and frenetic as always. Our landmark hotel-casinos and allied institutions are still puttin' on the glitz.

For a Las Vegas institution, I have always kept a low profile.

You do not hear about me on the nightly news. That is how I like it. That is the way any primo PI would like it. The name is Louie, Midnight Louie. I am a noir kind of guy, inside or out and about. I like my nightlife shaken, not stirred.

Being short, dark, and handsome . . . really short . . . gets me overlooked and underestimated, which is what the savvy operative wants anyway. I am your perfect undercover guy. I also like to hunker down under the covers with my little doll. So would some other guys, but they do not have my lush hirsute advantages.

Miss Temple Barr and I make perfect roomies. She tolerates my wandering ways. I play her bodyguard without getting in her way. Call me Muscle in Midnight Black. We share a well-honed sense of justice and long, sharp fingernails and have cracked some cases too tough for the local fuzz. She is, after all, a freelance public relations specialist, and Las Vegas is full of public and private relations of all stripes and legalities.

Our most recent crime-busting adventure took us deep into a conspiracy of magicians that resulted in a string of murders being solved, while some remain unsolved.

That Neon Nightmare club, now shut down, was also the site of a key incident in this ongoing tangle. That event was a shakedown, not a murder. And—I must blush to admit, if I ever do anything as wimpy as blush—I was not there to witness this event, in the course of protecting my Miss Temple. I hear on good authority that two takeover thugs (wearing concealing masks and cloaks à la Mr. Darth Vader of film fame) crashed a meeting of the conspiring magicians who called themselves "the Synth." The pair demanded at gunpoint the Synth members present hand over a hoard of concealed cash. In my absence, the Las Vegas feral cat pack, led by Miss Midnight Louise (no relation), made the invading pair into props for an Olympics-level scratching post claw-down. The Vaders fled, trailing blood, but remain anonymous.

So, there is much private investigative work left for me to do, as usual.

Then you get into the area of private *lives*. I say *you* get into that area. I do not. I remain aloof from these alien matters among humans. Why can they not be sensible and let

Mother Nature or a visit to the vet for what is called "altering" arrange these things? Or resort to breeders, aka "match-making sites," if you are of the tony, pedigreed sort? While it is important that humans assist in discouraging the over-population of our kind, when it comes to their own mating behavior, there is an overpopulation of indecision and angst.

I do not see how having two perfectly adequate males as a selection for one's life mate is a problem. If, unlike me, you have not had the happy procedure that allows me to be a bon vivant simultaneously entertaining multiple dating possibilities whilst not littering irresponsibly . . . you are out of luck, so get over it and go monogamous for life. Otherwise, I can recommend a good surgeon who tosses in a free tummy tuck with the deal.

I cannot give away the more intimate details of my roomie's life. Let me just say that everything it seemed you could bet on is now up for grabs and my Miss Temple may be in the lose–lose situation of her life and times.

Here is the current status of where we are all at:

None can deny that the Las Vegas crime scene is big time, and I have been treading these mean neon streets for twenty-five books now. I am an "alpha cat." Since I debuted in *Catnap* and *Pussyfoot,* I commenced to a title sequence that is as sweet and simple as *B* to *Z.*

My alphabet begins with the *B* in *Cat on a Blue Monday.* After that, the title's color word is in alphabetical order up to the, *ahem,* current volume, *Cat in an Alien X-Ray.*

(Obviously, a large dose of Weird has hit Sin City, the one blot on the map it is hard to out-weird. However, my breed is known for a mystical bent, not to mention reincarnation to the power of nine, so I am more than somewhat ready to tango with anything alien.)

Since Las Vegas is littered with guidebooks as well as bodies, I here provide a rundown of the local landmarks on my particular map of the world. A cast of characters, so to speak:

To wit, my lovely roommate and high-heel devotee, Miss Nancy Drew on killer spikes, freelance PR ace Miss Temple Barr, who had reunited with her elusive love . . .

. . . the once and future missing-in-action magician Mr. Max Kinsella, who has good reason for invisibility. After his cousin Sean died in an Irish Republican Army bomb attack during a post–high school jaunt to Ireland, Mr. Max joined the man who became his mentor, Garry Randolph, aka magician Gandolph the Great, in undercover counterterrorism work.

The elusive Mr. Max has also been sought—on suspicion of murder—by a hard-nosed dame, Las Vegas homicide detective Lieutenant C. R. Molina, single mother of teenage Mariah . . . .

Mama Molina is also the good friend of Miss Temple's freshly minted fiancé, Mr. Matt Devine, aka Mr. Midnight, a radio talk show shrink on *The Midnight Hour.* This former Roman Catholic priest came to Vegas to track down his abusive stepfather and ended up becoming a syndicated radio celebrity.

Speaking of unhappy pasts, Miss Lieutenant Carmen Regina Molina is not thrilled that her former flame—Mr. Rafi Nadir, working in Las Vegas after blowing his career at the LAPD, and for years the unsuspecting father of Mariah—now knows what is what and who is whose. . . .

Meanwhile, Mr. Matt drew a stalker, the local lass that Max and his cousin Sean boyishly competed for in that long-ago Ireland . . .

. . . one Miss Kathleen O'Connor, deservedly christened Kitty the Cutter by Miss Temple. Finding Mr. Max as impossible to trace as Lieutenant Molina did, Kitty the C settled for harassing with tooth and claw the nearest innocent bystander, Mr. Matt Devine. . . .

Now that Miss Kathleen O'Connor's sad, and later sadistic, history indicates she might not be dead and buried like all rotten elements, things are shaking up again for we who reside at a vintage round apartment building called the Circle Ritz. Ex-resident Mr. Max Kinsella is no longer MIA, although I saw him hit the wall of the Neon Nightmare club with lethal impact while in the guise of a bungee-jumping magician, the Phantom Mage.

That Mr. Max's recent miraculous resurrection coincides with my ever-lovin' roommate going over to the Light Side in her romantic life (our handsome blond upstairs neighbor, Mr. Matt Devine) only adds to the angst and confusion.

However, things are seldom what they seem, and almost never that in Las Vegas. A magician may have as many lives as a cat, in my humble estimation, and events now bear me out.

Meanwhile, any surprising developments do not surprise me. Everything is always up for grabs in Las Vegas 24/7: guilt, innocence, money, power, love, loss, death, and significant others.

All this human sex and violence makes me glad that I have a simpler social life, such as just trying to get along with my unacknowledged daughter . . .

. . . Miss Midnight Louise, who insinuated herself into my cases until I was forced to set up shop with her as Midnight Investigations, Inc. . . .

. . . and needing to unearth more about the Vaders and the Synth, a cabal of magicians that may be responsible for a lot of murderous cold cases in town, and are now the objects of growing international interest, but as MIA as Mr. Max has been lately.

So, there you have it, the usual human stew—folks good, bad, and hardly indifferent—totally mixed up and at odds with one another and within themselves. Obviously, it is left to me to solve all their mysteries and nail some crooks along the way.

Like Las Vegas, the City That Never Sleeps, Midnight Louie, private eye, also has a sobriquet: the Kitty That Never Sleeps.

With this crew, who could?

Chapter 1

Conduct Unbecoming

I am running ears-back, footpads flat-out down a dark alley.

This is not normally a problem for lithe ninja me. My skin-tight, full-body black catsuit is next to invisible in dark narrow spaces, and my hidden shivs are primed to scale any porous material I encounter, including the careless wandering person in my way.

The only thing in my way in this alley is a blank brick wall. I make a hard right, striking sparks off concrete with my rear brakes, and splitting enough nails to visit a pedicurist in the morning, were I a metrosexual sort of guy.

Which I decidedly am not.

Another blank and topless wall forces me left, and then right again. I sense my pursuers gaining on me, but I have no idea who—or what—they are. Or where we are. It feels like I have been running like this for blocks.

I spy a bright pinpoint at the end of my tunnel, put my paws to the pavement, and rocket toward it with my patented burst of cheetah-level speed. Midnight Louie is no easy catch.

I crash through the bright light like a circus tiger through a giant paper embroidery hoop. . . .

Only there is no sawdust to land on, just another inescapable tunnel, this one all spotlights and aurora borealis.

My pupils have slitted needle-thin, but the light is burning so bright, I am blind as I fall through empty air into apparent nothingness, my agile spine spiraling down like a drill bit.

"Louie," a voice calls, echoes.

Wait! Stop the action. I am being called back from the brink of annihilation by a familiar voice. My Miss Temple needs me. I cannot go splat on an unseen surface. I must fight gravity. My limbs thrash.

Then something from behind grabs me, shakes me, rattles and rolls me.

Never have I been so helpless.

"Louie."

Wait! The voice is not Miss Temple's. It is female but from another species speaking through my roommate's usual whispered little nothings.

Who has the nerve to come between a guy and his girl?

I am shaken more softly, and the light fades into the dark gray of a room without light.

I feel my pumping limbs slow and slacken. Around me are dim familiar forms, the most familiar—and acting like it—is indeed my Miss Temple.

"Louie, you are just dreaming. Nothing is chasing you but the Sandman. Wake up. You're tattooing my thigh with your thrashing feet."

She is slipping her hands around my cushy warm midsection to heave it upright, and me with it.

"Sorry, boy, but that stings. You are off the bed for the rest of the night."

I am ushered to the edge of the zebra-print spread and nudged until I have no choice but to puddle down to the cool wood parquet floor.

What a way to be awakened! Tossed out on my ear, although it is actually my feet that hit solid ground first, thanks to my native athletic ability.

I sit up and wash these exiled ears of the unfriendly decree from my very own roommate, whose bacon and backside I have saved on numerous occasions.

I am surprised to find my shivs still stretching and contracting, as if yet in that state of running for my life. I must admit I keep them highly honed.

They have never run so much as a nylon stocking (although women and particularly my Miss Temple do not much wear such things anymore) in my interaction with the human female population.

And I have never been kicked out of bed before. Is that a blow to a guy's ego.

And I have never been so sure I was one dead mallard as I was a couple minutes before.

What a nightmare!

I shake my head. I must be slipping. Speaking of that, I decide to slip through the French doors to the small three-sided patio Miss Temple's condominium offers. Perhaps the cool night air will soothe my ruffled feelings.

I stretch my frame full up to work the lever-style handle with my usual light-shivved touch and fall through to the stone patio beyond, turning to push the door gently shut behind me.

I breathe in night air as warm as cream of potato soup. We are heading into a Vegas summer, when the temperature never goes on vacation, particularly during these global warming times.

The palm fronds fan across a bit of full moon, making a splendid postcard shot. The neighborhood is as quiet as a harried cat could wish. No dogs barking, at the moment. No tires peeling asphalt. At the moment.

I yawn.

And then the hairs along my spine stand up and salute.

Looking up through the palm's fancy fans, I sense something hovering high above the scene. Some alert intelligence observing all, knowing all.

It is calling my name.

Louie.

My back twitches.

Louie. Come here.

No way.

Rise and climb.

It is not morning, and even if it was, I do not then rise and do anything except stretch and scratch my hard-to-reach places, which are none of anyone's business.

I stare upward anyway. Perhaps I will spot a lazy fly to take down. I need to restore my Great Black Hunter reputation after undergoing that craven dream sequence.

Yet, all my fly-catching instincts are telling me that something big is up, and not only up, but *up there,* in the vast Midnight Blue yonder.

Louie, do not fight my influence.

I cannot shake that unspoken "voice" in my head. This is more disturbing than any nightmare.

Or . . . am I hearing the moon?

That is not such a crazy notion. My kind are creatures of the night. We court and sing by the light of the moon. And hunt. Some writers have fancied that all of us leap up to the moon every night. (I do not know why we would. If it is indeed made of green cheese, it would attract taste bud–challenged rats, not cats. On the other hand, a planet-wide rat-chasing is an excellent fitness routine.)

Louie. Come up.

Manx, that moon is insistent! You would think it is Miss Midnight Louise, my liberated and obviously misbegotten (by somebody else other than me) would-be daughter.

The light dawns. That phrase is a metaphor, not a descriptive fact. A metaphor is a . . . sort of alias.

I leap to the palm tree trunk and ratchet up its scabrous curving height until I can leap to the frond that brushes the Circle Ritz roof. I slide down its bendable length, using my weight, and leap onto the patio three stories above my Miss Temple's place, a perfect four-shiv-point landing.

This equally small space puts me face-to-kisser with two round blue moon-shaped orbs, the slightly crossed eyes of Miss Electra Lark's reclusive, exclusive so-called sacred cat of Burma.

Her name is Karma, and she likes to play with everything from past lives to future predictions.

To add to my annoyance after climbing up to the penthouse level to join Miss Mystic Muse on her Juliet balcony, she does not even invite me in.

"You must stay out here, Louie. Miss Electra Lark has insomnia and just now fell asleep," she explains. "It was bad enough that I was drawn outside by the moon tides. I had to ease the door shut one toe at a time."

Insomnia is an inexplicable malady to me. I can fit in a catnap anytime, anywhere, and am about to doze off right here and now from boredom while Karma proceeds to extol the glories of the night sky.

"I know you are at home in the moonlight, Louie, but do you ever look up from your crude expeditions for prey and playmates to contemplate the vast clockwork motions of our universe?"

I am usually too busy looking down to make sure I do not lose my footing on whatever wall I am using for a serenading stage.

"Do you never sense, Louie, the presence of some thing, some entity, far larger than our petty struggles to survive?"

Uh, yeah. Like Animal Control.

And what is this "our" petty struggle to survive? I doubt

Karma has ever set one of her sacred white-tipped feet out of the penthouse apartment, other than onto this tiny balcony.

"Do you not think sometimes, Louie . . ."

The long pause after that sentence is getting to be insulting.

". . . that an entire universe of wondrous entities hovers just outside the reach of our hearts and minds?"

And with the defunding of the NASA programs, they can just stay out there hovering undiscovered to their hearts' content.

"Have you heard of astral projection, Louie?"

Her baby blue gaze leaves the heavens to finally focus again on my lowly self.

"Uh, yeah." Hey. I am the quintessential dude on the street and the Strip, supposed to be a hip cat up on every new wrinkle in this old town. I need to step up to protect my rep. "I hear that some venues are using holograms of dead superstars like Elvis as tourist attractions. Boogie with Bogey. Get down with James Dean. Mambo with Marilyn."

"Not holograms, Louie! You have such an impossibly material soul."

"Holograms are not material. You cannot get more ethereal than being a projected image of yourself."

"Actually, these crass entertainment technologies do touch on the magic of astral projection. I never need to leave my simple home here at the Circle Ritz—"

Hey! It is a penthouse. And you are the landlady's prize trust fund baby. I decide to tell her a thing or two for making me sit here to get drenched in mystical mumbo-jumbo.

"I hear Miss Electra Lark," I say, "has endowed an entire cat shelter to ensure you have 'most favored nation' status there should she exit for eternity before you do."

Karma sighs. Yes. Like a dog. "That is a sweet but useless gesture. I am the result of a thousand reincarnations. My heart will go on."

Apparently, the ditsy New Age brain too.

Karma is now subtly swaying as a deep purr vibrates her entire body to the ends of the long fine hairs in her ears.

I long to tell her that humans have clever battery-run devices to clear that ear clutter.

"Before many days are past," Karma warns in her lowest, most annoying tone of superior knowledge, "you will see signs and portents in the Las Vegas night sky."

Right, the Treasure Island curbside volcano spitting fake fire far into the dry desert air.

"You will face alien abduction. . . ."

"That already happened to me in Chicago, where the mob is an entire other species of lame."

"You will dance with the dead down a ten-story mountain. . . ."

Manx, is this lady on another plane, probably a discontinued SST! Nobody measures mountains in stories, but in feet.

Karma condescends to slit open one peeper. "That is a metaphor, Louie."

"Metaphor, mountain, right. All this is really interesting, Karma, but I have some bothersome, buzzing houseflies to catch on the first floor."

And a few zzzzz's.

"Duty calls," I say, braving the tickle of fronds as I leap onto the palm tree trunk and ratchet back down to my quarters.

"You are due for a great fall," Karma's fading voice calls as I flee.

I am not worried, although her whines of gloom and doom and my hasty retreat cause me to lose two nail sheaths on the way back down.

How come the mighty Karma did not predict *that*?

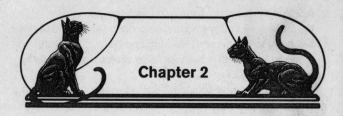

Chapter 2

Phoning Home

Temple yawned. It was only midmorning, but Midnight Louie had been thrashing about half the night, giving her dreams of being entangled by a giant furry black octopus.

The cat who deigned to live with her, a solid black, solid twenty-pound guy with a knack for showing up where needed, thumped atop her desk. Midnight Louie nosed her business cards aside to sprawl belly-down on the cool surface.

She eyed the smartphone on her desk as if it were a particularly large insect despite the serene graphic of nearby Red Rock Canyon on the home screen. She'd donned her headset because she expected this long-put-off call to last awhile. She didn't want to fry her brain . . . or her ear, which was already hot, and probably red. Her fingertips on the desktop were white. And cold.

Honestly!

Her gaze lingered on a pile of her business cards: TEMPLE BARR, PR.

Why was she indulging in cold feet now? She'd once done live stand-ups as a TV reporter, had repped a prestigious repertory theater where she ran into movie stars, for gosh sakes. She'd been a public relations freelancer in super-hyped, larger-than-life Las Vegas for more than two years. She was smart, single, successful, and had even developed a reputation as an amateur sleuth to the point that a homicide lieutenant had actually called upon her services a time or two.

If Oprah Winfrey—or Larry the Cable Guy, for gosh sakes—called right now, Temple could do an instant interview with either one. Or both at a time. She was a media maven and she'd had eluded murderers attempting to flame-roast her in a burning room only recently. Well, one murderer.

So why did she find phoning home so intimidating? Temple would be thirty-one in a couple of months. Past thirty and way past the age of consent.

Louie bent over to apparently study the cell phone screen displaying her "Family" contacts. One big black paw patted it.

"No claws," she warned, her hand snatching up the phone to safety.

Louie backed away, lifting a forepaw innocent of claw tips.

"Sorry, boy. I'm a little nervous."

Just do it, Temple told herself.

Temple tapped the familiar number in Minneapolis and waited for the ring. On Saturday her father and brothers would be off doing man things, like attending her nephews' and nieces' soccer games, performing strange rituals with their heads buried in vehicle motors, and sitting in battered wooden motorboats on lakes, pestering fish while mosquitoes pestered them.

Karen Barr should be home alone now, maybe doing accounts for her antique mall stand or . . . baking oatmeal-raisin cookies. Temple had such a sudden craving for those warm, homemade oatmeal-raisin cookies, her stomach spasmed and her mouth watered.

These autonomic system flare-ups were ridiculous. She called home every few weeks, but . . . But she hadn't been back to visit since coming to Las Vegas.

"Temple," her mother's voice hummed into her overheated ear. "I thought that might be you."

"Hi, Mom. How are you all doing?"

"Fine. The weather is warming up, so all the boys are out. We had hardly any snow this winter."

"I never thought global warming would hit Minnesota."

"So what's new in your world? Triple-digit heat numbers yet?"

"Not yet. Luckily, you don't have to shovel sweat. And it's a dry heat in this climate."

"I guess there's no prying you out of Sin City."

Good. Her mom had given Temple an out from this awkward conversation.

"There probably is, Mom," she said. "I was thinking about coming up."

"That's wonderful! Any special reason?"

"One."

"You're not changing jobs?"

"*Nooo* . . ." Temple could have said she was changing boyfriends, but she knew better than to drop the fiancé bomb right away. "I do have someone I want you to meet."

"Some*one*?" Her mother's voice was suddenly guarded. "Kit said you were the social butterfly of the Strip."

"What? Kit said that? When did you talk to Aunt Kit?"

"A lot of times. Temple. We *are* sisters."

"So you two talk about me?"

"Sometimes."

"And?"

"She said you'd really settled into that over-the-top city. That you had some key clients and a lot of friends. She particularly mentioned a big Italian family named Fontana that had given you a lot of PR commissions. I was so glad to hear that."

Oh, Aunt Kit, you devil you. Her mother was imagining a "Mamma Mia knows best" clan when the sophisticated Fontanas were Vegas venue owners and more like the Sopranos, but in a good way.

Obviously, Kit hadn't mentioned she herself had recently married the eldest of the mob of dreamy Fontana brothers. Their dark Italian good looks, attired in pale Ermenegildo Zegna designer suits, had become a Vegas brand for smooth, single, and sexy.

Temple understood why her aunt had kept mum with Karen. Kit had been a New York City single until sixty and then had married a younger man. Aldo Fontana was a much younger man. If Temple didn't have her own guy, she'd consider her aunt an ideal role model.

"Well, I'm used to having big brothers," Temple said, thinking of her hulking outdoorsy four, "and there are ten Fontana brothers."

"*Mamma mia.* Those Italians do reproduce! But I'm glad you still have 'older brothers' to take you under their wings."

"Sometimes, Mom, I take them under *my* wing."

Sometimes family couldn't see you as independent and grown up, particularly if you were the youngest and only daughter of five.

"Say, speaking of big families," Temple said, "I never

did find out why you and Dad had so many of us. A little out of step with the 'small footprint' philosophy of the times, although I've seen my birth footprint and it *was* tiny."

"Oh." A pause. "I suppose it was because we really wanted a daughter."

"You mean you were holding out for a girl the way families always used to hold out for a boy?"

"Yes."

"Way more liberated of you than I suspected, Mom."

"Thank you. I think. So who is this someone you want us to meet?"

"Well, duh. My fiancé."

A really long pause. The family had met Max, but had not been so enamored as Temple. No one could have been as enamored as much as Temple at that point, but her family would have resented anyone who'd take her out of the Twin Cities, especially to someplace as glitzy as Vegas.

"So it's not that magician?" she suggested cautiously.

"His name is Max."

"'Is'?"

"Well, sure. He's still alive and well"—just barely—"in Las Vegas."

"So there's someone new?"

Somehow that made Temple sound fickle. "Not so new. He lives here at the Circle Ritz too."

"I always think of a Western movie when I hear that name for your apartment building."

"Condo. I'm building equity."

"So it's over with . . . the magician?"

Temple smiled, sure that epithet for Max had originated with her dad. There was nothing Midwestern about Max except his origins, and that was an unforgivable strike against him in stable Minnesota.

"Pretty much."

"Not totally?"

"Yes, totally."

"So who will we be meeting?"

"His name is Matt. He's a couple years older than I am. He works in the communications business."

"That seems a good compatibility factor. Where is he from?"

"Chicago." The capital of the upper Midwest.

"Oh," This time the "oh" was stretched out on a rising scale of approval. For gosh sakes again, Max had been born in Wisconsin. Everybody was practically neighbors.

"Yes," Temple said. "We were just in Chicago to get together with his family."

"You were that close and you didn't swing up here?"

"Matt's job makes longer trips impossible."

"What is his job?"

"Radio."

"A disappearing medium, isn't it?"

"Not for Matt. He's syndicated."

"So when can you and this Matt come up?"

"In the next few weeks. I'm checking to see about family vacations."

"Your brothers go camping now and again in the summer. It'd be easier if you set a date and we go from there."

"I don't want to interfere with any expeditions."

"Oh, you wouldn't. The boys wouldn't miss meeting the new guy."

Temple rolled her eyes. She bet they wouldn't. They'd always had to hassle her dates from junior high on. One thing about Max. Nobody hassled him. They could try, but it never worked.

"It would be a quick trip," she warned. "Matt works nights."

"Not another one! Sorry. It's your business. I was just . . . surprised."

"Gosh, Mom. This is Vegas. It's such a twenty-four-hour town, it has its own time zone."

"Seriously?"

"No, just exaggerating for effect. I do that a lot in my job. So, we're good. I'll check with Matt and we'll figure a time to visit that works for you all."

"Fine, but . . . wait."

"Yes?"

"What's the young man's last name?"

"Want to check him out on Facebook, Mom?" Temple teased.

"I don't much go on there."

Temple smiled. It was a miracle that her mother was familiar with social media at all.

"It's Devine."

"I'm sure you think everything about him is, dear."

"Of course, but that's the last name."

"Devine?" This pause was the longest yet. "Not *the* Matt Devine."

"Well, he is to me."

"Temple, don't be coy. You're not really with that darling guy from the *Amanda Show*?"

Temple wanted to close her eyes but Louie reached up to pat her cheek with a velvet paw.

"If you say so, Mom."

"Temple, honey, that's amazing news! I don't know why you are so closemouthed about what's going on with you."

Try four teasing, overprotective older brothers, Mom.

"I love the show. But isn't he an ex-priest?"

"I thought Universal Universalists were open-minded."

"Of course we are, but I have to wonder if it's some kind of rebellion thing that you'd go for an ex-clergyman."

"I passed the age of rebellion over a decade ago, Mom. He's just a great guy to me, and the only issue with us now is, are we going to get married in Vegas, Chicago, or Minneapolis?"

"That serious?"

Louie leaned his intrusive black nose close to the cell phone as Karen Barr's deep audible intake of breath wafted into Temple's ear.

"Not serious. Exciting, happy, wonderful," Temple told her mother.

"Yes! Yes, of course. But, dear, it'll have to be a church wedding, and I don't know that Las Vegas is quite the venue for that."

"Are you kidding? There are more churches in Vegas than in most U.S. cities. Anyway, I'm not coming up to church-hunt, just to give you all a chance to meet my fiancé."

"It's great news, honey. We love you and can't wait to see you."

"Same here, Mom."

Mumbled good-byes ended the call.

Temple slumped in her ergonomic chair.

Midnight Louie lifted a lazy forepaw to bat at the wires as she returned her headphone to its usual position on her desk, curling the wires into a less tempting mass.

She took a deep breath of her own, then released it slowly. "Well, that's done," she told Louie. "You're lucky cats don't have families and civil and religious ceremonies. Mom's right. We'll have to come up with a geographical site and an ecumenical ceremony. No matter what, I am going to get one gorgeous over-the-top white bridal gown to do it in."

Temple dried her damp palms on her knit shorts and pushed herself to her feet.

Her spirits lifted with her first step back into the living area. She detoured to the kitchen to make herself a peanut butter sandwich, Louie at her heels and then up on the countertop. Louie was the Royal Sniffer, and the Royal Taster if he liked the sniff. He always smelled her food, but usually turned his nose and whiskers away in distaste.

Temple then went to cast herself down on the living room sofa. She pulled the *Review-Journal* sections across the coffee table to browse. Now that the May weather was growing hotter for the summer, Louie turned himself around by her side, twice, and cuddled up close.

His big furry body was going to get too hot to cuddle with soon, and she'd already had her sweat shop experience for the day.

A small headline below the newspaper's first section fold caught her eye:

UFOS AHOY ON THE STRIP

"As if my call to Minnesota wasn't totally 'phone home, E.T.,'" she mumbled to Louie, munching crunchy peanut butter. He perked a gentlemanly ear. Thank goodness cats didn't object to talking with one's mouth full. "Now Vegas is getting all spooked."

The article made much of a few tourists freaked out by low-flying UFOs they claimed to have spotted hovering over the Strip. Temple shook her head as she read of the darting round "ships" with a broad row of lights beaming a glow around the middle. Probably two Frisbees glued together. People will hallucinate anything, she thought. With all the exotic outdoor lighting in Sin City, a fleet of genuine flying saucers could land and probably be taken for a new restaurant's advertising gimmick. How would *she* engineer the effect?

With those silver flattened helium balloons, Temple thought, and a pulsing LED readout like the famous Times Square electronic billboard around the middle. That would work. Hey, the marketers behind this rumor had already scored newspaper ink and even a link to a site where people were mounting camcorder footage and cell phone photos of the phenomena.

And here Temple thought she'd been wandering through her own personal *Twilight Zone* already this afternoon. Still, inquiring minds wanted to know. Temple picked up her iPad and checked the sighting Web site just to laugh at what people will believe.

The usual jerky videos were fuzzy like all phony UFO footage, but she saw enough to get a sit-up-and-drop-your-jaw moment.

Anyone with a long memory or a thorough grounding in Las Vegas history would recognize this particular model of levitating saucer. The design was crude, the look was hokey, but this shape was not alien to Las Vegas at all.

In that case, maybe the UFOs weren't an alien visitation but more on the order of a haunting.

Someone should look into this.

She was sure someone would.

Temple tossed the newspaper section on the coffee table and went to relieve anticipated family stress by making another peanut butter sandwich, this one with bacon.

Imitating Elvis's eating habits was as weird as she wanted to get just now.

She had a forthcoming meeting that would make a call home to Mom look like a grammar school cakewalk.

Chapter 3

Ménage à Murder

An hour later, Temple was clinging to one concept: creative tension.

A public relations specialist could handle conventions hosting up to twenty thousand or more people, and Temple was well aware that major events weren't orchestrated in environments of tranquillity, concord, and camaraderie.

No, it often took chaos on the scale of Beethoven's "Eroica" Symphony—the one with the booming cannon—to move all the players and pieces around the board to reach a successful conclusion.

She was an expert at that.

Creative tension.

So.

One might think a mere party of three sitting at a round card-slash-dining table in her vintage condo could accomplish wonders with a minimum of fuss.

Temple shook her head mentally.

Two guys and a gal made a symmetrical but always awkward trio, especially if one guy had occupied the California king in the adjoining bedroom . . . and the girl was now a semi-permanent fixture in the other's guy's bedroom right above this very second-floor unit.

Would her mother ever be shocked! She'd think the Circle Ritz was some sort of swinging singles place when most of the residents were long-term and middle-aged-plus. Maybe what would shock her mother the most was that the triangle was still locked into place in mutual support because of criminal matters. How could Temple explain, if she ever had to, that each relationship was seriously monogamous? True at the time. Temple had never intended to be a serial monogamist. How had it happened?

Temple took the chance to study Mr. Now and Mr. Then from a distance as she hovered unnoticed in the kitchen archway.

A warm brown-eyed blond was as irresistible as a golden retriever, and Matt Devine had the inner warmth of empathy to light up her life and the room. A rotten childhood followed by years of dedication as a celibate priest had made him into someone who'd seen past his own hurts to tend to other people's pain. That included healing the unwed mother he'd defended since a boy.

On the other hand, and side of the table, Max's looks were compelling rather than handsome. His angular face, black hair, and pale blue eyes could make him seem mischievous . . . or dangerous. His great, all-American happy childhood had been followed by a hellish young adulthood that put his life on the line forever and had estranged him from his family and, ultimately, even her, despite his oodles of mercurial charm. She'd never before thought of the two men's histories as being in exact reverse.

She'd truly loved them both and they knew it.

Max Kinsella himself had "disengaged" from her, bowing to the inevitable draw of Matt Devine. She was Matt's first love, and nothing could stop their union . . . except themselves.

So now the three were joined into an uneasy alliance, forced to work together to declaw a psychopathic chameleon from Max's past, a possible serial murderess with as many lives as a cat.

That last thought made Temple smile. Midnight Louie, her alley cat roommate, was sitting as unnoticed as a furry black statue of Buddha on the narrow buffet, his glossy black velvet paws tucked in and his slitty eyes indicating either napping or a disgusted meditation on human follies. Such as romantic triangles.

Temple sighed. Aloud. Not meaning to attract either guy's attention.

Both men looked up from the centerpiece on the table and said, "What?" On that they were united.

"I'm in mourning," she said, matching her tone to the sentiment.

Both men frowned in concern.

She pointed to the piece of paper they were all staring at. "My wonderful, logical Table of Crime Elements is 'Mangeled,' rubbed out, and Xed-out to bits, thanks to recent deductions."

She followed her dramatic announcement by delivering bottles of sangria wine cooler to the guys. Max was Black Irish and favored whiskey. Matt wouldn't care what he drank.

Temple set down a tall glass of her favorite mixer, even when it was solo: Crystal Light. She sat at the third place and tapped the center of the table. "That single sheet of typing paper before you holds the most left-brained creation of my career. I feel ready to audition for *CSI: Las Vegas*."

A mutual chuckle broke the tension.

Matt spoke first. "It's brilliant. It's methodical. It's wonderful."

"What's wonderful," Max Kinsella said after a swallow of wine, "is that you've managed to rule out several unsolved deaths in one swoop."

"Yeah." Matt Devine sipped his drink. "How did that happen? One day this flaky group of disgruntled magicians who call themselves 'the Synth' are secretly running the Neon Nightmare club and hunting a hidden stockpile of Irish terrorism money and guns. The next day they've disbanded and the nightclub has gone dark overnight. Kaput. Closed. And you say—" He looked at Temple. "—they're no longer a danger and their recently murdered member, this Cosimo Sparks, is probably a serial killer."

"A multiple murderer," Temple corrected. "All his victims could have revealed his plans. He was the mastermind for the Synth's mounting the most astounding magical illusion ever staged in Vegas as cover for a huge heist and making off with the hidden IRA funds too."

"So the theory," Max said, "is that the Synth was on a recruiting jag for their illusion of a lifetime, treasure hunt, and heist in the making?"

"Yes," Temple said, for Matt's benefit. He was new to this scenario. "And the three surviving founders of the Synth and Neon Nightmare realized that Cosimo Sparks had the motive to recruit other professional magic workers. What if he panicked when they turned him down and thought they'd, er, squeal on him and the plan? The Synth founders even believed Sparks tried to recruit Gandolph, Max's mentor in magic."

"Ridiculous," Max said. "Once 'Gandolph the Great' retired, Garry Randolph was on his own crusade against phony mediums."

"He even faked his own death," Temple told Matt, "so he'd be available to help Max when the angry IRA guys from the past came after him."

"So." Matt pinned his finger on a row of the table in turn. "You think Gandolph's former onstage assistant, Gloria Fuentes, was also approached to be recruited, along with the Cloaked Conjuror's assistant, Barry, and Prof. Mangel at the state university. When they all backed off, Sparks killed them one by one to shut them up. Sounds like that board game, *Clue*."

Temple nodded.

"It's important we remember," Max said, "that the Synth members considered themselves the high priests and priestesses of magic, which had lost out on the Vegas Strip to artsy acrobatic productions by Cirque du Soleil and actual magic trick revealers, like the Cloaked Conjuror."

"And," Temple said, "they weren't primarily after the hidden stockpile of IRA loot and guns Kathleen O'Connor and her allies had amassed, now up for grabs. They wanted to provide the massive illusion that would astound the Strip and distract from the hoard being claimed. Maybe they were being used by the mob, and maybe by O'Connor. And who was using whom more, Kathleen O'Connor or the mob, I don't know."

"That's impressive," Matt said.

"My theory?" she asked.

"No, I don't know where the heck that's coming from. But you did employ the proper usage of 'who' and 'whom' in your last sentence."

She had to laugh. "Comic relief. Always welcome."

"Especially," Max said, "when you're unraveling a cosmic tangle."

"Cosimo Sparks," Matt said, "is now a murder victim himself, and any murders he might have committed are just speculation."

"So," Max noted, "is the Table of Crime Elements before us, but Temple's adjustment makes sense. There was a mini-attempt by the remaining Synth members and their followers to heist the million-dollar treasure chest at the Oasis last week."

Max glanced ruefully at Temple from under quizzical brows. "Now that you've cleared away the underbrush, we stand a better chance of finding out where—and why—Kathleen O'Connor was lurking during the past two years of unsolved Las Vegas crime scenes."

"Kathleen O'Connor." Matt picked up the sheet of paper, then tossed it back down as if wanting to wash his hands of it. And her. "She's become a myth, an invincible antagonist at the edges of all our everyday lives. If you believe," he told Temple, "that the Synth guy, Cosimo Sparks, accounts for several deaths, that doesn't leave much to blame on this . . . implacable banshee from Kinsella's Northern Ireland past. How and why did you get so cozy with the Synth that they told you all about these murders and then just faded away?" he asked Max.

"They may not have completely faded," Max said. "The IRA didn't either." His pause left a silence Temple didn't fill.

"Surely, Temple, you didn't go back alone to that hellish nightclub?" That's what Matt really wanted to know. "It was bad enough you were snooping around it enough to crash one of the Synth's meetings a bit back."

This was awkward. She indeed had gone back there, and Max had been on scene as well. She didn't want to lie to Matt. . . .

"I wasn't alone," she said.

She could feel the rising tension in Matt from two feet away. Max and she had not only once been live-in lovers heading toward marriage, but he'd also been the professional backup on her amateur investigations from the very beginning. Before Matt moved into the Circle Ritz.

"Midnight Louie and some of his feral cronies were there," she said, quite truthfully.

The cat took a bow by rising and thumping down to the tabletop. He cocked a head at the paper under discussion, then yawned and thumped down to the floor. And Midnight Louie, all twenty pounds of him, did thump. Yet not a thing on the table had moved during his ponderous passage.

He lofted up to the couch arm right behind Temple, a bodyguard settling into position.

"That cat follows you like Mary's little lamb in a Big Bad Wolf suit!" Matt sounded exasperated. That unlikely fact was true and they all knew it. Midnight Louie got around Vegas like a tumbleweed—fast, erratic, and often ignored. "After I saw his performance on our trip to Chicago, I have to admit he's pretty formidable."

Temple beamed with pride as she turned to view his latest perch. Louie had assumed a Cheshire cat position, his eyes narrowing, basking in the sunshine of full credit for his übercatness. He almost seemed to be smiling, but maybe that was because some of his snazzy white whiskers turned up at the ends. Any moment, she expected his lazily watchful form to vanish . . . everything but those whiskers.

"Plus," she said fondly, "Louie makes a darn good ring bearer at weddings."

"All hail the cat," Max said impatiently. He'd been out of the country during the recent weddings of Temple's Aunt Kit and Matt's mother, both mature brides. He'd never seen a dapper Midnight Louie wearing a white formal tie with a ring box tied to it. "We're not here to discuss weddings."

Temple and Matt exchanged a glance. She was struck

by how much of her life Max had missed during only a couple months of absence.

Max was still talking. "Tell Devine how you managed to solve several murders with one fell swoop of inspiration."

Matt's eyebrows remained arched inquiringly.

"First," Temple said, "we need to consult the Table of Crime Elements, because my new version shows the theoretical crimes committed by Cosimo Sparks before his own recent death."

WHO	WHEN	WHERE	METHOD	ODDITIES	SUSPECT
dead man at Goliath	April	Goliath ceiling	knife		Max?
dead man at Phoenix	Aug	Crystal Phoenix Hotel ceiling	knife	Effinger lookalike, his ID	unknown
Max's mentor, Gandolph the Great, aka Garry Randolph	Halloween	Haunted House séance	faked death	Disguised as woman	assorted psychics cleared
Cliff Effinger, Matt's stepfather	Jan. New Year	Oasis Hotel	drowning	Bound to sinking ship's figurehead	Two muscle men
Woman	Feb	Blue Dahlia club	strangled	"She left" on Molina's car	Unrelated killer
Cher Smith, stripper	Feb	Strip club parking lot	strangled		Stripper Killer
Gloria Fuentes, Gandolph's assistant	Feb	Church parking lot	strangled	"She left" on body in morgue	Synth/ Sparks
Prof. Jeff Mangel	March	UNLV campus hall	knifed	Ophiuchus body position	Synth/ Sparks

(continued on next page)

(continued from previous page)

WHO	WHEN	WHERE	METHOD	ODDITIES	SUSPECT
Cloaked Conjuror's assistant, Barry	April	New Millennium Hotel stage flies	beating or fatal fall	Masked like CC or SF TV show alien	Synth/ Sparks
Vassar, call girl	April	Goliath Hotel	fatal fall	After seeing Matt	Kitty/ Matt?
Shangri-La	May	New Millennium	fatal fall	CC's partner	Synth or Sparks
Cosimo Sparks	May	Crystal Phoenix Hotel Chunnel of Crime	stabbed	Ophiuchus position in old safe, wearing white tie and tails	Santiago? Or mob/ Kitty?

Matt tapped the paper. "I see you've still got me down for Vassar's death at the Goliath. Don't I get a free pass for being your fiancé?"

Max snorted. "You just don't like being paired with your slasher, Kitty the Cutter."

Temple had expected Matt to challenge that one, but instead he just glared for a second and looked away.

Awkward, awkward, awkward. She and Max had never been formally engaged, but Matt probably hadn't realized that. If she wanted to practice crisis-managing PR, doctoral level, she had the chance here and now.

"Sorry, guys. I am an equal opportunity speculative sleuth. I still have Max down for the Goliath murder that seems to have started this sequence."

"I have to admit I'm cloudy on the latest happenings on the Las Vegas crime scene," Matt said, "what with my career and family matters going full throttle in Chicago lately."

"Come to think of it," Max said, leaning back in his chair and then leaning back the chair to balance on its rear legs, "the *Chicago* mob was involved in founding Vegas. What?" he added, as Temple and Matt exchanged significant glances.

"What don't I know?" Max asked.

Temple and Matt spoke at once, the sounds gibberish because they were saying different things.

"Okay," Max said, "what I'm hearing is that Matt's evil stepfather, Effinger, was kidnapped by the mob."

"True, the unfortunate Effinger was bagged, gagged, and sent to a watery grave here in Vegas months ago," Temple went on solo, "but in Chicago, last week, *Louie* was kidnapped from Matt's mom's apartment by a couple of lame mobsters who wanted something from a locked file box Effinger had left behind long ago in Chicago."

Max leaned forward to stab the pertinent line on the table with his forefinger. "If any death on this list reeks of mob involvement, it's Effinger's. I happen to know that certain parties do not want folks snooping around at the Oasis and especially near that sinking-ship attraction. Or around that casino ceiling at the Goliath where the first guy on your unsolved list died and I was suspected of being the perp."

Matt folded his fists atop each other on the table and leaned his chin on them as he studied the paper again. "The other mob death could be Sparks's. Back in the day, they liked to leave their victims' bodies messy and where they could be found."

"True," Temple said. "The suspect in the Sparks death is a way-out Chilean architect who goes by one name like a rock star. Santiago. There's some blood evidence, but not enough to indict."

"He still in town?" Max asked.

"I doubt it," said Temple. "Speaking of 'mob,' in a good way, the Fontana brothers put the fear of God into him." She couldn't help smiling.

"What's to smile about?" Max asked.

"Oh, I just found out my aunt Kit has been reporting on me to my mom back in Minnesota, who now thinks 'a nice big Italian family' is looking out for me here."

"They are," Matt said. "Not to mention the alley cat Mafia."

"The Cat Pack," Temple corrected him. "Louie and the ferals make the human Rat Pack in '60s Vegas look lame."

"Who was that?" Matt asked, speculating. "Singers Frank Sinatra, Sammy Davis Jr., and Dean Martin, right?"

"Yes," said Temple, "and comic Joey Bishop and sometimes actress Shirley MacLaine, Warren Beatty's older sis."

"If you worked in clubs back in the '50s and '60s," Max said, "especially if you were Italian like Sinatra and Dino, you played by mob rules."

"Magicians were never under mob influence?" Matt asked.

"Naw," Max said. "As you've both noticed, we're too egomaniacal to control. Also, we're pretty good at defending ourselves. So," he continued, "did Midnight Louie find what Effinger had hidden away while the three of you were in Chicago?"

Temple nodded. "We all did, and it's pretty weird."

She lifted the Table of Crime Elements to reveal a crude drawing of a muscleman wrestling a serpent as thick as his gigantic quads.

"Ah." Max grinned. "Our old friend Ophiuchus, the lost thirteenth sign of the zodiac and the symbol of the vanquished Synth. I know Professor Mangel's dead body was found arranged in the houselike shape of the constellation's major stars. And that the Neon Nightmare zodiac lighting effects included that sign."

"So where else did Ophiuchus turn up?" Matt wanted

to know. "Obviously I've missed a lot by never patronizing this now-closed Neon Nightmare joint."

"Cosimo's red satin cloak lining," Temple said promptly. "It was arranged in that same houselike shape, with his body in white tie and tails on it."

Max gave a small theatrical shudder. "A magician would appreciate that 'hidden in plain sight' element of the death scene. Magic is all about loss, death, and restoration. Too bad a surprising resurrection wasn't in the cards and we could interrogate him."

"If Sparks hadn't been killed," Temple pointed out, "the Synth members wouldn't have tried their big plan out on a smaller heist that failed. I think Ophiuchus was just a cover. What the left hand is doing when the right one is robbing the bank."

"So his death spooked the Synth conspirators," Max explained to Matt. "They jumped the gun with the attempted mass illusion."

"I thought," Matt said, "that Oasis Hotel prize presentation Temple emceed was just . . . a piece of stunt PR."

Temple winced. She considered herself more serious than that, but couldn't deny that had been a larger-than-life event. "It was a heist attempt foiled in a way to look like crazy Strip business as usual."

"And the mob," Matt said. "Just how much mob is really left in Las Vegas?"

Temple shrugged. "That's a complicated question. Everybody's touchy on that subject now, with a forty-two-million-dollar mob museum operating downtown and the Tropicana and Gangsters Hotels adding smaller exhibitions of their own. Many iconic Vegas hotels, long ago imploded into nonexistence, were constructed with mob money. The Mafia skimmed profits from the front men and then invested in nightclubs and in country clubs and shopping centers and housing developments far afield from the Strip. That's what's meant by the mob 'going corporate.' They disappeared into the larger business climate. I know mob killings persisted into the '90s, even after the FBI came in and shut down the scene in the '80s."

"And," Max added, "there's still illegal activity from meat hijacking to running prostitutes and drugs."

"So lingering mobsters could still be active," Matt said.

"And, like the displaced traditional magicians of the Synth," Temple said, "they could still be hankering for that one last big score."

Max nodded. "The object of everyone's greed being the massive stash of money Kathleen O'Connor and her IRA hardliners collected from North and South America over the years and never delivered. Many former IRA malcontents want anything raised for their cause for reparation to the families who lost members in the struggle." He paused. "Not for collateral damage like my cousin Sean, though."

Temple hastened to move past that bitter truth. "We think much of the hoard is in bearer bonds, from what was found in the walk-in safe with Cosimo Sparks's body. They're not used much today, but are still valid. So the cache of cash, to put it in homonyms, would not have to be physically huge, although it might include serious weaponry."

"Cosimo Sparks. Not a forgettable name. Who killed him?" Matt asked.

"You're asking all the right questions," Temple said. "I'm thinking the mob or ex-IRA members after the stash. It could have been stored in the hidden walk-in safe where Sparks was found. But it's now gone. Someone could have suspected Sparks of moving it, and he could have. There were 'prod' stabs on the body, as if someone wanted to force him to talk."

"Like my stepfather, Effinger." Matt frowned. "Were the marks . . . slashes?"

"Ice pick," Temple said. She noticed Max eyeing Matt narrowly.

"Any of this theorizing provable?" Matt asked.

"No, but the other three surviving Synth leaders saw the light at the same time I did. Sparks indeed could have accounted for the magic-related cold cases that have littered Las Vegas lately."

"And your only witness to this mass confession is Midnight Louie—?" Matt asked skeptically.

"Yup. It wasn't a confession, Matt. More of a clearing the smoke and mirrors from their eyes to see the truth as the scenario came to me."

Matt took a long swallow of sangria and sat back. "So tell me the scenario."

"If I can stand. I was used to doing 'stand-up' on-scene reporting when I was at the Minnesota TV station." Temple did as requested and "reported" her overhearing the morose Synth survivors commiserating until she realized what the truth could be and stepped out of the dimness to say it.

"I don't think the Synth members were killers, and Sparks was probably pretty unhinged by grandiosity and paranoia. I wouldn't be surprised if he was bipolar."

"And you think the lady magician Shangri-La also was approached to join the renegade magicians?" Matt shook his head. "She was already suspected of being a drug smuggler, and now we think she was really Kathleen O'Connor in disguise under all that full-face Asian makeup."

"We do know she brought Temple onstage and made her ring disappear and then Temple herself," Max said. "Louie fast behind Temple, of course, into the understage escape area. The entire sequence was designed to kidnap Temple."

"For a ring?" Matt asked, surprised.

Temple glanced at Max. Kitty had claimed his "promise" ring to Temple.

"Yes," Temple told Matt. "A trophy of her power, I suppose."

"What happened to it?" Matt asked. He obviously sensed their unspoken thoughts.

"Molina kept it as evidence," Temple said.

"Molina doesn't strike me as having a leg to stand on in doing that, and she sure isn't into bling."

"It doesn't matter, Matt. We were having a girly showdown over that, and she finally gave the ring back to me."

Max was now staring at Temple with the same puzzlement and a new tinge of shock. "Where is it now?"

"In my scarf drawer, I guess. It was just something I bought at the women's exposition when I was handling that." She said the lie as casually as an amateur college actress could manage.

"Oh, that fatal bottomless pit," Max said, "your scarf drawer."

Temple laughed. "I know I'm impossible at managing scarves, but they're too pretty to throw away. Look. I don't know where Shangri-La fits in all this," Temple admitted. "She was sabotaged during her act with the Cloaked Conjuror at the New Millennium and fell to her death. The body was definitely that of an Asian woman. Unless," she told Max, "the corpse was switched on the way to the morgue and the tender mercies of Grizzly Bahr and his staff. Gandolph managed that for himself and a semi-switch for you when he spirited your unconscious body from the Neon Nightmare to Europe. Why couldn't the all-powerful Miss Kitty pull off the same kind of illusions?"

"She could," said Max. "Although I swore the woman who died pursuing me on a motorcycle was her, from information I got in Ireland, she's very much alive. Magicians use body doubles. Houdini did. Gandolph and I didn't. I suppose an international terrorism money-raiser like Kathleen could have insisted the doubles have facial plastic surgery to seem identical to her."

"And then she let them die in her place whenever anybody got too close." Now Temple shook her head. "What a totally irredeemable human being."

"Maybe not," Matt said, staring at the Table of Crime Elements. "The only person Jesus specifically invited to His Father's kingdom in heaven was the thief being crucified beside Him who went from reviling to believing in Him."

"Deathbed confessions," Max said, "are notoriously insincere."

"Still." Matt sat back. "I have to believe every human soul is redeemable."

"You don't *have* to believe it," Max said. "You just do. And I guess that's admirable."

He leaned forward, stabbing the Table of Crime Elements with a forefinger. "Here, here, and here. Somewhere in these unsolved crimes are clues that will implicate and lead us to Kitty the Cutter.

"We're getting closer than we know. I sense it. This time she won't die on me to run away and die another day in another guise, and another after that. This time it'll be a permanent demise. Even knowing what I know now about Kathleen's beyond-brutal childhood, I won't find peace until I know that she is off this planet for good, and unable to harm Temple, you, and me."

Temple felt a chill run up the back of her neck, sheer anger. What a rabble-rouser Max would have made.

She eyed Matt, sitting back, his expression both troubled and intense, his arms folded across his chest as if holding something in.

She wondered what thoughts or emotions held him captive. Something she didn't know, she sensed, kept him quiet.

And that couldn't be good.

Chapter 4

Home Alone

"I thought he'd never leave."

Matt shut the door on Max and turned to Temple.

"Me too," she said, moving into his arms. "Ever since we came back from Chicago, which was an all-business and too-much-funny-business trip, we've been caught up in your mom's wonderful-but-quickie wedding. You and I haven't had any real time together, night or day."

"I know." He pulled her into one of those first-time love-declaring, almost desperate embraces with a long kiss that migrated into a breathless series.

The new-old intensity of it made her knees and pulses quiver like a teenager's. "What was that for?"

"For us putting away all the old family business that's kept us worried and shot down our privacy, including who murdered whom on your darn Table of Crime Elements."

"I guess we'd better take a break."

His agreement was swift and no less intense, but he broke their kiss with a frown. "The cat's moved out to the balcony. He just pushed the French door open."

"Louie hates human 'mushy moments.' Forget him. Now we have the bed all to ourselves."

But Matt pulled out of their embrace to inspect the ajar French door and the balcony.

Temple sighed for full dramatic effect. "Matt. Louie is the original cat burglar. He always uses the French doors."

By now Matt was examining the levers and the latches as if they were a more fascinating erotic zone than hers truly's. Guys! They always had to examine anything mechanical. She wouldn't be surprised to learn there was a robotic blowup doll.

She couldn't help complaining about the French doors getting more attention than her. "You sound just like—" *Max*.

He whirled to face her.

Temple switched grips on the conversational footballs. "—like Lieutenant Molina making a house safety check. We can discuss changing the latches later. Meanwhile, 'I'm melting, I'm melting,'" she quoted the Wicked Witch of the West, as she had turned into another kind of puddle indeed.

He looked into her eyes, and seconds later she got a very satisfying bum's rush into the bedroom, although he shut the door behind them for the first time, as if intent on keeping Louie, or the whole world, out.

Temple had no complaints about that, or anything.

* * *

"You don't really hate my Table of Crime Elements," she said later, when they were entwined side by side on the living room sofa, bare feet propped on the newspaper-laden coffee table.

"It's brilliant, Temple, like you." He kissed her . . . temple, where her hairdo had devolved into damp tendrils. His sigh was deep enough to worry her. "I'm just more aware now of how dangerous this world is, and how much we're in danger every day."

"You mean, because of runaway buses or comets or recession? Or because of whatever your stepfather was mixed up in or—?"

"Because of all that, up to and including your tendency to solve everyone's problems, including the police's. It's dangerous. This last trip to Chicago, it was almost fatal to Louie."

"We can't sit still and wait for the bad guys and gals to find us."

"No," he agreed, his tight-lipped mouth a grim underline to that reality. "But *you* can be watchful." Matt shifted into a less cuddly position. "I'm going to have to be working late for a while."

She took that news, turned it over in her mind, and laughed. "You work late already."

"Later. A couple of hours later. I won't be able to see you after the show."

"Not until four thirty A.M.? I loved all our wee-hour rendezvous, the off-Strip world so deliciously dark. Why?"

"Ambrosia and I are running experimental tapes on a new concept. When your boss is the broadcaster ahead of you, that's the only time available for . . . experiments. I'm not giving up the earlier evening hours, because that's the time we can share going out and about like normal people."

Temple mock-pouted, though she was curious about the "experimental tapes."

"At least that means you'll be available for the post-honeymoon bash Nicky Fontana and Van are throwing at the Crystal Phoenix Tuesday night for my aunt Kit and his oldest brother Aldo."

"Really? There are post-honeymoon bashes? I'd love to have that for us."

Temple played coy. "I'm sure if I hint nicely to Van and Nicky. I do handle their PR. But why are you looking into new formats at WCOO? Oh. Does Ambrosia know about your network daytime TV talk show offer?"

"That's an exploration, Temple, not an offer yet."

"An 'exploration' that put a little deal tempter like a Jaguar in your driveway."

"In the Circle Ritz parking lot. And that's a problem because a car like that should be garaged. In fact, fancy cars are more trouble than the head-turning factor is worth. The only head I want to turn is yours."

"I'll never make you into a conspicuous consumer," Temple said, not complaining.

"Says the retro fashion recycler."

She smiled at his point, but frowned right after. "So did you tell Ambrosia about your career-change possibility?"

"On the air, 'Ambrosia' is all breathy empathy as she plays songs to comfort the troubled. As a businesswoman, Letitia Brown is sharper than a shark's tooth."

"So she knows you're in danger of leaving? You've caved and are trying out something the two of you can do beyond your *Midnight Hour* advice show, separately, following her sob story hour?"

Matt shrugged, looking unhappy. Poor guy, he had way too many scruples for the business world, Temple thought. She didn't want to add to his pressures.

"Okay. I'll give you up for those precious post–

Midnight Hour rendezvous, but you're all mine from noon to eleven P.M."

"I'm all yours around the clock, only I'll have to be absent for my work hours."

Finally. The men had left. Temple didn't believe she'd ever feel that way about either one of them. Still fretting over Matt's strange new indifference to his exciting job opportunities, she unleashed her own anxieties. She hied back to the bedroom and the small chest that housed accessories. The notorious scarf drawer was so full of its airy contents that it jammed a bit on opening.

She pawed through the contents for the few ring boxes and rings. Not a good hiding place, but she'd felt so safe at the Circle Ritz, when Max lived here with her, now with Matt just a floor above.

Her fingers found the heavy gold of a man's ring; the worm Ouroboros symbol of eternity, swallowing its own tail; and the box with the cheap cocktail ring she'd wasted her money on at the women's exhibition, something sparkly and girly that had fit her mood then. She *didn't* find the opal and diamond ring in its plastic evidence Baggie from Lieutenant Molina.

She sat on the bed, her heart pounding, the two rings in her lap. She shut her eyes, remembering the saleswoman behind the ring counter she barely looked at over the array of glittering stones.

That's when Matt's "returned" Ouroboros ring must have been slipped into Temple's bag and had emigrated with the boxed ring into her drawer unnoticed. When had Max's ring vanished—again—then? Much more recently.

Temple looked up, to the rooms beyond the bedroom. Midnight Louie jumped up beside her, nosing the two rings.

"Oh, Louie," she said. "Has Kitty the Cutter been breaking in here all along? Collecting 'trophies'? And what am I asking you for?"

His sturdy *merow* clearly meant he was just the one to confide in.

And then her phone rang.

Chapter 5

Wynning Number

"Am I talking to the greatest little stunt PR woman on Planet Hollywood or the Las Vegas Strip?"

Temple reared back from her own cell phone–holding hand. She welcomed new clients, but it was a bit early in the day for dealing with a carnival huckster.

"I *am* a PR freelancer," she answered evenly, "and I try to do a great job for my clients, but in all other respects, I find your introduction offensive."

"Sorry, sorry, sorry," the man's voice went on. "I'm a blunt businessman. I am not easily impressed, but you have caught my radar. Let me make a pitch in person, anywhere you say. Lunch, dinner, or even breakfast."

Temple didn't think she could stomach breakfast with this guy. He had the always "up," booming voice of a used car salesman.

"We can decide by phone if . . ." She paused, considering her next words. Temple seldom had to juggle words, but she already felt that "my services" or "our interests" were not phrases to use with this guy, like she should wash her cell phone surface after finishing the call.

"No, no, no." he said. "Nothing useful is done by phone except call-in sex."

Whoa! She reared back again.

"Silas T. Farnum, ma'am. I have a big investment property under way just off-Strip. Not much this size is going now in the Nevada economy. I sure could use a vice president of media. I could use the Wizard of Oz, frankly, ma'am, but maybe a munchkin will have to do."

Temple's jaw was nearly resting on her clavicle. Of all the insulting, off-putting idiots . . .

"You do know I'm—"

"Cute as a ladybug in a rug? Yes, ma'am. I saw pictures of you in the paper next to that elephant Jumbo, or Dumbo, at the Oasis. That was a slick eye-popping way to raffle off a million cash. That's when I first became an admirer."

Temple didn't think it necessary to mention that the event had become a crime scene and she had almost become elephant pâté.

"Well," she told him, "this 'ladybug in a rug' has a number of important, legitimate PR clients who aren't booking circus acts to keep me busy."

"Yup. I would be an illegitimate one, that's for sure. My mama was young and poor when she had me, but she's living in Versailles"—he pronounced it *Ver-sails,* not *Ver-sigh* as in proper French—"Versailles on the Intracoastal Waterway in Florida."

Temple sighed. "Why did you call me?"

"Love the business card: TEMPLE BARR, PR. I feel like I'm hiring Samantha Spade." And he chuckled with the enthusiasm of a clown.

"I'd have to know what sort of attraction you're financing, the budget, and the clientele."

"You've heard a picture is worth a thousand words?"

"Right. Unfortunately, I sling words, in whatever media. I don't take pictures."

"Now, now, now."

Apparently, Silas T. liked to repeat himself. Maybe that kept him from hearing that folks were tuning him out.

"I swear, Ms. Barr, this concept can't miss. It's so obviously meant for Vegas, and nothing like this has ever hit the Strip before. I dare not mention it to the cell phone towers, so you'll just have to trust me and agree to discuss it in person."

"Where?" she asked, intrigued despite herself.

Nevada still wallowed in a stagnant stew of recession. It wouldn't hurt to rustle up new business while Matt was waiting to hear on plans for his network TV talk show career. Even if they relocated to Chicago, she could always commute back to Vegas to finish projects in progress.

The Crystal Phoenix would need more than a fly-in-by-night PR person, though, she thought with a pang.

"What about the Wynn?" her caller was suggesting.

Temple was glad they weren't on Skype so her caller could see her twin elevated eyebrows. That was a high-end venue for this low-brow-sounding huckster.

"Lunch today?" he pushed.

She agreed, more out of curiosity than great expectations.

Steve Wynn was the self-made Las Vegas tycoon most known to the public. The crazy karma of his last name alone had been a gift. Daddy changed it from Weinberg. Naming an entire hotel-casino after it had been marketing genius. Talk about "branding."

So it was no wonder that his self-named hotel-casino had led the charge to super-upscale venues in Vegas. Not far from the Wynn's display area of high-six-figure Ferrari and Maserati sports cars was a charming restaurant.

The Terrace Pointe Café extended from indoors to outdoor tables overlooking an aquamarine pool and formal gardens with Italian pines and awnings and a cloudless blue sky. The hostess led Temple to a prime table for two with wicker chairs resembling small thrones. Just what the vertically challenged ego would order.

An elderly man at the table stood at her arrival, waving a pale linen napkin, having ID'ed her from news reports of the recent debacle at the Oasis.

Silas T. Farnum standing wasn't much of a production. He was barely taller than she and four times as round. He reminded her of a Mini-Me of someone she couldn't quite place, she realized. He hadn't been insulting when he'd called her a munchkin on that morning phone call. He was bonding.

"Sit, sit, sit. Do sit, Miss Barr," he urged. "We can have a delightful tête-à-tête here."

"Mr. Farnum," she greeted him as she set her tote bag on the floor, a bit dazed and wondering if Alice's rabbit hole wasn't far away.

She'd better avoid anything on the menu that called to her with an "Eat me" vibe, like—she glanced at the single placard menu faceup on her place setting—like the upscale turkey burger with sherry vinaigrette and pea tendrils in addition to the usual lettuce, tomato, and onions. She'd come to terms with her five-foot-zero plus three-inch heels and yearned neither to shrink nor expand. The same was true about her business, so her host had better have an interesting assignment.

"Now, Miss Barr, you must keep this discussion confidential, whether you decide to accept the assignment or not. Are you agreeable?"

"I'm always agreeable, Mr. Farnum. That's my job," she added with a smile. "However, anything you say will be between you and me and the wicker."

A bottle of pinot grigio was open on the table. The filled water goblets and wineglasses sparkled in the sunlight.

"I took the liberty," Mr. Farnum admitted with a bow as he reinstated the large napkin . . . behind his belt.

He still gave off a distinct whiff of "confidence man," but merry brown eyes under shaggy gray brows and Santa-style flushed cheeks intrigued Temple. Whatever this jolly little man had in mind, it would be original.

When the waiter came promptly, Temple relaxed and felt free to order salad for lunch. It was obvious Farnum was going to be doing all the talking and she wouldn't be caught with dressing on her lap or radicchio in her teeth while speaking and making notes at the same time. PR people had to think ahead.

Silas T. had no such concerns, ordering veggie burger sliders primed for disaster with a full complement of slippery edibles like red onions, zucchini, yellow squash, mushrooms, lentils, tomato pesto, and Boston lettuce. It was colorful, just like his peach-and-white-striped seersucker suit. She was surprised to see a straw boater on the table that seemed more like a prop for a summer picnic setting. Then she noticed that only five shriveled strands of gray hair crossed Silas T.'s bald head, reminding her of an impromptu musical staff.

"One thing I must make clear at the outset, Mr. Farnum: I am not a 'stunt' PR person."

"No? What about your performance on the elephant at the Oasis?"

"That was the elephant's idea. Apparently, she was a big girl used to working with a, well, petite woman."

"What about the headlines about the secret tunnel leading to several Vegas venues? While you were overseeing the live, formal opening of an old hidden walk-out safe for possible treasure—*voilà!*—a fresh corpse was found within?"

"That corpse was . . . unforeseen."

"And was wearing white tie and tails. What a terrific publicity coup for Gangsters, the Crystal Phoenix, and the Neon Nightmare club."

Temple sipped wine and squirmed. "If it was such great publicity, the outcome hasn't been great. Neon Nightmare has since gone dark."

"That club was always an iffy concept." Farnum leaned back as their orders arrived. His napkin migrated from being tucked into his high-waisted belt to covering the banana yellow bow tie at the neck of his shirt. "Off-Strip is tricky territory. Often it degenerates into cramped parking lots or ticky-tacky venues, say like from the corner of Paradise and Convention Drive all the way to Las Vegas Boulevard."

Temple took time to salad-dressing dive with some of her greens while she pictured that stretch of real estate. She recalled a cheap and happy-hour-heavy box of a nightclub/strip joint standing on that spot. The location was truly bared, standing cheeks-by-jowls with parking lots and the sleazy souvenir shops that popped up at any tiny gaps on the Mega-Million Miles of the Strip too.

Then she reminded herself that from such seedy sprouts major enterprises could grow, like Hooters, for instance. Which she Did Not Like.

Tourists thronging the Downtown Experience and the Las Vegas Strip might be amazed to learn that nearby real estate could support enterprises far more modest than billion-dollar hostelries. That was especially true now that grandiose expansion plans sixty stories tall stood abandoned in midair ever since the Great Recession had hit Nevada like a ton of bricks from the Luxor's giant pyramid turned landslide.

Temple was intrigued by where Farnum was placing his secret project as much as by what it was. That area had always been a difficult sell and was a boulevard of broken honky-tonk dreams.

Although her major client on the Strip was the Crystal Phoenix boutique hotel, she was also repping an innovative wine/beauty bar with an ancient Egyptian theme called Chez Shez that occupied the Strip's top end near the venerable Stratosphere, Circus Circus, and Riviera venues.

Its hunky proprietor was the bronzed Egyptian version of a Greek god in braided wig who played perfectly in person and on the Internet. The combo of custom cosmetics and ancient recipe wines had poised the pricey little place on the brink of becoming a franchise, thanks to her help. She was hoping to groom Shez into a cross between the new Fabio and an Iron Chef.

So she always kept an open mind when it came to offbeat clients with "secret recipe" ideas.

"What kind of new venue are you floating?" she asked, almost afraid to ask. Silas T. Farnum calling borderline venues tacky didn't mean he was above sponsoring just such a new venture himself, particularly if he wanted a "stunt" PR person.

"It's a secret," he said, lowering his voice and leaning closer.

Temple smelled peppermint on his breath, which was refreshing. "You have to tell your PR rep," she warned him.

"No, I have to show her."

"Look, Mr. Farnum. This lunch is already two hours out of my day. I don't work in the dark."

"Oh, it's a secret in broad daylight. That's what I have to show you."

"This is some . . . new nightclub?"

"What's old is new, isn't that true in the PR game?"

He chuckled and stuffed a slider in his mouth to avoid saying more.

"Granted, nothing is so old that it can't be spun into something new," Temple told him. "How can a secret be shown to anyone in broad daylight?"

"That's what you're going to be promoting. It's so secret, you can't see it right in front of your face. Even if X marks the spot."

With a flourish, Silas T. slapped his napkin to the tabletop and signed what was inside the discreet padded folder at his fingertips. It took him just a few seconds and no credit card.

He was staying at the high-end Wynn?

"Just where are you from?" Temple asked.

"That's a secret too. Maybe from somewhere out of this world," he said with a wink.

Temple expected him to bound up a nearby chimney or perhaps one of the clay Mexican chimenea fireplaces on the adjoining patio. The Vegas desert could get cold at night; in the winter, the hotels provided heaters for the outside lounges and restaurants.

The idea of the short but portly Mr. Farnum whisking like a genie into a patio fire urn made Temple swallow a giggle. She was thinking leprechaun now, more than seersucker Santa. The man was infectious and he'd make "good copy." That was an old newspaper expression. He'd make good multimedia would be the updated way to put it.

"Now," he said. "We can either go shopping for a Ferrari, or I can show you my mystery project." He leaned over to glance at the floor and Temple's four-inch heels on a one-inch platform shoe. "Not exactly Lady Gaga, but I'll warn you that we are heading for some rough terrain."

Curiouser and curiouser. Temple reached into her ever-present tote bag and pulled out a tiny drawstring bag and flourished roll-up rubber-soled ballet flats. Who was playing Santa Claus now?

"No problem, Mr. Farnum. I need only dash into the nearest ladies' room and I'll emerge as an Abba Super-tramper with utterly flat feet."

"Excellent footwork," Silas T. Farnum said with another wink.

Chapter 6

Louie Has His
Ups and Downs

Nothing is worse than having to do a 180-degree turn while working on a major catnap at my home, sweet home. It seems I have a new assignment: tailing my roommate when she is out on errands of a sudden and unscheduled nature.

That is to say, she is wearing her red high heels and is pulling her sunglasses out of her turquoise tote bag.

That is how I know she is in a hurry. Turquoise and red accessories? *Tsk, tsk,* and tangle my whiskers.

After our traumatic trip to Mr. Matt's family and network job opportunities, not to mention unsuspected family mob connections in Chicago, I have worried about my roomie's ability to handle everything that is in play, including a psychopath in the woodwork.

So it is out the French doors again. Then I am down the

rough-barked palm tree to the ground before the Circle Ritz elevator can creak Miss Temple to the lobby.

Next, I am under the little red Miata in its cozy carport before you can say Jackie Robinson.

Click, click, click. Miss Temple was never one to shy from announcing her oncoming presence. I crouch, vibrissae (whiskers to you) vibrating with excitement. I have a mere half a second to leap out, scramble up, and squeeze into the tiny space between Miss Temple's pushed-forward front seat and the trunk bulk head. Once placed, I blend with the black carpet.

I must protest to Mazda sometime for skimping on rumble seat room in Miatas for hitchhiking PIs of a feline nature. "Cute" is as cute does, and I look for function in a vehicle as well as cool looks. Just a little marketing tip.

You might think my Miss Temple is a bit dim not to notice that I am occasionally a third wheel, so to speak, on her expeditions. That would be underestimating my well-polished expertise as a stealth investigator. Given the prejudice against my kind running unfettered, I have been perfecting a low profile since a kit. Also, being petite, Miss Temple is a forward-charging personality and seldom looks back, which also serves me well.

I think this tendency will serve her well as she finalizes her transition from association with an alpha male who is too busy roaming and fighting to a more domesticated male who will settle down with her in a peaceful routine without, Bast forbid, any kits of any species on the horizon.

I have already conceded much in her behalf. There is eating the occasional putrid pellet of Free-to-Be-Feline health food for sissy cats. There is ceding one-quarter of the zebra-pattern comforter to offensive recreational activities of a personal nature that force me to decamp in the middle of the night. There is even occasionally using the disgusting plastic tray of grit she keeps in the second bathroom.

Despite my sacrifices, I am always ready to act as an impromptu bodyguard.

She uses the Wynn's off-Strip entrance, which avoids the endless lobby and casino areas. I have no trouble darting from one handy place of concealment to another while following her through the tourist throngs.

People in Las Vegas rarely look down, unless it is to puke, which is why the carpeting is always a busy multicolored design for long wear.

Nowadays, the upscale places are all marble floors, which clean up more easily but echo like crazy. "Stealth" is my middle name, so I make sure I am not seen and certainly am not heard in my velvet footpad mode.

Not so with Miss Temple, whose smart high heels add to the echo. She can trot faster than a Pomeranian on those spikes. I do not know how she does it and am all admiration. I certainly could not move so fast in any direction but up with my shivs out.

When she trots all the way through the casino areas to the Terrace Pointe Café, I am stymied. All the Wynn restaurants feature an indoor-outdoor ambience. I certainly approve because I am definitely an inside-outside kind of guy.

Still, the Terrace Pointe Café forsakes any tinge of Vegas casino shadowy décor. Simply put, the light and airy spaces mean my entrance would be like an inkblot trying to pass as Wite-Out on a piece of snowy bond paper.

Manx! I must glimpse what Pied Piper has drawn my Miss Temple from our cozy nest at the Circle Ritz. With Kathleen O'Connor lurking around the home front now that Mr. Max is back in town, I am super suspicious of all new contacts these days.

I could make out like a bandit with the hotel family buffet droppings just kiddie-corner from the café, but I am not here to feed my stomach, only my curiosity, which is almost as capacious.

Cringing with shame, I opt for cover in the resort-wear

shop opposite. At least they have hanging clothing areas I can conceal myself under, but it is not a locale of choice for the macho private eye. I would really rather be darting under the goods in the Ferrari–Maserati showroom at the main entrance. Ah. The fragrant drip of Italian motor oil and air of imminent Fontana brothers.

At least here in this domain where the women come and go, talking of mojitos and Michelangelo, I can keep my eyes on the restaurant entrance across the way. I can also spot the telltale style, color, and audible ring of my Miss Temple's current heels when she leaves. When I tail her, I can get a notion of whom she has met and for what purpose.

I will not bore you by reporting all the chitchat I overhear in the next hour or so. Or the extreme prices of so-called casual wear from an outfit named Dulcie and Gabby Anna.

The continual scrape of hanger tops on rods and incoming and outgoing waves of a dozen different designer fragrances lull me into something resembling a stupor.

My eyes pop wide when I realize I have gazed unthinking on my little doll's ankles leaving the restaurant in—she has cheated on me!—flats. Shoes that are all sole and no heel at all. No soul.

Someone in a pair of pale pants and oxford shoes was ankling along right beside her.

I throw caution to the caftans and corner like a Maserati outta the joint, immune to the *oohs* and *aahs* my exit leaves behind me.

Alas, the pathway between the casinos is a sea of legs mingling in all directions. I need height to spot my flat-footed roommate and her mysterious escort.

Sliding and dodging among the many hairy bare legs (the Terrace Pointe Café overlooks the hotel's main pools, which are about the size for a dozen orca whales, not to mention overweight gambling "whales"), I race to out-amble my prey.

I concoct a plan. The Wynn has a famous place where a two-story wall of glass overlooks a wall of falling water. Folks like to gather there for a quiet drink. (That is what anyone who spends four hours on the Vegas Strip requires, a quiet drink. I do not use addictive substances, but do take a wee nip now and then. I especially like mine organically grown. I know, that is very '70s.)

Anyway, I am planning to hitch a ride to the top of the magnificent white-plastered rotunda above the cocktail joint, from where I can spy Miss Temple's red hair and petite form with no trouble, even if she is going barefoot!

The beauty of my plan is that all the customers (I guess at the Wynn they are "clients") are facing out into this brilliantly sunlit façade. Anyone who happens to turn and spot me will be "light-blind" for many moments, and I plan to keep moving.

My ride to the top may be as yellow or red as a priceless Italian sports car, but it is a much humbler and common domestic object.

Yes, friends, I am going to be doing the Mary Poppins act. Not with the clumsy black bumbershoot the Brits favor, but with the floating fanciful umbrellas that constantly rise up and down in the area known as Parasol Up and Parasol Down, which will in future be known as Louie Up and Louie Down.

Everyone's ground-level focus faces away from me as I tumble into the belly of an upside-down yellow puffy number dripping tassels. Yeah, it is a girly sort of ride, but I use what is at hand, and the green piping matches my eyes.

There is nothing black here but me, so I will be clearly visible when I reach the second level, where viewers loiter to watch the parasols glide up and down like hot-air balloons.

Oops! Is it possible some of these open umbrellas are programmed to close now and then? I seem to feel my airy carriage turning into a deflated balloon and scramble to attach myself to a passing purple-and-gold parasol that is going . . . down, not up!

Below me lies the sea of white giant umbrellas covering the outdoor tables. Around and above me waft the Technicolor flock of floating parasols. I almost hear a Viennese waltz playing as they lilt up and down and leap like the pink-toe-shoe-and-tutu-wearing hippopotami in Disney's *Fantasia* while I spring froglike from one moving silken lily pad to another.

From the three viewing balconies on the second level (that would be Parasol Up) come exclamations and exhortations.

"How'd that cat get in here?"

"Maybe he thinks the parasols are birds."

"Dumb cat."

"Oh, the poor thing. He could fall and *die*!"

"He could fall and *kill* someone."

"Someone call Security."

"I'm filming. Get outa my way."

"Hey! They said at the desk, pets weren't allowed at this hotel. I had to leave my Mexican hairless at home."

"This is going on YouTube."

And, cruelest cut of all, "Is that a big fat bat, Mommy?"

Despite the rude comments, I paddle and churn and claw my way upward, hearing telltale hisses of fabric in my wake. Steve Wynn will be after my skin. Luckily, one of my type looks much like another on first glance and I doubt there will be any organized witch hunt.

I ignore the, uh, catcalls, and continue to walk on moving parasols, making a last daring leap to the brass top rail on the balcony and bounding off it to the floor.

"Get that cat!" a few someones yell in chorus, but there are so many tourists consulting smartphones or texting as they tour that I am soon lost in a welter of moving legs.

I am an expert at doing a serpentine do-si-do through that kind of crowd. My prey is heading for the exit. That means I only have to sprint through some luxurious displays of exotic plants and flowers. The fancy loam is clogging up my shivs, but dirt is great camouflage for me, and my trail can be detected only by a sinuous shaking among the greenery. I bust through to the south entrance and out in plain sight of Bast, parking valets, and everyone . . .

. . . to see the sassy rear of a little red Miata disappearing down the driveway.

What an expedition. What a day.

When I see sassy rears, I expect a lot better success rate than this parasol chase.

Chapter 7

Stunted!

Temple found the rubber soles of her "sensible" ballet flats no match for rubble.

She'd agreed to meet Silas T. on this uncivilized stretch of Paradise Road, but had underestimated the ability of her soles to deal with desert hikes.

Well, walks anyway.

Her tender arches strove for balance on the sharp irregular surface of stone-studded sand. It was like walking over a spike-embellished Hells Angels motorcycle jacket, not that one of those guys would ever do a Sir Walter Raleigh and throw his outer garment down for a lady to walk on.

Beside her, Silas T. Farnum hooked his thumbs in his trouser belt loops and gazed at the desolate sun-baked scene like Alexander the Great contemplating an empire extending from the Arabian and Caspian to the Black and Mediterranean Seas. She guessed that's why history called that sort "visionaries."

Farnum's vision was on the small side, like him. "That's it, right there."

Temple squinted despite sunglasses. No gigantic hotels shaded this backlot to Vegas Strip glory. Looking where his stubby forefinger pointed, she saw what seemed like a giant parking garage abandoned after going up a scant ten stories. It was just a skeleton of a building, intersecting girders and concrete making a dull gray brown plaid mostly obscured by giant tarps and plastic sheeting. Past its homely, raw structure, Temple glimpsed gaudy slices of completed Vegas Strip edifices.

"That's all you've got?" she asked Farnum. "I'm sandblasting my insteps to see another stalled construction project?"

"Not . . . quite. Watch the top of the building."

"Building" was an overambitious word for it, but Temple dutifully looked.

A blast of noise right beside her made her jump. That was some phone ringtone he had. Deep drums throbbed.

She glanced sideways, disapproving, only to see him holding a small recording device with a mighty big sound she was starting to recognize. . . .

Farnum beamed. "The symphonic opening theme to *2001: A Space Odyssey*. So glad a person of your generation recognized it. That confirms you're the one for me."

"Well, *I* may not feel confident that I'm the 'one for you,' Mr. Farnum."

"Are you watching the top of the building, Miss Barr?"

"All right, but if I'm watching that space, I'm giving it one more minute flat to impress me."

He just chuckled.

Had Temple been wearing her usual spike heels, she would have kicked herself for being dragged into this iffy outing with a certified fruit loop. Here she was always telling Matt he was too sympathetic to life's losers. At least that was his job. Her job was publicizing legitimate enterprises. . . .

Temple stared as she saw the familiar disk of the spaceship *Enterprise* rising like the Earth over the moon in the film *2001: A Space Odyssey*. No . . . that iconic *Star Trek* ship had big thrusters behind the main disk. This thing was all disk as it elevated against an ocean-deep sky of intense blue. This thing was a—

"It's you." She turned on Farnum. "It's *you* releasing those fake UFOs all over the Strip."

He shrugged modestly. "Well, my minions anyway. I've stationed operators in all the highest towers."

"Those otherworldly balloons are radio controlled, but I'm not, Mr. Farnum. My PR practice does not go in for cheap tricks. I am outta here."

She would have spun on her heel, but she didn't have one right now. The move just ground her sore soles deeper into the loose stones.

"*Ow!*" she exclaimed, disliking the weakness of her position both physically and mentally. She'd let herself be charmed and taken for a ludicrous ride. Being a hundred pounds and five-foot-zero often got her dismissed as young and silly, not serious, and now she'd earned that designation.

"Wait, Miss Barr. Just look at the building once more, for the space of a nanosecond."

Temple glared, but he'd produced another small black device from his summery suit jacket pocket.

She glared. At the building, not the man.

And it was gone. No, replaced by a dazzling tower with a glittering, spinning top. Blink. No, all that raw concrete and steel was still there.

Had she eaten something at lunch, something sprinkled over her salad while she'd gazed at the patio gardens?

Something in the wine? She hadn't seen the bottle opened. Careless. She was alone with this strange man and possibly doped in the medical sense of the word.

"What did you see?" Farnum demanded with almost a giggle.

"A magical illusion. A trick. I must admit it was a trick on a David Copperfield scale. A whole building shifting skins, I mean. But, I warn you. I've . . . associated with magicians. You're using some kind of controlled projection."

"On this size and scale?"

"Copperfield does it," she repeated.

"Do I look like him?"

"More like the anti-Copperfield," she admitted.

"I told you I would take you to where X marks the spot. This is the spot. This is the secret to be revealed in delicious bites by you. Sound bites, film bites, cell phone bites, old-fashioned print bites. Think. What did you see?"

"In a nanosecond? I saw a tower—as if Vegas isn't filled with them. It could have been the Stratosphere across the Strip. Something revolving, suspended. Again, like the roller coaster around the Stratosphere. I guess the icing on the layer cake could be a giant version of your annoying mini flying saucers."

"UFOs."

"UFOs. So I'm to 'sell' an alien slide show?"

"You're to sell a mystery."

"That's a disappointment." She saw Farnum's thumb click his creepy black box again and whipped her head around to spot the special effect it created. This second glimpse rang a bell in her cerebellum, or wherever memory cells abided, about an almost ancient local . . . landmark.

She pinned Farnum with her sternest look. She knew Vegas history better than anyone. "This site. It once hosted a Las Vegas landmark. In fact, Howard Hughes bought it before it opened, and when it was imploded, they used the footage in a movie called *Mars Attacks!* They called it the Landmark Hotel and it was a tower topped by a flying saucer and it was leveled in 1995. Are you telling me you have a freaking time machine?"

"Oh, no, Miss Barr. That would be an old, clichéd idea with little glamour and appeal."

Temple gave a relieved sigh. She wouldn't have to call for the men in white to take him away, after all, and she was sure he wasn't a Man in Black. He'd never make the height requirement.

"Although time travel is closer than you think," Farnum said. "What I have—what we have—is the latest in futuristic technology. I've created a stealth building that will soon be unveiled for gathering witnesses from the, shall we say, fringe scientific theory community. I have three thousand confirmed attendees driving and flying and possibly walking here at this moment. Also arriving will be media from all the alien-centered cable TV programming."

"Alien-centered programming" sounded even more sinister to Temple. Was it a fancy name for mind control? Meanwhile, she needed to grasp what was going on.

"When were you going to tell me that the circus was coming to town? Never mind. So they paved Paradise and put up a parking lot and now you've erected a 'stealth' building on it?"

Farnum nodded soberly. "Night crews have been working on it here for months, not knowing the building goes into hibernation once they leave. First you see it, then you don't."

She stared at the dreary unfinished mass of the parking garage. "How was I supposed to market an invisible building? What kind of a convention would anyone hold in an invisible building?"

"You must never underestimate the power of the human imagination when it boldly goes seeking alien life-forms. We have *Voyager* cruising out beyond the solar system after thirty-five years and now *Curiosity* scanning Mars. Soon Las Vegas will share in the wealth and debut the hotel-casino Area 54—'a little more far out than Area 51.' My motto." Farnum beamed at her.

"Beam me up, Scotty," she muttered.

Too bad that was just an expression and there was no way for her to turn into a sparkly silhouette and disappear.

When it came to alien life-forms, Silas T. Farnum was a doozy.

Chapter 8

Unlawful Entry

If Dear Abby ever needs another secretary, I believe that I am now fully qualified.

Talk about standing by your human. I am the poster boy for that theme song. I am sure my off-camera antics yesterday morning aided Miss Temple in handling the family business that often can be so difficult for her kind. I myself avoid phone calls in favor of a nose-to-nose meeting of the minds.

I do know something about large, untidy families, though. I sympathize with my little doll, being born the only girl kit—and the runt of the litter at that—with four hyperactive bruiser boys for what humans call "siblings."

I would call those brothers from the apparently savage and freezing stretch of northlands called Minnesota one thing: bozos. It is too bad my Miss Temple was not really born into *la famiglia Italiana* Fontana.

If anyone in Vegas could possibly fill my boots on protecting my little doll, it is a posse of Fontana brothers. Like me, they offer proper due respect to the females of our respective species.

My Miss Temple is no longer wishing to work as an official private eye, given the dangers she faced in her first run at the profession, but I could not allow her to trot out alone on her snappy platform heels this noon. Errands for her public relations business are not life threatening, and she returned from her Wynn meeting no worse for wear and ready to serve me dinner.

Me, duty done, I head for the living room couch for the night, stretching luxuriantly on my back. My role as an action hero is tabled for now and I can become the usual domestic sofa spud.

I gaze up at the unique arched white ceiling, which reminds one of sand dunes and makes the daylight seem like reflected water. This is as close as I wish to get to that irksome invention called "beach." Sand between my toes. *Ouch!* Sand dulling the polish on my concealed shivs? No thank you! Sand fleas hitching a ride on my shoulder blades just where I cannot reach . . . never again!

I curve into a comfy kittenish curl, since I am on my own and fancy-free. I twitch the only white feature on my whole black-satin bodysuit: my whiskers. A purr rumbles in my throat and rib cage. I am starting to dream about Topaz, the Oasis Hotel feline mascot, a sleek and nubile black-like-me beauty who—

Crash bang!

My world explodes. I do a double-axel twist. Ripping sounds up the back of the sofa raise the hairs on my spine from my hackles to the tip of my tailbone.

A speeding black bullet hits the sofa cushion beside me and ricochets off.

A few black hairs drift down into my face like falling eyelashes.

By now I have all four on the floor and am in full frontal battle mode. Only then do I realize this entire exercise in adrenaline has been a false alarm.

"Louise," I admonish the smaller black furry form facing me across the coffee table, a pile of tumbled newsprint between us. "That is no way to interrupt your superior's beauty sleep."

"Beauty sleep! My superior! I will give you a beauty sleep with a slap across the kisser."

My eyes widen. My mistake. I am not looking into the mellow yellow gold eyes of my partner in Midnight Investigations, Inc., but the green peepers that feature one fight-sagged lid and the snaggle-fanged visage of my long-lost and now-found dam, Ma Barker.

Damn.

"This is what you do on your off time?" she demands. "Lie about, you lackluster layabout? You would be a poor excuse of a leader if I ever abdicated from running the police substation clowder."

"I was taking a well-deserved rest. I only yesterday defended my Miss Temple during an uneasy phone call."

"No doubt a political solicitation."

"And you cannot break and enter here in your rowdy, alley cat way, Ma. Miss Temple might assume *I* am sharpening my shivs on her French doorframes and upholstery. I have always been the perfect indoor gentleman. What is the rush here?"

"Look, Junior. I have not got all day. My gang is waiting for us and it is only hours before the light of day, and that kind of exposure is dangerous. Those alien visitors that drop unidentified flying objects into our innocent midst to trap us and bear us away for medical experimentation are back.

"And this time, they are after not only us, but bigger prey too. We have stumbled on something fishy in the way of murder most mystifying."

Okay. My ma is a canny street fighter and survivor. Not every single black female of a certain age runs her own street gang. Yet she is of an older generation and has her stubborn misconceptions. I would not go so far as to say she is *superstitious.* I mean, it is pretty hard for her to avoid black cats crossing her path every which way but loose. Still, she does subscribe to some way-out ideas, like being a PI makes me a lazy lout and alien visitors are interested in a mass abduction of her precious clowder.

"Now, Ma," I say. "I have told you before that no alien force is coming to take you away, except the SPCA, and you all are in a TNR zone these days."

"Twilight Zone, I told you so."

"I am not referring to the spooky TV show. 'TNR' stands for Trap, Neuter, Return. The human do-gooders seek to prevent unwanted littering by whisking our street people away to low-cost neutering facilities. It is a good program for those who, unlike myself, are not able to avail themselves of such voluntary choices as vasectomy."

"Hmph," says Ma. "The way I hear it, you were captured and whisked away just like the rest of us, only you got dumped on a plastic surgeon rather than a vet. I tell you, what is going on now in town is a vast alien conspiracy."

Ma sits down to groom her mustache. (This does happen to older females, you know.) Sadly, her coat is terminally raggedy and she just manages to swirl the split ends around in a different pattern.

"It is just Planned Pethood, Ma," I suggest.

"Do not be an ignorant pup," she growls.

Now *my* back hairs are getting themselves in a twist. You do not call Midnight Louie canine, no matter who you are.

"Settle down, Louie." Her crooked paw pats my side whiskers. "We can have our own opinions about the alien conspiracy to whisk our population away to some hidden and forbidden planet, but you will not be able to deny what the Cat Pack has seen over on Paradise."

I am somewhat mollified, if not momified. "All right. Show me the way. But first I have to reverse engineer the claw marks you have put into the back of Miss Temple's sofa."

"From what I hear of her romantic life, she does not see much of the back of the couch."

By then I am using a single delicate shiv to restore the disturbed upholstery threads and too busy to take offense. It is true my Miss Temple has been distressingly involved in the mating game of late, and she does not have the handy on and off switch known as "heat" to moderate things.

But I would not be here if it were not for such urges, so who am I to complain?

"Ma!" I have now reached the breached French door. The lock is visibly sprung, and long track marks scar the exterior wood. "You are as bad as that renegade human known, not fondly, as Kitty the Cutter."

Ma shrugs and emits the short, almost gacking sounds that pass for amusement with her. "Kitty the Cutter—cute nickname. You can call *me* Cutter for short," she says with a sharp cuff to my shoulder.

I do not know why Ma is so fearful of alien abduction. If these so-called aliens were advanced enough to traverse space to get to Earth, they would not take her on a bet.

Chapter 9

Close Encounter

Had he always been a nightcrawler? Max Kinsella wondered about that as he wandered the brightly lit gaming aisles. The Goliath, an older Las Vegas hotel-casino, looked as tired as an aging bookie despite being tarted up with new carpeting and gaudier lighting fixtures.

He'd spent the day wandering the Strip, staring at familiar Las Vegas icons until his eyes could hardly focus. It worked like putting the pieces of a jigsaw puzzle together.

The Crystal Phoenix stirred rough cuts of Temple from a handheld movie camera, her red hair, her red car, her laugh. Memory hallucinations of Lieutenant Molina and her haunting ex, Rafi Nadir, appeared suddenly at other locations, even the elusive glimpse of a black cat.

The person or persons unknown who'd arranged his

almost-fatal fall probably hoped he'd remain a walking blind spot forever.

Now, though, he was back at the Goliath, where he'd performed the main magic show for a year, and it was feeling alarmingly familiar, like he belonged here. The up-late energy of a frenetic casino in the very wee hours seemed to spark even more memories.

A few passing faces looked vaguely familiar. Joy pulsed through him like a drug high. His traumatized memory was tiring of being a drag. It was starting to spark into life. He looked around, cherishing the familiar for the first time since he'd been back in the United States.

What a crazy scene Las Vegas was. He and his fellow post-midnight travelers were awash in a galaxy of winking lights, hearing computerized whoops and zings, pings and rings, inhaling stale cigarette smoke. Gaming, drinking, and smoking were the Three Musketeers of Vegas good times. The casinos would never ban smoking, so despite the air-conditioned chill, the scene was vaguely hellish.

Max weaved through crowds of grinning Vegas Strip zombies, haggard and staggering people refusing to admit it was nearly 3 A.M., when all good boys and girls should be at home and in bed with their significant others.

"Max Kinsella!" a hearty male voice hailed him. "What dead-end alley have you been hiding in?"

Hester Polyester, a dedicated octogenarian player of the cheapest slot machines, heard his name called too and looked up from the cartooned fruit and other icons floating before her red-rimmed eyes.

Max stopped and stared at the elderly woman. Her name and claim to fame were just "there." Could it be this easy?

Meanwhile, someone reached to grab and stop Max in his tracks just as Max realized he recognized the voice, Thumbs Kerrick, a veteran Goliath pit boss.

Max winked at Hester to put her next on the greeting list. He turned toward Kerrick and his question, which was being repeated.

"Where the heck have you been, you Mystifying Max, you? Just vanished after your gig was up. Not polite."

"Your shift over?" Max guessed.

Kerrick pulled him toward a couple empty slot machine spots. "On break." He released Max's arm in its linen sport coat. "Best biceps in the business still," Kerrick said, grinning. "For a tall skinny dude, you're deceptively strong."

"I'm a magician. We're all deceptive."

"You haven't been a magic man in this town lately. No, seriously. I thought you and your act would be moving up-Strip." He lowered his voice. "Then it went to hell. Rumor was the police were hot to question you on the dead guy found in the, you know—" Kerrick jerked his head toward the light-bristling ceiling.

Bells and chimes whooped from various areas of the casino, the siren sound of someone else winning far away.

"My contract was up that night," Max said. "I was gone the minute the greasepaint was off. So who died?"

"Mr. Nobody. Maybe that's why the Goliath became Cop Central. This tall lieutenant was all over the staff like a cheap leisure suit, gave the word 'grilling' the sniff of the Spanish Inquisition and burning at the stake. Sure wanted to talk to you bad."

"So in my absence, he endeared me to the staff by putting the heat on them. Sorry, Thumbs. I didn't know. I was long gone."

"*She*." Thumbs eyed Max like he would a potential card counter, with suspicion. He may have overdone the innocent act. "The lieutenant was a she."

"Good-looking?"

"Ah, Max!" Laughing, Thumbs punched him on the

cast-iron biceps. "That's why you skedaddled, isn't it? Woman trouble. I knew it."

Max considered, then nodded. "You're right. Woman trouble. And, Thumbs, this jacket is designer linen. It wrinkles easily."

"Well, I won't wrinkle your wearables again." Thumbs patted down the lapels like a tailor. He'd always been a hands-on kind of guy. Ex-muscle for the mob, went the rumor. "Still, it's good to see you. Some of us wondered if there were *two* dead guys in that incident, but only one body was found."

"I know I seemed to vanish. Too bad the murder happened the same night my contract was up. I heard about it later, but I didn't want to tangle with that pit bull of a suspicious cop. I needed to go away to reinvent myself."

"You're like a cat, Max. Always another life to live." Kerrick lifted a palm to slap Max's arm again, then just wiggled his meaty thumbs in a signature farewell wave.

Max remained still as Kerrick moved on.

What he'd confirmed to the pit boss was true enough. A woman had been in trouble, and would have been in more if he hadn't left town. Someone had been after him, and would have soon leaned on his innocent significant other if not drawn away by his disappearance. From what Temple had admitted just recently, Max didn't move quite fast enough. The thugs found her, and Matt Devine was there for her when Max was just some absconding guy without the decency to leave a good-bye note.

He sighed. It had been the only way. If some men's pasts were checkered, his was shamrock-patterned, none of them the lucky, four-leafed variety.

Turning, he approached Hester Polyester.

"That Kerrick," she told him in a cigarette-hoarse rasp as soon as he was within hearing range. "Always Mr. Friendly, but he keeps an eagle eye on things."

Her face had the surface of a suede walnut shell, all

furrows. Bifocals made her pale eyes child-huge as they looked up at him through the upper portion. She knew the Strip like the myriad lines on her wrinkled palms, but still seemed an innocent.

"He moves me along," Hester said with a grumble, "so I don't become a 'fixture.'"

"You aren't a fixture, Hester," Max told her. "You are a legend."

He smiled as he pulled over an empty stool and sat to give his less-than-rock-hard quads and calves a break. He could walk without a hitch in his step now, but the cut-bungee-cord fall still took a toll.

"So what's new here?" he asked Hester.

"Besides you coming back and the nickel slots clinging on in the old town like dandruff on a fancy Afghan hound?"

Max smiled, knowing that any casinos Hester didn't cover in her daily and nightly rounds, her husband, Lester, did. The "Polyester" surname came from the '60s-vintage sherbet-colored leisure suits the pair wore. Probably purchased at the Goodwill.

Characters like this were becoming rarer on the Strip, diluting the place's rich, eccentric flavor.

"That's a tasty mint green pantsuit you have on, Hester," Max told her.

"Exactly right, honey. 'Mint.' As in moneymaker. My lucky suit. Nobody knows that shade of color no more. You never miss a thing, Max Kinsella, not even about what a lady is wearing."

"That's because I'm a metrosexual."

"I'm too old to care where you have sex. I'm a suburban-sexual myself. You are still as charming as ever, Max. Now get outta my face and let me whip this rotating fruit salad on the ridiculous computer screen into tutti-frutti Jell-O."

Laughing, he obeyed and headed through the casino

for the lobby entrance, glad he'd put in an appearance so word would get out: Max is back. He was through with keeping a low profile.

He'd always been a high-risk kind of guy. Now that he'd tucked Temple Barr safely back in her cozy life as a PR whiz and newly engaged girl, he was ready to draw out his most lethal enemies for one last hand-to-hand showdown, including Kathleen O'Connor in any one of her myriad disguises.

He moved confidently onto the lobby's marble floors, hearing his feet hit the stone sharp and clean with no hesitation. *Yes indeed, Max is back.*

He stopped dead.

The last person on earth he'd expected to run into here was now moving toward him. There was no place to hide for either of them.

Chapter 10

Mother Ship

If there is anything a hip cat about town—particularly if that town is Sin City—loathes to admit, it is that he has anything in common with inferior species, namely canines and *Homo sapiens*.

Now, *Homo sapiens*—"saps" for short, in my opinion—is an easy enough breed to manipulate or avoid. Most canines are too herdlike to do more than pity.

However, it is possible, in our pursuit of ultimate felininity, we hip cats may show some symptoms we have in common with one or both inferior species.

That is why my extended family includes life partners and my so-called parents, Three O'Clock Louie and Ma Barker, along with Ma's clowder of street gangsters. Miss Midnight Louise, purported daughter, is my partner in Midnight Investigations, Inc., I being the capital *I* in "Inc." and Louise being the dot at the end of the "Inc."

Whatever our social ranking, we all have gathered on the fringe of desert that dips into the city proper on a night when the moon is a pale round mottled marble in the sky.

Coyotes and dogs may howl and bay at the moon.

Human beings may spoon and moon at the moon.

We of the Sacred Breed worshipped in ancient Egypt, however, sit in quiet contemplation.

That is because we have a mystical gene going back to our golden olden days when the cat goddess Bast oversaw the pinnacle of catdom.

So sometimes her call sings through our veins and to the very tips of our vibrissae, "whiskers" (oh-so-sadly human) in the common expression.

We suspend our daily struggles for food, warmth, zebra-pattern comforters, and Free-to-Be-Feline pellets and are drawn to a special spot, rather like '60s folks to a hootenanny.

Only we remain silent, sober, and soulful.

Our very presence signifies that something momentous is about to happen.

Naturally, I expect to figure out what it is first, because I am the private investigator of the lot and that is my job, to walk these lonely wastelands and restore order and justice.

Did I mention that we are meeting behind the deserted construction area—of which there are many in post–Great Recession Vegas—that sits opposite the Convention Center area?

Word on the street and around the Dumpsters is that something big is going up here, and going down tonight.

The construction is swathed in one of those gigantic plastic sheets that environmental artists like Christo employ to gift-wrap various iconic building and geographical areas, even whole islands.

Fear not. It is merely one of the many stalled construction projects turned abandoned slum by the Great Recession.

So there Ma and me finally stand on the stub-end of Vegas, looking around the shallow, sandy landscape, viewing a scene of ruin out of Hollywood's latest disaster movie.

I am a simple fellow. I suppose you could consider me a survivalist.

I wear built-in camo to blend into shade and shadow. If I cannot find, chase, and catch food, I know how to scout and score OPF. Other People's Food. I do not want my sovereign liberty to roam curtailed. I kowtow to no civil or religious authority, save She Who Must Be Obeyed, and, fortunately, Bast, the ancient Egyptian cat deity, keeps herself on the down low these days.

In a bow to modern mores (and because it was forced upon me by a vile enemy), I have had Planned Pethood thrust upon me and been rendered responsible to pursue my wildest dreams without fear of unwanted offspring. (If only my wildest dreams would let themselves be caught!) Oh, well, there is always another feline fatale around the corner.

Despite having angled a cushy position with a human roommate, I could revert to wandering wayfarer status in a heartbeat. Or so I like to think, though I would dearly miss the zebra-pattern comforter that makes such an ideal background for my reclining magnificence.

However enterprising I am as a small business owner and pillar of the community, I must admit many others of my breed do not have the luck and wiles I have had and do need a hand and a handout now and again.

This economy has been the pits for every life-form except rich roaches and other lowlifes that take and do not give—who knows?—perhaps alien visitors among them. Bring on more worry and woe!

I eye the blasted site that looks like the moon on a lush day and pick out members of Ma Barker's clowder hunkered in the shadows of isolated piles of lumber, rebar, coated concrete blocks, and other leftovers of stalled construction.

The Strip itself still glows, shines, sparkles, and glitters, but the backlot behind the façade is showing its age and decrepitude.

"So what is here to draw the gang?" I ask Ma as we crouch behind some burnt-out oleander bushes that died of thirst. Things wilt in Las Vegas if not watered regularly.

"In the dark before the dawn, vermin."

"I thought you were the darlings of the police substation and dined on fast food."

"Even they are on a budget. And we need to exercise our survival skills."

"This close to the Strip?"

"That is where the most deserted areas are now during the economic downturn."

It is a sad comment when your own mother starts sounding like a stockbroker.

"We arrived around three hours before dawn and were ready to leave in the still-dark. Only we were disturbed at the gathering."

"By—?"

"Small darting lights that enlarged and faded, flying in formation."

"Aw, come on, Ma. I am a rational dude. Trust me. The Strip is riddled by gimmicky dancing lights all over the place."

"This occurred above *this* deserted place only. But that is not all."

I sigh and wait.

"There was a mother ship. A huge, hovering flying thing just above the ground that emitted a blinding death ray."

"A death ray. Holy Flash Gordon, Ma! If you had ever been domesticated and moved indoors to watch movies from all eras on television, you would know that death rays are a corny invention of special effects technicians. FX, the humans call it for short. Special effects. A trick. An illusion. A delusion.

"What you saw was probably some advertising gimmick . . . maybe helium balloons loosed on an unsuspecting public. Right out in front of the Paris is this huge illuminated balloon and gondola. This stuff is all pure Las Vegas hype."

"Las Vegas is not so pure from what I have heard," she says with a sniff.

"So did anybody see this phenomenon? I mean somebody with an opposable thumb to punch in 911 on a cell phone."

"We go where we will not be seen. You know that is our kind's best defense, not to be seen. We did not do leaping lion but crouching tiger. We went belly-down to play rock and shadow. The security lights are dim here."

"They are indeed rather puny compared to the fireworks of the Strip and Downtown all around," I note.

"And anyway, the UFOs drove the men off, leaving behind their burden. We thought it might be traps to transport us to the mother ship, but we were too smart to fall for that trick."

"Men? Burden? That could have been . . . gym bags or something. There must be a 24 Hour Fitness club somewhere around here. I know life on the street makes one wary, but this all sounds like nonsense."

"Nonsense, all right. I sent Pitch and Blackula to sniff out the leavings after the men had fled. It was no burden, it was just very dead."

"Those gym bags can smell like death warmed over, believe me. I have hung out with humans way more than you ferals."

"The leaving was also about six feet long and most unfit, with a large pouch like you."

"Leave my body type out of this discussion. Let me get this straight. You saw grown men toting a corpse? They dropped it like a sack of potatoes and ran?"

Usually corpse-toters are not the fleeing type, much less the leaving-in-plain-sight types.

Maybe Ma and her crew *had* seen something weird. If I were a vast, hidden conspiracy believer, I might suspect secret government experiments gone rogue from Area 51. As I muse, I can almost hear *Twilight Zone* music pulsating in my head like annoying audio hail. I am definitely too domesticated, or too addicted to retro television.

Ma is nattering on. "I stationed the crew to stay here to keep the rats off the evidence. And bag a few for snacks."

"Please. I do not do sushi." I am afraid my palate at least has become totally domesticated. Which makes me wonder how suitable for survival I am these days, should it become necessary.

"Well," I say, "while I am willing to bet that these skittish flying tinfoil doughnuts are a scam, the scenario you have just described is genuine Las Vegas legerdemain from days of old, all right. It is a favorite game among the old mobs called 'bury the body.' Lead me to the remains. I am not a coroner, but I have played one on TV news cameras now and then."

Ma gives me the *sssst* hiss of reproval and heads to the darkest corner of the property. The scene certainly looks deserted now. The edifice-in-waiting is like the halted construction on a lot of Vegas sites, a skeletal hulk. Any light hitting the dirt around here is referred from distant sources.

We are talking a dead planet in the midst of one hyperactive, glitzy galaxy.

Come to think of it, we are talking prime body-dumping ground.

I start to feel like a Mars rover, churning up dust as I clamber over fallen cement blocks disrupting acres of sand. I will take a long, careful tongue-bath to restore my shiny black suit coat to prime condition.

The scene is a bit eerie, I think, looking up and seeing only a full moon above, an object not about to make a close encounter with Earth any eon soon. If that supposed mother ship swoops down tonight, I will have to swallow of lot of words as well as all this dust.

I am glad Ma's gang is backing me up.

A feature on the deserted landscape grows bigger by the second. It is too lumpy to be concrete. The meager light brings into focus a legendary feature of the planet Mars: the Mysterious Face.

Only I spot those facial features dead and on the ground on Paradise Road. They seem more ugly than mysterious, but that is how it often happens when one gets to the bottom of things.

Although Grizzly Bahr the coroner begins an autopsy with the buzz saw to the brain, the feline way is more delicate. While Ma Barker's gang hangs back, I walk step by step over the uneven ground until I can, like any intrepid explorer, plant a foot on the foreign territory.

My sensitive pads sense immediately that this guy is as cold as the stone that surrounds him. I lean in to sniff carefully at his sniffer. Not a breath of air stirs my hair-trigger vibrissae. Not a whisker is stirring, not even a fine, almost invisible one sprouting from my chinny chin-chin.

"Coroner cuisine," I diagnose.

"As if we did not know that all by ourselves," Ma Barker says. "What we need you for is dealing with the proper authorities to get this dead meat off our hunting grounds."

"Maybe," I say, "your flock of UFOs and the hovering mother ship will whisk him off before any of us can do anything. Anyway, I do not see your crowd rushing back to this place by dead of night as long as you are drinking the Kool-Aid about alien visitors coming to Las Vegas."

"Kool-Aid? We would never touch that sticky sweet stuff."

I do not bother to explain that is a human expression to denote the gullible.

"So you will have to devise a clever way to alert the authorities," Ma says.

"Maybe. Maybe not. The only thing I am sure of is that 'murder most mob' is definitely *not* alien to Sin City. Could this be a public relations ploy to draw attention to the new mob museums busting out all over town lately?"

"I am shocked." Ma sits down. "There is nothing that your human friends will not stoop to in order to make a buck, especially off the dead."

I glance down at the officially undiscovered corpse and have only one comment. "And they say *we* play with *our* food."

Chapter 11

Nightcrawlers

As Max froze in place, becoming an even more notice-able tall black island in the constant flow of people di-verting around him, the unlikely suspect was distracted enough to absently edge to the side with the crowds.

Then he glanced up and stopped. "You."

Now there were two immobile islands in the stream of tourists, who, like lemmings, were all intent on get-ting somewhere and oblivious of anything around them en route.

"Ditto," Max said before he played Kerrick, grabbed an arm, and pulled Matt Devine against the nearest mar-ble pillar. "What are you doing at the Goliath at three in the morning?"

Matt jerked his arm away and swatted out the crum-ples in his khaki poplin sport coat. "You first. I thought you were keeping on the down low. Or is the expression 'low-down'?"

"A crowd is the best disguise."

"It apparently didn't disguise me."

"You're being evasive. Does Temple know you're off leash?"

"Obviously she'd notice." Matt shrugged to loose the last wrinkled vestige of Max's urgent interception on his arm. "Temple assigned me the Goliath and Crystal Phoenix casino's ceiling bodies to investigate. I figure nighttime's the right time for that. You're certainly on the prowl, but we'd decided you needed to avoid the hotels where you're a suspect."

"Temple decided. She's a bit bossy, isn't she? Although it looks cute on her."

Matt frowned.

"Forget being territorial. I'm seeing someone else now."

Matt took a few seconds to react. Then he went with incredulous. "You're nearly killed in a murderous bungee cord malfunction at the Neon Nightmare club, end up in a coma at a Swiss clinic for more than a month, go on the run across Europe, survive a pursuit by both the old IRA and the new IRA, and slink back to Vegas with an AWOL memory. You've been back less than two weeks, yet have a new girlfriend?"

"'Love interest,' they say in the movie summaries." Max grinned. "She's followed me to Vegas; what can I do? I'll be happy to introduce you, should the occasion arise. Meanwhile, what are *you* doing here?"

"I don't have a lot of time to interview any of the night shift, do I, getting off the air on WCOO at two A.M."

"You might be getting off the air and night shift permanently if that daytime talk show gig in Chicago comes through."

"Maybe." Devine moved to brush past Max.

"Not the done deal Temple makes it out to be?" Max used the challenge in his voice as a rein to stop the guy's forward motion.

"Nothing in media's a done deal," Devine said over his shoulder.

"Nothing in life, either." Now Max had really jerked the cord.

Devine wheeled to face him. "Look, Kinsella. I get that you have to hang around Vegas until we settle who killed whom and might still do it to one of us, but who loves whom *is* a 'done deal,' and I'm not happy about you showing up again all needy and lame. You mess with Temple, and I'll kick you to the curb all the way down the Las Vegas Strip."

Max normally would mock and bow out of a scene like this. He measured the dark, repressed fury in Matt Devine's eyes, the bottom-line corrugated steel in his voice. . . . He was poised like a guard dog ready to rend. Someone far more formidable than Max had jerked his chain.

Max held up open palms and stepped back. "Better get on with it. The night shift clocks out even in Las Vegas."

Well. He watched Matt Devine's golden-boy head vanish into the ceaselessly milling crowd, reminding him of an angel fallen among the habitués of Hell in a Renaissance painting, all those faces around them masks of lust and greed and terror.

He'd been ready to consign Temple Barr to the necessary gal pal category, but Devine's bad boy behavior had him worried about her. He was hair-trigger touchy about something.

Max needed to get Revienne in the picture, if only to put paid to this broken romantic triangle so they could forget all that "who loves who" stuff tough guy Sam

Spade pooh-poohed in *The Maltese Falcon* and defend themselves from common enemies.

Meeting Revienne. Why did he think that Temple Barr would not take that well?

Chapter 12

Open Arms

Matt Devine leaned against the lapis lazuli lining the Goliath elevator car behind the jam-packed crowd of passengers. He spread his palms and fingers on the icy stone, and willed himself to let the unaccustomed rage drain out.

Of all the people to witness him coming here. Damn Max Kinsella! It was *his* darn fault Matt was stuck in this impasse now. They were all being toyed with by a wildcat who'd cornered a mouse, all their lives at stake. Everything depended on Matt's ability to break into and mind-meld with a twisted psyche, a serial killer's sensibility probably.

He pushed forward as happy drunks made way for him. This was the twentieth floor, from which the tormented call girl who used the name of Vassar had plunged to her death only months before.

Plunged or was pushed? If her death had been murder, he could be here to see her killer.

He remembered the route to this room as well as the balcony view down into the dramatic Hyatt-style atrium sparkling like endless levels of heaven, and hell, to the marble lobby floor below.

The door plaque bore the numbers *2032*. He knocked.

A woman answered.

She was brunette, beautiful, wearing very little, and she held a foldable straight-edge razor open in her naked palm.

Chapter 13

Graveyard Shift

Why do I always have to find the body? Especially if it is already dead.

It is not that I have any deep distaste for dead things. I mean, we all have to eat.

But I do shudder at the human race's ability to kill purely for pleasure or profit or sometimes just having a bad hair-trigger day.

Yes, I know my kind are considered cruel and prone to play with their food, but "play" is merely a class in survival of the species, Ma Nature being the imperative sort. In the wild, it is always about mere survival.

In the wilds of the Las Vegas Strip, that is seldom true.

So I circle around the body Ma Barker's gang has found. There is the constant hum of traffic in the distance and the roar of airplanes depositing and whisking away almost forty million people a year at McCarran on the south end of the Strip.

Like most sites hosting incomplete construction projects, here there is only the scritch of the night's scavengers over the rocks and sand, rats and mice, lizards, and big black bugs.

Occasionally, the distant muffled hoot of folks high on fun or various addictive substances wafts over the empty lot like an emission of hot air.

Managing to entice someone into "discovering" the body is looking hopeless. I pace the long distance to the street, gauging how far I have to lure a so-far-unseen passerby. Fifty yards at least.

If I were Rin Tin Tin or Lassie, or even that feisty little white Westie terror (I mean, of course, terrier) who pimps for Cesar brand dog food, I could howl, bark, and yip for attention. If I were a Westie, I could be seen at least. For once, my native coloring is working against me.

My whiskers are white, but far too few and too fine to make much of a showing.

I slump down on the lumpy ground so like giant sandpaper and gaze up and down the street. My only neighbor is the windowless concrete box of the Cabana Club, a strictly third-class bar and dance floor place covered with lurid murals of cavorting humans done in colors of yellow, hot pink, bright blue, and lime green that would make a rainbow nauseated.

I stand, sigh, and prepare to hoof down to that man-made music box that expels blasts of loud, discordant music and ever more hilarity-stricken people overcome by way too many rum drinks.

All the people are heading, as much as their stumbling feet can manage it, away from the (supposedly) deserted dark lot and back to the Strip.

I am thinking I will have to slip into the nightclub and perpetrate an act of such mad and bad behavior that Animal

Control will have to be called. Then I have only to escape their nets and traps and lead them back to the body.

First, I should be able to slip into the restrooms with so many rowdy and impaired revelers making frequent trips there. A bar of soap is too much to hope for, but there should be a wall dispenser of the liquid stuff.

Probably it is caked over with dried soap tracks and the prints of many human hands. How unsanitary!

I am walking faster, planning my break-in and subsequent shenanigans.

Once I smear my kisser with soap and some water from the leaky faucet (there is always a leaky faucet or two in these dives), I will chew up a good lather.

Then, apparently foaming at the mouth, I will return to the teeming, screaming crowd, jump up on the bar, and start knocking over bottles of beer like a champion bowler on a tear.

My next trick is to elude the would-be heroes in the crowd by climbing anything I can. Then when the Animal Control folks come, I pretend to be cornered and go quietly. Lulled into the usual complacency, the hunters will become the losers.

I will escape when out in the open again and streak for the abandoned lot next door. There I will evade tranquilizer darts as the posse closes in until they, stumbling over the dead body, finally have more important matters than little me on their minds.

Just planning the sequence reminds me that there are many junctures where I might be stopped, stomped, and clamped behind bars.

I sit and contemplate the lonely, dangerous life of the undercover operative. If I am caught and am regarded as rabid, that might be my last trip to the shelter with no witnesses of even an animal nature. It could be bye-bye Free-to-Be-Feline for Midnight Louie . . . and for what?

An old dead guy who would probably have kicked off without help sometime soon anyway.

This is not a case any of my nearest and dearest are at all

involved in. I have no stake in this death other than that Ma Barker thinks it our civic duty to alert the authorities. Fine for her to think. She has delegated the job to me! She may have faced off mad dogs and rabid raccoons as the leader of her pack, but she has no idea of the level of danger to be encountered integrating with humans, which are the most dangerous breed of all.

So. This is it. Midnight Louie plays the sap for no one, not even his own mother. Maybe especially not even his own mother. Am I a grown male or a mouse?

At that moment an intoxicated and intoxicating feminine giggle does an arpeggio up and down the scale of the human voice.

I look back to the Cabana Club. A solitary couple has exited, and turned my way. I cannot tell if he is holding up she, or vice versa, but they are entwined in a very friendly way and ambling, albeit shakily, right toward me.

I do an instant size-up. They are of the same age. She is wearing some dainty little dress and is barefoot, with her left arm dangling her high-heeled sandals over her shoulder. Not good. She is in no shape to pussyfoot over the building site ground.

He is about her age, early twenties, and wears the usual Las Vegas male tourist outfit: tennis shoes, baggy long shorts, T-shirt. He has now-useless sunglasses pushed atop his head.

He is putting one foot a bit too close to the other and they progress slowly, murmuring and laughing at their own condition.

Aha. They are a couple, not just a couple of strangers in the night who met at the Cabana Club. So far, so good. I need a Princess and a Galahad to make this con play.

They are too self-involved and too happily smashed to notice when they come abreast of me.

I move to brush the woman's ankles with a tantalizing swish of my glossy fur coat and supple rear member.

"*Ooooh,* honey. What was that, like a breeze on my legs?"

"No sidewalk grates in Vegas, baby."

They stop. Look down with great care.

I paw some stones against each other like castanets.

"Oh, look, honey. It is a cat."

"A black cat. Those things are unlucky."

I lurch toward them, then fall back, picking up my right mitt.

"Oh, no. It is hurt."

"Leave it. It will be all right."

I make a feeble objection to that idea.

"It mewed at me. It needs help." She leans down and holds out a hand with the shivs covered in neon pictographs.

I whimper again and stumble once in her direction.

"I can get it," she says. "We can take it to the shelter."

You can try, lady.

"That ground is awful rough," he says. "You can't go there barefoot."

"Then I'll put my shoes back on." She grabs hold of his shoulder and stands on one foot to don the spike-heel sandals one by one.

The dude has to hold her up or she would fall on her face, but he is not looking very happy about my interrupting their canoodling time. Tough. Tonight is your turn to play the good citizen.

"This is crazy," he tells her. "You will never catch it."

Right on, brother.

"It is just an old alley cat," he goes on, sealing his doom.

I sit up and pant laboriously. "Just an old alley cat" indeed, and a lot smarter than a six-mai-tais-to-the-wind young dude. Those rum cocktails will stir-fry your brain.

"Oh, honey." She teeters onto the sandy soil. "He really needs help."

I let her get close enough to bend down with hand outstretched; then I hop away on three legs, with a pitiful look over my shoulder.

She plants those thin-soled shoes and trots after me like my own Miss Temple on a rescue mission.

"God," the guy mutters from the sidewalk, but he has to commit to her quest and rushes after her.

It is like having a fish on the line. You must give them enough play and yet reel them in closer and closer. I am an old koi-catcher from my Crystal Phoenix house-detective days.

I give the silent meow and hobble away. I let her get near enough to almost grab me with one pounce . . . and spring away. Next time I limp even more.

"Oh, he is hurting himself," she announces. She has now decided I am a boy. Dames always go for me; Mr. "Old Alley Cat" should never underestimate the competition.

"We are never going to catch that cat," he grumbles.

You got it, bub.

"He must be at the end of his strength. Look. He is heading for those tumbled cement blocks. He will probably hunker down there for the night."

Uh . . . no, but you will.

I settle on my haunches in front of the John Doe and look up at my gracious rescuer with a happy little cry, almost kittenish, although it is hard to make my voice small and wee.

She gives a happy little cry in answer.

"Holy jalapeños, baby. That is a dead guy he is cozying up to."

"Oh. Do you think he killed him?"

Okay, not so much in the brains area, but her heart is pure.

They are much occupied in operating cell phones and calling 911 and fussing about if the police might question their condition.

"Don't worry, baby," is the last thing I hear the guy say. "I hate to say it, but we have been shocked sober."

"I hope the poor kitty is all right. . . ."

Poor Kitty is hot-footing his tender pads off this waste-land and getting back to his devoted roommate and their condominium at the Circle Ritz.

I pause before vanishing into the foliage and grounds of the major Strip hotels to see the squad car's headache rack casting bright colors over the arid scene. Ma Barker was right. This is our town. If something is wrong, we must do what we can to make it right.

But I can tell you one thing. I should get an Oscar nomi-nation for my "poor kitty" act tonight.

I am all the way home and preparing to shiv the bark off my living staircase into the Circle Ritz—the old leaning palm tree trunk—when someone hisses, "Mission accomplished?" in my ear.

I turn, spitting mad, but I am only facing my almost spitting image and certainly my almost double when it comes to names.

"Midnight Louise, why are you not getting your beauty sleep at the Crystal Phoenix?"

"Ma Barker wanted me to report on your body-revealing efforts."

"So you were there! And watching. And did not lift a claw sheath to help."

"That was unnecessary," she says.

"Quite right. I had the situation firmly in foot."

"That limping act was . . . a tad predictable."

"You try to get people to walk onto a rubble-strewn lot. When they finally came, Louise, I thought the fuzz was going to plant themselves on the site and grow there. And there will never be any credit to Ma Barker's clowder and me for taking the graveyard shift to keep their precious body pre-served in place."

"If you expect gratitude from the human race at your venerable stage in life, Daddy Dumbest, I have a cat condo in Atlantis to sell you."

Miss Midnight Louise cranks her head around to regard her fluffy train, which is covered in desert dust and who knows how many sand fleas, and gives it a mighty waft.

I cough in the downdraft, but cannot help bragging a bit. "Does Midnight Investigations, Inc., know how to preserve and reveal a crime scene, or what?"

"With you it is always 'or what.' What are you thinking of? Why are we here?"

"Not to answer eternal philosophical questions, for sure, Louise. Why do *you* think we are here?"

"Me? I am here to go back to Ma and report. You can rejoin your roommate and rest on your laurels, which you assure me you still have."

Chapter 14

The Thin White Line

Kitty the Cutter stepped back, her bare arm making a sweeping welcome gesture with the straight razor. "Enter, stranger."

Matt glimpsed himself, and her, in the floor-to-ceiling windows opposite the door. They looked like ghosts against the dark mirror of nighttime Las Vegas.

Kathleen O'Connor, Max Kinsella's adolescent Irish love turned IRA fanatic and eternal enemy, was a petite woman, not so small as Temple, and shared Max Kinsella's Black Irish looks. She was clearly obsessed with haunting Kinsella and anyone linked to him.

The first such person she crossed paths with, Max's cousin Sean Kelly, had died at the age of seventeen years ago. Only months ago, Kathleen O'Connor had assaulted Matt on the street with a slash to the side—just for as-

sociating with Max's significant other. With Temple now
his fiancée, she had Matt at the razor's edge again, threatening Temple if he didn't play her sick head games. So he
agreed to these creepy secret meetings at a place she may
have murdered another victim, desperately trying to find
some mental cutting edge that would disarm this severely
damaged and damaging woman.

Primed to dodge any sudden move on her part, Matt
was careful to amble inside as coolly as James Bond.

He moved into the opulent bedroom with burgundy
carpet the color of welling blood, with its marble-topped
furnishings. The immense brocaded bed was draped in
insanely costly linens and various sized pillows so elaborately embroidered, they seemed to be wearing suits of
metallic fabric armor.

He passed the hall's choke point opposite the entrance
to the bathroom, which was lined with marble and mirror, and approached the precipitous view of incandes-
cent Las Vegas Strip laid out below.

"See any ghosts in the glass?" she asked.

One.

This was the same room where he'd come to lose the
virginity Kathleen coveted, and ended up counseling the
troubled call girl, Vassar, instead. He'd been in deep but
unconfessed love with Temple by then and immune to
other women. He knew he'd had nothing to do with Vassar's fatal plunge off the balcony outside the room later
that night, after he'd left. Except for being a suspect. He
couldn't say the same for Kathleen O'Connor.

"Ghosts," he repeated. "No. You know I only believe
in one spirit."

"The Holy Ghost," she mocked. "What a ludicrous
concept. And he isn't here."

"The Holy Spirit is the spirit of truth. He is everywhere. Especially here."

"Truth." He heard a slashing sound and turned. Her

razor had ripped open the seat of the upholstered desk chair.

Matt shrugged. "You rented the room. I didn't."

"I put your name on the reservation." Her tone was childishly spiteful.

He eyed the destroyed property. "It can be repaired."

"And you'll pay for it."

The glare in her blue-green eyes was laser-intensive. Matt was reminded of the wicked queen in *Snow White*. Jealousy. Was that Kitty the Cutter's prime motive? He'd smiled at Temple's apt and quick-witted characterization of the demon haunting them all. Kitty the Cutter.

His calm angered her more. "I can cut you again as easily."

"Surface wounds. For show. Your own run deeper."

"So that's what you're here for? Comparing scars? Show me yours. Show me *mine* on you."

"It's shrunk to a thin white line, Kathleen, bloodless. Not interesting at all. *You* are interesting, though."

"Oh." She threw herself onto the pillow-mounded bed, her tight mesh skirt riding up to show white thigh and iceberg-sharp knees, seductive, the straight razor stropping back and forth on the encrusted comforter fabric, as if being wiped free of blood. "Mr. Midnight, counselor of the idiot wind, the Dysfunction Nation airwaves. You want to psychoanalyze me?"

Matt sat on the defaced chair, bracing his arms on its carved gilt arms. "I think 'psycho' is the operative word."

She laughed, mocking him. "You're trapped. You're trapped because you worry about other people when you should be worrying about yourself. You're trapped because you think you can still *do* good and *be* good. You're trapped because you know I can do anything."

"No, I don't know that, Kathleen."

"Don't call me that."

"Rebecca, then?" he asked deliberately.

She sat up. "Where'd you get that name?"

"Or Shangri-La?"

She relaxed back against the pillows. "Just how many people do you think I can be?"

"As many as you need to be, but that's an interesting question. You could have multiple personality disorder. Or just be an extreme drama queen."

"You're one to call *me* names. An ex-priest in an unsanctioned relationship. You'd do anything to keep your little redhead safe, wouldn't you?"

She rose, set the razor on the marble nightstand with a sharp click, and oozed across the bed toward him. Taffeta crinkled like dead leaves under a boa constrictor.

Matt couldn't help thinking his "drama queen" diagnosis was right on. A slinking femme fatale was pretty predictable, except he knew this one was no TV cliché, but a woman who had liked to play with her prey since her teens.

That meant she at least needed her victims alive to squirm.

Kathleen was fixated on tormenting men and he knew the reasons why. The question was, did *she*? On the surface, maybe she did, but deep down everyone has a "story," some deep personal blind spot. And around it they construct a distorted world view to justify what they need to believe of that world.

He stood and spelled out his terms. "You set the time and place for this session. I set the parameters. Temple is off the table. You mention her or her name and I walk."

"Oh, going all terse and manly. You knew when you came here that I can put you up against the wall with one slash of my razor on someone else's throat."

"No. You can get me to come out and play shrink with you, but one more threat and it's your neck that's in jeopardy."

"You'd kill me, Father Be Good?"

"*Ex*-father, and even if that weren't so, there's no vow against justifiable homicide."

"And since when did priests keep vows of poverty, obedience, and, particularly, chastity? Look at you, Mr. Ex. You've become wealthy listening to whiners on the radio."

"Poverty is not a vow made by parish priests, only within certain orders, such as Jesuits and Franciscans."

"So it's all right to rake it in on the miseries of others."

"I donate ten percent."

"Paltry."

Matt sat down, taking a negotiating tone again. "You're right. I set up that percentage when I wasn't making much money or anticipated doing that. I'll up it. Twenty-five percent strike you as fair?"

"You'd, you'd do that because I challenged you? Wishy-washy, aren't you?"

Of course, anything you'd say to a psychopath became a lose–lose for you.

"Not at all," Matt answered. "You've put your money where your mouth is. From all accounts, you've spent a good part of your life raising money for a cause. It was a just cause of human rights violations even if the IRA resorted to terrorism before the al-Qaeda terrorist extremism so appalled them that both sides in Northern Ireland saw the light and struck a peace."

Kathleen cast herself on her elbows at the foot of the bed, displaying deep cleavage three feet from his chair. "I put my *mouth* where the money was. Is that not a sin even in the service of a just cause? Can you absolve me of sin?"

Matt mentally kicked himself for using a careless expression that she could sexualize, this woman who'd used sex as a lethal weapon since adolescence.

"I can't absolve anyone now, not even myself," he

pointed out. "Besides, chastity was a vow for me at one time. You took no vows."

"And you honored none. No priests do. Chastity is a joke to that tribe of kiddie-diddlers, and obedience is only for their victims."

She was deep into the twisted truths of her "story" now, the lifelong narrative formed at dark moments of childhood that justified her hatred and anger and envy.

"That's not true of the majority of priests, Kathleen."

"Of course *you*'re in that saintly number that goes marching in to heaven."

"I was."

"But you ran away from your position as God Almighty's favorite son."

"I became laicized. I didn't just walk. I went through the full process of officially leaving."

"Mr. Ex, the rules follower."

Matt smiled. "Exactly your opposite."

Her precisely plucked raven black brows swooped into a frown. "You think you know all about me."

"I know nothing about you but your history."

"My history? Am I some kind of 'country' to you? A book you can read and figure out by this place or that event? You're making a huge mistake to underestimate me."

"Would I be here at your beck and call if I did?"

She sat up, leaning her hands on the bed and swinging her feet in their decidedly sinister cuffed and buckled black leather platform shoes. Every position she'd taken on that bed, stripped of the seductive clothing, was that of flirty teenage girl.

"You can tell me, Father Ex," she wheedled, whispered. "Was it earnest little tweens in the parish choir? Their plump unhappy mamas in the rectory? Maybe crushing teens in the confessional. You can't fool me. I know what you are and I know what you did."

Sexually abused children always believed their lot had to be the secretive norm of everyone around them, who just weren't telling. Kathleen was too old for that fairy tale.

"Sorry. Nada. I was even more abnormal than you. I was a virgin until way too recently. You said it. Rules follower. If I hadn't been, I probably would have killed my stepfather, Cliff Effinger, and murder for sure is a sin."

"You kill someone? Priests aren't good, they're just cowards." She leaned closer.

"I almost did." He met her eyes with all the darkness in his mind when he'd held a limp, wife-beating Effinger, himself the devil this time, who had his boyhood demon by the sharp lapels of checkered past and coat. Like the song said, Matt was here to rock the boat. "Maybe," he suggested, "you had something to do with his nasty death later."

She reared away from his words, or the truth in his eyes. You couldn't hide the hate that almost ate you alive. She didn't expect that of him, only of herself.

"Maybe you're more of a man than I thought."

"You don't know me, even if you think you know my kind. I'm not a country you can explore, a book you can turn into another kind of story. We each have our own dark fairy tale, Kathleen. So what are we going to talk about? Truth or dare."

"You'll sleep with me before I'm done with you. All men do."

It wasn't wise to end this game and unloose her elsewhere.

"I'll make you work for it. Tell me about the first sexual experience you remember."

Her eyes flared wide. This was territory she knew how to manipulate: sex and priests.

She rolled over onto her back and crossed her legs in the air, posed like the cover of a cheesy airport novel.

He sat behind her in the classic Freudian position of alienist and patient, only nowadays everyone knew a lot more about psychological kinks than Freud had.

Matt hoped what he knew was enough.

Chapter 15

Slugfest

Lieutenant C. R. Molina stood in the hot sun, staring down at the corpse planted under a bit of rubble in a deserted lot. It wasn't concrete that had killed him, but a .38 slug that had missed being an earring by two inches.

"Hey, Lieutenant," a voice said behind her. "What you got?"

"A bad feeling." She slid her eyes behind the sunglasses to Morrie Alch's tanned and seamed face. "You're old enough to remember mob hits in this town."

"As a kid, yeah."

"This guy's no kid."

"Pushing seventy before he stumbled, I'd say. He's sporting the mob-approved execution-style ventilation, all right. But, uh, dumping a body in public like this? It's just bad taste nowadays. Looks amateur. The mob is finally being recognized as the down-and-dirty influence on the making of Vegas with the official museum, the competing attraction, the *Ocean's* whatever-number 'son of Frank Sinatra' Vegas heist movies a few years back."

"Nothing ever dies here but people," Molina commented. "Certainly not the notion of mob activity."

"A cheesy body-dump like this looks small-time. Any remaining hoods would rather fling it than flaunt it."

"So that dead face doesn't populate a Ten Most Wanted list? There's something familiar about it to me."

Alch braced his hands on his knees and semi-squatted for a better gander at one dead goose. "Older guys all start to look alike."

"Not you, Morrie. It's that Justin Bieber hair of yours."

Alch snorted as he rose. He did have a handsome mop of hair, but it was the iron gray of an aging Scottie dog. "I know some CIs who are pretty senior. I'll ask around."

Molina nodded. "Actually, some leftover mob hit would be a nice change of pace on cases."

"Yeah?"

She produced her most sardonic face and voice. "This is nothing involving crazy public relations events or . . . critters. Old dead guy shot execution-style. Plain as dirt."

"Oops. Not quite, Lieutenant."

Alch pointed at a shadow near the large building construction.

Something was moving in it and vanishing.

A rat.

Molina raised an eyebrow over the upper sunglass rim. "Grizzly Bahr at the morgue will be glad our vic avoided being lunchmeat for the rat pack and losing any body parts that might be evidence."

Alch nodded. "That was a piece of luck. These empty lots attract a lot of vermin. Maybe this guy was a literal rat."

"A snitch, you mean?" Molina reflected. "Either that or a drug dealer or even a gambler who welched on a bet. Empty lots attract a large clientele of human vermin."

They backtracked in their crime-scene booties to let the tech team have its way with the body.

Chapter 16

Dead on Paradise

"Guess what?" the cheery voice cackled in Temple's ear way too early in the morning. She'd been inhaling coffee mug steam to clear her sinuses.

"Who is this?" Brain cell number 100,030 kicked in. "Silas T., is that you?"

"What'd you call me, chickadee? 'Silas T.'? I like it."

"I don't like 'chickadee.' Don't call me that again."

"If you say so, Miss Barr, but whatever I call you, you are a tip-top publicity genius. You've done it again."

"Done what?"

"Once again, a body has been found on the scene of your client's new attraction. Hip, hip, hooray!"

"I have found myself in a crazy phone conversation. What are you saying?"

"Better click, click, click those fancy high heels over

here to Paradise. I came by to check the site, and the authorities and their yellow ticker tape were all over the place. TV vans are lining the curb."

"Oh my lost ruby red slippers! I'm still in Oz. Your construction project has unearthed a corpse?"

"Even better, the scene looks rather mobbish. Ties right in with the latest trends in Vegas hot spots. I couldn't be happier if you had killed him yourself to make the buzz happen."

"Silas T. This is *bad* publicity. You are a bad, bad, bad client. Keep your mouth shut from now on or I'll . . . I'll do something drastic. I'll be there ASAP."

Temple wished she could "click, click, click" her red-shimmer slipper heels—ballet flats for around the condo—and get back home to a day earlier, in a past where she had declined to take a ride on Farnum's "stunt publicity" hurricane.

Before she left the condo, she looked around for Louie, but she hadn't seen him since he plopped on the bed a few hours earlier for an out-of-character purr-fest. He'd slipped away to some favorite condo haunt after that. Not to worry. He often knew what she was doing better than she did.

In record time, she and the Miata slipped into a just-right-size sloppy space left by two askew parked media vans. This was a "hot" scene, all right.

She'd worn her sturdiest shoes, black patent leather closed-toe pumps, and crunched across the rough bare ground toward a clot of what looked like the monsters from the *Alien* films, but were only media men and women bearing videotape cameras high on their shoulders to focus on the victim in their midst.

A mental mantra drummed in time to her steps. *I hope it isn't, I pray it isn't, I can't believe it is . . .*

"Here she is!" a voice from the ravening crowd of media monsters announced.

They turned, the cameras' mechanical eyes recording her.

"Mr. Farnum says you told him to 'keep mum.' What do you know about the body that was discovered on your client's property this morning?"

"I've just arrived, and I merely advised him not to speak about a crime scene that the Metro Police are just now handling," Temple said, not recognizing faces with a sinking feeling. She had contacts among the media, but not so much on the hard news side.

"We hear a dead body was recently discovered at another site where you were representing the attraction. Are you a jinx?" a tall guy with a soul patch asked.

Someone pushed to her side. "Now, don't you pick on the little lady." Farnum squeezed her elbow so vigorously, she almost lost her balance on the ridged ground.

They made quite a pair. A flashing image of him in a coral-striped seersucker suit with a yellow bow tie was emblazoned on her putt-putting brain. She'd never take on a client who wore straw boater hats again. He'd look like a carnival huckster on camera.

"Neither myself nor my client will be giving any statements," she said, "until we know what's going on and have been released to comment by the police." At the same time, she mulled how the police might just love the site's owner and operator mouthing off to the media unsupervised.

"And here the police are," said a voice from on high she recognized down to her balancing toes.

The noose of media people loosened and melted away. Temple was glad to know Molina had that effect on her newshound peers too. The woman was tall, dark, and commanding. *Not fair*, thought petite Temple.

She turned and looked up. "I'm sorry. We're sorry.

They intercepted us." Temple frowned. She knew Molina was more hands-on than most homicide lieutenants, but what about this abandoned lot was so interesting?

Eerily, Molina was delivering an answer to that very internal question. "Mr. Farnum arrived here practically with the uniforms. A partying couple from the Cabana Club was wandering around the premises, trying 'to see the moon.'"

Oh. Drunk, Temple thought. It was hard to see the moon with all the high-rises and competing lights in the dark of night. At dawn it would be a drunk's errand. The Cabana Club was an off-Strip joint where everyone partied hearty.

Silas T. narrowed his beady little eyes up at Molina and stuck out his close-shaven chinny chin-chin. "I always rise at the first, first crack of light and I always check the site first, first, first thing. Even before breakfast. Speaking of breakfast." He turned gallantly to Temple. "I'd be honored to buy you the tallest short stack of pancakes in Vegas, missy, for coming out so early at my call. Thanks for shooing the media people out so fast. We should make the noon news."

Temple rolled her eyes. She wondered if yellow bow ties were long enough for strangling, but offing someone in front of the fuzz was a trifle impetuous.

"I'll pass on the pancakes," she said. "So you can run along now."

"Yes, she will pass on the pancakes," Molina said. "She'll be here answering questions, but you can go."

"I don't desert a lady, ma'am."

Molina repeated, with emphasis, "You. Can. Go." That sent Farnum scuttling away like a Crayola-colored beetle.

Temple glanced to where it looked like *CSI: Las Vegas* was filming. Detective Morrie Alch would have to substitute for silver-haired Ted Danson. Temple couldn't spot his petite Asian partner, Merry Su. Su was such a fierce spitfire that her name always made Temple smile.

"Nothing to smile about this morning, Miss Barr," Molina said. "Your client is a very possible perp on this death. He'd look fishy in a desert. Fill me in fast."

"He is a bit eccentric, but he's putting up a new attraction." She nodded at the ten stories of raw construction a hundred feet away. "I had lunch with him yesterday and visited the site. Not many projects are going through these days, so I found it intriguing."

"What is it?"

"Um, that's a secret."

"What?"

"He's been really cagey about the exact nature of the building, and this has been preliminary exploration. We haven't signed a contract. He *is* staying at the Wynn," she added, trying to peer around Molina to glimpse where the body might be.

Molina adjusted her stance to better block the view. "Is that all the vetting you've done? Do you usually operate in this slipshod way?"

"No! I mean, this isn't slipshod. Everything that exists in Vegas, from Bugsy Siegel's Flamingo Hotel to ex–Mayor Goodman's Mob Museum downtown, was once a crazy idea nobody thought would fly."

"All I see, Miss Barr, is an empty lot, the skeleton of a building under very preliminary construction, and one very dead body that's been brought into the light of day on land your client owns. Why did he hire a PR rep at this early stage, anyway?"

"That's not unheard of. I've had only a couple meetings with him, so I'm not going to babysit him through a murder investigation. I'm not a criminal attorney, which I'll recommend he hire."

"And you have no insight on what he's really doing here, except it's a mystery?"

"Right. I'm worthless. To you."

"No, you're not."

That was an amazing statement. Temple was starting to think their few brief simpatico moments lately were beginning to pay off.

"Keep the client," Molina ordered. "And keep me informed on what he's really up to."

"Even if I have to eat buffet pancakes?" Temple asked, dismayed.

"Even if you have to eat dirt."

"I am not one of your detectives," Temple muttered to Molina's departing khaki-covered back.

Then her eyebrows lilted with an insty-epiphany. Maybe she was. But could she betray the interests of a client? No, she should look at this as protecting the interests of a client. She just didn't see Silas T. Farnum shutting his mouth long enough to murder someone.

Chapter 17

Short Stack

From the Wynn's Terrace Pointe Café located near a Ferrari showroom to a Circus Circus breakfast buffet was one of those weird juxtapositions the Strip offered. The bounteous, cheap breakfast buffet was fast becoming a threatened species. Las Vegas had gotten so high-end that low-end had become a nostalgic and exotic experience.

Young children cried for Cheetos over Cheerios, rejecting healthy for salty, air-filled, and permanently dyed orange fingertips. Harried parents loaded up on sausages and bacon and hash browns. And Temple found that pancakes with butter and syrup on the side were infinitely more nutritious and less messy than anything else at the copious food islands.

Silas T. Farnum piled his plate with such noxious

early-morning fare as bloody roast beef. Lotto numbers announced over the loudspeakers punctuated Temple's interrogation . . . er, breakfast chat with her would-be client.

"You really handled that long drink of Aquafina with a badge this morning," Silas T. chortled. Not many people chortled anymore, especially while eating, but Farnum did. "Not to mention witch-slapping those media people."

"I am not a witch," Temple growled, trying not to see his plate. Somehow it seemed very, very wrong to eat fried shrimp and fruit crepes for breakfast.

"Only a *good* witch, like Glinda." Farnum seemed prone to use *Wizard of Oz* comparisons. "But I warn you, I am a warlock, not a wizard."

To hear Silas T. Farnum make this declaration before 8 A.M. in the morning over a dripping forkful of kung pao scallops and pancakes was a sure appetite killer.

"What is really going on here?" she demanded, undercutting the surrounding clamor by using her best stage whisper, which made her sound hoarser than a B movie hit man. "Or I'll walk."

"And you do that so very well." The slightly lascivious twinkle in his beady eyes really wasn't forgivable in a man of his age, say eighty-two. "Especially over that uneven ground. Tell me, you've seen a corpse before. Do you think he was marched over all that rough ground before he was shot?"

"I didn't see this one. He was shot?"

Silas T. patted his lips with the linen napkin. "A small tidy hole right here, where headaches begin."

Temple put her own fingers to the knob behind her ear. Yes, that would probably do it. "Execution style. You saw that? How?"

Silas T. snickered smugly. "I'd gone over to check the site and saw the reeling young couple acting strange at a certain point on the site. They headed back to the disgusting nearby nightclub from whence they'd come. Probably to call the police and then vanish. So when I looked into what they were messing with, I saw the body."

"And left without reporting it? That's interfering with a crime scene! The techs will find their footprints. And yours."

"Maybe so, but I ruffled the sand around with my shoe toe. I used to dance the soft shuffle years ago, you know, which is tap dancing on sand. I'm used to keeping my balance."

"Don't tell me. You were in vaudeville."

"The club circuit, but that was more than fifty years ago, my dear. I'm a rich man now and don't have to shuffle for anybody."

"That won't help you. You interfered with a crime scene. I'm not going to defend you if the police find evidence of your tampering."

"Fine. It's good to have such an upstanding employee. I tell you, that body was old."

"I know he was a senior citizen."

"That too, but it looked longtime dead, maybe buried in the desert. Nothing as juicy as features on all the prime-time forensic shows. Did you notice how the corpses got gooier, the more popular those TV shows became?"

"Yes, I did, and the perps sicker, which is why I don't watch them."

"Just as well you live in Las Vegas, where in real life road kill nicely toasts away to nothing."

Temple pushed her plate away. "So what secret will that building reveal when it's done? *If* the discovered corpse doesn't queer all your crazy secret plans?"

"A surprise."

"Mr. Farnum, I cannot work with such an uncooperative client."

"You'll see," he said, sitting back against the leatherette booth and untucking his napkin from the neck of his shirt. "And sooner than you think. I promise I'll give you the big reveal once the police are through with the site. And that won't take long. There can't be much trace evidence."

"None of that will matter if I quit."

She got up from the table and stomped away through the crowds of couples with children.

"I'm paying for breakfast," he called after her.

You bet he was.

Chapter 18

Law and Order: Crimeshoppers

Temple hadn't managed to eat much for her breakfast with Farnum, and something was eating *at* her. She decided to risk a good chewing-out.

"I need to talk to you," Temple told the phone at noon when Molina answered with a bark of her surname and department.

"Aren't you doing that right now, unfortunately?"

"I mean . . . I need a . . . a meet."

"A . . . meet. Like mobspeak. Get thee to a Mob Museum downtown or at the Tropicana on the Strip . . . or back to your Chunnel of Crime."

"Not mine. I just publicized the opening of the attraction."

"You supervised the opening of a funky old underground walk-in safe and unveiled its freshly dead body, which is now on my unsolved case roster."

"Oh, that old dead body. I need to talk to you about the new one. The one on Paradise."

The line remained silent for three beats. "You have information?"

"I feel obligated to clear the owner of the new construction in the area."

"No, no, no."

"Yes, yes, yes. May I come in to your office now?"

"No! I may want you to keep an eye on this guy, but I'm not some Web site you can look up on a search function any darn time you please. I don't want you here."

Temple wondered why. Was Molina implying Temple wasn't presentable enough for your average homicide office?

"Still, I'm feeling generous about you today," Molina was saying. "God knows why. I can do lunch in . . . forty-five minutes."

"That would be fun."

"Not what I had in mind."

"Where?"

"Actually, I don't know." Molina's voice faded in and out as if she was looking around for someone to consult.

Temple would love to see inside the freshly built Metro Police facility and homicide unit, but she sensed her prey slipping away for a lack of ideas.

"Hey, the Premium Outlets–North mall is right near you. It has Stuart Weitzman and Cole Haan and Steve Madden shoes—and Adidas. And clothes from Calvin Klein and Ed Hardy and Hugo Boss and even a St. John Outlet to die for."

"I don't know any of those men."

Hopeless, Temple thought. "And a Chico's," she added. They had clothes for older and larger women.

"A Mexican restaurant? That'll do."

"No," Temple admitted, "clothes again. But there is China Pantry and Great Steak. It's mall food court eating, so you wouldn't be trapped by having a server."

"Oh, I'd be trapped, all right. I'll take the steak."

"Great. There's a north parking garage. When you enter the mall, take the Mountain Court down to the Tree Court. You hang a left and go past Juicy Couture, where you get to the Earth Court. The food places are between the Earth and Star Courts."

"Are you even speaking English now? Is this place a maze for tarot readings or some other New Age nonsense?"

"It's a nature theme. Relax. We had fun shopping for the reality TV *Teen Queen* show."

"You and Mariah had fun. I had overtime supervisory duty."

"Just sayin'. The new Metro Police building is right on top of some major retail at super prices."

"What I'm saying is you'll be paying for lunch and bringing me into that froufrou environment."

That ended their conversation, but Temple was not displeased. They'd actually had cocktails together in the Oasis Hotel Casablanca Bar after the literal "killer" dance competition that almost did in Matt. So Temple felt she was making inroads on C. R. Molina's no-frills life and work style.

The policewoman needed to access her inner Carmen again. Temple guessed the in-home stalker messing with her performance clothes, and her close encounter with a wardrobe slasher when she was snooping in Max's house, had soured her on what she already regarded as frivolous: being a girl.

Temple was happy to plead to that charge. It was the little touches—a bright color, a new bangle or bag—that perked up everyday life. It had nothing to do with youth or gender but joie de vivre. She knew she'd feel the same way when she was eighty.

She hummed as she looked up the mall on her smartphone. The Metro Police campus was in a traffic tangle north of Charleston and west of downtown, where Martin Luther King Boulevard ran parallel to Highway 93 before it split off before heading for Death Valley and Utah.

She checked her wristwatch. She was hooked on that second hand. Smartphone time readouts reminded her of looking at an alarm clock at 6 A.M. She checked the condo. Louie was out and about and could return via the small high open window in the second bathroom. She had no idea why he'd gotten macho and broken into the French doors, but the claw marks were inescapable.

Landlady Electra Lark had chained the doors shut until a locksmith could repair the middle latch's damage. Matt had promised to fill in the scratches and touch up the paint afterwards. Imagine, all that and handy too.

In three minutes Temple's Miata was tooling up the highway, she wearing a broad-brimmed hat with a built-in scarf tied under her chin to protect her hairdo from the wind and her skin from the sunlight. Convertibles made hats obligatory for a natural redhead, but were still fun. She felt very Grace Kelly in *To Catch a Thief*. Too bad her Cary Grant was off on errands today.

In no time the mall's low adobe-style shops were in view, painted the earth tones of a desert sunset. A Miata could breeze into a small space near the elevators, so Temple was soon through the Mountain, Tree, and Earth Courts and seated in the bustling food court. The echoing voices would make hearing—and overhearing—hard, but it was always a kick to see Molina out of her well-traveled road of home, office, and crime scene.

Temple started musing about Cary—Matt—wondering what he was up to today. And lately. He seemed distracted and yet amazingly unruffled by the lack of news from Chicago about his dream job as a network talk show host.

"Cat got your attention?"

Molina had sneaked up on her, hard for an almost-six-foot-tall woman in a khaki pantsuit. The ambient noise had muffled her clodhopper footsteps. Ugh. The usual unadorned brown loafers. Temple knew guys who'd buy better-looking shoes.

Molina nodded at the surrounding food stands. "Time to do our hunter-gathering thing?"

Temple, perhaps inspired by Silas T. Farnum's lunch order, got the Little Philly Sliders, in a "six-pack" with chicken instead of steak. Molina went for the Chicagoland Cheesesteak with white American cheese. Both went for dark drinks. Temple's was Dr Pepper, and Molina's was iced tea.

"Chicagoland," Temple noted of Molina's sandwich as she paid the tab. "Isn't that mob-appropriate, although the gourmet American cheese is a classy touch."

"Class is not on my wish list," Molina answered.

Temple disagreed. Those vintage '30s velvet gowns Carmen wore while performing were class personified, but it seemed C. R. Molina had stuffed Carmen permanently back in the literal closet. Naturally, a blues-singing female homicide lieutenant didn't want the guys at work to know she did occasional gigs at the Blue Dahlia supper club.

After they sat down at their little plastic table for four, Molina hefted the sub-style bun before taking a bite. "Isn't Chicago becoming Matt Devine's second home these days?"

"It was his first home," Temple said. "And not a happy one."

"Our first homes often aren't. That's why so many people end up in a pseudo-city like Las Vegas."

"That's only the Strip and all its works. Beyond that it's a pretty normal community."

"If you say so."

"And even crazy Vegas has its plus side. Matt's mother and her new beau just whisked in and out of town to be married here."

"Were you flower girl?"

"Maid of honor. Louie was ring bearer, though."

Molina rolled her eyes as she chewed. "Sometimes I think that cat has dog genes. What self-respecting feline would sit still for a bit part in a wedding ceremony?"

"Midnight Louie, as you know, has the self-respect and chutzpah to use this whole town for a litter box."

"His free-wheeling ways wouldn't go over in Chicago."

"Au contraire." Temple sipped the tangy Dr Pepper before adding, "He was kidnapped by the mob and got two made men arrested."

"Kidnapped by the mob? Grant you, the only places the mob still parties hard now are in the Northeast and Chicago. But people are too ready to attribute purpose to what pets do, and turn coincidence into beyond-natural motives and acts."

"What about your domestic pets, Lieutenant?"

"You've seen them. Two tabby cats of perfectly ordinary intelligence and instinct. They sleep a lot and always hear the can opener. So?"

"You've seen Louie inexplicably present on a few crime scenes."

"He follows you around like a dog. I don't suppose that's beyond the capacity of cats, though it's unusual. It may be some scent you wear."

"Like tuna toilet water?"

"Not an appetizing image right now, Miss Barr."

"We're sounding like we're at a tea party," Temple complained. "That's not necessary with cheese dribbling down our chins."

"I agree. I can call you Red."

"As in 'better dead than'?"

"You can call me—"

Temple waited breathlessly.

Molina shook her head ruefully. "Wait. You don't need to call me anything."

"I was waiting for Blue. You do sing them."

"The blues? Not so much lately. Now. What do you know about the body on the construction site?"

"It's more a matter of what I want to know."

"Me first. Just who is this Silas T. Farnum guy?"

"An out-of-state investor. Company name, Deja View Associates. I checked it out on the Internet and it looks legit."

"Ah, the Internet. That'll soon replace police departments and newspapers as 'impeccable' sources."

"I don't take everything at face value," Temple said, adding a tinge of indignity to her tone.

"Only Irishmen," Molina commented.

"I think I could come up with something to call you now, but it's not suitable for public consumption."

Molina laughed. "That was catty of me. I wasn't even catty in grade school. You're a bad influence."

"I hope so, because Chico's is just down the Sun Court."

Molina sipped iced tea with a grimace. "Everybody wants to remake me."

"Really. How 'everybody'?" To Temple's amazement, Molina answered.

"Teen singing phenom Mariah."

"Daughters always do that."

"You just brushed that off. Why?"

"Because I went through that creepy kid stage. The day you notice that Moth-er is Dow-dy. So embarrassing. Someone might notice you're Not Cool Too."

"You've got that stage down," Molina agreed. "Why do we always end up discussing trivial things?"

"Because you don't have any girlfriends?"

"Why would I want any?"

"I rest my case."

"Who have you got?"

"Well, Mariah, for one." When Molina winced, Temple went on. "I'm getting to be gal pals with Matt's mother. Not so much his lovesick younger cousin. Electra is a girlfriend. And a couple media women in town. And, oh, I mustn't forget my aunt Kit, who's hardly like a relative at all. And now that she's married Aldo Fontana, I'm some kinda crazy in-law to the ten brothers."

"Aldo Fontana is married? To your aunt? You're right. That is vaguely . . . incestuous. And you're asking *me* about mobsters?"

"You know the Fontanas are . . . vestigial mobsters. Mock mobsters."

"And that truly is all that's left of the mob in Vegas. The Metro Police and the FBI cleaned up the town in the '80s. Our big problem now is ethnic gangs."

"Couldn't there be a few vestigial made men hanging around town? That body dump on Paradise is very Jimmy Hoffa."

"What makes Hoffa a mystery is that his body was never found. This Paradise guy was old, though."

"Like the Glory Hole Gang? Those eighty-something rascals who heisted silver dollars in their youth and run a restaurant at Gangsters?"

"About that age. We don't see too many elderly murder victims."

"I suppose age takes people to a point where the usual motives—lust, envy, and vengeance—don't matter much anymore. Except for greed. That seems ageless."

"True. The Glory Hole Gang were holdup artists, not mob."

"Whoever killed Cliff Effinger was probably mob,"

Temple said. "Effinger was in on something. He knew something that got him killed. When Matt and I visited Chicago, someone was shaking down his mother for some old personal items Effinger had left behind."

"Really? What kind of items?"

Temple was not going to reveal the strange history of the constellation Ophiuchus and secret magicians' circle called the Synth. If Molina found the names of the outlet mall's various areas "New Age," she'd find all the Synth mumbo-jumbo, with bodies arranged in a constellation shape, too outré for the Las Vegas Metropolitan Police Department.

"We don't know," Temple said, guilty about lying. "Just that there was a fireproof locked file box full of memorabilia, and somebody wanted it enough to threaten and stalk Matt's mother—"

"Another stalking situation?" Molina's squinting eyes reduced her electric blue irises to high-intensity narrow beams. "That's . . . a coincidence too many."

"Her apartment was broken into and Midnight Louie taken to force her to surrender the box and its contents. The Chicago police went to the warehouse Louie had escaped from and found two 'minor crime figures' with Italian surnames in somewhat shaky condition."

"That's ethnic profiling, Red." Molina was sensitive about her half-Hispanic origins.

"Go to the mob museum if you want to see ethnic profiling spelled *M-a-f-i-a*."

Molina leaned back in the plastic chair, her meal and beverage dispensed with. And probably her patience. "I'll look into the Farnum character's company, but as far as we yet know, that dumped body was a murder in search of an unrelated site to be found in. The only prints around the location indicate the presence of rats. And cats," she added with a forbidding frown.

Temple knew when to pull back. "You can't have one without the other or else you get bubonic plague," she pointed out.

"The victim hasn't been identified, but I'd doubt he'd have mob connections. His hands were callused from heavy labor. I'd suspect the building trades."

"Shovels. Pickaxes. Maybe he knew where other bodies were buried."

"Will you get off this Jimmy Hoffa theme?" Molina was annoyed enough to make a speech. "With all the undreamed-of construction on the Strip in the past twenty years, any hidden bodies would have come to light. This is not a Big Crime case. It could be someone who welched on a bet at an illegal street gambling site. It could be someone who was bribed to use substandard building materials and was going to 'squeal' in the language of the gangster movies you favor." Molina rose, ready to go.

Temple would love to know what the woman kept in her pockets; she never carried a purse. "I agree that this was man-on-man violence, not some old lady going crazy with the family revolver after fifty years of unhappy wedlock." Temple gathered up her tote bag and stood as well.

"Stay put," Molina ordered. "I'll find my own way out. Maybe you should forget crime-solving, after all, and stick to what you know best. Shopping."

Molina had gone too far too fast for Temple to think of a snappy comeback. While she picked up the lunch remnants and consigned them to the trash barrel, she considered that she'd at least learned the official police position on the dead body on Paradise.

And that Molina was behind the times. A woman could work both sides of the street these days: career seriousness and self-expression.

Just to prove it, Temple would *not* stop in at the Juicy Couture 80 percent off sale on the way out.

Chapter 19

Honeymooners

"You and Matt make such an adorable couple!" Aunt Kit pronounced that evening.

She linked Temple's arm through hers and led her on a stroll through the lavish indoor tropical gardens and water features of the Crystal Court cocktail lounge. Although this was a private reception in honor of Kit and Aldo Fontana's return from a Lake Como honeymoon in Italy, a big and festive crowd thronged the Crystal Phoenix Hotel's bar area. The soaring spotlighted entry wall was frosted-crystal sheened by a thin veil of falling water. Very bridal.

A life-size wedding cake topper couple posed in the center of the space. "Living" statues as pure white as Carrara marble had been introduced at the Venetian Hotel. The specialty mimes looked frozen in place, but moved infinitesimally, disconcerting the unwary in a whimsical, charming way.

"Adorable couple, me and Matt," Temple repeated her aunt's comment. "Them too." She nodded at the statues. "And . . . I could say the same about you and Aldo."

Kit smiled like the Persian who'd lapped up the ice cream. "We Carlson girls are just the bee's knees. Luckily the genes weren't weakened by your father, Mr. Barr."

"Leave my poor father out of it, Kit. I hear you 'Carlson girls' have been chatting about me behind my back. Have you even told Mom you're married now?"

"Hell no. She'd make such a fuss. Have you told her you're engaged?"

"As a matter of fact," Temple said with a virtuous air she could seldom assume, "yes."

Kit grabbed her hand and sat them down on a white patent leather tufted bench with Lucite legs. It felt more like floating than sitting. "How'd she take it?"

"She was dubious until she learned the happy fiancé wasn't Max."

"Your mother recognizes a dangerous man when she sees him."

"Wait'll she sees Aldo."

"I hope to postpone that day until Aldo condescends to grow a respectable gray hair or two. These Italians are slow to turn distinguished."

"I hope 'that day' is at my wedding."

"Then you're going to do the deed in Minnesota?"

Temple sighed. "Maybe. Or Chicago. Or maybe there's someplace ecumenical in between."

"Iowa?"

Temple laughed. "Why not Wyoming, while you're at it?"

"Wherever it is," Kit said with a hug, "you'll make a beautiful bride."

That made Temple tear up a tad. "I'd better not desert

my bridegroom-to-be. It's really great to dress up and go out in Vegas together at an event that's not so late he'll have to rush off to the radio station."

Temple jumped up and fluffed the full skirt of her '50s vintage dress, now so "in" again. She and Kit strolled back to the main mingling area.

"Ah, *bella*." Tall, dark, and handsome Aldo Fontana intercepted them and so equally offered his glance that it was impossible to tell which woman he'd called beautiful, presumably both.

That was the Fontana touch, diplomatic to the bone. Imagine the movie *Godfather* having ten nephews who were maître d's at a five-star restaurant.

All the Fontana brothers were clichés: ridiculously tall, dark, and handsome. There were an incredible ten of them, here now mingling in suave social patterns to make guests feel welcome, whether it was steering a couple to the bar or kissing the ladies' hands.

Matt, bearing a tall frosted glass, joined them. "A mini family reunion?" he asked, smiling at Kit.

"Don't you look handsome," Kit said, embracing him and brushing his cheek with a kiss. "Family privilege, right, Aldo?"

Aldo responded by kissing Temple's left hand and winking at the engagement ring on it. "Family privilege, Matt."

"You'll all be pleased to know," Temple said, "that Kit has informed my worried mother in Minnesota that I'm under the wing of a large Italian family while in Las Vegas. She was much relieved."

"Then," said Aldo with a brush of his palms that ended with a gentle clap, "my function in life has been more than met. May I sweep you away," he asked Kit, "for a private family stroll among the camellias? I do have a lot of brothers."

"Your mother and mine," Matt told Temple after they

moved on, "would have a lot in common. Worrying. How do we stop them?"

"We get married and convince them we're grown-ups. If my mom knew that Uncle 'Macho' Mario's roots are as firmly planted as a corpse in Vegas's mob history, she'd be down here with the state police to pry me out of Vegas. Come to think of it, Chicago's a more notorious mob town. She'll pout when we settle down so close, but far, to her."

Matt's arm around her waist had tensed during her happy babble. Maybe she shouldn't have had that champagne cocktail when they arrived.

"Don't count your Chicagos," he said, "before they put out a contract on me. Media kingpins are fickle."

"It's not like we didn't totally blow the network bigwigs away. They were even talking about 'doing something' with me. We could be the hot new media couple of Michigan Avenue."

"It could all fall through."

"Anything could, I guess, Matt."

He remained silent, a shadow in his eyes. Then he deliberately shook off the mood, like Louie unseating an invisible flea. "Here I am, neglecting Number One fiancée. I think I'll switch to champagne. It's certainly given you a bubbly glow."

As they took a couple of steps toward the bar, Temple's idle gaze encountered a fixed point, and she stopped moving. "What's *she* doing here?"

He looked where she was staring. "Van von Rhine? She runs the joint."

"Not Van, the woman with her, the hot blonde from the icy Alps. Van's private school friend, from Switzerland. Funny, Max just spent a couple months in a coma and then on the run in . . . Switzer . . . land."

Temple's lower jaw remained frozen in position even as Matt frowned to identify the woman in question.

Moving through the crowd to join the two women, what at first impression seemed a Fontana brother, was Max Kinsella.

When she turned to consult Matt, he was already looking at her.

"Isn't that a shock?" she demanded. "I don't know why he . . . why she . . . why they're here. It's a reception for Kit and Aldo. That woman surely doesn't know them."

"Max does," Matt reminded her.

"If he remembers," Temple pointed out. "Though everybody in Vegas knows the Fontana brothers, and Kit met . . . ah, Max met Kit—oh, ages ago."

Temple had just remembered that her Christmas visit to Kit in Manhattan had ended with her aunt encouraging them to, er, reunite after the shock of Max's sudden exit of a year before, followed by as sudden a return.

"He and the blond schoolmate seem to be an item," Matt noted, unable to hide some smugness.

"That's wonderful," Temple said. "Max is creating new memories. He won't be so alone."

"Without you?"

"Without Gandolph."

At that moment, Van took the blonde in hand and headed toward Temple and Matt while Max turned to be hailed by Aldo and Kit. Temple wondered how much he remembered of the Fontana brothers . . . and Kit . . . and that night in Manhattan.

"Temple, Matt," Van said, "I'd like you to meet my finishing school friend, Revienne Schneider. I know, Temple, you've met in passing, but Revienne has a profession you, and particularly Matt, would find fascinating."

And with that, Van glided off, her hostess job done and her perfectly smooth champagne-colored French twist disappearing into the clusters of shoulders making conversation islands in the room.

Now Temple, Matt, and Revienne formed a new, alien clump of three.

What had Van been thinking?

First of all, even with Temple wearing her favorite heels with the sweet and clever bows (the '50s were all about bows), Revienne on her four-inch Louboutins bristling with cuffs and spikes and gladiator leather towered over her. Worse, like many tall women who boldly went for even taller, she was used to looking men in the eye about a foot above Temple's sight line, which put Revienne on eye level with Matt.

So Temple was automatically out of the conversation. She hated that!

Apparently, Ravishing Revienne also knew Max. From where? And when?

And what kind of name was Revienne? Temple was reminded of a vintage French perfume, Je Reviens. It meant "I return."

Boy, did that not bode well for Temple. She would have loved to equate Revienne with the similarly shod, over-whelmingly blond D movie actress Savannah Ashleigh, with whom Temple had crossed stilettos before . . . but that wasn't fair.

Revienne's hair was such a smooth blend of French vanilla and caramel, you could almost taste it. Even her aggressive shoes were the one runway touch in her ensemble, a silky summer suit even more meltingly luscious than one of the Fontana brothers' ice cream numbers.

And . . . an exquisite wisp of designer scarf flirted with her neck and shoulders. Temple had an entire drawer devoted to discarded and gifted scarves, with which she could do nothing even remotely fashionable.

"I've heard your radio show and have become addicted," Revienne was telling Matt. "You are such a brilliant and intuitive counselor. How can you relate so quickly to such an array of problems, having no personal contact with the clients?"

"I'm sorry if I kept you up late," Matt said with a smile. "They're 'listeners,' not clients. Maybe it's because I heard confessions for many years as a priest at a parish that had a Latin Mass and used confessionals for the older people."

"*C'est vrai?*" Revienne asked Temple in such apparent surprise that she needed confirmation, which was another churchly rite, Temple mused.

"Of course it's true," Temple said, glad she understood a few French expressions, "if Matt says it is. Are you surprised he heard confessions in an old-fashioned, uh, booth, or that he was a priest?"

"Both, I suppose. I'd taken you for a married couple."

Temple and Matt exchanged a smile and he answered. "You're a pretty good snap psychologist yourself, Ms. Schneider. We soon will be married."

"Ah." Revienne's new look at Temple included an eyebrow-raising appraisal of her vintage ruby-and-diamond engagement ring. "*C'est vrai* indeed. And please call me Revienne. Van and I were so close during our most formative years. It's a pleasure to see her again and meet her friends here in Las Vegas."

Like Max? Temple itched to ask. Maybe she could get the scoop on this blond bombshell from Van von Rhine in a private moment.

"What brings you to Las Vegas, Revienne?" Matt asked right out loud. "Van said you were in the same field as me. Surely you weren't in a convent at one time?"

Yay, Matt!

"A convent *school*," Revienne replied with an artful smile of her own. "Later I took degrees in Vienna and Berlin. A favorite instructor of mine has a visiting professorship at the local Nevada University branch. And I have engagements in Los Angeles later for my—I think you say 'pet'?—project."

"You do volunteer work?" Temple asked, surprised. This woman looked too stylish, too too-too, and too hot for charity causes.

"For eating disorders among teenage girls, yes."

"That's a global problem, for sure," Temple said. "When you and Van were at school together in Switzerland, was it a problem?"

"Yes, no doubt. But it was a secret one."

"It does seem sometimes," Matt said, "that teenagers' modern mania for 'posting' all the details of their lives online is a raw adolescent ego trip, yet it's exposed virulent problems like bullying and eating disorders."

"Public confessions, you could say," Revienne noted.

A waiter with a tray of champagne flutes paused beside them. Temple and Matt surrendered their empty glasses, and Revienne accepted one. Temple noticed the champagne matched her hair color perfectly.

"I should 'mingle,' as you say. I would love to stay and continue our collegial discussion, Mr. Devine, but Van wanted me to meet all her friends. *Je reviens*."

With a salute of her champagne flute, Temple noted sourly, Revienne and her scarf wafted elsewhere.

"One wonders," Matt said, watching her amble away as delicately as a fawn through the gathered people.

"That she had an eating disorder early on?"

His gaze narrowed just short of a frown. "Not that. It was someone close to her, all right, but not Revienne."

"What did you wonder, then?"

"What her real purpose in being here is. *We* sure didn't hear it."

"It seems plain enough. Her old teacher is here. She's visiting him on the way to her charity gigs in L.A."

Matt shook his head. "She's really interested in us."

"You maybe. *C'est vrais*. A man-eater!"

That made Matt laugh. "I've never seen your jealous gene acting up. Well, a little about my cousin Krys in Chicago."

"You are dealing with a hot-tempered redhead, fellow. Don't forget that."

"Speaking of hot-tempered redheads . . ." Matt nodded to Kit, who was talking to . . . Max at the bar.

"He's not the enemy," Temple said. "We do have to consult with him on various and sundry remaining mysteries and deaths, not to mention our Kitty the Cutter problem, but— Look! Kit is moving off alone. I'm going to plumb her brain on what's going on with Max attending this Crystal Phoenix party."

"Always the intrepid reporter. Meanwhile, I'll ask Aldo for tips on being married to someone from your family."

"Thanks for keeping him busy while I corner Kit," Temple said as her heels rapped a rapid drumbeat over the marble floors. "Kit!" She grabbed her aunt's arm just before she was about to join a group of Fontana brothers. She also snagged a passing waiter and scored champagne flutes for two. "Can you give me any idea of why my ex has been invited to a Crystal Phoenix party?"

"Sorry to be the bearer of bad news." Kit sipped before answering further, and Temple could have shaken her.

"What bad news?"

"For one, Max is Revienne's guest."

"He better watch out. She is one slinky slippery sister."

"Granted."

"Who told you that?"

"Aldo. He's putty in my hands."

"Please, I don't want to hear about any honeymoon disappointments."

"Dream on," Kit said, sipping once more.

"What did you learn from Max?"

"That he really doesn't remember a lot."

"He forgot you?"

"Yes, but he detected a resemblance and led me into talking about you and then me and my Manhattan career as an actress and then a romance writer and then as your madcap maiden aunt and your Christmas visit to my Manhattan digs."

"No! That was our big reunion after he came back from disappearing for my own safety and leaving me deserted in Las Vegas. I don't want him remembering anything . . . intimate about us. Just by talking to him, you turned his wandering memory in my direction."

"Relax. I did fill him in on his impulsive trip to my Manhattan place. The man knows you two were an item, whether he remembers specifics or not. He did remember Midnight Louie being there, but not you. He says."

"What a relief! Once again Midnight Louie comes in handy even when he isn't around, like here."

Kit sipped more champagne, fast.

"Going somewhere?" Temple asked.

"Preparing to duck and cover."

"What else is new? Kit. Tell me!"

"Nicky Fontana was talking with Max."

"I didn't notice, but I'm sure Van has filled her husband in on the fact that I'm with Matt Devine now, and Max Kinsella is firmly in my past."

"Maybe. But Nicky wants Max to work up a magic show for the Crystal Phoenix."

"He can't." Temple was stunned.

"Who can't what? Nicky can't commission Max to do a magic show?"

"Sure, Nicky can do that, but Max. His memory. How can he remember all his old illusions?"

"I'm sure he's got new illusions up his sleeve," Kit said dryly. "We all do. I can tell you, as an actress, that Max is very, very good at covering up his memory deficit.

Don't you want him to recover and get back to work again?"

"Sure, but not at the Phoenix, *my* account." Temple searched the busy lounge area until she saw Matt chatting with a tall man distinguished by a poll of ice white hair. "It's such a good thing Matt has a hot job waiting in Chicago."

"We'll all miss you," Kit said, her lips turning down into a mime's moue. Even when she made a sad face, she was charming. "I hope you two can commute to see us here. People live in the same city as their exes all over the world, and it's not the end of it."

"No, but—" *But Max is making it so obvious that he is back on the Vegas scene. Does he* want *to draw the attention of Kitty the Cutter?*

Temple started thinking about Max's almost-lifelong enemy, studying the cocktail waitresses, the female guests, looking for Kathleen O'Connor in another guise. That witch was so sneaky that Temple could almost believe Revienne Schneider was another incarnation of her.

Matt seemed totally occupied by a knot of female groupies, bless his humble heart, so Temple eased over to Max and the Mysterious Man. For one thing, she was dying to know more about how he'd hooked up with Revienne.

The men turned at the heel clicks of her approach, but it was the Mysterious Stranger who greeted her first. "Ah, Miss Barr, isn't it? I know your agile PR fingerprints are all over every successful event in this hyperactive city of ours, not to mention on the occasional crime scene. That Zoe Chloe Ozone persona of yours really hit with the teen crowd. And now I hear you've impressed some media folk in the Big Town."

Temple stood there, shell-shocked. Out of the corner of her eye, Max looked equally taken aback.

The man extended a veined but elegant hand and gave hers a waft past his lips. "Tony Valentine," he said. "I represent those close to you and hope for an even closer connection in the future."

Almost no one rendered Temple speechless. She saw that Max was in the same gobsmacked state and felt infinitely better.

"Adieu, Mr. Kinsella," Valentine said with almost a parting heel click. "Please think over our cocktail chit-chat and call me at teatime tomorrow for a true business conversation."

Temple had to stand on tippytoes to watch his majestic white head glide away through a crowd that parted like the Red Sea for Moses.

"Tony Valentine," she finally repeated. "He's Matt's agent. How did he know about my adventures in crime and punishment?"

"Probably from your concerned fiancé," Max said. "A good agent knows everything."

"Then I should ask him about the hot blond French babe you're suddenly escorting."

Max's laughter was so infectious, she rightly felt foolish.

"She's French-German," he corrected her.

"A quibble. You know she's as French as a Victoria's Secret Miracle Bra."

Max paused. Thought. "Actually, the French don't go in for artificial implementation. Au naturel, you know."

"So I noticed. Okay. What are you doing, exposing *your*self all over town? You know it's not safe."

"I know 'safe' isn't the way we're going to smoke out Kathleen O'Connor." Max gazed over her head at someone. He took a deep breath. "You realize her pattern is to torment next of kin, significant others, everyone but the true target of her rage."

"So you aim to make yourself Mr. Prime Target, against

the odds she even cares to torment you further at this point."

Max nodded solemnly. "Why wouldn't she? You do."

Temple wanted to sputter that she didn't. But couldn't.

"If I were you," he told her, "I'd keep an eye on the present, not the past."

"What are you saying?"

"Just a word to the sage."

Temple was frowning as he moved away.

Kathleen O'Connor was back. She'd never left, despite being mistaken for dead often enough to set a world record. Temple looked around. All the woman's favorite victims were gathered here. She tended to fixate on men. Matt. Max. Maybe she'd even dazzled the Cloaked Conjuror when she masqueraded as his partner, the Asian magician, Shangri-La. Supposedly Shangri-La had fallen to her death. Or a body double had.

For sure, Kitty the Cutter was a mistress of disguise. . . .

Temple's PR concerns could make her into a human security camera, and her last visual sweep of the area netted her a new idea. Sometimes the most obvious was the most concealed.

She eyed the slightly thinning crowd. Max had vanished. Tony Valentine had left. Even the Fontana brothers were down to a mere half dozen, including Nicky. . . .

In fact . . . Temple noticed that those two "living statues" powdered the solid white of marble were poised near Matt. The "groom" was apparently still at the moment, but the "bride" had edged over to . . . Max and Revienne, standing near the Crystal Phoenix movers and shakers.

How ironic if the "bride" were Kitty the Cutter, Max's teenage conquest in Northern Ireland, already then a human time bomb of hate and vengeance. Temple turned and stalked toward the motionless-yet-now-sinister bride, planning to step on her trailing train and jerk off the veil.

She was about to commit a huge public debacle, but her instincts screamed she had spotted a maybe suicide bomber in their midst. Kathleen O'Connor could take out all her favorite targets and a lot of innocents right here and now.

Temple headed toward her prey.

Only she was about four feet and six seconds too late.

Chapter 20

The French Connection

"They are so adorable," Revienne said.

"What?" Max asked. He'd been trying to overhear what Van von Rhine was telling her husband, Nicky Fontana, about . . . Revienne.

"Switzerland" had been the word in their conversation that had gotten his attention. He'd been astounded to learn during the introductions that Van von Rhine had gone to an exclusive boarding school with Revienne in Lucerne.

Small world. Or too small for comfort and credibility?

Max reflected that his spy instinct was obviously dominant.

"Max?"

"Sorry." He smiled with a shrug. "I was wondering whether my memory led me astray or not during my business conversation with Nicky Fontana. I hope that was Nicky. There are more Fontana brothers here than I would remember even without amnesia."

"You were fine, and I still say they are adorable."

"The Fontana brothers?"

Revienne laughed. "They as well, but I meant the honored couple. The handsome blond man and the lively little redhead. She'll age as well as her mother."

"Yes," Max said, a bit shocked. "That pair do make a handsome couple. But . . . ah, the older woman is Temple's aunt Kit, not her mother. And the honored newlyweds are the aunt and her recent bridegroom, the eldest Fontana brother. Aldo is over there by the bar."

"Ah, I see," Revienne said. "How European. I didn't know American women were enterprising enough to marry younger men. And the other couple?"

"Engaged."

"Friends of yours?"

"As of my return to Vegas, yes. And before."

"Poor man." Revienne took his arm. "It must be like walking on ice, living again in a city filled with people you don't remember. Not knowing who's a friend, or an enemy."

"Oh, I think I was used to that," Max answered, again surveying the people they'd been discussing. But their positions in the room had changed.

As he turned, he almost brushed the extravagant bouffant veil of the living-statue bride.

This concept had been charming when introduced but was getting to be annoying, he thought.

"What the—?" He moved Revienne so quickly aside that the champagne flute in her right hand spilled.

Temple was bearing down on them at a fast, determined clip.

"Oh," Revienne objected.

"Max, watch out!" Temple shouted.

Chapter 21

Let Them Eat Crow

I have been the perfect party guest. Unseen.

The copious greenery and potted plants make a perfect cover for the jungle-stalking kind, so I have observed this fancy social gavotte at the Crystal Court lounge from the cover of massive canna lily leaves.

My favorite humans are delightfully nimble, if predictable, at the cocktail game. If the soles of their shoes left fluorescent imprints on the pale marble floor, you would have a pattern showing enough to-and-fro traffic to emulate Times Square on New Year's Eve.

I, however, am not fooled by the usual ins and outs of the usual cocktail party. Like my Miss Temple, I am here to sniff out danger among the daiquiris.

"Hah!" comes an unwelcome greeting from the rear that has my tail hair as stiff and splayed as a radiator brush.

"Hanging about your old haunt, hoping for a job offer?" Miss Midnight Louise speculates. "I could use a pool boy."

I shudder as my flagship member settles back into its usual sleek condition. "Water is not my medium, Louise, especially chlorinated water. It is hard on the eyes and coat."

"Just saying. Your old spot by the canna lilies bordering the hotel pool is vacant, and the fishpond is teeming with fat, out-of-condition koi."

Of course, she knows just how to evoke my sentimental side . . . schooling fishies glittering in the sun, high-heel-sandaled bathing beauty feet passing to and fro. Bronzed bodies baking in the sun, and scaled golden torsos swaying just below the water level, plump and tasty . . .

"I no longer crave the swim-spa experience, Louise," I tell her. "I am on guard duty. If you had your ears perked right, you would know that the most dangerous female in Las Vegas could very well be within eyesight."

"I spot several suspicious females, including your roommate. She is dangerous to be around. Dead bodies have a habit of suddenly appearing."

"She is just curious. It is a characteristic of the human breed—only my Miss Temple has a double dose of that personality trait. Which other suspicious female has your hackles twitching?"

"There is that smooth blond foreign number."

"Are you talking sports cars or human beings? Miss Van von Rhine has not lived abroad since she came to Vegas after her father died and she met and married Nicky Fontana."

Miss Louise gives my whiskers a slightly exasperated boxing. "I know who the Crystal Phoenix boss lady is. I have been unofficial house detective here longer than you ever were before you decamped with Miss Temple Barr to the Circle Ritz."

"Oho. We are going into past history and 'he said/she said,' are we?"

"We are going into 'I am the law of the paw around

here now.' And I say Mr. Max Kinsella's new girlfriend looks like the calico that ate the cream cheese."

"Mr. Max has not already transferred his affections from my Miss Temple?" I feel indignant hairs stiffening all over my body. "The cad!"

"Or just absentminded," Louise says. "Like you sometimes."

Before I can get huffy about that comment, my sharp eyes focus on a movement as minuscule as a mouse might make. *Mmm.* I have glimpsed a white-slippered toe moving behind a snowy waterfall of bridal skirt.

I could swear I saw that toe *pushing* something not white out of sight.

"See, Pops. You have totally tuned out," Louise is whispering in my ear.

"Why should I tune in to nonsense when I have just spotted a major criminal on the scene? If the person under that white makeup and gown is not Miss Kathleen 'the Cutter' O'Connor preparing to attack Mr. Max and my Miss Temple and all those near and dear to her, I am the cat that ran away with the spoon."

"The *dish*," Miss Louise says in her best schoolmarm tone. "The dish eloped with the spoon. The cat just fiddled away."

"This cat is not fiddling around." I give a fearsome battle cry along the lines of *Tarzan of the Apes* vocalizations.

Then I leap three feet forward into the open as Miss Midnight Louise cries behind me, "Pop. Stop! What are you doing? Stop! You will humiliate yourself. Stop! You will cost me my job. Stop! This is my turf. Stop! They will think you are *me,* oh no."

You would think Miss Louise had gotten a job as a telegraph operator with all those "stop" commands.

I am about to unveil the psychopath among us, and nothing will stop me.

I barrel toward the albino bridal couple at full speed, watching their composure crack as I near and throw myself two-thirds up the bride's full skirt, clinging like a giant burr until my weight pulls a huge tear in the material.

"Stop!" a male human voice yells.

"Louie," Miss Temple wails.

"This cat is crazy," my stauesque victim screeches.

"Louise!" Miss Van von Rhine calls out, having indeed taken me for the house detective.

I leap higher to catch my shivs in the long trailing bridal veil, hoping to bare the black locks of Miss Kathleen O'Connor, human chameleon and Most Dangerous Woman Alive.

I pull down yards and yards of a cloud of tulle, that airy netted stuff, and uncover a . . . head of pinned-up brown hair.

Brown. That is not the hair color of a femme fatale.

I stand abashed, while human feet and shoes encircle me and human voices drift down in admonishment and anger.

In all the excitement, the living statues broke character and tried to escape my onslaught. Can an individual mount an onslaught? I do not know, but I am pretty impressive in ninja mode, especially against an all-white background.

"How did a rabid cat get in here?" The flour-decked groom's makeup is cracking. "We will sue."

"I am so sorry," Miss Van von Rhine is saying, wringing her hands.

"Oh, Louie," my Miss Temple is whispering. "He must have had some fright," she says in a louder tone.

Me? Subject to a "fright"?

I can spot Miss Midnight Louise's narrow gams through the forest of lower limbs. She is putting in an appearance to make sure that there can be no question that I am the culprit. Talk about family solidarity, not that we are family.

People are cooing over the disheveled bride, and they include some of the Fontana brothers. Is there no loyalty?

My name is indeed black. My reputation is in as many tatters as the gown wilting on this so-called statue of a bride.

The murmurs are getting ugly and I am hearing words like "cage" and "tetanus shots" and "isolation."

My Miss Temple is pleading for my life and freedom. I am thinking Marty Scorsese is the director for the biopic. He can move beyond fiction. He did a great documentary on Bob Dylan.

While they are all so exercised, plotting evil retribution for my apparent sins, I sneak out a long limb and stretch my shivs to the max. I am nearing the bride's stiffly starched skirt.

I put in a paw and pull out a plum . . . the sparkly bit I saw her bridal slipper toe sneaking under the giant white umbrella of her skirt.

I pull it across the smooth marble and into the custody of my folded forelimbs.

"What have you got there?" Trust my Miss Temple to keep a steady eye on me and my well-being in the midst of this mob. She bends to retrieve what I have captured. "Anybody in this crowd missing a screw-back ruby earring?" she asks loudly.

A muted shriek comes from the rim of the mob.

No guillotine for Midnight Louie today.

In another hour, hotel security and the Metro Police have hauled away the larcenous lovebirds in powdered sugar white. Only the inner circle remains, which does not include the Mystifying Max and Miss Dr. Revienne Schneider.

I am sitting atop one of those high chairs that surround tiny tall cocktail tables, lapping up an all-fat cream used for cocktails from a bell-shaped champagne glass that better suits my drinking method than those tall narrow flutes.

Miss Midnight Louise has done a disappearing act, so I get all the credit.

"Imagine the nerve," Miss Van von Rhine is telling the gathered Fontana brothers, including her husband. "I cannot believe all you crime experts had no idea a pair of pocket-pickers were working our party."

"Well, uh." Mr. Nicky Fontana eyes his sheepish bros. I have never before seen a Fontana brother looking sheepish. "Obviously we needed an undercover operative on the right level."

"It was a sweet setup," Aldo says despite his sister-in-law's small frown at that description. "You won't even feel a good pickpocket taking the gold fillings from your molars, much less anything dangling out there on your limbs or lobes."

"I could not believe," Miss Temple says, "how much jewelry they had slipped into the bags beneath the bride's skirts. A Rolex, even."

Miss Van von Rhine winces.

"Two things going on there to make this crooked gig work," Nicky said. "People will forget about living statues once they figure out what they are. Or they come close and try to make them break character in front of them. Either way, they are distracted, and a small move from, say, the groom will not be obvious while you are trying to stare down the bride through her veil."

"I am sure," Miss Temple says, "the police will discover this pair, or even the booking agency, has been ripping off clients and their guests for quite a while. I knew Midnight Louie had not lost his marbles."

She strokes me fondly on the head. Nice, but not while I am drinking.

I look up, glad to see everyone now smiling down at me like I was the genius crime-fighter I know myself to be.

It is a bit disappointing that my swift action did not unmask a psycho bride, but you cannot have everything.

Chapter 22

A Fine and
Secret Show

"The police anticipate murderers coming back to the scene of the crime," Temple told Silas T. Farnum as she looked from the deep, dark starless Las Vegas night to the lukewarm security lights dotting his shrouded building in a pattern resembling the Big Dipper.

"Is that why you're whispering in this huge deserted lot at midnight?" he asked. He was now accoutered with a handsome silver-headed cane, like a circus ringmaster.

Why had she come running back to the Paradise site at his excited call? Maybe she needed her mind taken off her personal woes.

She and Matt had so little time together lately, and after what should have been a romantic evening out too. When they'd gotten back to the Circle Ritz, she used the elevator ride to woo him from his mysterious overtime sessions at the radio station with the promise of a steamy rendezvous at the usual 3 A.M. He'd gotten off on her floor, but put her off with excuses again. When she persisted, he'd suggested that maybe she should call on Max for that, since she was so eager to rescue him from a Kathleen O'Connor who wasn't even in the room, and rushed up the stairs to his unit.

Talk about feeling drop-kicked all the way to Santa Monica! She wanted to be mad, but just felt sad. So, when Silas T.'s unfailingly cheerful voice chirped from her cell phone, she came running.

She gazed around the construction site, which reminded her of the remnants of the Forum in Rome, more in a state of fallen down than going up. Farnum at the Forum. It was not an enticing bill to envision on a marquee.

"Don't worry," Silas T. said, having read her mind. "I've had very discreet security . . . forces on duty here all along. The cops didn't detect them when they were swarming all over the place around the dead body, and they won't detect them now."

"Security *forces*? That sounds sinister, Mr. Farnum."

"If you have a secret site, you need to safeguard it, Miss Barr."

It was eerie how unpopulated this street was, how dark Las Vegas could be at night without its constant halo of neon and spotlights. She'd allowed Farnum to get her here so late because the Vegas Strip was pretty safe when it came to street crime and because she couldn't sleep and Matt sure wasn't going to show up at the Circle Ritz until the dawn patrol and she wasn't sure she wanted to see him if he did. And because even Midnight Louie had gone out after she'd put a favorite but frenetic movie musical, *Moulin Rouge,* on the TV before Farnum had called her.

"You don't want to daydream past the big reveal,

Miss Barr," Silas T. urged, tapping her on the shoulder and pointing up with his cane.

Her gaze lifted beyond the unpromising construction to the aurora borealis of the Strip peeking like the earth-rise shot from *2001* over the familiar silhouettes of its landmarks.

As she watched, some of the eye-blinking points of light flared even brighter. They separated from the huge nebula of neon and started moving slowly, moving together into a vee formation like migratory birds, only their size increased with motion and also the detail. Nine sleek silver UFOs bearing all the glimpsed futuristic bells and whistles Hollywood could invent swooped and spun over the Strip.

Even here, Temple could hear a rise and fall of excited screams, as if New York–New York's tower-circling roller coaster had broken—or been torn—free of its tracks and its passengers were howling for their lives.

Temple's jaw dropped as she seized Silas T. Farnum by his skinny forearm. "What is that? You must know. You concocted this."

"That, Miss Barr, is the girl in the fishnet hose and pink satin bustier. What you really want to see is right in front of you. There. Look."

She forced her focus down from the show in the sky to find one of the damn things had landed, silently, right in front of the new construction. It was gigantic, and hovered above a narrower shaft of swirling color and light, like a pseudopod it had lowered. She thought of a mushroom cloud equipped with a death ray the size of the Superdome tethering it to Earth.

This all being a conventional film version of a flying saucer spewing down alien lights was not reassuring. Her sky was now a huge hunk of alien metal hovering like a sting ray shadow over the entire lot, pulsing with

surface tension and emitting the odd watery phospho-
rescence of exotic undersea creatures.

The saucer's thick "edge" alone was two or three stories high. Its circumference was . . . not visible. Temple
was aware of shrill ringing in her ears, but that was
probably her blood pressure hitting a high C. As far as
she knew in her current altered state of stupefaction,
this UFO did not sing like the one in Steven Spielberg's
Close Encounters of the Third Kind. She heard no reassuring, blurted mellow chords that reminded Temple of
an engaging—and harmless—kiddie toy.

She barely heard a muted pulsing sound she'd describe
as the mating call of a sprinkler system and a legion of
seriously leg-chafing crickets. Mechanical yet natural,
and even somewhat . . . calming, like white noise. Her
fluttering pulses were evening out. She found herself
breathing more slowly and deeply.

The concentrated stalk of light, the softly shifting dark
shadows behind the saucer's beaming edge gave her a
sense of quiet and peace, as if she were meditating, chilling out in a rosé wine happy hour all of her own. As if
she was being . . . hypnotized.

And was that so bad? Everything light and bright
and . . . what was that small black dot, that minuscule
floater on an eye chart's lighted screen, that tiny, invasive, moment-ruining spot doing? Streaking across the
light-bathed ground, shifting shape into an arch of black,
and then into a vanishing point, a horizontal line?

Temple blinked. If she hadn't seen a startled cat streaking away like a superhero . . .

Her senses reassembled. That pinch on her elbow
was Silas T. Farnum's gnarly age-curled fingers. The rip-
ple pattern under her shoes she'd taken for that last
lick of waves on a tropical beach was the gritty, stone-
strewn ground. The dazzling gigantic magic mushroom
of an unearthly space ship was . . . once again a roughed-

in ten-story building with a few security lights glowing here and there.

Looking toward the Strip, she watched the last of the bouncing balloons vanishing south toward Arizona.

She turned on the only possible target. "Silas T. Farnum, this is a hallucination. Your entire project is a hallucination. And probably the money behind it. Unhand me! You've probably been dusting me with psychedelic something."

He released her and stepped back, leaving Temple to wobble without support, which she much preferred to being suckered.

She ground her soles deeper into the detritus. "I have friends in police places," she told him. "And here you are violating a crime scene."

"It's just dirt, Miss Barr. It's been released as a crime scene. The police are perfectly satisfied with my credentials and alibi."

"The police are never satisfied. They just let you think they are. This is Las Vegas. People here enjoy extravagance and make-believe, but they don't want to be hoodwinked any more than they are at the gaming tables."

"This is not hoodwinking." He stood his ground, planting his cane like a claiming flag. "You have just seen an astounding sight, haven't you? You have just heard the angels of our better beings singing, like the mermaids, for you. You have been transported."

Temple remained silent. Finally she said, "It was a pretty good illusion."

"That's just it. It wasn't an illusion. It's real. I needed to prove that. I needed you to see what I have here."

She glanced over her shoulder to the Strip. "That fleet of UFOs is fake. Radio controlled."

"Yes, yes, yes," he said, swaying on his polished tippy-toes in excitement. "Those are meant to be debunked. Rule One of stunt PR. First you raise expectations, then you flatten them, and then you bring them back from the dead to universal applause."

"All right. My First Rule of Ex-clients. First I evaluate their credibility, then I grade them on a scale of minus-five to zero, and then I kick them off my client list."

"I had to give you a preview of the attraction, Miss Barr, so you wouldn't lose faith. So I had to distract all of the Vegas Strip to give you a peek unveiling of my little beauty behind the curtain."

"Projecting your video concept on the deserted building frame and all that curtaining plastic and canvas is very clever, Mr. Farnum. In fact, a recent project of mine, a new attraction between the Crystal Phoenix and Gangsters, employs ultra-sophisticated audiovisual holographic effects, so don't think you can pull the pixels over my eyes."

"Exactly!" Farnum sounded triumphant. "It takes one to know one, and you now know I'm creating the real deal, with more advanced techniques than ever seen before outside of a secret laboratory run on the level of a Stephen Hawking operation. This is not only mind-bending, it is space and time-bending as well. And, after all, isn't that what aliens are all about?"

"I'm getting a terrible feeling, Mr. Farnum. One of your 'silent partners' wouldn't go by one name?"

"Yes! Brilliant deduction. You are such the right woman for the job. So intuitive."

"That man is a person of interest in a recent murder in town, and you have him working on a project where a dead body was found?"

"No, that can't be true." Farnum was so crestfallen, his five-hair comb-over seemed to shrivel to three. "Domingo has an international reputation."

"Domingo? He's not under suspicion of murder," Temple conceded.

The renowned international environmental artist had

come to town before to mass thousands of pink plastic flamingos around the Strip, making a statement about overblown popular taste, but that's as close to a crime as he'd gotten.

She couldn't imagine why Domingo would return and expand into fleets of mini-UFOs, but supposed it was another statement, perhaps about the usual suspect: the alienation of modern life.

"I'm not mollified," Temple told Farnum, "but I can see how Domingo would be interested in a similar stunt . . . uh, artistic installation."

"You do know 'spin,' Miss Barr." He produced a happy grin. "However, even better, Domingo is not the only international cutting-edge figure involved in my project."

"Oh?"

"Indeed. My other silent partner is as serious as Domingo, but in an allied field."

Well, that had her stumped.

Farnum literally tucked his thumbs under his seersucker suit lapels in the tried and true pose of pride. "His name is Santiago."

And that guy *was* under suspicion of murder.

Chapter 23

All at Sea

The pool was cool but felt like silk.

Matt pulled himself through the water, arm over arm, like pulling a liquid rope toward and past him. The underwater lights created a turquoise spring at either end that drew him like an aquatic moth. Then he pushed off the solid poolside and pulled into the second half of the lap, performing like a thread on a loom.

Swimming had always seemed a form of meditation to him, and it reminded him to breathe, deep and steady.

He pondered the Crystal Phoenix reception and the uneasy undercurrent he had sensed there, apart from the petty crime being committed . . . and revealed. Then he'd kissed Temple good night, more out of despair than passion, and she'd responded so intensely, it had driven him crazy because he couldn't be with her when he wanted to . . . and he'd said something crazy and horrible and left her to move on to two hours surfing waves of everybody else's pain coming over the telephone and spreading across the country. He'd finally topped off an angst-ridden evening with a wee-hour overdose of Kathleen O'Connor.

He'd left a profoundly apologetic message on Temple's cell phone, and hoped he could atone in the morning, which would soon be here.

It must be five in the morning. The sun never quite set on the Vegas Strip, given the halo of bright lights playing aurora borealis on the skyline. Here, though, he glimpsed a bowl of black sky through his water-spotted eyelashes. He was moving too fast to stargaze, but that was the idea, to rinse off his latest encounter with a woman so volatile, even using her given name could set her off.

Tonight she'd set *him* off. Not really. It'd been a bit of psychodrama on his part. Her life had been so extreme, it took extremes to get her true attention. To find some genuine emotion other than anger buried under manipulation.

Still, he needed to rinse off the last couple of hours. Their jousts made him feel like the man in the constellation wrestling a huge serpent, Ophiuchus brought down from the skies to Earth, if you could call Las Vegas Earth.

What significance *did* the shape and stars of that unlucky ex-thirteenth sign of the zodiac hold for the rogue magicians who called themselves the Synth? Why would his dead stepfather keep, hide, and be hunted for a drawing of the entwined man and huge serpent the ancients had seen in that distant cluster of stars?

When Matt's hand hit the pool's end, he turned automatically, picturing an ancient Greek statue at St. Peter's in Rome of the same subject, only it had been a man and his two sons who found themselves in the giant serpent's toils. The Trojan priest Laocoön had suspected the Greeks' giant horse might conceal soldiers, but the gods who favored the Greeks, Poseidon and Athena, sent two giant serpents to kill Laocoön and his sons before they could warn the Trojans.

Laocoön had always warned them to "beware of Greeks bearing gifts."

Matt was willing to bet that no Greek warrior hidden in the Trojan horse was bearing a razor.

Kitty the Cutter was always waiting for him at their Goliath Hotel rendezvous. He was stuck signing off the air at WCOO and could never get to the room before her, never sit in the catbird seat.

And she always had her straight razor cocked open in plain sight. It was almost like a pet with her.

"You're looking a bit harried," she had greeted him earlier this morning, stirring her room service cocktail with her pinkie finger and then sucking it with an X-rated movie flourish.

Matt had never seen an X-rated movie, and now he didn't have to. Kathleen O'Connor had obviously frozen in the teenage Lolita stage years ago. Serial killers liked to torture their victims for sexual satisfaction. Kitty had substituted the adolescent tease to the murderous mix, but with her the payoff wasn't sex—it was control.

She lounged on the beaded brocade bedspread like a road show Cleopatra clutching her queenship and her ever-present poisonous asp.

He sank into his accustomed chair across from the bed. He'd booked the room for two weeks after she reserved it in his name the first night they'd met here. He hoped his self-imposed deadline would prove correct. Whether it would or not depended on his ability to "reach" her and release the self-loathing that made her so dangerous.

"Extra hours at work," he told her, "takes a toll. You must have noticed that too."

"You must be running short of excuses back at the Circle Ritz."

Matt celebrated a little victory. He'd warned her any specific mention of Temple would terminate this charade. She'd conceded enough to come up with a code phrase for her.

"Not really. This is just an extension of my radio advice work, only more in-depth."

"And in person."

Matt nodded. "Although I'm just a stand-in for Max Kinsella."

That had her squirming on the bed, and not in a sexy way. She tossed her head back with an angry swallow of liquor.

"You know he's back," Matt said.

"Of course. And still an elusive bastard."

"Really elusive this time. You know his memory is shot," Matt added.

"Poor boy hit his head in a very bad fall." She eyed him slyly. "Just like the poor call girl who met with you here before. Only she died. Much good you did her. Jumped down to the casino's glass ceiling far, far below."

"Or was pushed."

"Are you confessing, Father?"

"I rather hoped you would." He watched her. She wasn't mad, with no grasp on reality, he was convinced, just very damaged. "Tell me about your relationship with Max Kinsella."

"You priests like all the filthy details in the dark of the confessional."

"Those dark confessionals are passé, Kathleen. And, from what I've heard, you were a lot less dark then.

Wasn't it a romp with the two naïve American boys lighting up dreary Belfast with high spirits and healthy but innocent hormones?"

"Oh, quite the engaging lads, they were," she said between her teeth, her Irish accent strengthening. "Still blushed at first kiss, but that didn't stop them from wanting one thing. You all do."

"Boys, you mean. Men, you mean. That's nature. I went against nature for a long time, but it didn't work, because it was out of cowardice, not conviction. Not for the reason I thought it was."

She settled back against the pillows. "Tell me about your deflowering and I'll tell you about mine."

"I know about yours and I'm sorry that I do."

"Sorry! Don't be sorry for me. Be sorry for yourself when I'm done with you." She'd leaped up from the bed and grabbed her constant talisman for these sessions, the straight razor, from the veined marble top of the nightstand.

"Your skin is very white, very sensitive," he observed.

She immediately unruffled her defenses, as a cat's bristled fur settled down at the sound of a familiar voice, a familiar hand. Seducing, bespelling a man was the only way she could permit herself to be petted.

"Have you used that razor on yourself?"

"What?" She glared, hardly believing the question.

"The thin pale scars would hardly show on that skin of yours. I imagine that was some comfort, to hurt yourself and feel it, rather than being hurt by somebody else and trying not to feel it."

She flung a string of gutter Irish expletives he could barely understand, much less take offense at. "Manipulating, lying, Judas priest and freaking bastard," was the decipherable end of it.

"I guess we share that 'bastard' label," he said mildly. Very mildly. "Toast to that?" He lifted his lowball glass.

She slammed the razor back down on the marble and paced between the bed and the wall, a mirrored wall that reflected the long mirror on the opposite wall, so she met herself coming and going. "Smug, superior professional eunuch," she spat at him, quite literally, her lips wet from a series of savage sips at the drink in her hand. "You're not man enough to bother seducing."

"But Max Kinsella was, and is. You seduced Max once, when he was seventeen. Is that why not finding him is so maddening? You need to seduce Max again, but can't, now that he knows what you are?"

Her knuckles went white on the shaft of the folding razor. "You underestimate yourself, priest. You're my target now."

If only, Matt thought, the Northern Ireland peace hadn't deprived her of a "cause" to justify her fury and sexual manipulations. She had to seduce and bedevil someone.

"Ex-priest," he said again. Calm. "Tell me about the ones who abused you."

She sat on the bed's foot, the razor under her supporting palm, and leaned near. "I'm sure you'll find this very exciting."

She certainly did.

Chapter 24

Law and Order:
Truce or Consequences

"I thought," Max said, "I was to be allowed a long leash."

He was still gobsmacked that Molina had invited him onto her home turf for a conversation, instead of to the usual scuzzy confidential-informant meeting place.

The unexpected civility put him off his game. He actually was sounding apologetic. "I've barely had time to survey Goliath and the Oasis Hotels for any lingering taint from the time dead bodies occupied the casino ceiling and were shanghaied onto sinking-ship attractions."

"Circumstances change," Molina answered.

They sure had; she'd gone from hunting him as a murderer to accepting his secret counter-terrorism past and finding him a useful covert investigator.

"Your bias against all things 'me' certainly has," he

agreed. "You're asking to see me so often, I'm beginning to wonder if I'm a candidate to take Mariah to the Dad–Daughter dance next fall."

"You know about my daughter's school events? How?"

The truce was still iffy. Max laughed. "Scrub that Mama Grizzly look off your face and relax. Since the leading favorite for that honor, Matt Devine, is making visits to Chicago with Temple and cat in tow, he may not even be in Vegas by then. I smell a job opportunity for our golden boy."

"Really? Apparently you still keep in touch with old acquaintances, even if you don't remember much of them?"

"I'm here, aren't I?"

"Devine has always visited Chicago regularly for TV talk show gigs. Your rival is a media darling."

"Ex-rival. I've conceded. This most recent Windy City visit by the happy couple is enough to plant suspicions. Your daughter would be crushed to lose her Prince Charming."

"Maybe not so much now." Molina sat back on her slouchy family couch. "Mariah is all about becoming a YouTube sensation these days. Why do you think I can even consider . . . entertaining you at home?"

"She's off with her girlfriends," Max speculated, "singing into home karaoke machines and trying out new Girly Gaga looks."

"Something like that." Molina's smile was nostalgic.

"I can see that's in the genes. How did your secret singing career get started?"

"Church choir."

Max nodded. "Makes sense. Singing alto on 'Little Drummer Boy' is perfect training for crooning torch songs at a neighborhood club."

Molina wouldn't be baited. "Your sarcasm," she said, "is not going to make me 'sing' about how my undercover hobby got started. One good thing about today's teen mania for fame and fortune and *American Idol:* It keeps them off the streets at night."

Max smiled to hear that. He knew Rafi was getting what he wanted, quality time with his kid. And, because of that smart parental compromise, Max was getting a mellowed-out Molina. She'd actually given him a beer when he arrived.

"So what can a man with no memory tell a homicide lieutenant?" he asked, back to business.

"What are you getting from those two cold case deaths? Casino robbery interrupted?"

"Probably."

"Does it seem . . . like the mob?"

"The mob?" Max repeated. "Vegas mobsters are only in museums now, aren't they?"

"Are they?"

"You're the one who's supposed to know, Lieutenant."

"Call me Molina."

Max donned an impressed expression. "Sure thing. I could even shorten it to 'Mole.' "

She did not look amused. "Maybe," she said, "someone is trying to fake a fresh mob presence on the Strip. We did have one nasty murder that recalled the old-time mob methods of threats, torture, and death."

"Anybody I know the victim?" Max asked carefully.

"You know about him. That scumbag named Clifford Effinger. He was bound to the prow of the sinking Treasure Island boat attraction and drowned."

Max found his most disinterested look. "Yes, but it sounds a little too bloodless and histrionic for the mob."

"Agreed. But it was a message to somebody."

"Why do you say 'fake' mob presence?" Max asked.

"This department and the FBI cleared the mob off the Strip and out of town in the early '80s."

"For real?"

"For real. Listen. You should contact Frank Bucek."

"Frank Bucek?"

"Yeah, the ex-priest FBI guy." When Max's face remained blank, she realized she'd entered a memory-free zone and explained further. "He was an instructor at Matt's seminary. He comes to town now and again."

"Ex-priests seem to find interesting new occupations."

"They have a lot to offer—intelligence, diligence, discipline, knowledge of human psychology."

"From what I remember of grade school, the parish priests and nuns were pretty good cops, now that you mention it."

"You remember that far back still?" she wondered.

"The oldest memories are the last to go."

Max let his mind drift back to summer twilights in a grassy climate and ball games in the street, then snow and cold and hockey, the prick of ice skate blades slung over his shoulder through his down-quilted jacket. Sean's ears scarlet under his stocking cap. They'd reddened when he was in Northern Ireland, drinking beer with him at pubs, two underage young guys behaving foolishly but harmlessly. Sean waving him off. Max felt the small soft hand in his, the girl bewitching and ripe and as easy to acquire as that illegal-in-the-U.S. Brit version of beer. Smiling, flirting, pulling him away from Sean, the beer, the pub to slake other thirsts at a private place she knew, for him to become a man in Ireland. . . .

Then the memory exploded.

"Whoa." Molina caught the beer bottle before it crashed from his numb fingers to the coffee table top in front of them. "Brain crash?"

"Memory flash."

"Not a good one."

He nodded. "Mixed reviews, good and bad." He placed the one-third-full bottle as carefully on the table-top as he would if it were made of blown glass. "I just remembered I don't drink beer if I can help it. Your hospitality has overwhelmed me, Lieutenant."

"Me Molina. You Kinsella." She picked up the bottle and left the room.

Max threaded his fingers, suddenly icy, together. This was a hell of a place to have a guilt attack, right in front of a homicide lieutenant.

A lowball glass with an inch and a half of amber liquid descended to the coffee table in front of him.

"It's not the prime brand you keep at home," she warned him, "but you need it."

He did. He took a stinging gulp. "My legs are almost normal."

"But not your head, yet."

"Head and heart."

"Regrets?"

He looked up. Her eyes were nonaccusing, and as blue as the Morning Glory Pool at Yellowstone. Memory, he thought, might hide in the depths of such eyes, eyes so like Kathleen O'Connor's.

"Regrets? Do you mean about a certain engaged couple? No. Only that I'm the cause of a lot of the grief that people I've known have faced."

"I hate to puncture your cozy, self-hating cocoon of ego and guilt, but you are *not* the cause. You are the mere pretext. The cause is this highly damaged and damaging psychopath you and your cousin had the bad luck to encounter."

"So I'll chase another will-o'-the-wisp. If I have a surviving psychopath, maybe Las Vegas is still haunted by vestiges of the mob, some greedy and retired old don who still wants to squeeze filthy lucre out of the trillion-dollar city."

Molina sighed and sipped. "Vegas has indeed had an explosion of entrepreneurial interest in the mob," she said. "There's the forty-two million dollars of official

civic museum in the same civil courts building that held
Senate hearings to bust the mob in the '50s. Now the
Mob Attraction Las Vegas at the Tropicana is vying with
the underground Chunnel of Crime that links the sepa-
rate venues of the Crystal Phoenix and Gangsters."

"What is this fever for interactive attractions?" Max
asked rhetorically. "It used to be that a magician inviting
an audience member onstage to assist in an illusion was a
biggie. Now people are expecting to see whole buildings
disappear before their eyes."

"Or elephants," Molina said with a toasting gesture
of her beer bottle.

"*Ahh*, you're talking about the elephant, the girl sitting on the elephant trunk, and the disappearing trunk-
ful of prize money last week. I assume you got a report
on that incident at the Oasis."

"I got *film*, Kinsella. Not all of the street hucksters
milling around that million-dollar giveaway were street
hucksters." She eyed him hard. "And you of all people
know that from firsthand experience."

Max took the fifth by not responding.

"The only thing I'm wondering," Molina went on, "is
if you and the Cloaked Conjuror switched places. You
have the height to do it, and I imagine the Cloaked Conjuror might have enjoyed a few minutes performing out
of his disguising carapace."

"Carapace. Interesting word for a full head mask and
a bulletproof padded costume that weighs sixty pounds.
CC leads an insanely constricted life. I suspect someday
he'll take the money and run, never to be seen in Vegas
again."

"I'm guessing Matt Devine has the same hopes for
you."

Max shook his head. "I'm no threat. I'm not only
crippled in mind and body, but I've got a brand-new
girlfriend."

"Lay off the 'poor me' stuff," she was already saying, then exhibited the same indignant reaction as Matt Devine. "Wait a couple months or three. You're performing in disguise as the Phantom Mage—the Cloaked Conjuror should sue you for that—when you get your bungee cord sabotaged and crash spectacularly. You're spirited away to two months of coma and leg casts in a fancy Swiss clinic, end up on the run across Europe and Ireland, and come back here alive, crippled, and memory impaired. Yet you've replaced Temple Barr in your affections, presto change-o?"

"Yes," Max said simply. "Want to see a photo?"

Before Molina could open her lips or shake her head to indicate "no," he had his phone screen in front of her face. The first photo showed Revienne showing a lot of leg on a slot machine stool at the Paris Hotel. That was his favorite. He clicked through a couple of smashing portraits of her full face and in profile against the Paris's beautifully lit balloon.

Molina sat speechless, a state that Max enjoyed more than he would ever let her see.

"That woman's . . . a stunner," she finally got out, "but I don't see—"

"And überbright. Don't let the façade make you underestimate the foundations. She's a noted psychologist in Europe and here, works gratis on teenage eating disorders. Gutsy too. Went on the lam across the Alps in a Saint Laurent Paris suit and Charles Jourdan pumps. Hacked my casts off and begged food from Swiss farmers and other . . . necessary things for us.

"By the way," he added, suddenly serious. "This is just a hunch from an accidental half-wit, but from what I've seen, no one could replace Temple Barr." Max leaned back on the sofa, took a long satisfactory draft of whiskey, eyed Molina, and tapped the phone photo of Revienne. "I want you to run her through Interpol."

"Okay. You have my jaw dropping. You must be very proud of yourself. And, meanwhile, you're sleeping with this wonder woman?"

Max gave an affable shrug. "Or she's sleeping with me. There's a difference." He turned the phone image to face him. "I hope I'm wrong, but I don't believe in convenient escapes with bright, beautiful strangers. Remember *The X-Files* catch phrase: 'Trust no one.'"

Molina stirred uneasily on the couch. "What makes you bring up that old cult TV show?"

"Not old, classic," Max corrected her. "Like us. And the songs you sing." He grinned before going on. "Now, what did you want to see me for? I'm at your service for anything not horizontal. I do have some standards."

It took a couple of minutes for Molina to exhaust such nouns and adjectives as "gall," "arrogance," "amoral," and "treacherous."

All he said at the end of it was, "I've e-mailed you her photos. Her name is Revienne Schneider, and it's real. Dig deep. This could involve your career."

"As if you care about my career."

"Deeply," he said. "I need solid contacts."

"Look here, Kinsella, I am using you, not the opposite."

"Let's compromise. We're using each other, in a purely platonic way, of course. There's one big nasty conspiracy underlying the sometimes silly excesses of Vegas. You might look into the movements of Cosimo Sparks for the past couple of years."

"He's a victim of an unsolved murder."

"No reason he couldn't also have been a perp beforehand."

"You give me a headache."

"Great. Then we can never have sex."

"As if I would—"

He cut her off, as fun as it was to smash into the iron wall of her professionalism. "I know. You're all business and no personal life. So . . ."

"Anybody else you want me to investigate for you?" She'd reverted to sarcasm.

"Well, in the larger picture, why Las Vegas is going prerecorded and interactive. Artifacts from real life and movie crime on display, guests interacting with 3-D holograms of movie mobsters and live actor guides, deciding if they want to become part of the 'Family' or else—"

"An 'immersive experience,' they call it," Molina said. "Ask your ex-fiancée. She was up to her pert little nose in using that Chunnel of Crime ride to freak out a possible murderer."

"Cosimo Sparks's murderer," Max said.

"He was a magician, not a mobster." Molina's tone tightened. "Or was he both?"

"I hear the suspect for his death is some notoriously flamboyant international architect. Not your usual slasher."

"He had his suspicious hands on the murder weapon—an ice pick—but I'm not convinced he used it lethally. Sparks was known to you?"

"Most likely not. Different generation. Different level of professionalism."

"By that, I'm to gather that he was a penny-ante has-been?"

"You seem to be admitting that I'm a high-dollar up-and-comer."

"You were. Once. Do you even remember your signature illusions?"

"You ever see me perform?"

"Not on my wish list."

"Too bad. You'd know that magic is as much in the fingers as in the frontal lobes. The hands remember." Max waggled his particularly long and strong hands.

"Really, how viable is your memory nowadays?"

"Going forward, it's wizard."

"And backwards?"

"Dicey. Arbitrary. I don't seem to remember intense emotions."

"Lucky for the happy couple at the Circle Ritz."

"I wish them eternal bliss," he said seriously. "But most of all, I wish them safety, and that won't be possible until I solve what will stop this nemesis on my tail from endangering anybody else."

"I solve that." Molina said, "It's my turf, my city, my job."

Max raised his glass. "And you do it superbly. Las Vegas is lucky."

Her olive skin flushed again, barely detectable. Not from anger, but from pride. That was a step forward. "So who is our common enemy?"

"I didn't say that."

"It's obvious," she said.

He nodded. "Okay. I had a stalker in my house when I was gone, as you know, since it was you."

"Good thing I stopped by. Someone wanted to cut you to shreds."

"Instead my wardrobe—and you—got shredded, I hear. So you were stalking me," Max asked, "because you thought I was stalking you?"

"Someone was. You were the only suspect I was after who had the obvious . . . skills . . . and gall to do such a subtle and thorough job in my own house."

"More kudos. I may take up my abandoned onstage career yet." Max grinned.

"You still want to remain a mystery man for some reason. Until it suits you."

"We've both had 'closet' issues."

She didn't quite get the connection at first. Then she tumbled. "You think *my* stalker was your stalker?"

He nodded. "My closet's contents were obliterated. Yours apparently acquired alien articles of clothing."

"Why me and mine?"

"She wanted to make you more suspicious of me, angry enough to hunt and hassle me even more."

"*She?* I hadn't figured on a woman stalking a woman. Why would it be your nemesis? You're just habitually cynical about women."

"I wasn't always. Not until *her.*"

"Weren't you very young then?"

"Seventeen."

"Only . . . three years older than Mariah." Molina seemed stunned by the comparison.

"Kids were more naïve back then."

"Your same-age cousin died in a pub bombing at the same time."

Obviously Temple had thoroughly briefed Molina on Max's history with the IRA, probably to defend him.

"More like a brother," Max said brusquely. "So how were you stalked in this house? That takes a lot of nerve, going after a police detective."

Molina hesitated, reluctant to change the subject, then moved on. "It could have been someone I closed a case on. What happened . . . ended. It was a warped, sick scenario. I don't want to talk about it."

"Temple Barr knows."

"Yes," she admitted. She stood, walked around the sofa behind him, leaned her hands on either side of his shoulders, and asked, "Matt Devine knows?"

He paused to decide what to say, what to admit. "Yes."

Molina took an audible deep breath. She leaned in, so the meter of her words huffed across his skin. "That's too many already."

"Why can't I know?" Max asked.

"Why do you have to know?"

"It might affect your detecting ability. I want your objectivity working for me."

"You think I could be objective about you?" Molina asked.

"Yes, I do."

She came around to the front of the couch, looming as only a five-foot-ten woman could. "The stalker tried to manipulate me. I'm willing to concede now that wasn't you. Probably. But even I don't claim I'm objective about you."

"Everything and everyone needs to be questioned now—motives, goals, what strings are being pulled by whom. We all do the best we can to pull back the curtain, don't we? While still keeping a veil over our deepest fears and oldest sins."

"Heavy." Molina let herself sink back onto the couch. "This time *you* fetch *me* a beer from the fridge."

The second soldier was empty on the snack bar between the kitchen and the living room, and Max was crawling around in the bottom of Molina's closet. "A shrink would have a lot of fun with your shoe collection."

"More so with Temple Barr's, I'm thinking."

"It's all about height, or the lack of it, with women. She overcompensates for short physical stature, you temper your ability to intimidate male coworkers with an array of low-heeled loafers for work. Even at home you wear moccasins."

"I see your association with Miss Barr has made you a sidewalk connoisseur of shoes and psyches."

"And sometimes you just want to break out of the career closet. What's this?" Max looked up, one forefinger dangling the ankle strap of a pale nile green satin sandal with a half-inch platform on the sole. "Lady Gaga boots it isn't. Don't tell me you share a vintage clothing jones with Temple Barr."

Molina snatched the slipper up, up, and away.

"And Cinderella you're not," he commented. "Also not a size five, looked like—"

"None of your business."

"Wrong. It's my business. Any of your shoes or mates go missing during the stalking incidents?"

"No. I told you. The stalker *added* to my wardrobe."

Max let his fingers page through the soft five-inch swatch of floor-length hanging gowns in deep jewel-toned silk velvet. "These are Carmen's, your warbling alter ego's. Which one didn't you buy?"

She reached out to one. "The blue. At least I didn't remember it."

"It looks a lot like the others."

"Gowns of that 1930s' vintage are very similar and there isn't much good light in the closets of these old houses."

"So you can't be sure." Max leaned back to study the gowns. "They're all the same length."

She nodded. "That's what made this first discovery creepy. I sensed it didn't belong, but it looked like it should."

"What was the next leaving?"

"Nasty. Obvious. Meant to chill."

He waited and she averted her eyes.

She answered in a monotone, turning away. "It was a gift-wrapped slim little box on my bedspread, looked like candy. I couldn't conceive that Mariah would do that, although teen girls often do owe their mothers an apology. But I opened it."

"Not a letter bomb," he said to diffuse the tension.

Her laugh was short. "A filmy piece of cheap lingerie, with a note: 'You dress like a nun.'"

"And of course, that sealed the deal that it was me."

She turned on him, blue eyes blazing like midnight specials. "You always like to . . . taunt me."

"I honestly can't remember."

"You were doing it just now."

He thought. "Yeah, I was—"

"You think I'm too buttoned-down and uptight."

"I am getting a bit of that vibe, but it's hitting me more like . . . that's there because you'd be a lot hotter if it wasn't."

"That comment is sexist, not sexy. Like that invasive 'gift' was stalking, not . . . not courting behavior."

"But you know now that it wasn't me."

"Mostly." She sounded almost as sullen as a teenager fessing up. Learned that from Mariah, likely.

"Look. I'm sorry. I don't think I'd do that. A magician gets used to manipulating people, to getting a reaction from an audience. It's nothing personal."

She shrugged, her anger and embarrassment spent.

"Um, I have to ask. Was the article of lingerie black?"

Oops. She was annoyed again.

"'Articles' like that usually are."

"Then, Lieutenant. Molina. I think there's a clue you've missed because you couldn't possibly know it. That 'gift' wasn't a sexual come-on. Not at all."

"What?"

"You went to school with Catholic nuns."

"I'm half Hispanic. Of course."

"And the habits they used to wear were—?"

"Black."

"You don't wear black. Navy maybe, but not much in this broiler climate. I think that gown was left by a woman."

She looked doubtful.

"Who was out to get me."

"It's always all about you."

"In this case, it really is."

"And the next time, when I came home to find the radio on and a trail of rose petals down the hall to Mariah's bedroom?"

Max sighed. Kathleen O'Connor had done a job on Molina. No wonder she'd risked her career to break into Max's house to prove he was the stalker, and then had the bad luck to run straight into Kitty the Cutter.

"She likes to play with her prey, but she is armed and dangerous. She slashed Matt Devine trying to get at me."

Molina let herself sink down upon the bed, in a way reclaiming it from being a scene of a crime. Max didn't want to loom, so he sat beside her, with no protestations.

"This monster was in my house? How do you know all this with a flawed memory?"

"My mentor, my foster father really, was the one who spirited me away from the Neon Nightmare. He filled in my history from the age of seventeen. And I have . . . flashes of recovering memory."

"This woman, you think she has something against Catholic nuns?"

"And priests."

"Hence Devine." Molina nodded. "So it's a vast anti-Catholic, anti-Max conspiracy?"

"Anti-me mostly."

"Why?"

"I saw through her early. That made me the enemy. I've only just learned, in Northern Ireland, what a hellish history she had. People have died because of that." Max bestirred himself to leave his recent, all-too-vivid memories. "I'll tell you a story, all I was told and remember, about a girl named Kathleen O'Connor, who became a murderous, mad, vengeful force aptly renamed 'Kitty the Cutter.'

"I think she's safely out of your private life, Molina, but not your professional one. I once loved her, then hated her, and now I hunt her. As she hunts me and mine . . . and even my 'frenemies' . . . is that the word for us now?"

Molina nodded solemnly.

"I need your help, Carmen Regina, Lieutenant, sir." He mustered a crooked smile. "And we none of us will sleep well until she's cornered and confined."

Romance on the Rocks

"I need drinks and a dinner," Temple briskly instructed the person on the other end of her home phone at 11 A.M. the next day.

"Ah, isn't it usually dinner and drinks?" Matt sounded a bit fuzzy. "And are we still talking, much less dining and drinking?"

Temple knew he was just waking up after a long work night, poor guy, but she couldn't wait a moment longer. "The message you left was suitably desperate. I am mollified. Matt, I know the insane pressure you've been under with your mother being threatened and then getting married and the job thing and us having to work with Max and knowing that Kitty the Cutter is out there somewhere. It's completely normal you might feel a little jealous. You've never been in this position before."

"You're way more generous than I deserve."

"Just keep that in mind." Temple couldn't contain something else a moment longer. Her indignation. "Just remember, this outing is drinks first, food later. A special occasion. I just fired a would-be client."

"I thought the fir*ee* was the one who went out and solaced herself with good liquor and bad food."

Temple sighed loud enough to be heard in the back row of a community theater building. "I've never had to give up on a project before, but this was the last indignity. Silas T. Farnum is a deceptive, screwy, irresponsible nutcase, even if he has the most mind-blowing venue in Las Vegas, and I have flacked my last flack on his behalf. Details at six o'clock."

"Okay, okay. I see this calls for an emergency evening out. What would soothe the savaged soul? The Four Seasons, Palazzo? Or something down-home like the Bellagio?"

"Maybe," Temple conceded.

"Maybe . . . which one?"

"Surprise me."

"What? So it's not the right one and you can fire *me*?"

"No such luck. I'm done firing people. I don't want to talk about this until we're sitting someplace wonderful and I've had at least three sips of something very high proof. I'll see you at my door at seven thirty."

"Aye, aye, sir."

She was smiling as she hung up. She'd seen the strain on Matt's face lately and should have held back and given him some space. Now she was getting the romantic time out they both deserved, and needed.

It was high time to cut Silas T. afloat and concentrate on her chaotic personal life. Temple was not liking the fact that no further word had been heard from the Chicago network execs. They'd been so interested in Matt's talk show future during the recent trip to the Windy

City. She knew media plans could fall flatter than a French crepe, faster than a three-minute egg, but . . . Gee, listen to her think. Crepes and eggs. She must really be hungry.

Tonight while Matt was properly attentive and consoling her on public relations bloopers, she could pump him on major career matters.

The Bellagio it was. The Circo restaurant was surrounded by gleaming vaulted traditional woodwork with sophisticated big top touches and offered Tuscan delights from octopus appetizers to gourmet pizza.

Temple let herself soak in the setting as if she were sinking into a buoyant, bubbling hot spa. Matt was watching her relax with eyes as warming as brandy. Temple sighed.

"Matt, this is exactly what I needed after spending days, it seems, on an unshaded dusty, grimy construction site. And this restaurant overlooks the Bellagio's Lago di Como. Lake Como, where Kit and Aldo went on their honeymoon. Did you know—?"

He just grinned, an expression Temple was surprised to realize she'd not seen for a while. "And did you buy that dress during your lightning shopping session with my mother?" Matt asked. He'd already learned to ask, not assume.

"No, that was totally for the bride-to-be. I *saw* something during that raid on the Venice shops and realized I had an '80s lookalike version among the vintage stuff in my closet."

"Lavender is definitely your color," he said as the waiter brought them something wickedly scarlet in martini glasses. "Your high-powered drink, madam," Matt said. "The Web site says the Bellagio pours twenty-five thousand cocktails every twenty-four hours, but the hotel pioneered upping the quality on mixed drinks in Las Vegas in recent years."

"You researched my druthers! That is so sweet, Matt."

"I hope this candy apple red drink isn't." He sipped and offered a considering expression.

Temple said, "You realize I can't be a 'madam' until I'm married."

"Not a problem." He watched her sample the cocktail.

"Wow. Like a Cosmopolitan made from White Lightning. I like." She sighed. "I need. My shoulder muscles have been in lockdown since I first heard the name Silas T. Farnum."

"So what did Silas T. Farnum do to earn your wrath and swift execution?"

"Farnum," she snarled. "The surname alone should have alerted me. He's the P. T. Barnum of modern hucksterism." She lifted her glass. "A toast to toasted hucksters." She sipped again before reluctantly lowering her glass. "Although his building concept was pretty awesome."

"We're not talking about his personal presence here, I hope. A Web site maybe—"

"No. He's invested in the unlovely area on the Paradise Road bend, the beastly backside of the Strip's beauty parade. His project is so high-tech, it takes futuristic to the moon and back. But how do you sell a building people can't see?"

"Ran out of construction money, huh?" Matt shook his head. "A lot of people with big dreams and even bigger bankrolls did when the Great Recession hit them."

"Don't cry for Silas T. Farnum. He's got the site lot, he's got the dough. He's got a sure-thing prize for the 'Most Unusual Vegas Design.' If people could only see it."

"Maybe he'll attract more customers than you think."

"Don't keep looking on the bright side! How do you sell . . . nothing?"

Matt was looking lost. And that made him look weary, with new fine lines around his eyes.

"Forget about my troubles," Temple said. "What's up with you? Or, rather, what's keeping you up past your two A.M. quitting time? I don't understand why you need to work up new show ideas with Ambrosia when you're on the brink of leaving *The Midnight Hour*."

"I'm not." He took another slug of Red Ruin.

"Not working up new ideas? I can understand how you hate to leave her and WCOO in the lurch—"

"I'm not leaving *The Midnight Hour*."

"Matt!"

At that instant, her cell phone yodeled for attention. Temple had to dig in her crowded envelope purse to pull out a smartphone with a loud ringtone of Leonard Cohen singing "Hallelujah" and set it back to sleep.

This was definitely not a "hallelujah" moment for either of them.

"Sorry," she told Matt, hating the interruption at such a crucial time.

Out of the corner of her eye she saw Matt looking relieved. He didn't really want to continue this conversation. And she really did need a good long talk with him. . . . As she watched her phone screen, she heard Silas T.'s voice: "Look at this."

She lifted the dang phone, ready to hurl it to the floor.

Sound and motion filled her screen. A YouTube clip showed a Spielberg-like hovering spaceship as a hysterical voice-over did the "color" coverage.

"Holy flying cow! It's not a bird! It's not a plane! It's a super spaceship, and I'm filming it on my camcorder from my Riviera Hotel room window. I'm watching this thing descend—hell, *land!*—in a vacant lot off the Vegas

Strip. The aliens are *heeeere* and they couldn't have picked a better place to colonize."

Matt had risen at hearing the hysterical voice and came around the table to watch the tiny screen over her shoulder. "Is that your ex-client's freaky new attraction? Looks like a winner to me."

"That's just the thing. It's not an attraction. It's invisible."

"Coulda fooled me. Temple, you need to tell me what's going on."

She looked up into his worried but true-blue brown eyes. "I think I could say the same."

Matt was right, but first Temple needed to consult with . . . ditch . . . her not-client. She excused herself to head for the ladies' room. This was Vegas, so it was a mini-nightclub all on its own. Dark and glossy with furtive reflections and pink fluorescent lights framing the over-sink mirrors so every woman looked like a movie star.

"What is going on?" she demanded when Farnum answered her call.

"We've an accidental reveal. Those fleeting seconds I showed you Area 54's bells and whistles were captured by dozens of amateur videographers from hotel room windows all around. Talk about stunt PR. This is premature but sweet."

"This is a huge pain in the alien patootie. It will have Unforeseen Consequences. Trust me. Meanwhile, I'm off having a private life, if you don't mind."

When she came out of the bathroom, totally unprimped, she eyed Matt sitting at their table, swirling a swizzle stick around in his virtually untouched drink, frowning.

Something invisible was going on here too, and she

doubted it would ever be accidentally revealed. She needed to find out why the Chicago deal had gone cold and why he didn't want to talk to her about it.

Temple sighed, turned off her cell phone, and headed for her fiancé with a feeling of dread.

Chapter 26

Going, Going, Going, Gone . . . Viral

Temple jerked upright in bed, in the dark, her heart pounding. She'd finally fallen asleep after an awkward dinner with Matt. He gave reason after reason for not taking the job in Chicago: his relocation, her relocation, Louie's relocation. Loyalty to WCOO and Leticia Brown and her "Ambrosia" syndication. Too many relatives in Chicago, including his clingy cousin Krys, his mother who needed a stable family atmosphere to start out her new marriage.

It was all absolutely true and reasonable and Temple didn't buy a bit of it. You can't snow a professional snower, a spin expert. The only thing that rang true was the deep, troubled look in Matt's eyes.

What was going on?

They'd parted when he had to leave for work, both of

them miserable, the would-be festive evening out a debacle, thanks to her crazy day job and his late-night job and everything being knocked out of its orbit by some hidden planet Matt *would not* reveal to her to save his soul.

She'd sobbed her way through *War Horse* on the DVD and finally was exhausted enough to sleep. She was a fixer, she decided, and she would fix this if it killed her.

Now her cell phone was trumpeting "Hallelujah," and from the condo's large living room her landline was chiming in, very much muffled.

She'd shut the bedroom door to keep the dawn's early light from flooding through the row of glass-paned French doors to the patio. So she didn't know what time it was until her cell phone face told her—6:10 A.M. An ungodly hour in Las Vegas, when all bad gamblers kissed their assets good-bye and bedded down for the night at 5 A.M.

Jeez, was that unreliable Silas T. Farnum pestering her again? She fumbled for the bedside lamp switch, being careful not to kick her feet as she rolled over to sit up. Didn't want to give Midnight Louie a punch in the paunch.

The distant phone rang on as she answered the cell.

"Silas T.—"

"This is Temple Barr?" The female voice was brisk and urgent and not Molina's.

"Yes."

"This is Madison Wiswallson."

Madison, Wisconsin? Something to do with Max?

"KXTP-TV news, L.A."

Alphabet soup. Temple was still disoriented.

The voice continued. "You're representing Deja View Associates, it says in this release. A Mr. Farnum directed me to you about the UFO scare infecting Las Vegas."

"UFO? Oh. He's not officially my client." No legal agreements had been signed. "I do know he released some helium balloons on his own. I have nothing to do with them, uh, him."

"Well, he plastered the Internet and media e-mails with a strangely vague release and you're listed as the contact. And I beg your pardon. We're not talking 'helium balloons.' Do a YouTube search for 'Vee Is for Vegas Visitors' and, oh, let's see . . . 'Alien Intervention' . . . 'UFOs Unleashed' . . . 'Elvis's Asteroid Belt Lands on Strip' . . . 'Flying Saucer Convention' . . . 'Little Men in Green' . . ."

Temple had done as instructed and was following a string of tiny films of Farnum's supposedly quick-peek at the UFO design. *Oh, my unmentionables!* She quashed any expletives that occurred to her and would be better directed at Silas T. Farnum.

"I know nothing about this, Miss Wisconsin. I mean, Miss Wishywallson. I have *no* comment. Mr. Farnum is not a client." *And he won't be quotable the minute I can reach the sneaky old scam artist and shut him up.*

She clicked on the bedroom TV, set to a local channel's morning news show. A huge photo of the revealed UFO top of Farnum's stealth building occupied the entire screen. It looked as impressive as a movie still from *Close Encounters of the Third Kind.*

It was replaced by a live shot of the parking lot, the real building invisible to the TV videographers, thank God. A male reporter was doing a stand-up job of a stand-up, gazing soberly into the camera. *Oh, no!* It was sleazy promoter Crawford Buchanan, with a soul patch and a pea-sized diamond earring. *Gross. When did he get a real TV job?* His deep, mellow, and oily radio voice oozed into the room.

"Hundreds of people have gathered overnight on this

deserted Las Vegas construction site on news that an un-identified flying object was captured in mid-descent by dozens of cell phones and camcorders."

The camera panned across the milling mob before returning to the reporter.

"Complicating matters," he went on, "is the fact that part of the area was a recent crime scene when an unidentified body was discovered here three days ago. Many of those gathering now include some who claim they had signed up for a 'UFO convention' at this location—an empty lot, as everyone can see."

Another camera pan of the towering buildings hundreds of feet away on the Strip and the unimpressive shrouded pseudo-building made the point.

"So who invited all these true believers to an empty lot? Did the people just arriving miss the main attraction? A real UFO landing? Or is it all a come-on for a new magic act on the Strip? Maybe the New Millennium Hotel's Cloaked Conjuror can pay Paradise Road a visit and pull away the curtain."

How right the annoying twerp was. Temple knew she had to get there to do damage control, whether she was representing Farnum or not.

"This is Crawford Buchanan, the KSOS-TV Night Crawler, up bright and early to see what the cat dragged into Vegas now."

Temple remembered the small four-legged silhouette streaking away from the temporarily revealed spotlight the saucer's neon green pillar of light made. *Oh, no!* Where was Louie? Not here safe in bed.

All she needed was Molina on the warpath and her cat caught fleeing the scene on film.

Chapter 27

We Are Not Alone

I knew there was something fishy about that high-rise parking garage the old guy in the seersucker suit was wanting my Miss Temple to see the other night. So I went along undercover (of darkness) to view the sneak peek.

Manx! Those UFO lights nearly sizzled my unmentionables.

I rocketed out of there, but when the waft of something fishy undulates past the area between my whiskers and chin, I leave no stone unturned or nook and cranny unexplored.

What are these nooks and crannies, anyway? More of those insanely popular e-readers? I am sure that it goes back all the way to middling English, which is no skin off my sniffer, as I do not deign to speak anything other than key phrases of cat.

Humans would be a lot better off if they restricted themselves to only a few choice words of absolute necessity, such as "This sunlight spot is mine" or "You are sleeping on my tail." Instructions to lesser beings, that kind of thing. In that line, I will broadcast a mental command to Miss Temple: "More shrimp risotto sauce on that former rabbit food that is served to me in the guise of army brown Free-to-Be-Feline health kibble. Pellets in and pellets out, if you know what I mean, and the ants will play pinochle on your snout before I munch a bit of it. It does not fill my nook or cranny.

Anyway, I am again on the same site, and it is almost unrecognizable, mostly for the crowd of gawkers it has attracted.

I wander now among the gathered weirdos, fans, and true believers of all things UFO and alien. If any murderer was going to return to the scene of this crime, the discovery of an unlabeled corpse, he or she would have an instant cover.

I recall when my gang of three—Miss Temple, Mr. Matt Devine, and a younger and more amenable Mariah Molina—attended TitaniCon, the world's largest (and most disastrous) science fiction convention at the New Millennium hotel. That was when *Star Trek*: The Experience was in full bloom, and all sorts of alien beings got to parade around as waiters and guides wearing assorted alien heads . . . Klingons and Ferengi and such.

Did you ever notice that most aliens always have something weird about the head and face? Whether they wear rubber masks for a TV show or are drawn by purported victims of alien abduction, there is always some new wrinkle in the unfortunate human skin condition called . . . well, skin.

You will also realize how much more attractive media aliens are when they wear fur, such as the charming Chewbacca of the *Star Wars* franchise or, my personal favorite, those delicious little *Star Trek* morsels called Tribbles. Born to be snacks, and so prolific.

I do not chew tobacco, however, and I do not like it when the usual stew of milling human presence is supplemented by various latex smells from items called Spock ears and Bajoran noses. To confuse the crime scene even more, various vendors have set up illegal carts to hawk green glow-in-the-dark alien-faced soap.

Holy Madam Curie! Anyone addicted to that glowy stuff ever think about radium exposure? I suppose there are "trace" amounts, but for one of my build and size, that is a lot of "trace." Perhaps they have a new safe potion for the same effect.

I gaze at the rows of slanty-eyed faces with the green visage of a seasick Siamese. I never noticed before that those big-eyed little gray men much resemble those furless fancy cats called the Sphinx breed.

I want to make tracks out of this madhouse, but instead dutifully thread my way around the occasional potentially lethal Klingon boot and plenty of flip-flops, looking for Miss Temple's arrival. I know she will be here somewhere. She cannot resist trying to straighten out a public relations disaster of this size and momentum. Misguided loyalty is her main flaw. She responded to what seemed to be a nice old gent, and now he has got us all in the soup.

I have been suspicious of Mr. Silas T. Farnum since the first time I took a ride on the Wynn's floating parasols to keep an eye on him. Now he has imported a masquerading mob that could disrupt any unfound evidence at the crime scene.

This makes the savvy operative suspicious that that whole scheme is a put-up deal for just such a purpose.

One purported to be far wiser than my kind, but also dead (so I still have the advantage), noted "Where do you hide a leaf? In a forest." This melee is just the thing to put the murder case on the back burner of public interest.

Fortunately, I am beset by my breed's hallmark curiosity. The minute I realized Miss Temple was being drawn to this site someone had settled on for a body dump, I put my nose into overtime.

It is not enough that I see the lay of the land. I must also sniff it. Of course, I am attracted to unfinished construction, which is a jungle gym to those with my athletic prowess. Ever since I could put one paw in front of the other, I was fond of heights. I can run along the business edge of a construction two-by-four like nobody's business, except that it *is* my business, since I am a shamus or a private eye or what you will.

Imagine my surprise when I start to scale this lovely conglomeration of concrete and steel and wood and plastic sheeting, and I find I have to break and enter.

That is right, folks. I never am for a moment deceived about there not being a building on this site hidden by whatever string theory, Einstein premise, or difference engine thingamajiggy Mr. Silas T. Farnum has funded to create an illusion.

I will not believe it until I smell it, and what I smell here (fresh paint, carpeting, electrical wiring) tells me that spectacular spinning UFO is just a Big Brother to the floating parasols at the Wynn. I am guessing it is another revolving restaurant togged out as an alien ship.

You know that famous book and movie where Miss Dorothy Gale's little dog, Toto, pulls the curtain aside and the Wizard of Oz is proved to be just a puppeteer?

Well, anything a dog can do Midnight Louie can do better, and I am about to pull several stories of plastic sheeting down on this phony "third encounter of the weird kind" act.

I start climbing an exterior spiral staircase made of Plexiglas. The central core of this structure is the Guggenheim Museum in Manhattan turned inside out. How do I, a humble Vegas gumshoe, know about tony Frank Lloyd Wright classic designs in the Big Apple?

Simple as making Baked Alaska.

All things crass and cultured come to Vegas sometime.

Thus I was able to stroll through the Guggenheim Hermitage Museum during its seven-year tenure at the Venetian Resort Hotel-Casino.

Naturally, my strolls were of the wee-hours variety, when I had a much less obstructed view of the treasures and minus human lower extremities in an odiferous array of vented and unvented footwear. That is to say, sandals and sweaty tennis shoes. It is hard to say which style is most repellent to the ankle-level nose.

Anyway, here I am now, making architectural connections and scaling this giant spiral shell under the cover of lots of canvas and plastic swaddling. I plan to reach the top and schuss down the unanchored billowing canvas so like a wooden ship's sails.

I am pretty sure this act of derring-do will be the disruption that can break the spell of the stealth machine, which is the only real science fiction item on-site, and unveil the actual structure in one heroic, guaranteed viral media moment.

(I am miffed by my junior partner, Miss Midnight Louise, going viral first by hopping a ride on a Segway tour on the Las Vegas Strip not too long ago.)

This little stunt will put the *V* in "viral" and make the "Midnight" in "Midnight Investigations, Inc.," a household name. Plus, it is a much better curtain-pulling-back act than any little black dog could manage. This is ten stories, folks, a small step for Las Vegas and mankind but a giant leap for Midnight Louie and catkind.

Like the movie stunt boys and girls do, I will land safely on several feet of piled canvas and plastic and my own legendary feet.

Uh-oh. I hear a strange whirring sound above. So does everyone present.

Great Bast's Ghost! The entire doughnut-shaped revolving UFO restaurant is spiraling down on me like the head of a screw in the grip of a giant alien screwdriver.

Abandon mother ship!

I look down in horror as my nimble frame twists and plummets like Mr. Max Kinsella on a bungee cord.

I am not alone in this fall to earth.

A hitchhiking scene-stealer has crashed my act and is falling much less gracefully.

I am heading down at thirty miles an hour in the close company of some dude with a terminally dark George Hamilton tan who one-ups me as the main attraction, being both naked and dead.

Chapter 28

The Unusual Suspects

Molina stood with her back to Temple, boot-toed cow-boy mules planted wide on the sandy soil, hands on hips. The stance reminded Temple of a gunfighter poised to draw, except, instead of carrying six-guns, she probably had a fancy foreign pistol stashed in a shoulder holster or tucked in the back of her pants or strapped to an ankle. Ruined the whole look.

Still, wearing her David Caruso *CSI* sunglasses as she turned sideways, Molina looked ready for a shoot-out in Miami, if not Las Vegas.

Temple saw another thing that ruined Molina's whole Metro detective hard-nose look. She was interrogating the nervous dwarf at her side. Silas T. Farnum wore a gray-and-white-striped seersucker suit reminiscent of a con-vict's outfit. His polka-dot tie also ruined the whole look.

"This has been a crime scene for more than forty-eight hours," Temple heard Molina say, the words spit out like a Thompson submachine gun spraying bullets, actually. "You have had a concealed experimental scientific device on this site and did not report its presence? I don't know how many charges an inspired assistant DA could string together, from violated city ordinances to one big mama of an illegal parking ticket."

"But, Lieutenant. I'm an entrepren—"

"Now," Molina went on at the same furious but controlled pace, "some poor soul who got caught up in your UFO fever scheme has plummeted to his death. Was it a construction worker? A tourist who glimpsed the shenanigans going on here and tried to climb his way to an answer? One of your so-called silent partners or fans or detractors? Homicide wants to know."

Temple had been ordered to "stand there."

So she was kept mute five feet behind Molina and her victim but every word nailed her guilty conscience as well. She'd worn her dust-shedding red patent-leather pumps to the site, but she wasn't comfortable.

"Explain yourself," Molina barked at Farnum. By now Temple was envisioning the woman's dark bobbed hair above a khaki pantsuit as the black-and-tan of a German shepherd guard dog on the attack. She really must rein in her imagination.

"I—I'm an entrepreneur, ma'am," Farnum said.

"So was Bugsy Siegel," came the icy response, "and look how he ended up. You'd be downtown getting your pinkies scanned for fingerprints if I didn't need you to explain your science fiction device."

"It's not a device."

Molina's face donned an *Are you contradicting me?* glower.

Farnum continued his explanation. "I'm trying to explain the inexplicable here. It's a process, actually. The structure employs metamaterials with a light-bending technology. You combine polymer substratas and gold and copper, which forcibly bend electromagnetic waves *around* an object. Light hitting the object is diverted around it. The light is not reflected nor refracted."

Molina absorbed this cascade of technological terms, then shoved the sunglasses up onto her head and whirled to pin her gaze on Temple's. Temple had always found the effect of intense blue eyes in an olive complexion like being hit by a blinding blue laser.

"You're the PR whiz kid," Molina said. "Explain what Farnum here has said in simple English."

Temple tried. "From what I've found out, researchers have been working since the early 2000s to develop a material that can bend visible light around three-D objects. And it's working. These metamaterials can conceal small objects, but are rapidly being applied to bigger projects. The implications for the military and, uh, police departments are enormous if this technology leaked into the wrong hands."

"That's an understatement." This time Molina's gaze snapped like heat lightning between Temple and Farnum, who shrugged at each other, hoping the other won the hot spot. "So the first commercial use of these 'metamaterials' shows up—or doesn't show up—in Vegas? Tell me another fairy story."

Temple directed her own steely look at her errant sorta client.

He caved. "It could *only* happen in Vegas, Lieutenant Mojito."

"Molina!"

"Molina." Farnum doffed his straw hat and wiped his sweat-beaded forehead with the back of his stubby hand at the same time. "The hotel consortium billionaires of the Strip are the only ones who could bankroll a weird science project like this."

"Even they aren't that crazy," Molina said.

Farnum turned earnest, his huckster's enthusiasm for his con coming forward. "Look at the space program. The U.S. government? Outta there. It's up to the Russians and Chinese now. And to entrepreneurs, billionaire entrepreneurs from the U.S. and beyond, like Sir Richard Branson of Virgin Everything. Entrepreneurs are sending manned rockets into space. You don't think one or more of them wouldn't mind building a real Space Mountain in Vegas?"

"So," Molina said. "You've been working on this secret construction under the cover of darkness and cutting-edge technology. What people saw was not really there. It was a . . . reflection of all the stalled projects around us?"

"Not exactly, but it'll do."

"And what exactly is the real construction I'm seeing now?" Molina sighed and turned to view the unveiled Disneyland structure of space ship top and residential tower. "It's not much of a building."

Farnum had the answer. "It's the biggest building yet shielded from view."

"Not now. Now it's a crime scene. And how do these metamaterials turn off and on?"

"Trade secret," Farnum answered promptly.

"It's no secret that two bodies have been found on this site." Molina lowered her sunglasses and looked sideways at Farnum. "This entire lot is a crime scene, including your trickster building. I'm posting officers around the clock, and not even Harry Potter will slip past them."

Temple remembered that Harry had an invisibility cloak. Molina had read Harry Potter? Probably when Mariah was a kindergartner.

"Prepare to give me a list of who bankrolled what, or I'll get a court order to view all the permits," Molina told Farnum. "Even invisible buildings can't go up these days without plenty of paperwork."

Farnum backed away, bowing like a spurned suitor, his straw hat clutched to his heart.

Molina turned to Temple. "I see you've been chatting up the gathering UFO *Looney Tunes* division. You're coming to headquarters with me to give a full oral report."

Yo, ho, ho and little green gray men on a dead man's chest.

Chapter 29

Fringe Benefit

Only in Las Vegas.

In only an hour or two, my spectacular Olympic-level performance in Downhill Racing is forgotten in the resulting chaos, although I am sure it will soon go viral and reality TV will be calling . . . and calling my name.

Police DO NOT CROSS tape has expanded to encompass most of the lot and now includes the nakedly exposed building. Crawford Buchanan is in all-too-prominent evidence, chatting up the crowd for a slot on the ten o'clock news. Onlookers and schlock-sellers form a thick lunatic fringe between the tape and the curb, creating a street circus atmosphere to mirror the Strip, although in small scale.

Still, it is hard for a dude of my stature to make an evidence-gathering stroll of the grounds. My Miss Temple captured me while I was still a bit disoriented from my ten-story slide. She hugged me and petted me and called me her very own, in full public view, which was terribly humiliating, then admonished me and locked me "safely" in the Miata convertible and flounced off to do spin control and snoop, as she is wont.

Foolish girl. She ordered the Mazda model with the push-button top. The day, or night, Midnight Louie cannot paw-punch a button with enough force to operate it is the day I hang up my crime-busting credentials. She should know that by now. I have pussyfooted over enough of her landline and fax buttons in the past.

Granted, Miss Temple is somewhat dizzy from being the PR person in charge of this big-time would-be alien side-show despite herself. I had heard her muttering about being stuck as "Molina's Junior G-string Girl" or some such as she left me in temporary custody in the Miata.

I do enjoy the sweet smell and cushiness of leather seats, but I like a crime scene—no matter how grimy and bizarre—better.

So now I am footloose and fancy free, and following in Crawford Buchanan's nosy newscaster footsteps, which smell of rose-scented athlete's foot powder—*oof!* Above me, his oily baritone is drawing sensational comments from the gathered loonies—er, legions of UFO believers—and the usual Vegas suspects: onlooker tourists and local gawkers.

"I saw that UFO thingie just swallow up a building whole," testifies an elderly dude wearing a Hawaiian shirt and flip-flops that sport gel-green frogs on the toes. Definitely a keen eyewitness. "This is obviously the first scout ship," he adds, "but these alien thingies will be downing the Monte Carlo next. We are witnessing Armagideon."

And Joshua and Jericho too.

The next camera subject wears jeans and Earth Shoes. I would have sworn that this '70s' artifact would have vanished from the earth, but no. It is a pleasure to see long pants in Las Vegas, and lots less human hair that looks like it escaped a coconut shell. I delicately walk my foretoes up the leg of the oblivious wearer and spot a halo of un-governed Einstein hair on his head.

Perchance this dude will share a brainiac perspective.

"I was able," he confides to Crawford and myself and the camera, "to shoot a cell phone pic of the unfortunate fallen corpse. This is clearly a returned alien abductee who either died in custody or was . . . experimented on to the death. Just like the helpless animals in our research labs. Our own sins are being visited upon our abducted members."

This guy has a point. Should the wrong individuals spot me on the loose, I am in danger of going from confinement in a locked Miata to a wire crate on death row. This thought has me hotfooting into a swarm of tennis shoes, which are bulk-ier to hunker down behind.

However, the Crawfish's two-tone loafers catch up with me.

"Your theories on the visitation to Paradise?" Buchanan asks the Nike-clad feet of a female of the species, holding out his mic like it was as tasty as a licorice lollipop.

People today gravitate to the sweet smell of self-advertisement. Resistance is futile.

"Obviously," says a woman in a MISKATONIC U T-shirt, "this is a close encounter of the sixth kind."

"Sixth kind?" Buchanan sounds confused. "I've heard about the first kind and the second and third, but—"

"You reporters are so behind the times," she enlightens us all. "The body expelled from the alien ship is obviously a captive of ancient aliens who'd preserved his life for hun-dreds of years before some space accident or just time caused him to finally expire. Surely you glimpsed the swar-thy complexion, the noble Mayan profile, as etched into the stones of Calixtlahuaca. This is an ancient Mayan astronaut whose extraterrestrial duty has sadly ended after hundreds of years, yet . . . too soon."

She flashes the face of her cell phone at the video camera eavesdropping over Buchanan's shoulder. "This man was *hot*."

I cringe in embarrassment for Miss Temple's species.

Looks like alien abductees are the new multimedia, multi-cultural sex symbol, and then some.

Chapter 30

Fallout

"You don't need to take me downtown, honest," Temple said when Molina escorted her to a parked squad car.

"I should," Molina answered. "I said to keep me informed, not to take us all to Oz, and your big cat too."

Lieutenant Molina's face wore a slightly sour professional scowl. Detective Su, Alch's partner and a petite Asian woman who could out-scowl her superior officer, was leaning against the squad car's door, keeping Temple sitting tight in the passenger seat.

Temple remembered she'd left Louie locked in her Miata ten minutes earlier. She needed to get him out before it got too hot, although he actually liked to snooze under the dashboard on the passenger side in the Circle Ritz parking lot . . . a spot that was warm, dark, and defended. And also kept close watch on her comings and goings.

Often she wished the shoe were on the other paw.

Molina was in the driver's seat, one long leg jackknifed in the crowded under–steering wheel area, the other on the street through the ajar door.

The black-and-white's interior was hot, crammed with equipment, and smelled like a spilled strawberry soda, thanks to an odor remover. Temple was thinking if she stayed here too long, she might throw up.

"Things," Temple said, "went horribly wrong terribly fast."

"Just your speed." Molina was tapping the keys of the built-in computer. "I want to know why your cat was the only one to understand that building had a fully climbable, completed interior."

"Legendary curiosity?"

Molina's scowl deepened into furrows, and her fingertips beat the keys even faster. Temple decided to go for it. "Speaking of curiosity, why all the crowd rumors about the corpse being a Mayan or an Aztec?"

"Cruise YouTube."

Temple did, pumping in the words "Mayan" and "Vegas."

A bronze-skinned nude figure like a broken starfish came up in blurry focus.

"Ouch," Temple said. "How'd anybody get crime scene photos to post on social media?"

"Not us. Paparazzi and wannabes. The pros have been stalking the morgue for years. Coroner Bahr has metal shades on his windows, and they still smuggle themselves in."

"But these were taken here, where the man fell. Where did the ancient Aztec-Mayan rumor come from?"

"Profiling," Molina said sardonically, leaning back as

an actual color crime-scene photo popped onto the screen.

"Oh." This photo was Kodak sharp from the days of yore when there was a Kodak camera and color Kodak film to boast of, like back in the '90s. The body had landed in a swastika-sign position. The man's naked skin was as deeply bronze as the male figures on ancient Egyptian tomb paintings, and his build was lean and toned, which, again, brought to mind the peoples of ancient empires.

The face was in profile, untouched on the revealed side. But his profile, with the strong frontal ridge over the prominent nose, looked a lot like those Mayan stone carvings of elaborately unclothed warriors UFO believers liked to identify as wearing astronaut gear instead of mere ceremonial headdresses and battle armament.

Temple had always found that claim far-fetched, but she mentioned that astronaut theory to Molina, who snorted.

"The Incas, Aztecs, and Mayans didn't die out entirely under the Spaniard conquistadors," Molina said. "You can still see contemporary people with faces from the monuments all through Mexico and Central America."

"This guy sure wasn't old, like the first body."

"In vigorous health, Coroner Bahr says, after a fast look-see," Molina agreed. "About forty-five to fifty."

"Okay, so he's super buff for that age. The tabloid sites are screaming about 'scars of alien surgery.' I can see some faint lines curling onto his front torso, but they're about as clear as the canals on Mars. Did Grizzly have any conclusions on that?"

"Cozy with the coroner, are we?"

"I have a wide range of acquaintanceship."

"Sadly, that's sometimes of use to me. The amateur alien experts are texting that the marks are . . . 'purposefully placed shallow track incisions, some in positions on the ribs almost like . . . gills.' "

Temple gasped. "That does sound alien."

"According to Grizzly, they're recent but healed. They do mark primarily the back, curve around the sides, and some are down the backs of the legs."

"Gang initiation?" Temple asked.

"No tats. Besides, he's too old and well cared for. This man's teeth were in great condition. No fillings."

"That's rare."

"But not impossible. There are geographical areas where the water naturally contains fluoride."

"So Midnight Louie's explorations managed to unveil an ancient Mayan or Aztec abductee, or alien, returned to Earth, lightly scarred but otherwise in superb physical shape, somehow concealed in Silas T. Farnum's now-you-see-it/now-you-don't building?"

"I'll believe that when he shows up as Hillary's running mate in 2016."

Temple had to give that joke a quick smile. "How can people swoon over this poor dead guy?" she wondered. "What an awful way to die."

"Social media swooning is unstoppable." Molina tapped the screen with one of her seriously short fingernails. "Part of the 'rich Corinthian leather' skin color is self-tanning lotion. Interesting, isn't it?"

Temple recognized the "Corinthian" phrase from an old TV car ad featuring the rich Mexican-accented voice of pioneering Latino actor Ricardo Montalbán, dead a lot longer than this guy.

"I doubt the ancients went in for tanning preparations. Hey, maybe this guy was an actor?" Temple said. "Maybe Silas T. had hired him to add some alien color to his big revelation."

"He ever mention an ancient Mayan theme to you?"

"No, but I've been visiting all the UFO and alien Web

sites lately to figure out what Farnum was up to, and the ancient-alien theme is a whole industry."

Molina shook her head. "Talk about alien visitors, you are one on those Web sites."

"True. I don't believe any of it. You can take any image or custom or artifact from history and theorize that 'ancient alien visitors' left signs of giving the culture a sudden technological boost. I'm quite satisfied with the way public TV says the pyramids were built. Slave labor is a lot more likely than alien tourists who lent an ancient hand and then left us to stew in our own slow mambo to modern times over centuries of ignorance and war."

"Mercy. You're pretty indignant about these fringe theories."

"I've been pretty mercilessly misled by Mr. Farnum and his undercover enterprise," Temple answered. "And the sad part about all this is that his magical disappearing act is the real deal. That's on the Web too. Scientists are learning to bend light, and time, to make our eyes fool themselves."

Molina's mouth went thin-lipped and grim. "That just makes my job harder. It's bad enough Vegas is a 24-hour cabaret of crime, my friend. What I don't need are alien interlopers. Your cat is about all I can handle, just barely, in that department."

Chapter 31

Short Stuff

Much as I loathe treading in Crawford Buchanan's foot-steps, he makes a good cover.

He has now buttonholed a lady wearing an outfit my vintage clothing–loving Miss Temple would give the Revival Stamp of Approval: plaid Bermuda shorts and crisp light blue shirt with rolled-up buttoned sleeves. Then again, this lady may have just bought from the Lands' End classic mail-order catalog.

Her sensible navy canvas boating flats are refreshingly odor-free, but I can't say the same for her boon companion, whom she has released from a canvas doggie tote to the arid ground and swift perusal from my world-class sniffer.

This critter is so small, the dogdom bit is questionable. However, it has the intelligent and sturdy look of the noble and industrious sled dogs known as huskies.

I confess myself confused.

"Hey, shorty," I greet this ambiguous animal.

I am answered by a round of yapping, which settles the species question.

"No offense," I say after another long inhalation of its essence. *Hmm.* Attar of taco sauce. "I gather that you are familiar with the ruins called 'Calix-tla-hua-ca.' Pardon my accent, but my breed is not geographically centered, as yours is."

"Whowho Whoareyou? Whadayoudoinghere? Iguard-myhuman. Iwillchewoffyoureartips."

Manx, that is one territorial Chi-hua-hua! Fierce little fellow. I sense a story here, and they are a talkative breed.

Meanwhile, above me, the Bermuda shorts lady is enlightening Crawford Buchanan far more than he wishes to be.

"Why are you and your TV station making a mockery of this event?" she demands. "Alien visitation is no joke."

"Ah, no, madam." Buchanan's feet do a little jiggle as his mind seeks to catch up with her challenge. "But . . . people saw this thing land. Including you? Miss—?"

"My name is Penny, and this is my dog, Rens."

I hear echoes of Sergeant Preston of the Yukon and his dog, King. I am most fond of vintage TV.

"I do not know," she goes on as if she is sure that *he* does not know, "if you realize that our age's greatest scientific mind has warned that our incessant search for life beyond our planet may have unanticipated results. If they are smart enough to be 'out there' and find us, we may not want to be found by the likes of them."

"Aw, yeah? 'Our greatest mind'?"

"Surely, even you have heard of Stephen Hawking."

"Aw . . . sure. The guy who wrote *The Stand.*"

"Not Stephen King. Stephen *Haw*king. And I'd bet you haven't a clue about string theory."

"String theory? Ah . . . yo-yos?"

I hear a huge sigh above me. "Yo-yos, yes. Like you."

"What did this Hawking guy warn against?"

She leans close to the mic and articulates every syllable. "Watch out what you wish for. The aliens we are searching for may be out there, all right, looking to take us over. The human rider from that spaceship is dead, isn't he?"

I comment off-camera to my new compadre, "She may have a point. What do you think?"

"I think there are a lot of food stands around here where the pickings are dropping to the ground and free for you and me."

I always bow to the superior sniffer. With one chomp, I pull the tongue of leather on his collar through the metal buckle and Rens and I are off on a culinary scouting mission of our own.

We know our moments of freedom are few. Our respective associates will soon be tracking us down. Miss Penny will not remain deeply engaged with the shallow Crawford Buchanan for long, and my Miss Temple will not appreciate my cavalier ways with her convertible top control.

Meanwhile . . . free food!

Our loving ladies mean well, poor souls.

Chapter 32

Identity Crisis

Temple didn't know whether she was relieved or worried to find the Miata's top down and Louie gone. Given Louie's record of going rogue whenever he pleased, she was very, very afraid. For everyone else.

She grabbed the wide-brimmed hat with the built-in scarf she kept in the car. The unshaded lot was as dangerous for her redhead's sensitive skin as driving a convertible with the top down. She put up the top to protect the car's leather seats and steering wheel from frying in the sunlight.

As for Mr. Midnight Louie, missing "purrson," she figured she'd find him, or vice versa, in the crowd. He'd just become another lead to follow.

While she was talking to Molina, Temple's PR genes had stayed active and entered Eavesdrop Mode.

An ace public relations person could nod attentively and talk to one person, even an authority figure like a cop, while locating the presence and identity of at least half a dozen people around her at the same time.

Given the extreme appearances of the pro and con UFO crowds gathered, that was much harder right now. Basically, the crowd was fifty shades of weird. Being a PR person, Temple enjoyed every shade of weird. It made for easy publicity. That was surely true now, with vans from local TV stations jumping on footage of this event before L.A. could even hope to get a unit here.

During her almost subconscious pans of the crowd, Temple thought she'd spied a local personality who might at least know Midnight Louie if he saw him and help her corral her cat before Louie unearthed another body.

Looking for Crawford Buchanan's head in a crowd was as bad as someone looking for hers, given his short stature. Having to want to find the sleazy cad-about-town was even worse.

She needn't have worried. Buchanan had some PR vibes himself, because she heard a baritone voice from the mob intone, "And here's a local light on the Strip PR scene," just as someone grabbed her arm.

Temple turned into the bright light of a shouldered camera and smiled at least half as brightly.

Buchanan had switched to wearing a local cable TV gold sports coat with the station call letters on the breast pocket and ditched the crass diamond ear stud.

Luckily, the glare kept Buchanan's regular but smug features in temporary darkness. "Miss Temple Barr," he announced to whatever audience he represented at the moment, "feminine flack extraordinaire."

She winced inside at his hokey and demeaning intro-duction, but maintained her broad smile. Flunk electronic media exposure these days, and it would be all over the world instantly.

"You are," Crawford went on, "the presumptive PR rep for the shadowy individuals who own the murder site. I believe."

"Goodness. You make me sound like I'm running for president with a PAC behind me. Yes, I've been in talks to represent one of the individuals who back this construction, but there was no desire on anyone's part to own a 'murder site.' Besides, the coroner has not ruled on the cause of death, so any suggestion of 'murder' at this point is utterly irresponsible."

Temple smiled demurely into the camera while Buchanan sputtered to think up a new question.

"So, Miss Barr, are you saying you don't believe in UFOs?"

"Certainly many people do, and it's not for me to say they're wrong."

"Rumor is the dead body was a plant."

"Oh, no. I'm very certain he was some sort of *Homo sapiens*."

"And naked as a jaybird."

"I don't think he was a bird, either. Or Superman sans costume. We just don't know enough about him. This is not *The Day of the Triffids,* Mr. Buchanan. And I doubt 'space spores' have escaped a *Star Trek* set to invade a desert climate."

The surrounding believers were muttering and pressing closer. "However," Temple said, "his presence and death certainly give one reason to wonder. 'The truth is out there,' and I do believe that 'we are not alone.' "

Scattered applause.

The videographer turned to pan on the crowd. Temple grabbed Awful Crawford's mic and fisted her hand over it. "You've got your interview," she told him vehemently. "Now you'll answer some of my questions."

"Absolutely, TB. I'm at your disposal."

"I couldn't put it better myself. Listen. You know my cat, Midnight Louie?"

"That black back-alley escapee. I'd expect a cute chick like you to own something more upscale, like one of those fluffy white numbers on the TV commercials."

"Louie was on some TV commercials."

Buchanan smirked at having irked her to the point of defending her cat.

"Anyway," Temple said, back on point. "I need to round him up. Have you seen him in this mess?"

He gave her a reproachful look. "Don't I have my finger on the pulse of everything that goes on around Vegas? Sure, I saw your alley cat, and I would have interviewed him if I could have. He did tumble into the scene of the body dump—"

The crowds muttered again.

"—or landing," Crawford said quickly.

Temple dragged him away from the current eavesdroppers by pulling the mic with her. He was as attached to his on-camera persona as a dog to its leash.

Surrounded by a fresh crowd of imaginatively attired folks with rainbow skin and artificially altered noses and ears, Temple resumed her interrogation. "Louie? Where? When?"

Buchanan looked around. "Well, he was making eyes at the strangest little critter I ever saw."

"Female?"

"How do I know?" He was indignant. "It was like a miniature sled dog. You know, a husky, only a foot by a foot, say, and that thing was with a woman I interviewed. . . ." He craned his neck and even went a bit on tippytoes in his height-assisted '70s-style platform shoes. "That woman, there."

Temple released the mic from her now sweaty hot little hand and started edging past ridged spinal frills and fairy wings (fairy wings?) to the relatively normal-looking woman twenty feet away.

A sound of labored breathing behind her revealed she had not quite shed the intrepid dork called Crawford Buchanan.

Temple immediately began scanning the ground, but the woman wore deck shoes unaccompanied by any miniature Siberian huskies or a particularly large black cat.

"Excuse me," Temple said, by now a trifle breathless herself. "This gentleman"—that hurt—"says when he interviewed you earlier, you were accompanied by a small . . . dog? And a black cat was in the neighborhood."

The woman gazed at her with shock. "I've never seen this man before in my life. And, frankly, if I had, I'd make sure I didn't see him again. He looks like a really self-satisfied aggravating twit."

Buchanan was sputtering again. "I must disagree, ma'am. I did a brief stand-up with you not fifteen minutes ago."

"'A brief stand-up'! What a phony accusation. I am not that sort of woman at all, and even if I was, I would not be that sort of woman with *you.*"

"You don't understand, that's a technical term," he said hastily. "And I don't understand. You were perfectly cordial when I talked to you earlier. Surely you remember me."

"Surely I would do my best to forget your manners."

"I have it on film. Where's that cameraman?" Buchanan gazed around wildly.

A crowd was gathering again.

"You would actually *film* yourself making such offensive overtures? I saw some police people here just a moment ago." *She* gazed wildly around this time.

By now, even Temple was gazing wildly around at both foot and head level.

"This is a misunderstanding," Buchanan was saying. "I interviewed you. You must remember me."

"There's no law that I have to!" she shouted as the missing videographer, a tall portly guy, appeared and ushered Buchanan away. "What a putz," she told Temple.

"Thanks for getting rid of him. I'm Temple and I'm looking for my cat."

"I'm Penny, and I'm looking for my dog. He slipped the collar of his harness." The woman pulled up her left hand, holding a leash and empty harness.

Temple had a feeling Midnight Louie had been the harness undoer. "That's a tiny harness. What kind of dog do you have?"

The woman chuckled. "He's a husky Chihuahua."

"I've seen a few overweight Chihuahuas, but that would be big even on them."

"Rens is not overweight, but he does look more like a Siberian husky, only tiny."

"Gosh, he could get lost underfoot." Temple looked around at the carelessly milling crowd taking photos of Area 54.

"He has a lot of sense, small body, big brain. But I do want to find him."

"What brought you and Rens here?"

"We like to see the passing parade, and this sure is a doozy. I don't believe in this stuff."

Temple nodded.

"Besides, if aliens did decide to enter our solar system and check Earth out, I believe they'd be galactic conquerors or so different than us, they'd regard stamping us out the way we'd stomp on a scorpion." Penny's shoe stamped in demonstration.

Temple jumped. No scorpions were underfoot, but a cat tail . . . or a little dog paw could be.

Then she spotted a familiar street sight. "I'm going over there to look for Rens and Louie."

Penny turned her head. "Good thinking. I'll go the other way."

Glad she'd hadn't had time to don the hat before her impromptu "face time" in front of Awful Crawford's videographer, Temple tied it on. The wide brim softened the glare and made searching the scene easier, and Buchanan—and Molina—might not recognize her, always a good idea.

When Temple reached the mobile "pop-up" hot dog stand, a little dog, who did sport the coat color of a husky, was sitting up behind the counter with the operator, getting hot dog bits from time to time. It was amazing. He had the bigger breed's widow's peak coloration on his forehead, and carried his feathered tail over his back in a wolf–spitz curl. Yet he was the size of a Chihuahua.

Temple's sigh of relief could have launched a model sailing boat. This was definitely Rens.

Temple eyed the deep black shadow under the truck. She spotted a flash of iridescent green from a cat iris before it winked out.

She was willing to bet that Midnight Louie would be back at the Circle Ritz before she was.

Meanwhile, she needed to reunite Rens with his Penny.

"Hi," she told the pop-up stand operator, a burly guy who could have played a marine recruiter in a movie.

"You want a dog, lady?"

"Yes. That one." She pointed at Rens.

"This little fella?"

"That's the one."

"He just showed up, so how do I know he's yours?"

"He's not, but I've just been talking to his owner, who's pretty distraught."

"I don't know . . . everybody's been wanting to claim him."

Temple didn't have time or energy left to trek back and

forth in this mob. She set her heels, opened her arms like someone about to burst into song, and called, "Rens!"

The little dog bounded into her chest like a furry bullet. Temple swayed on her feet, but got heel traction fast and closed her arms around one happy fluffball.

The burly man looked about to cry. "I guess this little guy knows his name, and you do too. I was thinking we'd make a good team, Big Mike and Shorty. My customers were eating him up."

Temple hoped he wasn't speaking literally.

"Visit the local shelter," she suggested over her shoulder as she toted the lightweight dog away. "I bet they have more in need of homes."

Shelters were overflowing with Chihuahuas and Chihuahua mixes, she knew, because of the "purse pooch" fad. Rens was sure a lot lighter than Louie.

She spotted a down-faced Penny gazing back and forth like a scanning camera as she returned to where she'd discovered Rens was missing. Then she saw her dog being toted along at shoulder level.

"That's my dog!"

"Yes, I know."

"Did you take him?"

Temple was stunned, and people around them were suddenly paying attention. "No. I found him for you."

"How did you even know he was missing? How do I know that *you* didn't take him?"

They were now the center of a circle of animal lovers. Holy jalapeño! Penny was even more suspicious than the hot dog vendor.

"We—we talked," Temple said, Temple who never stuttered, who always had even the worst public relations disaster firmly in hand.

"I don't know you."

Temple felt the crowd pressing closer. Rens whimpered.

"Do you have any distinguishing characteristics?" Penny demanded.

"Uh, a few freckles, but I usually use a cover-up."

"Besides your face."

Temple thought. She looked down, where Rens's tiny harness still hung empty at the end of the short leash. "My red high heels?"

"Oh. You're that lady. Okay. Thanks so much!" She reached to take Rens into full custody as people turned away and moved on.

"My little Rens, where have you been?" She rubbed noses with the alert mini husky face.

"He got as far as the hot dog stand. Say, um, Penny, why were you treating me like a petnapper?"

"Oh, that." Penny shrugged. "You should have told me you had red hair under that hat you just put on, not that you had freckles."

"I guess my red hair is more memorable than my freckles, but I'm more self-conscious of my freckles." Then Temple had a wild hope. Were her freckles really that minor and she didn't know it? Could she throw out the vanishing cream?

"Your freckles don't register with me." Penny smiled. "To me your face is a blank space on a map. I have a learning disability that affects only two and a half percent of the population. It's called prosopagnosia. My brain doesn't process faces. And it's hell. The condition has been covered by TV shows like *Sixty Minutes*."

Temple nodded. She'd heard of that problem. She'd also heard that one facility humans had that animals didn't was . . . the ability to recognize faces.

"I'm sorry. That must be . . . surreal for you," she told Penny.

"I've learned to focus on pieces of a person. Like hair color, clothing, mannerisms, posture. Freckles! No go. Can't see 'em. You're freckle-free with me, kiddo! Just remind me about the red hair and high heels next time we cross paths."

Temple doubted their paths would cross again.

"Do you know what the worst things about this condition are?" Penny asked.

Temple shook her head. She was almost afraid to hear.

"One, it makes me brutally honest, so I have a hard time keeping friends. I can't lie, because I won't recognize the person I lied to. So I tell the truth at all times. That can get to be a real pain."

"So you genuinely forgot Crawford Buchanan," Temple mused aloud, remembering his confusion.

"Yes, at first. But then I remembered his oily hair—way too much product, dude! So I played dumb just to tick him off because he was a stuck-up, phony sort of person. I got to snub someone for a change. Everyone always thinks I'm snubbing them in public, like you did here, when they see me in passing on the street and I don't recognize them."

Temple couldn't begin to contemplate the adjustments such a condition would demand of her and her job, but she had a suggestion for one issue: "Just be a smiley person and nod at anyone you pass who makes eye contact. Strangers will think you're a bubbly personality, and people who know you will probably stop to chat and you can use your ID system, or get a clue from their conversation."

"*Hmm.* I'm not a bubbly person. I told you, I have to be brutally honest."

That *was* a problem. No wonder Penny was so attached to Rens. His love was unconditional. He'd leap for the sound of his name and know her voice.

"Can you recognize Rens's face?"

"It's the same, except dogness is easier to isolate."

"One other thing I'm curious about," Temple said.

"Only one? You're easy."

"With this problem, why come out to join a mob of people like this, all faces you can't really see? And you are really skeptical of the UFO fever all around here."

"Simple. It's a great laboratory. I practice remembering strangers in the crowd by things beside their faces. Plus, I think they're all silly for getting caught up in this UFO and ancient-alien stuff. Any aliens who are out there, we definitely don't want to meet."

"Even if you don't have to see their weird alien faces."

"Especially if I have to remember them by other traits. I mean, who'd want to have a memory of tentacles?"

Chapter 33

Synth You've
Been Gone

Once Rens—that walking contradiction in genetics, the mini husky Chihuahua—was restored to his person, I begin to think I could safely lock myself back in the Miata with my Miss Temple being none the wiser.

I am about to make myself scarce on the alien flash mob scene when something familiar flashes across my field of vision and kisser like a chorus girl's black ostrich fan.

I sneeze, not the suave reaction I hope for during an encounter with a chorus girl. Once my eyes blink open again, I am disappointed to discover the firm's junior partner has joined the melee.

"Off cadging free lunches again, huh, Pops? This time with the local vermin of a canine nature," Miss Midnight Louise admonishes me.

If she really were my daughter, as she claims, she would

defer to my parental role and let me do the admonishing. Or . . . maybe not. Miss Midnight Louise does not take correction well at all. She is what they call liberated and I call impertinent to her elders.

"A guy has got to keep his energy up."

"For what? Naps?"

"Research has shown that the dude who naps lives longer to nap again." That comment does not quite come out right.

"You were not napping when you did that swan dive off the top of the so-called parking garage. You are drawing the public's attention to a lot of bodies of late. You could damage Midnight Investigations, Inc.'s reputation."

"You know I did my earlier body-discovery work for Ma Barker's clowder."

"Yes. I am also invited for lunch with them at the police substation from time to time, and get caught up on all the gossip then."

"*You* lunch on Big Macs and Red Lobster?"

"And Tastee Crème doughnuts," she adds in a *nyah-nyah-nyah-nyah* tone.

"I have never been invited. I am just asked to do the dirty work."

"Oh, come on. I have dipped into the trash containers at the Circle Ritz. Your Miss Temple is lavishing oysters and shrimp and sirloin beef tips on your Free-to-Be-Feline bowl."

"Yes, but it all has a certain odor of—" I cannot contain a shudder. "—FTBF."

"Yeah, there is a definite army green vibe to your roommate's health food of choice. Have you ever tried putting some of it in her half-used cereal boxes and forcing her to face the stuff first thing in the morning?"

"I would *never* subject my Miss Temple to such a dirty trick.

"Although, Louise . . . maybe it would banish Free-to-Be-Feline forever. I would have to make it look like Miss Temple had mixed up the bag and the box contents. That could be done if I woke her up earlier than usual in the morning with one of my purr-massage-love-rub sessions. . . .

"She would stumble into the kitchen half-asleep and—presto!—Free-to-Be-Feline in her bowl, with low-fat milk.

"No, I cannot do that to low-fat milk."

"Anyway, Pops, I am not here to discuss cuisine."

"No kidding. What harebrained scheme are you laying on me now?"

"We need to break into the coroner's office on Pinto Lane."

"What!? Are you crazy? Do not answer. That was a rhetorical question. Louise, the facility will be screwed down tighter than a rusty bolt with all these *Alien* nut jobs in town. Everybody from paparazzi to amateur bloggers wants to break in to eyeball and photograph The Hunk Who Fell to Earth. At the moment, he is more popular than Elvis. And that is going some in Las Vegas.

"Do they fret about me? Are they worried about my delicate limbs being broken, along with my shivs? Am I on their cell phone and camcorder films? No. I am just a dust mite in a media-mad world, a tiny Cinderfella at the ball. An unsung hero."

"Yeah, yeah. Fame is fleeting, also YouTube hits. I am telling you. This is serious. I was there when you fell—"

"You were? I did not see you rushing up to succor me."

"Hah. I was busy rushing up to the falling body once it hit the dirt, before any curious onlookers got a glimpse of it."

"So some dead human is more important than your supposed old man. I am *really* glad we are not related now."

"That is your unlikely story."

Louise can be merciless, but she is the female of the species. Bloodthirsty. Her mind is back on the corpse. She mews on. "I cannot say for sure—unless I inspect the body in the morgue. But . . ."

Females are ferocious hunters and killers, did I mention

that? Forget the cliché of them quailing at violence and mayhem.

"And . . . ," she says after a final pinprick of her claw into my shoulder just in case I am not paying enough attention. "I think the scars on this guy's back and sides were put there by the Cat Pack I led to defend the Synth from the two armed individuals in Darth Vader outfits at the Neon Nightmare, now defunct."

I catch my breath. What Miss Louise is calling defunct is not the Synth magicians' club, or the invading Darth Vaders from that recent meeting I was not privileged (or invited, I guess) to participate in. No, it is only the Neon Nightmare nightclub that is closed and defunct.

Louise does not know I was there much more recently with Miss Temple and Mr. Max, when my roommate's speculations made it clear that some of the Synth members and wannabes are, um, dead, possibly by the hand of Synth recruiter Cosimo Sparks, himself now slain by person or persons unknown.

So here I am being asked to consider that one of the two masked leaders and predators who fed on the Synth's thirst for revenge might now be dead at the morgue, his body bearing identifying marks of the Cat Pack attack on that night when Miss Louise and her minions swarmed to protect Miss Temple and divert attention from her undetected presence.

Whew. That is a lot of dead people, but then, Miss Temple's Table of Crime Elements is longer than a grocery list for a reality TV cooking show.

I sit back on the pillow of my most operative parts, stunned.

For months and years, I have been protecting my main gal and her associated humans against renegade magicians, IRA terrorists, possible mob remnants, and a psycho serial killer.

Now, it could be likely the secret malefactors at the top of the pyramid of crime are possibly from out of this world.

Can it be that I am dealing here with murder most extra-terrestrial?

Chapter 34

Law and Order: LVMPD

"What is the Circle Ritz these days?" Molina asked him the moment Matt identified himself on the phone. "The new home of the Hole-in-the-Wall Gang?"

He was confused, maybe because he'd been mentally planning an approach to his problem.

Molina relieved him of answering that seemingly irrelevant question as her voice on the phone answered for him. "Your inventive fiancée has been showing up at bizarre sites all over town, messing up crime scenes."

"Temple?"

"You think I'm talking about Lydia, the Tattooed Lady?"

"I've never met that entertaining individual, and don't hope to," Matt said, more confused than ever. He'd been too distracted to hear about any other crimes than the ones committed by Kathleen O'Connor.

Also, he was uneasy anyway about trying to pump Molina for information when he was secretly playing psycho cat-and-mouse with the most wanted suspect on her—and everybody's—unofficial Wanted Lists.

"Temple's trespassing on crime scenes? News to me."

"The significant other is always the last to know." Molina sounded dire. "A client of hers happens to own the crime scene property."

Matt obviously needed to be brought up to date on his fiancée's current events, but he wasn't going to let a homicide lieutenant give him the first spin on what was going on.

"I just called to see if I could make an appointment to talk to you about—"

"Don't tell me."

Had she somehow found out about his nightly 3 A.M. "sessions" at the Goliath Hotel?

"UFOs," her firm contralto boomed in his ear.

Curiouser and curiouser. "UFOs? No, I'm interested in another mythical Las Vegas apparition. Mobsters."

"Hie yourself over to the three new mob museums or, better yet, to the Crystal Phoenix or Gangsters Hotel and convene a flock of Fontanas."

"I'm not talking about the Beretta of brothers in the Fontana clan. They're as much for show as those mob museums popping up all over. But . . . I wondered how seriously mob their uncle, Macho Mario Fontana, was? Is."

"Before my day. Remember, I moved here from L.A. Are you serious?"

"I did say so. Aren't there a few leftover elements from the bad old days still bouncing around town?"

Molina's laugh was wary. "They're all over at the

Museum for Law Enforcement downtown, signing autographs."

"I am very serious." Matt was aggravated enough to sound like it. Serious and steamed. "Can we talk or not?"

"*Sheesh.* You Circle Ritz residents act like you have a private line to the police. If you're that serious, visit me at the office. You know where Metro headquarters is located now?"

"Sure, it's Temple's second-favorite Las Vegas site to point out on jaunts around the Strip."

"What's our girl's very favorite?"

"Grizzly Bahr's morgue on Pinto Lane. That innocuous street address just cracks her up. Says it sounds like a pony ride."

"Some days it is. That's where you ID'd your dead stepfather after someone sank him at the sinking-ship attraction. Is that what's got this new 'mob' fixation going?"

Matt sighed loudly enough so she'd hear him over the phone, then waited.

"All right. I agree that ugly incident had the whiff of an old-time whack job. Fifty minutes. My place. Just follow your fiancée's ruby red slippers to South Martin Luther King Boulevard. I'll have a visitor's ID ready for you."

The new headquarters, almost 400,000 square feet, had recently united departments housed in various leased facilities around town in two five-story blocks of dark gray stone with regimental square windows. It had reminded Matt of the supposedly impregnable Bastille stormed during the French Revolution.

Yet the soaring glass central structure had a slightly curved and raised roof that also reminded Matt of folded angel wings as he drove up to the main doors.

Tender little trees edging the parking lot resembled ar-

chitects' 3-D miniatures so prissily placed on model building sites. The mirrored central window-wall reflected the
cloudless blue sky common to Vegas. That made the solid
structure look like it was only a hollow gridwork on a
Hollywood backlot, one you could see right through.
Matt supposed that architectural "trick of light" was appropriate to a city built on illusion.

Matt parked the Jaguar near an oval of concrete holding the skimpy trees. He scanned the central glittering
plinth for the entry doors, watching the sky reflection
vanish as he got closer, until he met his reflection at a
door, then pushed through . . . and straight into a waiting Molina.

She was, as always, tall and plainly dressed and sardonic. "Fancy car," she said. "You sure you don't want
to valet-park it?" she joked.

"It's not mine—"

"This a confession?"

"It's a gift I'm not sure I'll keep."

She shook her head, causing her shiny brunet bob to
shimmer. Was Molina doing a Hillary Clinton and letting her businesslike chop cut grow out?

"Relax," she told him. "I know you're a syndicated
radio personality and all things pretty and perklike flow
your way."

"You think the car is pretty?"

"Gorgeous, but my Prius is greener. Mariah would
swoon over your Jaguar, though."

"Do teenage girls still swoon?"

"No, they text—dear Lord, how they text."

She started walking and he fell into step beside her
through a big modern space sprouting rows of sleek and
skinny gray-upholstered visitors' chairs. As they neared
the office area, there was chaos, there was crowding,
there was heat generated by computers and noisy phone
calls, like in a newsroom.

Molina shut a door on them both. They were boxed into a small but slick private office.

"You've got something new, too, don't you?" Matt asked. "Fancy private office instead of a cubbyhole."

"You betcha."

She sat in the desk chair, spun a quarter turn, and gestured at an angular guest chair. "Have a seat."

"This is big," he said, eyeing the horizontal file cabinets, a sideboard with a single-shot coffeemaker, a photo of Mariah in the uninspiring annual-school-photo style.

"Comparatively small, but mine own. It's new. It'll get that used look fast." Molina nodded at her computer, all screen and no visible tower. "So what do you want to know about mob remnants in Vegas?"

Matt started to answer, but she interrupted him.

"I should say, first, *why* do you want to know?"

"That's the key question. Why would some aging mobsters out of a Danny DeVito movie stalk my mom in Chicago? They ended up kidnapping and holding Temple's cat for ransom while we were in town last week."

Molina had leaned forward during his recital, resting her elbows on her desk and her chin on her fists. Matt doubted she'd fall into such an informal pose with anyone else, but it gave him a chance to suffer the concentrated effect of her truly electric blue eyes. Like his Jaguar, they were gorgeous. No wonder she was a mesmerizing cabaret singer on the side. He blinked and she drew back, either satisfied or, like him, surprised.

"Miss Barr mentioned that," she said. "You tell me more. Midnight Louie's fate was in question?" She'd resumed sardonic cop mode. "Should I send flowers?"

"Only catnip. The nappers, Benny 'the Viper' Bennedetto and Waldo 'the Weasel' Walker, were caught."

"You're describing a movie script, right? So what's with the cat?"

"He escaped the warehouse where they were holding

him. The hoods apparently had a falling out and beat each other senseless. The only sign that Louie had been there was the empty leopard-print carrier Temple had bought him."

"So we have Midnight Louie now at large in Chicago and living large? Is that hoping for too much?"

"He, uh, made his way back to my mother's apartment."

"Chicago is a big city."

"Louie's a big cat." Matt shifted in the chair. Visitors weren't expected to stay long anywhere here, and the Spartan seating assured that. "Look, Lieutenant. The thugs were mobsters on their last legs and pretty lame, but what they did to my mother was extreme. They followed her to her workplace and left threatening notes among her papers. They broke into her apartment and left notes on her pillow. She rooms with my college-age cousin, Krys, and was scared stiff her niece was in danger too.

"But the notes insisted she'd regret going to the police."

Now Molina had leaned far back in her chair, her eyes narrowed, a pen she'd picked up beating hushed time on her desktop. "What did they want?"

"A lockbox my late stepfather, Cliff Effinger, had left behind in Mom's old Chicago-style two-flat place."

"And somebody had killed Effinger here in a particularly torturous and grisly way. He must have mentioned the lockbox was with his ex-wife before he died."

"You'd think they could have let him live."

"You might. Not me. I'd think they'd consider him a loose end that they would see tied tight and sunk publicly enough to scare off anyone else interested in the contents of Effinger's lockbox."

"And my mother wasn't his ex-wife. They'd never divorced."

Molina put a finger to her lip. "Keep those personal facts to yourself. My first thought is that maybe you'd want to off Effinger to free your mother from a rotten marriage."

"Effinger had moved on to Vegas years before I came here. Besides, it took more than one person to do him in that way."

"True. Not that you don't have loyal groupies here in Vegas now. What was in the lockbox the Chicago hoods didn't get?"

"That's just it. Nothing much. Tax returns, probably doctored. An old high school yearbook, some school stuff a mother would have saved."

"Speaking of mothers, why did yours get mixed up with a rotter like Cliff Effinger?"

"He came from the same neighborhood. I was heading off to preschool and you couldn't have single mothers in my Polish Catholic neighborhood then unless they were widows."

"Oh." Molina sat back. She was a single mother too.

"That wasn't a problem, with you?" Matt asked. "You and Mariah, I mean? You grew up in L.A."

"Yeah. Latino Catholic community." When Matt tilted his head, wanting more, she delivered. "My mother was like your mother. Unwed. I always fantasized my father was Paul Newman."

"The blue eyes."

"He sure wasn't Latino. When she married, she made sure my stepdaddy was."

Matt pulled out his cell phone and held up a photo. "Mom just got married again. Here in Vegas last weekend."

Molina took the phone. "That's a very familiar-looking wedding party . . . you, Temple Barr, Electra Lark as justice of the peace. Even Midnight Louie present and accounted for. The groom looks like a nice guy, but if the blond woman in the middle is your mom, she looks like your slightly older sister."

Matt took the phone back to survey the shot. "Louie was ring-bearer. Mom was very young when she had me. 'And naïve' is the expression."

"Not my problem," Molina said. "I was old enough to know better and protect myself, but it didn't work." She sat back again. "Easy for me, I just got the hell out of Dodge and changed jobs and locations. Lots of cops get divorced."

"Being a single mother can't ever be easy."

"Easy in that I was too old to be shamed with the 'unwed mother' label, and I was pretty distant from my family by then anyway."

"Yeah. Mom and me were the odd ones out too."

"Thing is, I was just old enough that I got to babysit all six of my younger stepsisters and brothers from the time I was practically a toddler myself."

"I would have loved to be 'lost' among a family of other children."

"Try it before you convert." Molina tapped a folder on her desk. "Back to the undying rumors of the mob. So you and Temple Barr are now the chaperones of this interesting treasure chest of Effinger's?"

Matt hesitated, not sure how much he wanted to reveal. Certainly, talk of the Synth and Ophiuchus would get him laughed out of Molina's spanking new office and destroy this new personal rapport over their lives as bastard kids, an echo of his recent sessions at the Goliath.

Molina wasn't lingering on personal revelations anyway. "Aren't you two setting yourselves up to get the unfriendly attention Effinger and your mom got?"

"That hadn't occurred to me."

"If there is anything suspicious going on in your family link to Effinger, it always defaults back to Vegas, where you and Temple Barr and even that annoying cat live. That should have been the first thing on your mind."

It would have been, Matt thought, if he hadn't been distracted by becoming the sole target, he hoped, for the unfriendly attentions of Kathleen O'Connor.

Could the mob or any undying remnant really be any worse?

Chapter 35

Black Ops

If anybody had told me I would be playing the role of co-cat burglar with my maybe-baby Miss Midnight Louise in order to break into the Metro morgue ... well, I would have taken them off at the anklebones, or hocks, depending on the species.

We have interrupted our tour of the outer limits of a low municipal building on the southern fringe of Downtown, where the nightly light show is bright. Here are silence and shadow.

Morgues tend to be sedate sites, and the residents even more so.

Still, this is a morgue in a city teeming with celebrities and paparazzi. Every window is shuttered and locked tight, and the entry door requires checking in and ID. The only "ID" me and Miss Louise could ever have is that brand name of medically approved canned pet food only the terminally ill would deign to touch with a pooper scooper.

The warm Las Vegas night seems to have been put to bed early around this place. I led the perimeter search and now we are sitting by the parking lot door planning our next move.

At least this is one occasion on which the know-it-all Miss Louise has not a clue.

"You admit," she tells me, "you have never been inside the morgue."

"But I have often been on very close terms with individuals destined for the morgue."

She sniffs. "I was closer than you to the current victim under discussion."

"My dear girl, the dead man—or whatever species, domestic or feral alien—and I fell ten stories together. That betokens a closeness a mere postmortem sniff cannot match."

"Boots on the ground count more than aerial displays, Daddy-O. I was first to reach the body and the first to detect those 'unusual cryptic marks' all the tabloids are making a front-page fuss about. Laughable. Even bad journalism has slipped to the level of fish wrappings."

"You simply recognized the Cat Pack's handiwork. That was no leap of brain power. Some commentators have come closer to the truth."

"*Chupacabra* tracks!" Louise's longish jet-black best coat is having an electric static hair attack, she is so outraged. "These dumbskulls are too blind to see the obvious."

"Look at it their way, Louise. They have already been conditioned to think that the dead guy fell out of the sky or at least a revolving high-rise restaurant-to-be. Who would suspect that an avenging pack of domestic cats would have scratched him up one side and down the other, and his partner-in-crime too, and disarmed them both?"

"The Cat Pack is not composed of domestic cats," she growls. "We are all feral and semiferal, except for the one indoor lounge lizard of our acquaintance, you. And you are not the boss of us. Ma Barker is."

"And you are a floating member, as am I. You do your lounge lizarding under a tanning bed by the Crystal Phoenix pool, so that exempts you from true feral status. Whatever the fine points, you all need a link to the ruling human class, and I am the expert at that."

"You mean the *dominant* race. Cats rule—dogs just wish they did, and people are fooling themselves."

"Now is no time to talk politics. I am thinking up a plan to storm this jail of the dead and get a good look at the ancient alien."

"My testimony is not good enough?"

"I see the big picture, Louise. That is my job. Now, here is the plan. We need to stake out the back entrance and make like we rode in on a Black Maria."

"A Black Maria? What kind of jimsonweed have you been masticating now? You always were of the slacker generation."

"That is what meat wagons were called back in the day when the classic detectives walked the mean streets."

"As I recall, we hitched a ride on a meat wagon a while back during one of your so-called self-assigned cases."

"That was a genuine meat wagon, and that is one place where the mob still operates in Vegas, selling illegal meat."

"That is not very glamorous. I do not see a revival of the *Godfather* movies on that subject forthcoming soon."

"You gotta admit there is a gore quotient."

"So is there inside. This expedition is not a crabcake walk."

"It will be." I say, "All we have to do is slip under the next incoming deceased's gurney and keep pace with it. Morgue attendants have a lot to do at above-the-waist level, which is always a boon to us."

"But we need to see a body already in the morgue. It will be in a freezer. Those have one-way doors."

"A trifling detail, Louise. That is why there are two of us. One to dare the frigid freezer and one to keep watch outside, ready to release the other."

"Who does what?"

"We will see when we get in."

At that moment, we hear the low peeling sound of a Band-Aid being ripped off. Tires turning onto sandy asphalt. We duck behind the nearest thicket of pampas grass.

Sure enough, a big black van, all its windows blacked out, is grinding our way, its headlights poking nova-sized holes in the night. I feel my eyes switch to built-in infrared night vision mode. No bulky headgear for yours truly.

Las Vegas is one of the few metropolitan areas where we still have a "coroner" as opposed to a "medical examiner." As far as I can see, dead is dead and one title will do as well as the other to deal with it.

Out of the now-stopped vehicle comes the clatter of a collapsed-for-travel gurney being uncollapsed.

It is a chilling sound. This process smacks of a ritual, and humans and dogs are big on those. Our kind is so much more independent, which implies we need no care, and are likely to retreat on our own to some elephant graveyard to fade away never to be found. Of course, if we are lucky enough to have a human base, we too will benefit from last rites and memorializing.

I am sure my Miss Temple would provide some suitable stately urn if—Bast forbid!—I should ever lick my last flake of koi. Perhaps something classic in lapis lazuli stone, or no—malachite. That is green to match my eyes.

"Old dude!" Louise whacks my whiskers. "It is time to do the limbo under the dead departed's skateboard. Hustle."

"That is 'dear' departed, Louise." I manage to get in one last jab, verbal and physical, before we whisk into place and atune our slowest trot to the pace of the gurney. These workers are wasting no time and muffling no noise. I guess their passengers cannot complain of a bumpy ride. I could complain of a distinct odor of decay, but it is not my place.

Momentarily blinded once we hit the fluorescent lights of the receiving area, we are happy to stop with the gurney.

It is hard to describe the condition of the air inside a morgue. Of course, Louise and I are more fitted to detecting undertones and overtones, to analyzing stages of decay, than your usual human.

But there is the dominant whiff of Febreze to overcome. Which, I find, tends to make me want to . . . sneeze!

Catastrophe!

I feel Louise holding her breath next to me to resist the same overpowering instinct. At least the people are talking.

"Log in and then store it in the decaying-body room. Metro says this guy was not found for a while."

Louise is shaking her head at me. We both realize the decaying-body room is likely to be colder, less often visited, and a really bad place to get locked in. I mean, our deepest instincts are to prefer fresh kill. Not that we exercise them much these days, each having our own private chef.

I must admit that Louise benefits from the personal attentions of Chef Song and his palette of Asian-infusion menu items at the Crystal Phoenix (the little suck-up) and my Miss Temple, being a working woman, can be a bit cavalier about her menu planning.

We trot under the belly of the beast as its wheels start spinning and peel off when we spot a large stainless steel trash can. Not ideal cover, because it reflects us, but black is a very fine color because it shows up in almost any room you can think of.

We immediately eel around the circular trash can into a room of tables surrounded by four lightweight chairs. *Hmm.* Is this place a morgue or a bridge club?

In fact, I become almost hypnotized by the blaring fluorescent lights and the stainless steel cabinet fronts that stand in a U-shaped row like robotic servers on parade.

Snack dispensers. Louise has made a tour from the other side and we meet in the middle.

"Awesome," she says. "I must admire these people for sustaining such a prodigious appetite in the face of daily death. Although it is all junk calories."

"Cheetos? That is dairy protein. You know how we like our milk. Pepperoni 'n' cheddar. That is dairy *and* protein."

"Pretzels?" Louise's tone is withering.

"Ah, salt is the saline solution that is the staff of life, along with, uh, wheat."

"Gluten." She glowers. "High-fructose corn syrup."

"Fiber. Low, er, sodium."

We have faced off over this bounty we do not have time to break into.

Louise nods as sagaciously as a babe of her type can. "If we can contemplate breaking into the fast-food automat, we can crack any autopsy cabinet in the place. Do you think they will make it easy for us and have drawers?"

"One can only hope, Louise."

Of course, identifying one dead dude among so many is a challenge. I somehow think our ancient alien will not be in any old drawer, so we tour the rooms off the main autopsy area.

"Where would Grizzly Bahr stash a prime candidate for illegal paparazzi snapshots?" I ask.

Midnight Louise sits down, curls her flurry tail around her neat forefeet and pretends to meditate like Bast. "I would mislabel the most desirable exhibit."

So. Looking for "ancient alien" on stainless steel drawers as if they were file cabinets is not likely to be successful.

Suddenly, Louise lifts her head. "Idiots!"

People certainly are.

"We have overlooked the obvious," Louise announces without giving me a hint of what she is referring to.

"Obviously. And that is—?"

"Where do you hide a leaf?" she asks.

"In a forest. Father Brown, the priest-detective I have cited before, figured that out before your one-thousandth great-grandmama was born."

"Where do you hide an alien being fallen to earth?"

"Under . . . oddities?" I hazard.

"Under . . . suspected suicides?"

"It is true that there was not a mark on him, except ours, and no Cat Pack attacks are fatal. Is there a suicides room?"

"There should be, in Las Vegas," she says.

"Yes, people win, and most people lose, and lose and lose. I believe," I decree, "I would file him under 'Anonymous.'"

That is how we locate the one unlabeled room. We sit upon an empty autopsy table—excellent construction, sturdy stainless steel with the look of those modern recto-linear sinks all the best home redos feature these days, almost an old Roman grandeur to them. I feel quite importantly supported by a pedestal, always a flattering position for my breed, from Bast on down.

Together, we leap, and push open a door that takes the force of a human palm in ordinary circumstances.

We are in! And, more important, the door has sprung wide and is not creeping closed again, as in all the best summer slasher movies.

We loft up in tandem to view the sole corpse occupying this unlabeled room. Talk about anonymous.

"He looks perfectly human, almost alive," Louise comments reverently.

"They did a good job. The broken limbs are straightened to fit the table, the Y-incision in the torso is neatly sewed up, and the cranial sawing looks almost like a hippie headband."

"A sign of respect and excellent workmanship."

"He might become a museum exhibit ultimately."

"Not so good," Louise says, wrinkling her nose.

"They can freeze-dry him. No odor."

"It is not that. Observe the faint white lines to the sides of his bronzed torso and legs."

"Almost like the scars of a wire whip."

"Or . . . these." Louise lifts the spread four shivs of her right mitt.

"Our slashes tend to be a bit ragged."

"These wounds are healed," she points out (quite literally, running her fanned ninja knives through the air just above the rib scars). "I would like to see the back."

"Not possible without human cooperation. This dude must weigh one-eighty. Could this man have contracted the Cat Pack slashes here in Las Vegas and still be from outer space?"

"Possibly. What do you think of him?" she asks.

"He does have an exotic look."

"More of a human model, say a romance novel cover hero."

"His hair is oddly slicked down close to his skull for that," I say. "I have heard my Miss Temple quote Mr. Grizzly Bahr, our esteemed coroner, that faces relax in death so that the features may seem entirely alien."

Louise pats his cold dead face with one velvet-soft mitt. "Poor mystery man. I have the oddest feeling that I have seen him somewhere, but that is not likely."

In Las Vegas, the unlikely is always possible.

Chapter 36

Stunt Double

Temple sat in her condo in a funk as she grazed through the morning paper, viewing what Silas T. Farnum hath wrought.

She was probably the last person at the Circle Ritz who subscribed to the local paper. Staring at that day's "second front" with its slightly out-of-register color photos of the parking lot crowd wasn't the kind of promotion she'd want to get even a not-quite client. It was a sea of Spock ears and tinfoil hats.

She was even in one pic, caught in the act of turning Rens over to his happy owner. Temple wondered if Penny could recognize photos of herself. Or see herself in the mirror even. Just then, Louie skittered through the living area from the second bathroom litter box, his tail fluffed to radiator-brush size. He dashed across the glass cocktail table, claws razoring right through the opinion pages and classifieds section, a bizarre marriage in modern journalism, and raced on into the bedroom.

"Louie! Slow down, Mr. Black the Ripper." Cats did that, suddenly tore through the house as if they'd gotten a moth in their ears or laid a major stinky in the litter box.

Temple bent to retrieve the scattered papers, thinking she should save the savaged second section, half-client or no half-client, and then stared at the paper's yet-unread front page.

DEAD "ALIEN ASTRONAUT" HAS CLASSIC JUNGLE TEMPLE FEATURES, read the headline on the story below the fold. A sketch purported to be "obtained" by a freelancer was obviously based on smartphone shots caught on the run when the body first fell. Next to it was a photo of a purported "alien astronaut" from a Mayan temple. Temple squinted at the image—it did look like "air hoses" were coming from his head, and the figure was tilted at the angle of astronauts leaving Earth's gravity.

This whole mess made "good print" and YouTube these days. She turned to the story's "jump" to make sure no one had mentioned her name, and there was Farnum in a photo, beaming like he'd just ballooned into Oz.

Temple's mind was on a mad, mad, mad merry-go-round.

She had no idea how she'd answered one phone call and was now involved with a notorious site of double murder, or at least of double body-dumping.

Not to mention a "ghost" hotel-casino building that was expected to attract hordes of customers by being invisible.

Or how Las Vegas's mythical "mob" and "Area 51 alien" presence had met on one scruffy lot owned by one dapper oddball.

She ran the last few days past her mental movie screen. Standing on that hard-packed sand and watching Silas T.'s revolving spaceship restaurant appear and disappear ten stories up.

Standing on that same spot with the sand now burning in broad daylight and trying to explain herself and Farnum and his high-tech magic act to Molina.

The awful moment when the actual plastic and canvas that hid the real construction came billowing down in slow-motion, carrying one bronzed, naked male human body and a black feline figure that was twisting down like a furry screwdriver to disappear near a ground-level swell and strut out like a stunt cat when next seen again.

Cats could walk away from falls from extraordinary heights.

Dead men couldn't.

Temple pictured the corpse on Molina's cell phone. One hesitated to stare at naked dead men, or women. Well, one would if one was not a person professionally charged with dealing with such bare facts of life and death.

But those faint pale lines, the so-called alien scars, could have been made by wire. She was sure Grizzly Bahr, no relation, had considered that possibility. Bundled in a sheet and wire for transport and then left naked at the top of the building. Why not? Great place to stash a body, in a hidden edifice.

Yet, had it been so precariously placed that a misstep by a house cat had given the game away, not any nearby perpetrator?

Somebody had "dropped" bodies there for some reason, which would mean somebody wanted Farnum's project to be the hot public potato it now was.

So was Farnum the instigator or the victim, the perp or the target, of the dead men?

Temple turned to the sensational front page. You'd think the *Review-Journal* had morphed into the *Crackpot Gazette*.

She studied the stone figure. Then looked at the sketch. She attired Las Vegas Man in Maya Man's headdress and gear. A definite resemblance, but in the features and the profile, not the context.

Omigod! Penny and Rens. Facial features not registering, blurring out, needing . . . context. Clues. She sent newspaper sections flying as she frantically patted down her cocktail table top for the slim outline of a smartphone.

Search and . . . seized!

She ignored contact groups labeled "Friends" and "Family" and went to one named "Iffy." She checked her faithful wristwatch with the second hand. *Please, please, please be in.*

"Molina," came the familiar bark.

Yes! Good doggie, reliable doggie.

"I need to see the body."

"Which body of the two in question are you hankering to view?"

"The ancient alien."

"Of course. He's off-limits to the public, the press, even the President of the United States."

"*They* wouldn't be able to help ID him."

"And you are?"

"I think I know him from somewhere."

"Won't happen, even if you met him on Mars during your lunch break."

"I'm dead serious. I need to look at him out of context, not in it. I have temporary prosopagnosia."

"I don't care if you have terminal halitosis. That body is on lockdown."

"Grizzly Bahr would let me in. I know he would."

"Am I to infer that he has performed some highly unprofessional courtesies for you before?"

"Uh . . . no. I just suspect he would, like I suspect I know the body. I mean the dead man. I wouldn't know his body, since I hardly looked at it on your cell phone, and of course I haven't seen any naked strange men. Or strange naked men. Recently. Ever. But I didn't really see his face. That's what I think I subconsciously recognized. The face. But the context temporarily blinded me."

Molina suddenly snapped at someone nearby, "Just leave the reports.

"I'll call the coroner," she told Temple. "If Bahr okays it, you're in. I'll let you know later. Much later. Some of us work on actual cases as a career, not a hobby."

Temple hung up with a smile.

Molina was going to find out that Temple and crusty ole Grizzly Bahr had an affinity that went a lot further than a last name that sounded the same.

Chapter 37

Bad News Bearer

"Van von Rhine."

The voice on the phone was as smooth and controlled as its owner's platinum-blond French twist. Temple knew she was also going to have to get Van von Rhine's fancy French panties into a double-pretzel twist pretty soon.

"Hi, Van. It's your PR consultant en route to the Phoenix. I've got to talk to you immediately about a nasty public relations turn of events that so far is known only to me, the Metro Police, and the coroner."

"It involves our hotel-casino?"

"Peripherally."

"What on earth—?"

"It's not on Earth anymore. It's very alien territory."

"Tell me this has nothing to do with that UFO fiasco

on Paradise. Talk about bad publicity for the entire Strip."

"I'll tell you that I'm not willing to commit any more info to the cell phone towers. Don't talk to strangers with media credentials until I get there."

"Now I'm really alarmed. I'll call Nicky."

"No."

"No?"

"No. We need to be forewarned and forearmed before anybody else hears this, and everybody else will, all too soon."

"Drive fast," Van said before signing off, sounding terse.

Temple buzzed the Miata around any lagging traffic, although the Strip was typically a slow-flowing river of hot metal. Temple always felt like Nancy Drew in her roadster in the small convertible. Now she raced like Nancy on a hot crime trail.

"Where's the fire?" the Phoenix's parking valet asked as her little red car sped up to the dazzling glass-and-mirror entry canopy.

"Hi, Wayne. Emergency meet inside. Put her someplace in the shade to cool down."

"Sure thing, Miss Barr."

Crystal Phoenix parking valets were attired like bellboys from a Fred Astaire and Ginger Rogers '30s movie and had the same pep.

Temple dashed inside.

"Whoa!" She ran into—literally—one of the Fontana brothers.

"You're breaking the sound barrier," he commented.

"No time to say hello-goodbye, I'm late," she threw behind her, White Rabbit–style. She didn't even have time to ascertain whether she'd nearly slammed into Eduardo, Giuseppe, Rico, Ernesto, Julio, Armando, or Emilio. She knew it wasn't Nicky, Aldo, or Ralph.

Her toe on its one-inch platform sole (she would go no higher, not even for precious stature) tapped the marble floor in front of the elevators until a set of doors opened.

Temple eeled past the departing passengers and punched the button to the top floor before the elevator had time to change gears and rise instead of sink. And she punched the CLOSE DOORS button on six falling faces of tourists left behind this trip.

Inside, Temple took floor orders from the handful of people who'd slipped in with her and punched them in, toes tapping in rebuke. The other riders got the message. They stayed clear and haunted the elevator doors so they could squeeze out as soon as the car arrived at their floor.

There were times when being petite concentrated a surge of pure energy.

Van's male assistant was standing by the inner office door to whisk it open while handing her a glass of Crystal Light—her favorite beverage, but one not served at the Crystal Phoenix.

Temple came to a stop at Van's glass-and-chrome desk and slung her tote bag to the floor. "I'm going to be going to the morgue to identify a body."

Van, already as pale as the vanilla she was named after, stood behind her desk, caught up in the drama. "Oh, no. Not anybody we know?"

Temple nodded.

"Not anybody we love?"

Temple shook her head, still trying to catch her breath. "Somebody we know and don't love, which is worse."

Van was perplexed. "How can that be worse?"

"It's a murder victim, and I, for one, found him a murder-deserving individual. We could be suspects."

Van sat in her channeled white leather executive chair. "Us? All? Suspects?"

"Especially the family Fontana."

Van shook her head and exhaled a hushed "*Nooo.*" She looked up. "All right, what can we do about it?"

"You don't want to know who the victim is?"

"I'm sure you'll tell me when *you* sit down and catch your breath."

"Santiago," Temple said as she did so, "the Phoenix's Chunnel of Crime designer, personally hired by your husband, Nicky, and suspect for the Cosimo Sparks murder in that very locale."

"Santiago? Was he still hanging around town?"

"Evidently. That international architectural superstar seemed phony from the get-go. He and Sparks may have planned some shady scheme that kept Santiago here, even under suspicion."

"The police didn't have enough evidence to hold him. Oh, if only he'd skedaddled out of the country as fast as he could, Temple! We didn't have to murder him, we fired him. Given his larger-than-life personality, I'm sure his murder would be spec-tac-u-lar."

"It was. He's tabloid news now."

Van looked puzzled. "Nothing in town has been tabloid headlines lately except that loony UFO dustup on Paradise . . . . Oh, no!" Van thumped a fist on her glass desktop. "You're telling me the purported ancient astronaut deposited on ground zero at that loopy UFO project on Paradise was *our* Santiago? How can you ID him? Wasn't that man nude?"

"I assume Santiago was capable of that state."

"And why was he there?"

"He was consulting on the UFO project."

"Of course. His kind of scam." Van rested her paler face on her pale hand. "We've taken his name off all the publicity for the Phoenix–Gangsters Chunnel of Crime once he was suspected of murder. Isn't that enough?"

"I'm afraid people—and especially media people—will remember what, and who, brought him to Las Vegas. We need to create a short but sufficiently vague press release saying Santiago had consulted on remodeling projects at the Crystal Phoenix but that position is over and so was all contact with him."

Van nodded through Temple's presentation, still stunned.

"And, Van, luckily I'm in place to control the Phoenix link from the other end too."

"What other end, Temple?"

"Ah, the place on Paradise."

"You don't have anything to do with that UFO nuttiness?"

"Don't I wish."

"You do! What would make you take on such a flaky client? A supposedly invisible building with a spaceship restaurant on the top?"

"I didn't really take it on. Officially. I had just started talks with Deja View Associates when the first corpse on the site was found."

"What?" Van was livid with shock, almost as livid as . . . a corpse.

"The death didn't happen there," Temple assured her. "The police are pretty sure. The site was just used as a body dump."

"'Pretty sure'? 'Just used as a body dump'? And now a *second* body has been dumped, one associated with the Phoenix. I'm not at all happy about that, Temple."

Van was amping up her Ice Queen act. She ran a Strip hotel-casino and could take the heat . . . and dish it out in that icy *Devil Wears Prada* fashion Meryl Streep had mastered for the film.

"I understand, Van. That's why I have Plan B."

"What was Plan A? That whizzed past me."

"The press release. Believe me, the Area Fifty-four concept and site are so wacky that they'll get all the ink and pixels and mass digital recordings. What I need to know is how much background research you did on Santiago after Nicky hired him."

"Temple, you think I'd second-guess my devoted husband and the hotel owner like that?"

"Absolutely. I would. Nicky is a doll and sharp as a nail gun, but he can get overenthusiastic about over-the-top schemes. He thinks that Fontana charm will smooth all roads to Rome."

Van leaned forward to consult her sleek computer screen. She was Apple all the way. "What do you want to know?"

"Santiago wasn't born an international phenom. Where'd he come from?"

"This was tough to find out. My father was a European hotel manager, so I met many hotel owners as a child. They form a network through the major cities of the world. Luckily, Santiago had consulted for the Ritz-Carlton in his home city before he became internationally known."

"His doing Vegas projects isn't that far-fetched," Temple said, "though I don't understand why he was still hanging around the Strip after being tainted by the Cosimo Sparks murder."

"A crime uncovered on our premises," Van reminded her. "Was that another 'body dump' I shouldn't worry about?"

"We're lucky that the Crystal Phoenix is too classy to hold public attention. Silas T. Farnum with his invisible hotel and revolving spaceship restaurant makes much better copy. Ordinarily, Santiago's working for Farnum wouldn't be that strange. Santiago did have a strong reputation in immersive entertainment and cutting-edge technology and special effects. It was his specialty."

"Not in the beginning." Van looked up from her screen. "He actually had a last, middle, and first name, although he hadn't used it in decades. Carlos MacCarthy. *M-a-c,* not *M-c.* That last name's unusual spelling made it easier to track."

"His father was Irish? Maybe . . ."

"Maybe what? There are many mixed Latino-Irish names in South America. Ireland's always been so poor, her citizens emigrated to survive or thrive."

"Maybe Santiago took a 'city' name because he wanted to hide his origins."

"I'm sure it was a career decision," Van said. "Look at John Denver and Rick Springfield. They needed something more memorable."

"And those two had real last names that were a mouthful. Although 'MacCarthy' would be an awkward surname, given Santiago's strong Central and South American looks." Particularly, Temple thought to herself, if the father had been devoted to the IRA and Irish liberty. "Thanks for the info, Van, and stay cool," Temple told her. "I have the inside track with the police on this. In fact, I'll probably be seeing Lieutenant Molina later."

Van sighed and kicked off her cream patent leather Cole Haans under her glass-topped desk. "Molina? That's impressive. Go to it, then."

Temple left, considering what had always seemed likely: Santiago may have been one of Kathleen O'Connor's South American sources of funds for the IRA back in the day. Maybe, though, he hadn't been the usual rich seducee. Maybe he'd been a bankroller who knew about the hidden Las Vegas stash because he'd been a political partner.

There were still people in Ireland who deserved reparations for lives lost in the Troubles. An IRA fanatic might want that money to go to them.

So . . . had Kitty the Cutter been the *other* Darth Vader at the Neon Nightmare during Temple's inadvertent but memorable visit?

Chapter 38

Body Double

"I've never thought of the coroner's office as open twenty-four/seven, like the casinos," Temple said when she met Lieutenant Molina at the rear entrance where the bodies came in.

"Death doesn't take a holiday," Molina answered, looking down disapprovingly at Temple's Jessica Simpson high heels. "Those will echo in there."

"As if the dead would complain. We all don't need to sneak around on moccasins and rubber soles."

"You manage to sneak around plenty." Molina eyed the area. The coroner's van was parked outside the garage area. "It's the late afternoon shift change. Let's get inside before some paparazzo decides our visit is worth covering."

Molina punched in a security code at a high-enough

position that her body concealed the entry number from Temple . . . and any lurking paparazzi bearing infrared cameras equipped with long lenses.

Once the women were inside, fluorescent lights turned both their skins slightly green. Temple assumed she had the more ghoulish pallor. Molina's olive complexion was harder to tint.

Molina was wearing one of her summer khaki pantsuits. Temple wondered why beige colors looked so dull and institutional on Molina and so casual and dreamy on Matt. This was an odd comparison to make in a morgue. It had definitely been too long between assignations, Temple thought, if engaged people could accomplish anything that sounded so naughty.

Or maybe her mind was already trying to go anywhere else than here. It was the casual gore of the place that got to her. A white-coated worker slicing a brain into cold-cut thinness on a lab table that would have looked at home in a high school biology lab. A naked body parked on a seemingly abandoned gurney in a hall.

She was sure that the alien astronaut guy would not be in open sight.

"Here you are," the coroner greeted them, as if they'd gotten lost already. "Lieutenant. Miss Barr. You'll have to excuse my appearance. I've just returned from dinner at the Monte Carlo. What a savory rack of lamb."

The appearance he apologized for was a navy linen sports coat and old school tie glimpsed under his wrinkled white lab coat. Dr. Graham Bahr had a curling head of whitened black hair with werewolf eyebrows to match, but it was his robust weight, imposing height, and sometimes his temperament that gave him the "Grizzly" nickname.

"I imagine you two have no time to waste in viewing our current 'savory rack of lamb,' eh? An unlikely pair," he added.

Molina was gathering herself to take offense when Temple realized where his focus was: on her feet. She hurried to answer his comment.

"Thanks. Your orange and burgundy snakeskin boots really rock that navy coat and tie."

Molina frowned. "Down is the last place I'd look in medical examiners' facilities," she said. "How long have you worn cowboy boots?"

"Forever, Lieutenant. I guess my dazzling pearly whites distract visitors from my footwear."

His teeth, and Molina's, were probably the only unwhitened choppers in Las Vegas. Everybody Temple's age used a whitening toothpaste at least, even Matt.

That thought spurred another one. "What color are the teeth of the ancient astronaut?" she asked.

"Not ancient," Grizzly said with a grin, "but they are naturally whiter than most. I suppose you girls are champing at the bit to see my hunky mystery man."

"I'd appreciate you using the honorific, Doctor." Molina was not smiling.

"Now, are our titles really 'honorifics,' Lieutenant? I'm not too sure. More like horrorifics in my field. Anyway, come with me; we keep our alien visitor in a special room, the celebrity suite, if you will."

Temple was counting on Febreze to cover any scent of decay, but also wished she'd put some Mentholatum near her nostrils. She tried to walk on her soles to mute any high-heel clatter, but Bahr's boot heels made enough noise for both of them.

Molina strode beside him, leaving Temple trailing two tall people like a child.

Huh! She was the one who might be able to fill in the blanks on their many official forms.

The facility was eerily quiet, apparently running on a skeleton crew. One siren or phone call could stir up staff like a stick energizes an anthill, she was sure.

"Here's the bunker." Bahr pushed through an unmarked steel door and hit the inside light switch. The warming fluorescent tubes spotlighted a man wearing only the incision marks around his forehead and skull and the Y-incision on his torso.

You couldn't help but think of Frankenstein's monster as depicted in a slew of films. At least Temple couldn't. She was glad she was here to look at a face, not a fig leaf.

And maybe she didn't want to look it in the eyes either.

It. Already she'd objectified the victim in her mind, and emotions. If truly alien, maybe it was an "it." If not, it was a "him." A him she thought she could recognize. What had she been thinking? The people she knew were animated, and that made recognition a whole different task.

"Five-ten," Molina said, bringing the tension down to the facts on a driver's license, which this guy certainly had not been carrying. "Maybe one-eighty or -ninety. Brown/brown. Skin tone natural?"

"Sort of, Lieutenant. The skin is naturally dark, with added self-tanner. What about this individual does Miss Barr think she might recognize?"

"Dr. Bahr!" Temple was taking offense now. "Just the face, of course."

"Of course," he said, chuckling.

Temple walked around the top of the stainless steel gurney, unable to avoid seeing the back-of-the-head incision that had exposed the now-missing brain.

The Scarecrow from *The Wizard of Oz* film crooned, *If I only had a brain . . .* , in her head. In her brain.

She stepped away from the table. Dr. Bahr's and Lieutenant Molina's faces looked serious and seriously scary in the harsh light. Did hers?

She tried to think like a computer image, tilted her head to imagine the man vertical. To see the slicked-back black hair clinging to the skull over the incision. It would fall all the way to his collar-top if he wore a shirt and suit coat.

If he were tilted up a bit at an ancient astronaut angle, he would have the strong brow bone and nose of the carved temple warrior. Those genes had not died out in Central and South America, despite the best efforts of the conquering Spanish explorers many centuries before. Empire had always been about genocide.

Temple walked the length of the body, looked back up to the face with its staring dark eyes that reflected fluorescent tubes.

Can you see a face, and not recognize it again? Yes, if you have prosopagnosia. But if you have mental prosopagnosia? She eyed the hands and nails, the hair, the neck; she tilted the whole man upright and clothed him in a great suit to wear for his funeral. Wait. One borrowed from a Fontana brother.

Because that was the vibe her subconscious associated with this man, not some ancient warrior culture. Something primitive, predatory even, but clothed in complete modernity, down to his buffed fingernails and that razor-cut nape-line of his hair. Smooth, slick. Smart, glib.

"He's from an ancient South American line, all right," Temple told the doctor and police lieutenant. "This is the world-renowned conceptual architect who came to Las Vegas to dream up special projects around the Strip. He was even a consultant on Silas T. Farnum's decidedly third-class construction site."

"You're saying he was somebody important?" Molina asked.

"*He* thought so. He goes by one name, like Cher or Madonna. He's Santiago." Temple was as stunned she was right as they were.

Chapter 39

Murder Ménage II: Naked Came the Clue

Temple called a meeting of the Murder Ménage that evening.

Max purposely arrived late for the meeting.

He wanted the lovebirds to have a chance to establish their couplehood before he intruded on it. He wanted to be clearly the "outsider." Creative consultant, say. This was purely professional.

When Temple opened the condo door to his knock— ringing the doorbell was too akin to the unwanted solicitor—Midnight Louie uttered the first word of welcome as he weaved protectively around Temple's calves.

Correction: The couple was already a triumvirate. He was the fourth corner of a quadrangle. Temporarily.

"This is starting to feel like a three-person poker game," Temple said when she'd seated Max across from

Matt Devine at the round dining table on one side of the main living room.

"What's up?" Max asked as he sat. Unwanted snap-shots of memory from the time he'd lived here with Temple clashed in his mind, and he could hear majestic strains of Vangelis echoing from the unique barreled ceiling.

He kept his head down and his expression blank. Only Max's amnesia made it tolerable for them to gather in such a cozy, private way at all.

"I thought you two should know what I and Molina know," Temple began.

The men exchanged glances, Matt looking edgy and a tad guilty, which was the way Max felt. Guilt? What was that about with Devine? Max would have to figure it out later.

"Look, guys," Temple said, "I've got the most shocking information. It's like being hit by a . . . death ray from Jupiter. I've ID'd the 'ancient astronaut' body from the construction site on Paradise for the police," she announced, sitting back to receive accolades.

Matt leaned forward with a frown. "Temple, I thought you were distancing yourself from that crackpot developer guy with the invisible building."

"So the dead guy is a crackpot developer?" Max asked.

"No," Temple said, sighing. "That's Silas T. Farnum, who wanted to hire me to PR the project. The ancient alien abductee who fell back to Earth in a flash of UFO fire is . . ."

"Don't milk it too long," Max warned.

". . . Santiago."

She waited for applause, but got silence.

"This is big, guys. Santiago is the South American architect-cum-showman who redid the 'immersive' Chunnel of Crime attraction connecting Gangsters and the Crystal Phoenix Hotels."

"So you provided the police with the right name for the most notorious corpse in Vegas?" Max wondered. "Didn't this Santiago have links to the bizarre murder victim in formal dress found in the underground safe?"

"Yes, and yes, that is a bizarre scenario," Temple said. "Cosimo Sparks, that dead man in the safe, was also the head magician who was running the Synth," she added for Matt's benefit.

Max already knew that. She and Max had paid a midnight visit to the disbanding Synth at the Neon Nightmare only days before. And there Temple had discerned from the forlorn magicians' conversation that several unsolved murders on her Table of Crime Elements could have been committed by the now-dead Sparks to keep their failed conspiracy secret.

Matt mustn't know that, at least not right now, when Max's return to Vegas made him uneasy.

"South American architect," Max repeated to change the subject. He'd been on the run in Europe when Santiago debuted in Vegas. "That's Kathleen O'Connor IRA-donor territory. How could this apparent technocrat be mistaken for an 'ancient alien'?"

"Being found naked. In this case, clothes made the man," Temple explained, "and his living look was all Fontana brothers gone Latino."

Max nodded. "That Italian greyhound pack of 'instant sleek' wears the 'cool clothes in a hot climate' look that sells designer suits."

"As if," Matt said, "you didn't ever work that look."

Max raised an objecting forefinger. "Not the same. That tropical look requires an off-white or pastel palette. I'm all about midnight black."

As though called, Midnight Louie gave a yodeling greeting and lofted atop the table, managing to avoid any elbows or glasses. He settled into an alert lying position, his huge black paws elegantly crossed.

"Hi, Louie," Temple said. "You are the epitome of elegant black."

Louie blinked as if accepting tribute and slitted his eyes almost shut.

"Enough *Gentlemen's Quarterly* chat, boys," Temple decreed. "Santiago was pumped enough under those high-end suits to look like an ancient Central American civilization warrior and, without the product inflating his black hair, had the classic Mayan profile. At least when dead. That's what tipped me off, visualizing the face upright on a modern, clothed man."

"Lying horizontal on a stainless steel autopsy table will indeed give the profile a new emphasis," Max noted dryly.

"Agreed," Matt said. "I had to ID Effinger and wasn't sure at first. When the living expression falls away . . . they look different enough to confuse people who knew them, the coroner told me. So, Temple. You figured this out, how?" Matt was looking skeptical, and suspicious.

"Well, I never did regard the guy as anything more than a pricey con man, but I'd seen some photos of the body online. Combining that with the rumored 'alien surgery scars,' it suddenly clicked that he might have been one of the Darth Vaders at Neon Nightmare and been cat-mauled. So I called Molina and demanded to see the body. And I did. And it was just as I'd thought."

Max eyed Matt. "She and Molina are becoming quite a crime-solving duo. Are we being cut out of the action?"

Matt didn't bother to answer, instead asking Temple, "Someone wanted Santiago to be mistaken for a figure from the UFO-ancient alien cult?"

"Maybe. Maybe not," she said.

"Ancient astronauts." Max shook his head. "People are so gullible, but I shouldn't complain, given my profession. That 'Chariots of the Gods' stuff trades on some temple carvings looking amazingly like a space-suited astronaut. One of the most famous figures happens to be a long-lived Mayan king, Pakal, tilted forward as he died and fell into the afterworld. A happy ending and place in that mythology, by the way."

"You're awfully current on lunatic fringe lore," Matt noted.

"Given the elevated nature of my magic act, I'm interested in the 'falling man' iconography."

"And," Temple said, "we've had a lot of 'falling' deaths and maybe-murders and attempted murders around town. The Cloaked Conjuror's assistant, Barry, fell, and so did Shangri-La and. . . ."

Temple let the list trail off as her glance caught the tense look on Matt's face.

"And Vassar, the call girl at the Goliath, fell to her death," Matt told Temple. "After I visited her at the Goliath."

Max turned to Temple. "So what do you think? Was Santiago's body set up to fall and cause a stir?"

"Not sure," she answered. "Maybe someone just got him out of his clothes to take away any trace evidence. The cause of death is the usual suspect, a blow to the back of the head by a blunt instrument."

Matt nodded. "A construction site would be thronging with those."

Temple agreed. "I am thinking someone wanted to cause a stir at the Area Fifty-four site, though. In the professional and amateur media furor over the body, the building, the UFO adherents showing up for a pretty secret convention, everyone's forgotten that the body of an elderly man was dumped on the same site days earlier."

"And that man is still unidentified?" Max said.

"Yes," Temple said. "The body dump smacks of old mob habits. Have either of you guys come up with any contemporary links on that?"

They eyed each other, obviously equally guilty of ignoring that line of inquiry.

Matt jumped in. "I just got a lead on a retired cop who might have some insight on that."

The others stared at him.

"Molina," he admitted, a bit lamely.

"Molina." Max almost purred. "She has been very cooperative with our bunch lately."

"Why was Santiago killed?" Matt shook his head. "The man was rich and famous. Was it a kidnapping gone wrong?"

"I think I know everything but why he was killed," Temple said.

She was about to push a pitcher of cold beer she'd set out like a good hostess toward Max, then retracted the gesture. She'd already almost forgotten he didn't like beer or ale. Too reminiscent of an Irish pub.

"Let's see." Devine put down his mostly untasted beer glass. "You'd already suspected Santiago's motives for coming to Vegas to work on the Crystal Phoenix hotel and casino. And the next thing we know, he's plummeting naked off the top of an invisible building."

She put out a hand to pat Louie's head. "If this cat could talk, we'd know a lot more, because he was sniffing around up there and may have triggered the landslide effect that brought the concealing plastic and canvas sheets down."

"And survived," Max noted. "Midnight Louie and I have more than one thing in common now." He smiled at the cat and then noticed the silence growing awkwardly long. "We're both acrobats with black hair," he added, fooling no one.

Louie yawned, and Max agreed with him. "We can discount the UFO brouhaha," he told the others. "The gullible are always ready to gather at any hint of a paranormal or conspiratory event. But maybe we're wrong in assuming the cat being up in the construction started anything. Sorry, Louie. Maybe Santiago was thrown off the top of the building at that time *because* a crowd had gathered."

Matt spoke suddenly. "Maybe it was suicide."

"Who gets naked to commit suicide?" Temple objected. "This guy ate ego for breakfast. And the coroner did find the usual suspicious blow to the back of the head."

"Which could have happened in the fall," Devine said.

"Removing his clothes removed a lot of evidence too." Max frowned. "It does look like someone was trying to stage something for maximum publicity. Why?"

They looked at Temple. This was her area of expertise.

"It could have been someone out to get Silas T. Farnum, my semi-client, who conceived and, as far as I know, bankrolled this project. He mentioned silent partners. He mentioned that both Domingo and Santiago were working on the project design. So . . . he could have done it. He has a warped idea about publicity. Thinks stunts are the way to go."

Matt shook his head again. "And you're still mixed up with this character?"

"Lieutenant Molina wanted me to keep an eye on him."

"Junior G-girl," Max teased, getting an *I am not amused* glint from Temple's blue-gray eyes and a suspicious narrowing from Devine's.

He put "humor" on his list of what not to do when with Temple from now on, with or without her fiancé present.

"Look, guys," Temple said. "I'm the one who figured out who the UFO corpse was. By a process of deduction, I might add. When everyone is used to seeing a fairly public figure spectacularly clothed, like a Fontana brother, and he turns up naked and dead and horizontal on a dusty construction site, his features no longer animated . . . maybe his own brother wouldn't recognize him."

"Be sure you don't tell the Fontana brothers you used them to make this kind of point," Max couldn't help saying.

Devine laughed, one short guffaw. Temple put her hand over her mouth. "The Flying Fontana Brothers. It's not funny, but . . ." The more she tried to stop laughing, the less she could, until they were all caught up in helpless mirth.

The only one not laughing was Midnight Louie.

"Please don't tell the Fontana brothers I envisioned them as candidates for ancient aliens," Temple implored them when she regained her sobriety. "We've had a fit of the black humor that crime pros depend on to keep them sane." She sat up straighter, like a schoolmarm.

"Okay. Santiago's South American features spawned the ancient-alien mania. No one could have known that. The crowd jumped to the conclusion. Was revealing his death deliberate, or just an accident? He was bound to be found soon, now that the secret of the 'stealth' building was out and workmen would be doing their jobs by daylight, instead of as Farnum's night crew."

"You still haven't said how you made the identification?" Matt pointed out.

"It was the scarring left by so-called alien surgery. I was just sitting here alone at this very cocktail table—"

Midnight Louie roused himself from his "seated sage" with forepaws tucked in posture and sat up commandingly, to match Temple.

"I was studying the newspaper's photo of Santiago right after his fall to earth, sent by some reader from his cell phone, and the temple carving of a Mayan 'astronaut.' And I not only began to see the resemblance to an upright Santiago, but for some reason I also thought about the scars and remembered the pair dressed in

Darth Vader–like masks and cloaks who tried to intimidate the magicians' cabal at Neon Nightmare . . . were attacked by a bunch of black cats who jumped on their backs and clawed them into submission—into dropping their firearms and running away, at least."

Midnight Louie had started growling softly during her recital. When she finished, he leaped onto the cocktail table, skidding across the folded newspaper section and making a sharp cut across the pages as he hightailed it out of there for the office. They all gasped.

Max lunged to keep the beer pitcher from overturning.

"I wanted to keep that section with the photo and sketch," Temple wailed, leaping up.

Devine had already gotten there to grab it and smooth the cut, not torn, section in question. "Look," he told Temple, "the cut's below the graphics. You still have Exhibit A."

Max couldn't help smiling at this tableau: Temple wanted to preserve the evidence, Devine wanted to heal the wounded and solace the lost, and he wanted to save the beer that he loathed, the tabletop, the rug . . . and the day.

"It's my fault," Temple said, sitting back with a sigh. "Louie just reminded me. He did that paper-cutting trick the other day, which is what made me think of cat scratches at the same time I made the connection between the dead man and Santiago."

"Uh," Devine said, "you're attributing a lot of motive to a cat. Not only in the first place, but in the miffed second place."

"Get used to it," Max put in.

Temple glared at them both.

So did Midnight Louie.

Chapter 40

Frank Talk

Matt sat in his living room directly above Temple's. He was glad she couldn't see through ceilings, or read thoughts. His fingers were entwined, prayerfully, but the grip was white-knuckle tight and he didn't know what to pray for.

He ran what he knew through his troubled mind.

Two armed and masked people in Darth Vader–like garb had confronted members of a secret cabal of magicians calling themselves the Synth. They'd invaded the group's hidden clubrooms at the now-defunct Neon Nightmare club. Temple had just found and entered the scene, undetected. So apparently had Midnight Louie and his alley cat cohorts.

Matt had seen the cat act as Temple's guard dog and realized Louie shared a remarkable bond with his one-time rescuer. So Matt wasn't surprised that a gang of cats had gone feral-wild and attacked the invaders from behind, climbing their robes and clinging to their masks and inflicting multiple claw trails on their bodies.

Matt supposed it was like having Freddy Krueger's razor-tipped gloves slicing you on Elm Street. He'd never liked horror movies, but he'd had one razor wound from Kathleen O'Connor that earned her the Cutter nickname. He remembered the painless puzzlement of the strike and then the shock and burning sensation. That was just from one cut. Having your body used as a scratching post for a pack of fifteen-pound cats clawing and hanging from your skin would be like medieval torture.

No wonder the corny but scary shrouded figures had dropped their weapons and escaped the way they'd come.

Now a prominent international artsy architect had been found stripped and striped with vertical healed wound tracks on his rear torso and legs. One Darth Vader down. One to go.

Neither Temple nor Max knew—and they could not know—that Matt had been blackmailed into consorting with the number one suspect for the role of Darth Vader Number Two. Kathleen "the Cutter" O'Connor.

He looked at the expensive watch the TV producers had given him as part of the courting procedure for his own TV talk show. It was only 5 P.M. His *Midnight Hour* advice radio show ran from midnight to 2 A.M. By two thirty he'd be at the Goliath locked into another battle of wills with Kathleen O'Connor.

She needed to prove any priest, even an ex-priest like him, was corrupt and seducible. He needed to keep her busy so Temple was safe. He could tell no one.

Now, he needed to see the bare back of her torso and legs to discover whether or not she'd been with Santiago that Neon Nightmare night.

Dear God, how was he going to do that without confirming her contention that all men were corrupt? Without losing all chance of keeping her hooked on an interaction that was more about finding and growing some tiny remnant of trust in the heart and soul of a psychopath than playing cat and mouse with a career seducer.

Drugs? Was there something mild but effective he could dose her with? Kinsella might know, but Matt couldn't do anything that might make Kathleen's other targets aware of Matt's desperate game. Kinsella would be sure to interfere and defeat the whole point.

His cell phone rang. He jumped as if guilty of something, then dragged it out of his pocket. He hesitated to check the caller ID, hoping it wasn't Temple, because he'd have to lie to her again.

But the caller wasn't Temple.

"Frank," Matt said, hearing the unconcealed relief in his voice.

His spiritual director from seminary heard it loud and clear. "Matt. Anything wrong?"

"Uh, no. Just a lot of stress at work."

"You're the one who made yourself a nightly sitting duck for every crazy out there in Radioland."

"Only five nights a week, and most of them are just uncertain and lonely, not crazy."

"Listen to you." Bucek chuckled. "Made to minister."

"Everybody's gotta have a vocation," Matt said, a bit offended by the glib line.

"Listen, I'm in Vegas. This is sudden, but are you available for dinner?"

"Yes." Matt jumped at an unexpected lifeline. Maybe he could get some inspiration from a veteran ex-priest now in law enforcement. "This another quick visit?"

Bucek's vigorous baritone didn't boom right back. "Uh, no. I'm staying for a while this time."

His tone and the vagueness told Matt his former mentor was not going to reveal more. Handling anonymous calls in the night had sensitized Matt to vocal nuances.

"Great, Frank. Where do you want to meet and eat?"

"What else? A steakhouse. How about Planet Hollywood at seven?"

"Done."

"I'll make reservations. It'll be good to see you again, Matt."

Matt echoed his sentiments and put the phone on a sleek gray cube table fronting the long red vintage couch. Temple had found the '50s sofa for him when he'd been new to Vegas and didn't have a stick or stitch of furniture.

Soon they'd all three be moving in together, he and Temple and Louie, one small happy family.

If he could excise Kitty the Cutter from their lives. He hoped that wouldn't come down to razors.

The Strip House steak house at Planet Hollywood reminded Matt of a Chicago or New York venue, very red with black-and-white photos on the wall, like Sardi's famous theatrical district restaurant in Manhattan. Sardi's featured Broadway stars on the wall. This was Vegas. Vintage black-and-white semidraped pinup girls ruled here.

As Matt glanced at, comprehended, then studied the "art" work, he realized it was highly appropriate to his current problem: how to undress a woman without any sexual element in the act whatsoever.

"You're looking a bit glum," Frank said as Matt joined him at the table.

"Just thinking about logistics." That was true.

"The wall art is a bit racy," Frank said after they'd ordered drinks, "but the steaks are prime. So what logistics are you wrestling with?"

"Temple and I are getting married."

"Finally! When, where?"

Matt laughed. "You're reading my mind. Those are the big questions. My family wants a big Polish Catholic wedding in Chicago. Temple's parents are Unitarians in Minneapolis."

"That makes 'ecumenical' as complex as a corporate merger."

"Yeah. Makes you want to run away to Vegas for a civil ceremony."

"You live with an adjoining wedding chapel for the job."

"You know about the landlady's side business?"

"The Lovers' Knot Wedding Chapel, sure."

"I'm shocked."

"That I suggested it or knew about it? I'm FBI now. I know everything." Frank smiled as he sipped the scotch on the rocks drink in front of him.

"I find that declaration somewhat sinister, Frank."

Bucek shrugged. "Business has brought me to Vegas now and again. This time I'm staying for a while."

"Are Sharon and the kids coming to stay too?"

"No. I'm solo for now." Frank glanced at Matt. "Now, wait a minute. Don't worry. Nothing personal is going on. I'm just needed here for a while."

"Terrorism?" Matt wondered.

Frank tilted his head from side to side in that *maybe* way.

Matt sighed. "My logistics problems shrink to atom size when that word comes into play."

"Nothing that serious, Matt. I just can't talk about it. Let's get back to the wedding. We married guys always like more fellow sufferers."

The steak had been great, and Frank's humor made discussing the intricacies of marrying a non-Catholic more amusing than discouraging.

"You've got to think like an American nun," Frank had said during dessert. "You're not going to let a bunch of old guys in dresses in Rome affect what is good and true to do here in the USA. You know that, Matt. There's been a big disconnect between many of the American faithful and the overseas hierarchy for a long time."

Matt had agreed, but he couldn't tell that to Father Frankenfurter from seminary, even though almost everyone from those days had moved on to secular jobs. He couldn't say his real problem was how not to be seduced by a psychopath.

During a conversational lull, Matt considered he might be making a mistake in labeling Kathleen the way she wanted to be categorized. Maybe he should forget her horrible sins against everyone he knew, including him and herself, really. Maybe he should regard her as just another troubled person calling in because she needed attention.

He leaned away from the tiny after-dinner liqueur glass. "All the abuse issues aren't likely to endear the Catholic church to Temple's parents, Frank."

"Child abuse crosses all faiths. And professions, for that matter. Anyone who wants to work with youth these days has to tread carefully." Frank shook his head.

"So what is the worse sin? The violation of children or that our culture covered up that issue for so long? Even the social workers went hush-hush on it."

"That the caretakers failed the children all the way up the line."

Matt nodded. "How do you heal the survivors?"

"You know. Counseling."

"Words won't erase their total distrust of anyone."

Frank eyed him suspiciously. "You don't get that deep into this topic on your radio show."

"No. But . . . I'm dealing with a person who's actually turned to striking out against others. It's hard to blame her. She's a second-generation victim. And they *are* victims, legally and in every other way. We can have them rethink themselves as survivors, but that doesn't do it for anyone who's been so . . ."

"Twisted?" Bucek leaned closer to Matt and dropped his voice. "Matt, you sound like you're taking on a job for a psychiatrist. I'd advise you to leave any abuse survivor who's turned to violence alone. That person is a ticking time bomb. That person could turn to mass violence."

"No. This one is acting out against the one decent person in her life."

"You?"

"Not me. Not directly."

"Indirectly? Good God, Matt. You're on the brink of an insanely great career and marrying a woman you've been lucky enough to find and love later in your life than most men. Don't mess it up with some crusade to save a nut job."

Matt recoiled as Frank went on.

"'Love the little children,' but a psychotic abuse survivor is no one for an amateur to deal with. We have FBI profilers who've plumbed the depths of human misbehavior, and even they don't personally interact with the damned."

Matt nodded as Frank sat back, relieved, taking the nod for a concession.

Matt had been nodding to himself. Yes, he'd have to continue going this alone. Bucek wouldn't be any help.

Matt just had to be something more than Kathleen O'Connor was. Something smarter. Something more determined. Something more stable. And fast.

Chapter 41

Northern Exposure

"*Hmm.*" Kathleen cooed at Matt, trying to circle him in the narrow hotel room entry hall. "I smell expensive booze and steak sauce and cigar smoke on you."

Had she been tailing him?

"What a high-end nose you have."

He moved to keep her face-to-face while he checked out her clothes. The filmy skirt was short in front and long in back, the way women (other than Temple) were wearing them today. And she wore some hip-length floaty top.

Maybe he could see through the back of it if he positioned her correctly against the bedside lampshades, which were about at back level.

"Oh, you want to tango tonight," she said.

He gently avoided her clinging ways. "I guess you did

a lot of that in Rio and Buenos Aires, Lima and Santiago when you were courting South American money for the IRA."

He watched for a reaction on the word "Santiago."

She backed away. "And what have you done to support a cause besides simper from a pulpit?"

"Nothing," he said. "What made you fall in with the IRA at such a young age?"

"I escaped the Magdalene 'school.' None did, you know."

"I do know. I've looked all that up."

"So you can divine my entire life story from the Internet?"

He took his customary chair without turning his back on her, yet making the movement look natural, not defensive. He'd studied marital arts, but was finding the philosophy more helpful than the fighting part.

She tossed herself on the bed, reminding him that she'd made her political point on her back the world over and that she still struck him in some ways as a rebellious teenager. "How do you know how young I was?" she asked with a bit of a preen in her voice.

If Max was at his mid-thirties, his teenage "older woman" must be pushing forty, like Molina. Vamping it up might not get the instant results it once had. Besides, peace had made her cause moot.

"Max thought of you as an older woman."

That had her sitting up, indignant. "Only six years!"

"Double that in the emotional age between you. And then there's your vast sexual experience edge, no matter how wrongfully you came by it."

"Max was an infant. A baby. He knew nothing of the world but being a privileged American and underage drinking and having fun and wanting to go far from home to seduce and screw his first girl."

"That sure didn't work out for him, thanks to you.

He thinks the only reason you went off to the park with him was to have his cousin Sean killed in that IRA bombing. Divide and destroy."

She shook her long black hair and wriggled to expose more leg in the front high-rise of the bipolar skirt. Nearing forty or not, she was a world-class beauty, born of abuse and compelled to think sexual power ran the world. "I thought we were here to talk about me. About how you're Father Pureheart and want to save me."

Her mockery held some pulse of hope she'd deny, Matt thought. Unfortunately, at the moment, Father Pureheart was not only no longer a "father," but he had to figure out a nonsexual way to check out her back for cat-scar marks, as well.

"Tell me about it all," Matt said.

"How much 'all' do you want?" She crossed her legs high up, legs in sheer black nylons visibly supported by a black garter belt. Matt was not susceptible, but he allowed her to see him glancing at her thighs, looking for marks. Nothing to see at this distance. The back would be the telling section.

"Tell me," Matt said, hoping to overwhelm her, "about your mother and father, about your daughter. Then tell me about you and Max."

"You don't want much, do you?" She picked up the razor from the marble-topped bedside table. "One strike across the eyelid, and you're blind."

He couldn't deter the chill of fear.

"My mother was a whore. Sounds Victorian music hall, doesn't it?" She'd veered off the threat. Maybe she'd always craved an audience for her wrongs.

"So far," Matt said, "I'm getting that she was unmarried and pregnant, like mine."

"Don't try to 'identify' with me."

"How do you know she was a sex worker?"

"Because in the orphanage they called me a bastard

child of a whore. Are you too holy to say the word 'whore'?"

"No, but it's a word meant to hurt, label, denigrate. And most often, it isn't true." Matt wanted to strip the shock value from her words, to depersonalize the dialogue.

He realized he was being as manipulative as she was, but maybe that was what it took to cut through thirty-some years of abuse, fury, and hatred.

He went on, "If your mother was put into a Magdalene school, she was an unpaid laundry worker, a virtual domestic slave. Those are labels I'll accept."

"With nuns and priests as the warders."

Matt appeared to mull her words. "Yes. Warders is a good way to put it."

His agreement aggravated her more than any diatribe would.

She grabbed the razor again and leaped to the floor. She jumped at him, flying hair almost blinding her. Matt stood even faster, intercepted her right wrist, and pulled it down toward the floor. It was easy to push a foot out from under her, so she tumbled over onto her side.

She curled into a ball, the reflexive position revealing more about her early life than a hundred hours of "therapy" talk. He could hardly hear the low keening, but saw a trio of ruby red blots on the marble floor.

He bent over her. "Have you hurt yourself!"

"No! You did!"

The razor had fallen a few inches away. He grabbed it before she could. Her hand must have hit the floor with the open blade clutched in her palm. He shut it to get the blood-dewed cutting edge out of her sight and put it in his pants pocket.

"Come on. We'll clean that up."

He was careful not to use her name. Anything that put her back into the dreadful past might push her into hysteria again.

Funny. Everyone took her for a stone-cold killer, including himself. That was only a pose. What she really was might be even more dangerous.

She let him lead her into the bathroom, to the marble sink with its 24-karat gold-clad faucets.

She hung over it, panting, as he ran cold water on her bloody hand and jerked tissues from a golden box to wrap her palm. King Midas must have had a frenzy in this bathroom.

Kathleen let herself sag against the sink stand, ironically accomplishing his dangerous and touchy mission for him. His supporting arm had pushed up the filmy top, exposing her spine and a lot of back.

White. Clear of scars. He almost let her slip in shock, and had to clamp her ebbing body close, her heavy hair against his chin and chest.

He realized this was supposed to be seductive, but his now ruefully regarded years of wrought-iron celibacy had made him seduce-proof.

"Here, a towel." He grabbed an ornately embroidered finger towel and wrapped it around the cut hand. "Let's get you back into the bedroom." She'd take that move as a sign of victory.

He steered her out onto the bed, then peeled open the towel. It had absorbed some blood from the short cut, but the flow was already slowing.

He plumped the scratchy brocade pillows behind her and settled her back like an invalid.

Then he sat again in his usual chair against the wall.

It was hard to be seductive with a huge towel wrapped around one hand.

"You're good at first aid," she said, unaware of delivering her first compliment. "Did your stepfather hit you?"

Matt shrugged.

"Did he, did he? He must have!"

"Then why ask me?"

"I want to make you tell the truth."

"You don't have to make me. Yes, he yelled at me, cursed at me, and he hit me when I stood between him and my mother."

"When was that."

"Every time."

She fell silent. No one had stood in front of her.

"Look," Matt said. "I know Cliff Effinger was a piker in everything he ever said or did. He was even a failure at being abusive. I know now what I went through was minor compared to some."

"And I'm that 'some.'"

"No. You are the one. A one. The only one I'm talking to at this moment."

"But you don't want to be."

"True."

"You don't want me to exist."

Matt didn't have to think before he spoke. "I don't want anyone who's been through what you have to exist, but the world won't let that happen."

"*You* are the world." She spun away on the bed. Again revealed the back he'd needed to see. He was glad no signs of further abuse showed, even from the cat pack. "We are the world."

She quoted the title of the mid-eighties song Michael Jackson, Harry Belafonte, Lionel Ritchie and other major artists recorded to aid African famine relief. Matt remembered crouching on the floor in front of the TV set in an unhappy house and seeing all those happy people singing . . . just as he'd seen a similar upbeat chorus singing a happy, sappy soft drink song of eighteen million commercials ago, wishing they could teach the world to sing in perfect harmony.

Yeah, he had felt that he could do that at one time. Still did.

It occurred to him that Kathleen's dedication to the IRA might have been genuine.

I'd like to buy the world...a soft drink and then what? Call man's inhumanity to man, woman, and child done?

He approached the bed. He pulled the shut razor from his pocket. He opened it. He laid it on the bedside table.

She didn't move. She left her vulnerable back—that he'd so needed to see to convict her of another wrong—exposed.

Mission accomplished.

He left, without her moving or speaking for once. Just bleeding a little.

And breathed a deep sigh of relief outside the door.

He walked to the edge of the hallway and the railing that overlooked all the tropical greenery and flitting, chatting birds of the atrium.

He said good night to Vassar, who'd plunged from this height eighteen stories to her death.

Perhaps her murderer rested inside.

Chapter 42

Track of the Cat

It had taken Max a few nights to determine which floor Matt Devine was visiting.

It took another day to target the exact room of the many that circled the Hyatt-style atrium of the Goliath Hotel.

First, he'd called the front desk on his cell phone—thank God for smaller, brilliant portable devices—and asked for Devine's room over and over. That service was automated, so no human would notice the repetitions.

Then it was a matter of prowling the halls of the twentieth floor until he heard a phone ringing at the same time. That was not an easy task. The central atrium was a thirty-story aviary, thronging with whistling, chattering, calling exotic birds. As pleasant as the effect was, it made it hell to determine where normal human sounds, like ringing room phones, had originated.

Max couldn't say why he was doing this. Was it to protect his ex–significant other from news of a philandering fiancé? Or to protect—or nail—Devine, who was clearly uncomfortable with whatever was going on in room 2032? Was it a matter of prurient curiosity? Or life and death?

His new secret mission certainly wasn't uncovering the possible mob activity Temple was obsessed by. That was the task assigned him and Devine by their lead detective.

Max chuckled. Temple certainly put the "dom" in "indomitable."

Tonight he'd gotten here ahead of Devine, ducking into the entry niche of a lavish suite.

He'd seen his expected prey arrive, looking unhappy, and depart about ninety minutes later, looking unhappier.

About ten minutes after that, he heard the room's door open and close. His back was to the hall as someone from the room passed a man bent over to open the room to his suite. Max had worn the gangsta fedora so popular in music videos, and had pushed his blazer sleeves up to his elbows to complete the look.

When he thought it safe to come out, he passed only bleary-eyed gamblers, all male, as he headed for the elevator area, arriving just as the middle one of five closed its doors on nothing visible.

He called for another, pacing. At this hour, past 4 A.M., it came quickly. Gamblers either gave up the ghost of a chance around 3 A.M. or stuck it through until breakfast at six.

Once on, Max hit LOBBY and pressed the CLOSE DOORS buttons. This trick happened to work at the Goliath. He'd used it when performing his magic act here to get around the hotel without delays and in privacy.

One elevator essentially out of service would force the other four elevators to stop more frequently.

When the elevator car lifted almost imperceptibly before stopping, Max released the LOBBY button and hit OPEN ELEVATOR DOORS at once.

He burst out of his silent womb into the bright, bustling lobby of milling people.

He stepped aside. Waiting people pushed past him into the elevator car. Max studied the master board that showed each car and the floor it was on. The first and last were too high to have touched bottom during his own trip down. Number two was about to come in for a landing, and number four had just disgorged a clot of passengers.

Max joined those debarkers, quickly studying them for any possible clue to being Matt Devine's secret contact. This was hard, with his memory bereft of 90 percent of what Matt Devine was about besides the bare facts of his history, ex-priest and now disc jockey to the depressed. Actually, he'd listened to the evening programming at WCOO-AM radio.

It was Devine's predecessor on the air, Ambrosia, who played the songs. Devine just talked the talk afterwards. He had a good voice, and an obvious gift for teasing reason out of troubled people. No surprise he was on the brink of a national career.

Could that have anything to do with these nightly assignations? Not unless the wooing network brass had given him a free room at the Goliath with call girls on tap as a contract perk. Highly unlikely, given the guy's mind-blowing celibate history. He'd known how to resist temptation for years. Devine had "straight shooter" written all over him.

The Bermuda shorts–clad tourists of both sexes who'd left the elevator were also highly unlikely to be Devine buddies, and most of them high on alcohol too, at this late hour.

Whatever was happening in room 2032, it wasn't a party. He'd listened at the door, but all that marble and mirror wall sheathing deadened sound.

Max whirled to see the spate of passengers from elevator number two fanning out like electrons deserting a nucleus.

He had half a second to make a decision. His eye focused on the only blur of black, and he swung into step behind it, knowing people crisscrossed in all directions and they both were caught in a basketweave pattern that made a simple attempt to follow almost impossible.

Woman, though. Not that tall, even allowing for stiletto heels.

Max shrugged and shouldered his way closer, keeping his knees bent and his face down, looking past the hat brim.

She was leaving the hotel. That conviction sent a shock wave of jubilation through him.

Outside it would be much easier to follow her, even if she used a cab.

But she didn't. She was walking down the long, curving pavement toward the Strip, on heels but walking fast.

Max slouched after her, taking in the shiny black-patent trench coat so much more costly than the hooker heels. She wore real hooker heels, extreme and cheap enough to glitter and be easy to follow. She too wore a hat, black with a floppy brim. Made it hard to see what was hair and what was hat.

Max ran the stats through his mind. Around five-feet-three. Black hair. Max got a sudden vision of aqua eyes, probably contact lens enhanced. No doubt about it. She must be Kathleen O'Connor, his implacable enemy.

How the bloody hell had she ended up in nightly collusion with Matt Devine?

For a moment, he savored outing ex–Father Perfect, but that was petty.

Even as he paused in shock to absorb his conclusion, the crowds were thinning enough for him to realize another shocking fact.

He was the second in line.

Someone else was tailing Kitty the Cutter—and from the way she kept her right hand buried in the coat pocket, she might well be carrying a switchblade—another guy, not so tall as he but as unremarkably dressed. In a hat. A baseball cap.

Not law enforcement.

Some new player in the game.

Max stuck his hands in his black denim jeans and fell into step where he belonged . . . behind everybody.

Max Kinsella watched the dawn come up on the desert. He'd driven east after his long night of surveillance. It wasn't hard to leave Las Vegas if you drove east or west.

Kathleen had lost them in the Treasure Island's tropical greenery. Not Max, but by then he'd been more curious about who was following her than where she went. There was always tomorrow night to track down Kitty the Cutter.

The other guy was either an amateur or aware of Max on his tail and not minding it. He not only lost Kathleen, but he did nothing to lose Max. Maybe he didn't know Max was behind him all the way to his home ground.

Max's suspicions were uncertain as to his exact identity, but the possibilities gave him a chill. In fact, what he was concluding was impossible. *Isn't it?*

No way he could throw out this new development for speculation on Temple's round table of crime. This was even more shocking, to him personally, than Matt Devine's hookup with Kathleen O'Connor.

Chapter 43

Cat Tails

I pause in a shadow made by the slight instep rise on Goliath's left sandal.

One of the wonders of the ancient world was the Colossus of Rhodes, a mighty 110-foot statue of a giant man guarding that Grecian island's harbor before the turn of the first century.

Naturally, this is just the thing to re-create in the Mojave desert.

When Las Vegas hosts a hotel named the Goliath, one can be sure the several-story statue of the biblical giant David toppled with a slingshot will be even taller, if less tasteful, than the Old World inspiration.

Essentially, every man, woman, and child who enters the Goliath Hotel and casino must walk under the figure's skirt. Perhaps I should describe it as a battle kilt. Those Greek and Roman gods and men were not ashamed of showing a lot of knee and thigh.

Call it statutory gape.

Anyway, I would not normally pause under a landmark of such vulgarity, but I am a wee bit weary and the hour is even more wee. My quarry has gone to ground inside the Goliath, and it is now nigh on four o'clock in the morning. I have been on the prowl since before midnight, being carried concealed during two car rides and now wondering what to do.

People still stagger in and out, under and even around Goliath's mighty legs. Perhaps I should give up the quest. I yawn and glance around the mostly empty driveway.

A flash of neon light attracts my fatigued gaze to Goliath's other sandal. It appears something gaudy is glittering beneath it. *Hmm.* I only recently uncovered a ruby earring under a bridal hem. I scan the area, then slink fast and silent to the other sandal, nosing into the shadow.

Whomp! I have run face-first into a thornbush, or a bee, or a porcupine.

As my eyes adjust to the change from dark to light to dark, I realize what drew me was the green reflection at the back of a golden eye.

"Louise! What are you doing here and why are you whacking me?" I stroke a mitt across my kisser, feeling the slight sting of four claws to the chops.

"This is *my* temporary territory," she announces. "When did you show up?"

"I was here first. I had staked out the other sandal while my prey vanished inside."

"Really? I was here first, but my prey has performed the same dirty trick as yours."

"It is diabolical when these humans escape into pigeon coops with three thousand cubicles. Perhaps we are tailing the same individual?" I suggest.

"You say first."

I am reluctant to commit. Discretion is a professional responsibility. "I came from the south," I concede.

"I came from the northeast."

We settle down to sit and mull that information.

"You are not tailing your roommate, as is your wont?" she asks.

"Nope. Not my want right now."

"Then you are tailing Mr. Matt Devine. The Circle Ritz is south of here."

"And I suppose you, Louise, are on the trail of your crush, Mr. Max Kinsella."

"Ridiculous charge! I merely keep an eye on him because he is always after someone who is up to no good."

"*Hmm.* I am here because I fear Mr. Matt is up to no good."

"Maybe he is whom Mr. Max is tailing?"

"That is not good." I sit half-up, senses sharpened. "Mr. Matt is leaving."

"Poor man. He looks very downcast and . . . furtive."

"My poor Miss Temple!"

"*Aha!* You are an idiot if I say so myself. Your Miss Temple is following him out on her high heels."

"My Miss Temple is home in bed, where she should be, and I should be there with her."

"I am sure your devotion goes over well with Mr. Matt."

"None of your business! And are you blind? That is not Miss Temple. She does not wear high heels of that instep-mangling height. That woman wears true stilettos."

"Sharp," Louise purrs admiringly.

Meanwhile, I am frowning. Mr. Matt is hunching his way to the side parking lot, but this woman wears a black trench coat and hat. Hot for Vegas, but hot fashion items nowadays. She is clicking away in the opposite direction, face obscured.

"We will have to split up," I decree. "Louise, you follow Mr. Matt. If you hurry, you can slip into the backseat of the

Jaguar when he opens the door. I will take on the strange woman in black who seemed to follow him out."

Miss Midnight Louise pulses her shivs in and out on the pavement while she considers.

"Midnight Investigations, Inc., has only one motto, Louise. Divide and conquer. Go!"

I give her an encouraging pat on the back, and she shoots out into the open, spitting her farewell as I flex my shivs. It is tit for tat. She must dash away without dawdling to escape the blinding entry area lights and catch up to Mr. Matt.

I turn to follow the well-heeled mystery woman. Then the soft scrape of a shoe on stone makes me pause.

Now I see whom Louise has followed here. Mr. Max Kinsella. His height and recovered stride gives him away despite the fedora he wears like an old-time PI.

Since he is heading in the direction of the woman in question, I pad into the line behind him . . . just in time to spot a heavyset man in a ball cap step out from an idle hotel van and follow the woman on the long walk to the parking areas behind the hotel.

The adventuresome individual can find unlikely paths through and around and beyond the tourist-frequented areas of the massive hotel-casino buildings.

I am wishing I had the stride length of the long-left-behind Goliath statue by the time the woman cuts through some thick parking lot foliage and the man following her veers off the trail.

So does Mr. Max.

Now I shadow two men, until the first heads into the looming shadow of a parking ramp behind the usual mega-looming shadow of a major strip hotel. I must say Mr. Max's walking ability is back to normal and making tracks.

Mr. Max follows him inside, but by the time I work my way into the parked cars, I hear footsteps coming my way. I dash under the nearest SUV. He is heading away from the hotel and I am in no mood to follow.

My pads have been worn to nubs and all I want is to settle down where I am and enjoy a peaceful snooze. I wiggle my posterior farther under the vehicle . . . and feel I have backed into a cactus.

"Yeowww!"

"Quiet, Pops," Louise mews contentedly. "I decided to tail you. It is a long hike back to our main bases. I say we head for Ma Barker's territory at dawn and recruit some temporary tailers."

"We were two short," I agree. "And if that is not Miss Kathleen O'Connor who has drawn all the male attention, I will eat her hat."

"You will eat *your* hat," she has to correct me.

"No, Louise, I will eat hers, and you can chow down on your Mr. Max's fedora."

Chapter 44

Cop Shop Talk

"Hell yes, kid. In the old days, they'd jerk out your finger-nails and force-feed 'em to your dog for good measure. They'd weld you into a drum and send you down the river. The Mexican cartels are just now revving up to that level of plain deviltry."

Molina had given Matt one crumb at the end of their meeting: contact info for Woodrow Wetherly, a Metro cop who'd retired in the '80s. That put him in his own eighties, and his skin looked every centimeter of it. He was as spotted as a hyena on face, hands, and forearms, further embellished by enough blue and black splotches to give a tattoo artist envy. It was all just sun damage.

Matt resolved then and there to use the high-octane sunscreen Temple was always after him about. The three golden hairs left on Wetherly's mostly bald head remained a permanent reminder of his original blond coloring, like Matt's.

"Call me Woody. I don't get why the lady lieutenant would send a civilian to me for mob gossip. You write for one of those digital rags, Mr. Devine?"

"No. Radio's my medium."

"Radio." Wetherly nodded and relaxed enough to light up a stogie that was waiting half-smoked in the big crystal ashtray on the table beside his lounger chair. "I did a lot of radio interviews in the 2000s. Nostalgia about the mob mostly, and how Metro and the FBI rid the city of all that jazz.

"The end of the '80s, that's when they started imploding all those mob-financed hotels, and as they hit the dirt, so did the gangsters that laundered money through them. I'm thinking of writing a book," he added, which sounded like a line he'd used for years. "Would you want me on your radio show to talk about all that stuff?"

"Sure, someday." Matt didn't have Temple's ease and maybe lack of conscience about jollying people along for his own purposes.

"What's the name of your show, sonny?"

"The Midnight Hour."

Wetherly puffed on his cigar, releasing an odor of burning tires. "Sounds like a good tough crime show."

It did, so Matt just nodded.

"What are you wanting to know about any of this stuff going on now?"

"I wonder if there could be mob interest in illegally stockpiled money and guns. Something that had been accruing for a few years."

"'Accruing.'" Wetherly laughed heartily until his aged tobacco mirth died off into a gagging cough. "Gang interest, for sure." He hacked a bit more behind his spotted, hairy hand. "Punks. Criminals are just punks now. Mean, yes, and stupid. And greedy. Always greedy. But the mob. Those guys had organization. You worked your way up, like in a bank. You did okay with the little jobs, you got bigger ones, and *you* got bigger. And those guys didn't talk. No jailhouse confessions from them. They went to the grave with their lips sealed, just like Jimmy Hoffa."

"But . . . he was a union bigwig the mob turned on."

"And he paid the price. But his death and the body never being found . . . that was old-time merciless mob boss stuff. No one ever found his body. Forever. That is mob vengeance."

"So a . . . flashy brutal killing?"

"That's mob too. That's mob sending a message. Usually to shut up the troops. Making an example."

"They say the mob is out of Vegas."

"In a wholesale way like years ago, yeah. But there are still operations, like in other cities."

"So the survivors might be organized enough to . . . plan a heist, say?"

"Heist? No. Nope. Nothing that obvious. Amateurs-ville. Heists are the work of small-time grifters who think they'll get away with it, and they never do. Vegas was always a town that did business under the table, not in the street, assault rifles blazing."

"But if the prize, the money or the guns, were someone else's hidden stockpile, would traditional mobsters go after it?"

A wheezing laugh sounded like it might do the old guy in for good. Matt sat forward, ready to catch him if he toppled.

No risk. Wetherly slapped the arms of his faux-leather upholstery and leaned back so far, the footrest popped out with a metallic snap.

Matt jumped.

Woody laughed even harder. "Scared you some, didn't it? This is one scary chair. Anyway, the answer is yes. I know a few old-timers who'd go after a secret stash. One in particularly."

Matt saw a story coming on and just nodded, something he couldn't do on the radio to encourage a shy caller. Wetherly was too old to be shy.

He leaned close enough for Matt to smell his cigar breath. "This is between you and me, not for the radio, right?"

Matt nodded again, fighting not to pull back from the foul breath.

Wetherly's smile broadened, showing crowded yellow teeth. He leaned back. "There was this old kingpin. Jeez, he'd be in his nineties now. Or almost there. But back in the '70s, he was big. We never could nail him for nothing, but pills, prostitution, protection—he was all over those rackets. Jack the Hammer, they called him."

"After Jack the Ripper?" Matt wondered.

Wetherly shook his head from side to side with a tight-lipped smile. He leaned forward again, and Matt was too mesmerized to draw back.

"Cross him, and he'd drive you far out into the desert, which wasn't that far in the old days. There was always a construction site. There was always a compressor with a jackhammer. . . ." Wetherly grinned.

"He killed people with a jackhammer?"

"Not people, kid. Rivals, upstarts, petty crooks who got greedy. You'll never see anything on him in all those mob museums, not old Giacchino Petrocelli, because they never caught him and nobody ever killed him."

"You're sure he didn't end up on the business end of his own jackhammer?"

"Only God and the buzzards know, sonny."

"Jah-keen-o, how is that spelled?"

"It's Italian. The *J* names always start with *G-i-a*, then two *c*'s give you *k* pronunciation. *G-i-a-c-c-h-i-n-o*. You jottted that down right. And 'Petrocelli' is right too.

Okay. So what you up to? You want to make a headstone for the old mobster?"

"I might want to research him, for my show."

"I'd watch myself. My theory is Old Giacch-o is still out there, all alone and sitting on his millions. And maybe floating a few deals or corpses even today."

"Like that dead body of an old man that was dumped off Paradise behind the Strip a week ago?"

"Never knew that guy was old. Who'd bother offing someone my age?" Wetherly wheezed out a laugh that neared a cackle. Then his narrowed eyes almost disappeared in the dunes of flesh surrounding them. "I see, sonny. You're thinking it might be some old-time mob guy."

"Yeah," Matt said. "Like that guy who was tied to the pirate ship prow after dark at the Oasis, and drowned with the ship when it sank."

"Ooh, that was a nasty do-in, wasn't it? Buried in the paper, though." Wetherly nodded sagely. "Just like that. I hadn't thought of old Giaccho, but maybe he wanted to change his MO to keep the police away from the fact that he is maybe still out there somewhere."

The chair squealed as Wetherly slapped himself back into reclining position. He was still a big guy.

"I slam back a few at the cop bars around town. That 'victim,' Effinger, was known as a bad lot. Ran errands for anything shady around town. But he never was big enough to merit a mob offing with full honors. Weird case."

"There's a rumor Effinger knew something about the loot from an old heist."

"Rumors." Wetherly had turned scoffing. "Effinger was a rat fink, a pathetic hanger-on scratching out a few bucks now and then. If Jack the Hammer is still out there, he would have rubbed him out on principle."

Wetherly's contempt of his dead stepfather warmed

Matt's heart, not a very charitable reaction. It was always good, though, to learn his own opinion was shared by leaders in their field . . . in Effinger's case, cops and crooks alike.

Matt thanked the old cop, who actually rose to see him out.

Wetherly whistled when he spotted the Jaguar at his curb. "Must have robbed a bank yourself."

Matt smiled modestly. "My show does all right."

"Keep it up," the old man advised, "you'll be seamed and freckled and useless like me before you know it."

"You've been really helpful," Matt assured him, surviving a crushing handshake before he finally got away.

Old people liked to talk. He often had to hurry them along on the radio. This old guy, though, had given him some solid information.

Maybe Molina would find the first dead guy at Area 54 had links to this Petrocelli character or his old-time operation.

Meanwhile, he checked his cell phone. Temple had texted him to come home. Max had found some new evidence to review.

Matt gunned the Jaguar away from the house, a rare expression of aggravation. Max Kinsella and his precious "evidence" could be abducted by aliens and never heard from again, as far as he was concerned.

Chapter 45

Murder Ménage III: The Thirteenth Sign

Max finally had his magic moment. He looked at Temple and Matt to gather their attention as they sat at the round table.

Then he produced the scrap of paper he'd rescued from the Professor Mangel magic exhibition at the University of Nevada campus here several days ago, saving it for this savoring moment, flourishing it between his fingers like a paper bouquet.

"Voilà!"

"You're sounding very French lately," Temple observed.

"The language of love and mystery." Max would not let guilt over his recent French connection deny him his *ooh-la-la* moment of revelation. "I found this inside a coin box, a magic trick box, at Professor Mangel's exhibition on the university campus."

"A puzzle box?" Matt asked.

"It's a small box with hidden chambers."

"Kind of like the human heart," Matt said.

Max paused. "Exactly. Magicians meant it to be impenetrable by the average person, and I've seen the clever average person buy such puzzle boxes to hide pot from the police. I gamed the mechanism after a thorough inspection."

"Why did you tamper with the Mangel exhibition?" Temple asked.

"Magician's instinct. I psyched out where I'd hide something there. I figured if someone killed him and left his body in that Ophiuchus position, it must have been because he knew something about the Synth. Something dangerous to them."

"And if he had," Temple broke in excitedly, "he would have hidden what he knew someplace safe. His mind worked like that. He delighted in the illusions-inside-illusions aspect of magic."

"Or maybe," Matt said, "you just took it because you could."

Max laughed. "It was a particularly unusual coin box. Call it instinct, call it luck, call it fate. Inside the box, once I figured out how to open it, was this map, for what I don't know. That's where you people with a memory of Vegas need to help out."

"I love puzzles." Temple snatched the bait with her lilac-enameled fingernails and smoothed out the paper. She reminded him of a terrier playing with a toy hiding treats inside.

Matt balanced his chin on her shoulder to see better. Revienne had been right. They made the coziest couple. Max silently applauded. Apparently he'd been an excellent matchmaker before his memory had gone south.

"It looks like a bare branch with Christmas tree lights on it," Temple said.

"Or forked summer lightning," Matt suggested.

"Or fireworks," Max said. "Yes, there's something organic about it and artificial at the same time. You're both right."

"It could be a night view of an airplane landing field," Matt said, exercising his left brain.

"Bravo," said Max.

"Or . . ." Temple was waxing imaginative. "Or . . . Area Fifty-one."

"So you think this is an alien-landing map?" Matt asked, his vocal tone just this far south of ridicule.

"We must think outside the box," she answered. "What would a cool metaphysical guy like Jeff Mangel have?"

"A string of chemical formulas," Max said, just to be confounding.

"No." Temple sounded discouraged. "It's too skeletal, too sketchy. Unless we had a key to this map, it'll never mean anything but gibberish. Darn you, Jeff Mangel."

"You said his philosophical outlook fascinated you," Matt reminded her. "That's not science. We need to look for something more symbolic in this . . . arrangement of dots or points."

"French pointillist paintings? Sand paintings. Tattoos?" Temple suggested, a bit huffily.

Max sat back, enjoying their . . . process.

Temple tumbled to his amused voyeurism. "Max. You must have a theory. What? Do these dots repeat the arrangement of doves in your signature illusion, for instance, or the number of angels dancing on the head of a pin or the back of an elephant?"

Her pointed interrogation and references made his smile broaden. "It's something to do with Jeff Mangel's obsession with magic. Not angels or elephants, Temple, much as I find that combination stimulating. Maybe for a new act."

"Oh, that would be so cool, Max!"

Matt frowned at her instant engagement with ideas for Max's act. "We're not here to reinvent the Mystifying Max."

"The Mystifying, Flying Max," Temple corrected. She thought like P. T. Barnum.

Even Matt was forced to smile and make eye contact with his former rival. "She's the gift that keeps on giving, isn't she?"

Max nodded. "I will admit, this pattern leaves me bewitched and bewildered. It looks so deliberate, but must be random."

Temple leaned in to study it. "I'm no expert at three-dimensional layouts. I mean, before I flew into O'Hare, or even LaGuardia in New York, I printed out the terminal and baggage claim layouts from the Internet."

"No." Matt shook his head. "That's taking organization to insane extremes. There are overhead signs and arrows everywhere."

"And sometimes they're ambiguous," Temple said. "And you're short and being outpaced by everybody from your flight and dragging and toting bags—and maybe overweight alley cats"—she was offended now, and both men chose to let her rave on uninterrupted—"with *no* superior upper body strength, I might add. So you want to know where you need to go before you get there. Savvy?"

"Aye, aye," Matt said, saluting.

Max chuckled, but remained mute.

Temple heaved a five-foot-nine sigh, drew the paper near, and folded her arms on the table to study it some more. After an intense minute or so, she said, "I know what this reminds me of."

"We're all ears." Max fanned his fingers behind said appendages.

Temple mock-frowned. "This is how my dad laid out the Christmas tree light strands before he put them on the actual tree. He didn't wrap them around the tree, three-dimensionally. He laid them on in a zigzag pattern for each viewable 'side.' "

"There must have been some crazy overlay." Max squinted his eyes to visualize the method.

"Not much," Matt said. "That's how we did it for the big tree at the church. Wrapping those twelve-foot balsam firs would have required altar boys on skateboards at the bottom."

Temple giggled at the mental image. "I hope I never see you on a skateboard," she told Matt.

"I promise," he said ardently. "Maybe a Segway, but never a skateboard. I see what you're getting at with this sketch. This might not be a full three-D image, but a skeleton. Like the pine tree and its branches."

"Which is thinking with*in* the box," Max added. "I did a lot of that in my career as a magician."

"Wait a minute." Temple turned the drawing left and right and then upside down. Then she lifted it up against the ceiling light.

"That would be backwards," Matt pointed out.

"That would be a mirror image," Max said. "The basis of numerable illusions."

"And," Temple finished, "exactly where the magic-oriented person like Jeff Mangel would turn if seeking to create confusion." She frowned at the image again. "I know the Strip pretty well. And, gentlemen, I think this is a 'tree' of Las Vegas Boulevard and some famous off-Strip attractions, and if you drew an outline around the dots, you'd have the 'house' image of the major stars in Ophiuchus."

Max was so stunned, his forefinger slid the paper to his side of the table. "You mean that it's a drawing of the *inside* of the box. Brilliant!"

"I don't know," Temple said, "whether to be miffed by your takeover move or flattered."

"Maybe that was always your problem with Kinsella," Matt murmured.

"Charity," Max answered him. "The first of these is charity, Devine. He's right, Temple. I'm being possessive of this clue. But I wanted to check if there was any invisible writing on it. It looks straightforward." He lifted it to the ceiling and the light again, like a priest elevating the host, Temple thought, remembering attending Mass with Matt, as she would be again.

"Stop it," Matt ordered.

Temple wondered if he'd made the same connection and was offended. Max sure was.

"I'm the magician here," he told Matt. "If there's anything hinky about this paper and the scrawling on it, I'd be the one to figure it out."

"No," Matt ordered. "Put it down. We need to lay it *over* something before we can see anything in the light." He turned to Temple. "You took custody of the stuff from Mom's fireproof file chest in Chicago."

"Yeah. I have a safe place to store it."

"You mean your scarf drawer," Max said sarcastically.

They stared at him.

"You said that like you *remembered* it." Matt sounded accusing.

"No, you or Temple mentioned that fascinating depository . . . or do I remember it?"

"Maybe," Temple said, "and maybe you're remembering the safe you had built in the bedroom closet side wall. I have my own fireproof file box in the same closet."

She turned to Matt. "You should invest in one too. I keep the sketches Janice Flanders, the police artist, made for us there, along with my Table of Crime Elements."

"Let's get that file." Matt stood, heading for the bedroom, and Temple did likewise.

Behind them, Max cleared his throat. "Don't be too long, kiddies."

"We really need tracing paper," Matt suggested as Temple crouched to dig through the file folders in her closet. "You're usually uprooting shoes in there."

She stood, flourishing Effinger's detailed drawing of the constellation Ophiuchus, man versus giant snake. Those Greeks, so imaginative. Those Synth members, so bewitched by conspiracies and their trappings.

They charged back to the living room and presented the prize to Max. "You can get this closer to the light," Temple said.

He stood and elevated the two sheets of white paper together, spinning the Ophiuchus drawing around the stripped-down "tree" skeleton from Professor Mangel's box.

"*Hmm.*"

Matt gazed up, rapt, and nodded.

"What?" Temple was almost jumping up and down in frustration at being too low to see. She kicked off her shoes and hopped up on her chair seat. "*What?*"

Matt turned and lifted her up on the table, though she had to squinch down to keep her head from hitting the ceiling.

"It doesn't jibe," Max was saying, already lowering the papers.

"No," Matt said, "flip the snake over. I think there's some convergence."

"They're a different scale," Temple suggested.

"Scale? Snake?" Max mocked.

"Get me down from here, and I'll use my copier to enlarge and reduce the map until this Ophiuchus image either matches somehow, or doesn't."

This time Max lifted her down. Temple noticed he'd

left Matt to do the heavy lifting, probably because he still didn't have full leg strength.

"Before we all get bent out of shape," Matt said, "including Ophiuchus, what exactly would explain my no-good late stepfather having custody of any kind of key related to a fringe group of magicians in Las Vegas? The same Synth being apparently abetted by some vague mobster connections and Irish political extremists of either stripe?"

Temple sat at the table again, chin on elbows atop the table. "Looking at my Table of Crime Elements—"

Both guys groaned, realized their mutual agreement, and shut up.

"Effinger died," Temple went on, "before Gloria Fuentes was found dead and Professor Mangel was, well, as good as slaughtered a month later." She shut up before she choked up.

She'd had a couple talks with Jeff Mangel, the way a reporter or an investigator would. He was a model of the idealistic, always enthusiastic teacher. She'd liked him instantly. And he'd loved Max's onstage work. She sensed the guys looking at each other over her head, at a loss.

Because of her emotional upsurge, it was way too awkward for either of them to make a move, like the impasse between the china images of the gingham dog and calico cat on the mantel in an old poem. Because of her, they were frozen into incompatible roles.

Then she'd just have to unfreeze the moment with her incisive logic. Easier said than done.

"Look, guys. It's pretty clear that Effinger knew or had something that got him killed, likely without talking. We've always speculated that the mob and the Synth were after the same prize, and now we know that Cosimo Sparks was the Synth headman."

"'Major recruiter' is probably what you'd call him,"

Max put in. "And he wasn't too persuasive if he left a killing trail of would-be recruits that turned him down."

"Effinger talked to somebody with mob connections," Matt said. "The events in Chicago proved that."

Temple was starting to see the light. "Santiago probably got something out of Sparks. The body had what the coroner calls 'hesitation marks.' "

"What was the weapon?" Matt wanted to know.

"Ice pick."

"Cold," Matt said. "And he hasn't been indicted?"

"He confessed, but without a lawyer present, so he retracted it."

"He confessed?" Now Max was incredulous.

Temple grinned. "The Fontana boys took him for a ride from hell, and he wasn't too rational after that."

"So now he *is* in hell," Matt said, nodding. "According to Dante, there's a whole circle of hell with murderers being harried in a river of blood."

"Gosh," Temple said, "we encountered a few of those killers."

"Think Kathleen O'Connor will go directly there?" Max asked Matt with gusto.

Matt looked troubled. "I think that's not up to us. There still may be the soul of a lost child within her."

Temple hadn't been following the interchange. She was busy writing Santiago in as the latest corpse on her Table of Crime Elements.

"Why was Santiago killed? By whom? And why there?"

Both men opened their mouths to speculate, but Temple suddenly jumped up. "Hold the fort and the mayo. I've got an idea."

She grabbed Professor Mangel's map and the Ophiuchus map and ran for her office, to rev up the copier. There was some murmured conversation between the guys but the noise from the rackety copier kept Temple from hearing what they were saying.

"I'm back!" she announced breathlessly from the doorway to the main room. "I reduced and enlarged until I went through fifty pages, but I finally herded these two images into cowering submission and they are one. Now I know why Santiago was murdered and why it happened where it did."

"And who did it?" Matt and Max asked together, in concert for the second time in the history of their sessions.

"Well, no. On that, I haven't got a clue. Specifically."

"Specifically is kind of important," Matt said.

Max nodded.

"So are maps," Temple said, slapping two pieces of paper to the tabletop. One was copied at a very dark setting.

Both men leaned close to view the usual guidebook map of Las Vegas Boulevard from Downtown to Mc-Carran Airport on the south end, the footprints of all the major hotels and landmarks drawn in and named.

Temple lifted a faint reproduction of the Ophiuchus figure from Effinger's file box, only a few dark spots inked in: the major stars that formed the crude shape of a kindergartner's askew house outline.

Matt reared back so abruptly, he almost butted skulls with Max. "It's the Vegas Strip. The star sites are places that could be hiding the IRA hoard. Why so many, though?"

Max's forefinger pinioned a dark spot. "The Synth was the keeper of the hoard for outside interests. It's like Cosimo Sparks kept the map to himself, but some map site points may have been phony to confuse other seekers, perhaps even the intended keepers of the hoard. Or the 'star spots' may indicate an order in which the hoard could be moved if in danger."

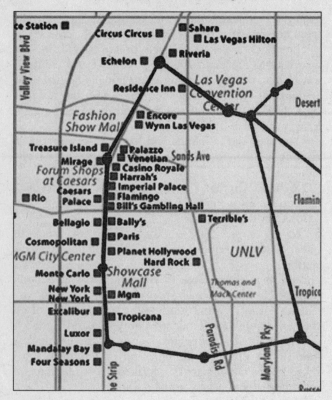

"This one," Temple said, "is right under 'Area 54.' Now we know why Santiago was snooping around that site. He'd tormented another copy of the map out of Sparks before the magician died: then he in turn was killed to keep the hoard safe for somebody else."

"Somebody who may have moved it," Matt said.

"Doesn't this feel like an outtake from *Treasure Island*?" Temple said. "A hidden hoard wanted by many parties, as in the *Pirates of the Caribbean* films, and, for drama, 'the Black Spot,' only several of them."

"The Black Spot was a note delivered to pirates, warning they were marked for death, not geographical markings," Matt said.

"Death *has* followed this 'treasure,' " Temple pointed out. "It we find it, we can end the mayhem being wreaked by the factions fighting over it."

Max had been silent while Temple and Matt went into their pirate-treasure riff.

"Max?" she asked. "What do you think?"

"More than I'm willing to say yet." He ran his hands through his hair, looking troubled. "My balky brain isn't running on high octane, but I do believe I'm . . . we're finally on the right trail."

Max sighed. "And who knows what unlikely suspect we might find at the end of it."

His intonation hadn't made that speculation a question, but a statement.

Poor X-man, Temple thought, *ex-spy, ex-magician, ex– main man and now operating with an X-factor memory.*

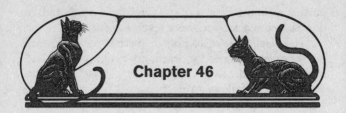

Chapter 46

Max's Midnight Hour

Max wondered what Matt Devine was doing right now. Probably talking down some depressed ex-boyfriend on the radio and preparing for another wrongheaded but good-hearted attempt to deal with and deflect Kathleen O'Connor. She'd always found the ex-priest a favorite second-best target.

Max couldn't worry about that now. Last night he couldn't believe where the trail of Kathleen's follower had led. Once again the hulking high skyline of a major strip hotel loomed over him. Max had dodged around Ford 150s and Tacomas and Expeditions in the farthest area of the hotel parking garage to track his prey to an unlighted wall in the structure's top level.

Max had heard the soft wheeze and snick of an elevator door closing and rushed to find only a concrete block dead end. Several dark gray metal doors promised to lead somewhere, but all were hinged and locked. A very private elevator must lurk behind one of them. They all had security pads, not locks to pick.

Max had pressed like a lover against each in turn, seeking some slight warmth or tremor from the only operative one.

Nothing. The elevator was elaborately camouflaged. Max could, and would, get inside the hotel to find whatever was on the other side of this wall there, but he expected to encounter another dead end.

What that said about the man he'd been following was chilling.

Talk about a cloak of invisibility. Silas T. Farnum's technologically invisible Area 54 hotel-casino had nothing on this guy.

And here Max himself had made what he needed to do next even harder than it was before.

"Darlin' girl," Max told the stunning New Millennium cocktail waitress wearing a liquid silver catsuit over a silver-paint full body and face job. "I need you to assist me in a street magic illusion. First, who is your favorite president, William McKinley or Grover Cleveland?"

"Grover Cleveland," she answered promptly, proving she was no babe in the woods.

Max rolled the fingers of his right hand, and a thousand-dollar bill materialized. He'd already expected to dip into his emergency stash. Big bills were easier to conceal.

"All I need is you," he said, "with a tray of two vodka martinis and a cool head. Follow me and I will follow you later."

She cocked an inquiring silver eyebrow, but Vegas casino workers were used to eccentric big spenders and often shared in the bounty.

On his order, the bar produced two princely looking, and costing, martinis embellished with gourmet onions, and more of Max's big bills went to the cause.

"What flavor martinis are those?" the cocktail waitress asked.

"They're called Open Sesames."

"That's a new one," she commented, shrugging.

"Now, head backstage," he told her.

She raised both eyebrows. "We only go there on orders."

"These are my orders, and we'll be as welcome as whales . . . once we get in."

Max followed her through the casino, donning the white *Star Wars* helmet with black eye visor he'd also bought from the bartender.

Now they were a cocktail waitress and her personal *Star trooper* guard en route to a Very Important Prestidigitator Max wanted to surprise.

The girl glided past the hotel's huge theater and down a low-lit side ramp most people would overlook. She paused at a heavy steel door, with a keypad entry showing both letters and numbers.

Max thought he knew his man, but he thought some more. His fingertips tapped a rhythm on eight buttons. Nothing happened. The girl sighed heavily behind him. He tried three more combinations. The fifth unlocked the door, which he pulled open to admit her before him. Always the gentleman, but this was the riskiest part of the plan.

Two heavyset men who probably held black belts in several varieties of exotic martial arts and also held high-caliber automatic weapons bracketed the door.

They didn't have a silver-metal almost naked girl, though, and from the looks on their stolid faces, this was the best part of their day.

Knowing her power, the waitress approached without

hesitation. From the next look on their faces, she had smiled at them.

"Legacy liquor-crafted cocktails from Mr. Akihiro on a radiant performance," Max intoned in an insufferably snobby English accent. The major Vegas hotels could charge thousands for drinks made from obscenely aged liquors.

Max knew their voices would be piped into the next room. So did the cocktail waitress, who probably believed this entire farce was the gesture of an immensely rich "whale."

The interior keypad allowed the door to be cracked enough for Max to again usher his glamorous guide right through.

And like that, he was in the fortress of the Cloaked Conjuror's dressing room.

As the door shut automatically behind them, Max took the cocktail tray and placed it on the dressing table. The next moment, he wrenched off the helmet and made a deep bow with it playing the part of a cavalier's hat.

"Yo, Max Kinsella!" The man in the massive easy chair rose slightly. "Testing my security again and finding it lacking. I'll have to put you on retainer."

Max gave another courtly bow. "I live to serve."

"What did you use to take out my doormen, a Vulcan neck pinch? A bit physical for you, isn't that?"

"Nothing crude and violent. My intercepting you coming offstage last time made that route null and void, so I improvised with a lovely distraction, the trick of our common trade."

"Jolly good."

The waitress flashed Max an approving look and offered another to the Cloaked Conjuror, who'd retained his helmetlike but animalistic head mask after leaving the stage for the night.

"Have a seat, and your gorgeous cocktail waitress friend can fetch you any drink you desire."

"Sparkling water," Max ordered. "In fact, I see some on ice on your dressing table. That'll do," he told the waitress.

He fancied he would have seen CC's eyebrows rising if the magician hadn't been wearing the head-encompassing mask.

"You a teetotaler suddenly?" CC asked, incredulous. Max was probably the only drinking buddy he had.

"Just for the moment." Max accepted the Baccarat crystal goblet showcasing totally unalcoholic bubbles fizzing like mad.

When the heavy door shut behind the departing cocktail waitress, Max set down the glass and leaned toward CC. "I followed you following her last night."

"Me? Out following someone?" The mask's voice-altering mechanism made CC's laugh sound like a pack of Santa Clauses on a toot. "Max, you're good, but you're not so good you can follow a figment of your imagination."

"The figment of my imagination was my first thought about the identity of the portly guy who trekked from the Goliath to the Treasure Island to the abandoned Neon Nightmare to the New Millennium here. I actually thought at first it might be Gandolph."

"And why wouldn't it be? He's a foxy fellow and could have led you a merry chase."

"He was shot and killed in Belfast a few weeks ago."

"God, no." CC slumped back in his chair, the sagging of his costumed shoulders conveying sorrow, but in an exaggerated way, like a forlorn clown. "I'm sorry, Max. I know how much he meant to you."

"Then take off that mask and talk to me face-to-face."

The Cloaked Conjuror put his bare hands to the striped sides of his leonine face mask. Then they paused.

"You broke in here, but you're also going to have to break out, if I say you can't go."

"I'm aware of that." Max finally drank some water, never taking his eyes off CC and the mask at his graceful fingertips. Magicians were used to making flourishes.

"Risk." CC pulled off the headpiece. "Always your long suit, Max. I envied you that. My risks are well cloaked, and I don't have any sense of personal credit when I win."

"I'm not after credit. I'm after justice and truth." Max heard himself and laughed. "And the American way."

"You'd make a good Superman, but I don't think red and blue are your colors." CC chuckled, setting his iconic headpiece on the dressing table.

Black greasepaint circled his eyes and nose so they'd blend with the mask, and red surrounded his mouth, which made him look like a part-time member of Kiss. Sweat shone in his hairline. Max doubted it was fresh.

"Cheers," said CC, leaning forward to click his drink glass with Max's. He sat back. "So how did Garry Randolph come to be shot in Northern Ireland?"

"We weren't just magicians when we toured the Continent years ago."

"That was such a lucky gig for a young pup like you. I was doing birthday parties and nursing homes. Then, years later, you came back and hit Vegas like a storm with that strobe light and walking-on-air act of yours. Why'd you vanish after your first year? You must have had offers bigger than the Goliath by then?"

"I did." Max sipped fizz water, feeling his throat tighten. To get info, you had to give info. First rule of manipulation. "Also several firm offers to leave the planet. Garry and I were undercover counterterrorists during our tour of Europe. I'd run afoul of the IRA when my cousin was blown up in a pub bombing, and they've been after me ever since."

"No shit." CC was shocked to the soles of his five-inch platform shoes.

"So now you know why I slink around Las Vegas like a cartoon spy character. I have a lot at stake. Now I want to know why *you* slink around like a bad cartoon spy character and how long this has been going on."

"What? You're hallucinating, Max. You don't know what I look like out of mask and makeup and this costume, not to mention the padded body armor because of all the threats on my life. You thought you were seeing Gandolph, Garry Randolph. That shows you're a bit off your rocker, and I don't blame you."

Max got up, got an empty glass, and poured the Grey Goose vodka on a side table into it straight.

CC tensed as Max moved, yet kept very still.

Then Max poured the vodka into his sparkling water. "Not exactly a James Bond–approved martini, but it'll do. Yes, I am a bit off my rocker. Someone tried to kill me and racked up my legs and memory."

"You . . . walk just fine." CC frowned his puzzlement at where this was going. "And you remember me."

"I remember bits and pieces of back then and back now, and bits and pieces of people. Confession time. I always admired your guts in making an act out of exposing other magicians' tricks." Max settled in the chair as if for a long winter's nap, stretching out his legs. "Those ticked-off magicians are short-sighted. They'll still get audiences trying to see them do what you show they do, and the audiences still won't see through everything."

"I never exposed one of your specialties."

"I appreciated that. That's why I've been acting as your guardian angel."

"I didn't know about your double life, Max, but I've always felt a kinship with you, probably because I sensed you had your own secrets. You understood my isolation and loneliness, and I sensed that in you."

"Soul brothers." Max leaned forward to butt glass rims. "But you're not at the top of my save list. My ex-girl is, for instance."

"You do pretty well for a multi-client guardian angel. I get that totally." CC sighed, then took a three-swallow hit of straight vodka. "I had a girl. Why is your ex an 'ex'?"

"I don't quite remember, mercifully." Max eyed the uneasy mix of liquor and water in his glass, not a shaken or stirred cocktail but two elements in opposition. "I think I felt she was safer without me."

CC stared past him to the metal door and nodded. "Yeah. We're both targets. Our survival can come at the risk of collateral damage."

"Yet you're out in plain clothes prowling the Strip after your act."

"Damn it, Max! I'm confined in this heavy, hot, itchy false skin five nights a week, three to five hours depending on the day of the week. I need to get out to breathe."

"You have that big estate out on Sunset Road."

"Big for a prison yard." He shifted his sturdy frame, and his mood changed. "So what's new?"

"What's new is that I think we're in the same boat on significant others too, and I hadn't realized until last night that you were in a position to do something about it . . . in fact, anything you damn well please." Las Vegas was a place where no one knew his face.

"Am I?" The man's laugh was bitter. "Can I bring back the dead? Is that a trick I can work into my act? Maybe you can do that, Max Kinsella, Mr. Mystifying Max, magician and IRA target and counter-spy. You can't bring back Gandolph."

Max saw the Cloaked Conjuror was doffing his masks, getting down to a face-peel of the soul. He shut his eyes, accessing his own. "I saw him die."

"I saw her die."

Max took a deep breath. This was probably the most important interview of his life, and he didn't know where it was going except it was someplace he damn well didn't want to be.

"Look," Max said. "I don't know your name—and I've tried to find it. With that greasepaint mask you lard on beneath the headpiece—black, white, red—it'd be like trying to ID a clown from his makeup. I don't really know what you look like, not enough to give the police for a BOLO. In fact, the police find me a highly suspicious character. What I also don't know is if we're in this together, because the woman you followed the other night is the devil in snakeskin who indirectly killed my cousin Sean, and maybe Gandolph directly. What have you got against her?"

"Devil is right." CC turned to the mirror and began swiping cold cream over his face with a tissue, wiping off sweat and greasepaint in such hard repetitive strokes that Max winced for his skin. The man of masks was scraping himself raw.

Max knew that feeling. He'd been doing that himself since the age of seventeen when Sean was killed. He let CC talk. It was a monologue to the real man in his mirror anyway, to the meaty, middle-aged face in his mirror. Ordinary was a good disguise too.

"She seemed like a rich amateur, Max. A hanger-on. A groupie. We magicians don't get many of those besides wannabe adolescent boys. Maybe we're supposed to be satisfied by the hot babes in our acts." He glanced at Max. "I know, you didn't have any assistants, except feathered. But she brought me Shang." CC's smile was rueful. "And Shang brought me her furred Siamese cat, Hyacinth. Damn thing ran away, after her death."

"Wait. The woman I'm after, who's after me, *wasn't* Shangri-La?"

"Sometimes she got herself up as Shang. They had

similar body types, but Shang was fine-boned, more graceful, a true tiger lily of a girl. She worshipped this woman, this Rebecca."

Max recognized Kathleen O'Connor's latter-day persona, based on the amoral and manipulative psychopath in the novel of the same name. *Rebecca*.

He couldn't restrain a shocked move.

"You hate her too." CC's voice contained wonder, and hope.

"Hate isn't the word. I know her for an enemy. Once we were lovers, for a day."

CC blinked, his eyelashes oily with cold cream. "That witch?"

"I was seventeen, and no judge. I've long suspected she knew my cousin was in harm's way, and seduced me to safety . . . and a lifetime of guilt. That's her modus operandi, to 'take away' love and life."

CC set his glass down so hard on the dressing table, the fine crystal cracked. "She did that with me, dear God. Her games left Shang dangling by a thread during our act. I know you were there, guardian angel. I know you did everything to save Shang from the fatal cut bungee cord, but even you couldn't do it. At least you tried."

"I didn't know then there were . . . two. I thought I was saving Kathleen. Ironic. I questioned trying to save this woman, but my reflexes betrayed me." Max shut his eyes. "And so another of her victims perished. Shang had been set up as a body double. We often use them. I'm still not sure if yours, Barry, fell or was pushed from the top of your set. This woman has used body doubles before to deceive the living and cheat death. Shang's not the only one who's died in that woman's demented script of vengeance."

"Vengeance? Hers? That's crazy. We need to avenge ourselves on her."

Max recalled the horrific childhood abuse he and

Garry had discovered she'd survived in Ireland. "She was sinned against early and often."

"Shang was the only woman I ever loved." CC pounded his padded chest in emphasis. "I've used eight private detectives to find this vicious woman from her looks alone. She shows up on film of my show that was done for TV spots." He leaned back, spent. "Now you've found both her, Max, and my recent secret outings. She made a mistake creating a pattern at the Goliath. One of my hired guys spotted her. I've been following her, but I've never found where she goes to ground. I should have gone to you in the first place." CC gazed into the pool of priceless vodka in his glass.

Max decided to wait until he knew more before asking his friend and colleague in magic and vengeance the question he most wanted answered at the moment. He stood, and set his unsatisfying drink on the dressing table. "I'm following her now," Max said. "Stay out of it. I'll let you have the leavings."

He left before CC could answer, as unsatisfied with the situation as with the drink. The guards gave him dirty looks, but he noted them only in passing. He was thinking hard.

O'Connor and Santiago MacCarthy were old allies and likely after the hidden money they raised for the IRA that the Synth had protected. That's what really had brought Santiago to Las Vegas. If Santiago was in town, Kathleen would have seen him.

And so could CC have when he was following her.

Kitty was good at finally slipping away from the amateur-detective magician whose antisocial lifestyle made him less agile on the street, but maybe Santiago hadn't been. Max could imagine CC recognizing Santiago as someone he could trap, following him somewhere deserted like Farnum's building, and trying to throttle Kathleen's whereabouts out of the man.

Yet . . . Max *couldn't* imagine a scenario that put both Santiago and CC on the top floor of the mysterious building on Paradise Road.

Max needed to figure out not only motivation, but opportunity. Motivation was all too plain. He wondered how sane a man could be who'd lived hidden behind a literal false front to the world for years, once he lost the one woman he'd loved.

Max and the Cloaked Conjuror had way too much in common.

Chapter 47

Falling for You

Why did he feel more guilty, Matt wondered, the longer he let himself be forced into nightly meetings with Kathleen O'Connor?

Maybe that was because he was getting somewhere with her, which meant she was getting somewhere with him. The last thing he needed was for her to transfer her love–hate fixation on Max Kinsella to him. The fact was, Temple was still in danger from the woman either way, because she'd been loved by both men.

At Temple's Table of Crime Elements meeting today, with the exciting revelation that Jeff Mangel had secreted a Synth map in his exhibition of magic and Max had found it, Matt had wanted to shout, "Hey, I found out that Kathleen O'Connor isn't the second Darth Vader who intimidated the Synth members. She is cat-scratch free."

Yeah, explain how he knew that to Temple with Max Kinsella looking on.

Speaking of Kinsella, he'd broadcast the same air of stress and guilt Matt felt. And Temple had obviously picked up their unease.

Last time Kitty the Cutter had cut herself. He'd tended the wound and left her the razor. She'd seemed much more docile tonight, even subdued. They'd discussed her abuse, his abusive stepfather, Cliff Effinger.

She'd first approached—and cut him—because she'd believed his following Effinger made him a rival for her interests. That alone tied the IRA hoard to minor mob errand boys, at least.

It was almost a normal counseling session.

That made Matt nervous. Normality made Kathleen O'Connor even more nervous.

The session was breaking up early tonight.

"Do you see *her* after every time you come here?" she asked as they'd left the room together, like a fornicating couple leaving an assignation.

At least that's the look they got from a late-returning gambler shambling down the hall toward them, his short-sleeved shirt darkened by damp rings around the armpits. His build was as baggy as his eyes, but he spared each of them a knowing leer that said "hooker and john" before passing by.

Matt had stepped to the brass-and-steel railing, turning his back. He was a radio "personality," to be heard but not seen . . . except for the station billboards. MR. MIDNIGHT IN THE WEE HOURS. He didn't want to read any headlines like MR. MIDNIGHT'S TRYST IN THE WEE HOURS.

Kathleen, of course, had leaned back against the railing as the man had passed, stretching her arms out to display her torso and leering back. "You took the risk in the first place," she whispered just loud enough for it to be a hiss, "seeing that whore here, for counseling, at night, an upstanding ex-priest like you."

"That used to be called 'giving scandal,'" he admitted, relieved that Kathleen had been referring to Vassar, not Temple.

"The Church has a name for every little move a man could make."

Her answer echoed a song Ambrosia played sometimes, about the usual unfaithful woman. "Sundown." It was sure place- and person-appropriate now.

He couldn't help smiling, which infuriated her.

"Smug. You're so sure, so smug. So 'right,' like all the rest of them."

With the graceful wrist movement of a flamenco dancer poising a castanet for playing, she unfurled the straight razor.

Matt's small smile didn't fade. Who did she think *she* was, a femme fatale or "Bad, Bad Leroy Brown" with a razor in his shoe?

Yeah, she'd accosted him on a dark street and cut him once, when he'd been new to Las Vegas and innocent of her existence. He'd had warning now.

He could have done a mind-bending riff on how the razor was an emasculating weapon for a woman, and also an artificial extension that grew longer and a phallic symbol as well. But she wasn't interested in academic theories now. The leering man had set her off. She was back into terrorizing.

She leaned far out to look down into the tunnel of hanging jungle foliage with colorful birds flitting in and out like escapees from an animated Disney film.

"If you fell from here, like Vassar," Kathleen speculated in a playful tone. "Just saying. If you fell and were declared a suicide, you'd never be buried in a Catholic cemetery. No St. Peter's or Paul's or Stanislaus's in Chicago for you or your family."

She spun and put her back to the railing, still flirtatiously threatening.

"And why shouldn't you fall, with a razor at your throat? Why shouldn't there be a 'scandal'? 'Ex-Priest Radio Personality Dies on Site of Apparent Tryst.' Why shouldn't everyone who knows you weep and wail and say they can't explain it? . . . I could leave some indicting trinkets. Hints of a secret love affair gone wrong. Who'd be around to deny it?" She lunged toward him. "Not. You." The point of her razor pressed against his carotid artery.

He could feel it pulsing, but kept his voice calm. "So this is how you extorted money out of your wealthy IRA 'donors'? Sex wasn't always enough, was it, Kathleen?"

"If you don't care about *your* postmortem reputation, I'll remind you that someone's Circle Ritz balcony is only one story above the parking lot," she told him. "And it's a tiny, triangular toy of a space where a woman wearing high heels—like Vassar up here on this very spot—might twist an ankle, or let her cell phone slip away and lean over the railing too far and fall . . . not far, not twenty stories like Vassar, but . . . enough."

He'd warned her about threatening Temple again.

As she leaned close, confident in her faithful cutting edge, Matt caught her left hand in his right as if they were dancing, used his left to exert pressure on her right wrist, twisted, and then pulled her torso against the railing, facing down.

The falling razor flashed as it glinted and sliced through the hanging foliage like a mini machete. Exotic birds, disturbed, rustled up into the air, a fractured rainbow of color. The razor vanished into the long empty distance all the way to the illuminated stained glass ceiling far, far below, where Vassar had been found dead.

"You. Hurt. Me." Kathleen was aghast. Surprised. Her hands flexed closed and opened, bereft of the weapon that was almost a sentient extension of her hatred and power.

"Sorry." Matt held her immobile, on the brink of falling herself. "You've been hurt plenty before. I could easily toss you over this railing and then all your pain would be gone and *you*'d be the suicide."

She shook the strands of black hair out of her eyes and lifted her face. "Deaths like these are always suspicious. Vassar's was. Twice, Mr. Devine? You're on the scene when two women go over the railing?" She didn't notice she'd dropped the taunting "Father" before his name. She was worried.

"I had a chance to off Effinger, you know," Matt said in a reminiscent tone. He could play the stone-cold killer too. "I could have throttled him. Instead, I left him for your lot to fasten to a sinking ship and slowly drown. My way would have been kinder."

"You're not—" She was trying to slide away down the railing, but his grip tightened.

"I'm not playing the usual patsy? That's thanks to you. I've watched your anger and hate strike at everyone around me, and me once. Once is enough with you, Kathleen. You can't carry around as much hatred as you do and feel entirely justified. Some maybe, but not enough. You are a bad woman, Kathleen. You need to get clear of your past and become a happy person."

"They don't serve Kool-Aid in this hotel, but you've drunk plenty elsewhere."

"Right. I'm the demented one. So before we resume our . . . dialogue, I'll tell you something you don't know about Max Kinsella."

Just mentioning the name tautened every sinew in her

frame. Matt felt it all the way through to her slender wrists. Her build was dainty, but she felt like a guitar string that had been tightened to the snapping point.

"He's your rival," she said.

Matt shook his head. "He's harmless."

She almost spit at him, but glanced at the chasm below and reconsidered.

"He's forgotten most of his past, you know. That's right. You wouldn't know. He's forgotten you, thanks to that bungee cord act of sabotage at the late, great Neon Nightmare club. Was that you? No, you like live victims. But you knew about that so-called accident. It's your business to know everything about all of us."

"Us?"

"Anyone close to Max Kinsella. As I said, he's lost and misplaced most of what made Max Kinsella before he was the Mystifying Max. His mentor's death in Northern Ireland probably blasted the rest out of him. Do you know anything about that, Kathleen? The old IRA and the recalcitrant 'New' IRA are still fightin' and fussin' some, and Max and Garry Randolph got caught in the crossfire. Do you know anything about who betrayed them? Speechless? Thinking hard? Never mind.

"Max is back in Vegas putting pieces together. He remembers the past few weeks since he recovered from his coma, of course. He remembers his travels with his mentor to Belfast. I'm not sure he remembers you, Kathleen. Except for what his mentor learned about your mother and your birth and your own motherhood and passed on."

By now her glare had frozen as if this Medusa had finally glimpsed herself in a mirror. Her breathing was hardly detectable, but her pulse was galloping in her wrists.

"He has odd flashes of memory, you understand? And he's a very bright man. Brilliant. I'm counseling him too.

Helping him to rebuild his life. To remember. But it's often just the offbeat emotional flash. Something simmers, then he blurts it out.

"During one of those moments, when we were talking about you . . . you can imagine how much we talk about you lately. Max said, regarding those crazy teenage times in the Auld Sod when he and his cousin Sean went waltzing up to Londonderry into the teeth of the Troubles. He said, and we can't put much stock into what a man in his condition, not to mention recovering from the violent loss of his mentor, thanks to some unknown assailants, says. But he said, with amazing and sudden certainty, that he'd been in love with you.

"It's ironic that you'd hate forever the only man who ever really loved you."

He pushed her away and left, knowing he was done with this charade and that, if she did go over the railing, she would never scream on the way down.

At least he'd learned something major, if he was inclined to believe anything Kathleen O'Connor would say, but he did believe she was lurking there that night. Vassar hadn't killed herself. She'd fallen, grabbing for her cell phone while gazing out at the pseudo-tropical foliage, inhabited by birds no less, twenty stories up.

Had she been calling the advice hotline he'd suggested? Had he turned her despair around, just a little? Or was Kitty the Cutter just toying with him again? Hope was an antidote to guilt, and she knew how to work that combination lock to the emotions very, very well.

Chapter 48

After the Fall

So there I am at the Goliath, on tailing duty, having shad-
owed Mr. Matt Devine into the hotel and up in the elevator,
when I overhear that interesting interlude.

Las Vegas hotel elevators are the easiest to slip into and
out of, like loafers. Folks are always counting their chips or
their money, and chatting or planning their forays around
the Strip. Many are rotund enough that they cannot even
see where their toes are, much less me and mine.

And the management prefers dark-floored elevators to
resist stains.

I was even able to follow him to the door of room 2032. I
cozied up to it in hopes of hearing something useful, but the
door was too well built to hear through, especially with the
air-conditioning running.

The recent balcony scene outside the door was no

Romeo and Juliet rerun and I heard every word. At last Mr. Matt knows from someone on two legs who was there that Vassar's death was accidental and his counseling had encouraged her to call for more help while Miss K the C spied on her from down the hall.

I knew that all along after coming here and interviewing the wildlife on the scene. I learned that Miss Vassar had come out to gaze on the flora and fauna and make a call on her cell phone after Mr. Matt left. She reached down as the phone slipped from her hand and, sadly, fell.

There was no way for me to bring the eyewitness evidence I obtained from a macaw and cockatoos to human attention, so Mr. Matt has labored under a bit of suspicion and his own sense of guilt ever since. Now he has stepped up and found the truth.

I cannot rejoice overmuch at the moment, though, because when the pair left the hotel room, I had flung myself down under the railing to cling to a thick but thorny length of exotic flowering vine and am now desperately fighting two fatal impulses: To sneeze or to fall, that is the question. Or do both.

Hopefully, neither of the above.

Unfortunately, Miss Kitty the Cutter is alone now and wringing the brass top rail with her razorless hands and cussing out Mr. Matt, Mr. Max, and Miss Temple something awful.

I dare not climb up to resume tailing Mr. Matt because the awkward positions required to achieve solid ground again would leave me at the mercy of Miss Kitty and either a swift kick to the gut and the curb twenty stories below or a lusty neck-wringing.

Inquiring members of feather nation gather around me, chirping and calling and clicking their beaks in admonition, drawing unwelcome attention to my secret presence and generally twittering it all over the atrium.

Fortunately, I am recognized.

"Oh, not a predator," comes the sweet tweet of a gray parrot I recognize from my last assignment here.

"Begone, begone, begone," tweet a flock of cockatiels, and I would be obliged if Miss Kitty would depart.

"I need a diversion," I tell the gray parrot, who is amazingly verbal and intelligent for a featherhead.

"Troops," the gray orders, "Disneyize that woman at the railing."

Well, you have never seen a more colorful array of sweet little feathered nothings twining in and around Miss Kathleen O'Connor's form, swooping into her black locks and lifting edges of her filmy clothing in their little yellow beaks and chirping oh-so-sunnily.

It is as if one of the Ugly Stepsisters became the object of a Cinderella makeover. Miss Kitty is soon batting and turning and making like Miss Tippi Hedren in an Alfred Hitchcock movie.

I undulate up the sinuous branch, never looking down to twenty stories below, and scramble over the edge onto the balcony.

The last I see of Miss Kitty the Cutter, she is batting off birds and much resembling the Wicked Witch of the West surrounded by her flying monkeys.

I race to the elevators, heading for the main floor and the parking lot, determined to get to Mr. Matt's silver Jaguar before the big automotive cat takes off without me.

That would not be a brotherly act from a fellow feline. I need to keep my tail.

I can only hope the rest of the Cat Pack is pursuing their assignments with equal savvy and vigor.

And less dependence on our feathered friends.

Chapter 49

Left Behind

Max couldn't sleep. He often woke up before the dawn, listening. That was said to be a sign of depression, but so was oversleeping.

The house was quiet without Garry there, with no hope of Garry ever being there again. Gandolph the Great had truly died and wouldn't come back, as Gandalf did in *The Lord of the Rings*.

Max nursed his whiskey, relaxing in the big lounge chair, feeling his frame settled into the upholstery as all of one piece, not leaning away from a twinge there, an ache here.

Whole.

That was the physical accomplishment. The next step would be mental in two stages: truly accepting Garry's absence and teasing his own memories into the present.

He shut his eyes, wondering what person, what place would undam his barricaded mind.

His thoughts jittered away from anyone he'd been emotionally connected to in the recent past. The issues were too delicate. Molina. Maybe that was his entry point. Their edgy, distant association invigorated him.

Max was disturbed to consider she had become more like a boss, more like a superior, and therefore more like his mentor. Why not? She was a leader of men. Max quirked a smile on the crystal rim of his glass. And she owed him. Falsely accused, poor boy, he was. He sensed something sheepish in her attitude toward him. Now that he'd been chased and half-killed by ex-terrorists, she'd come around to Temple's view of him.

Stubborn woman.

Not too sure which one he referred to.

Max smiled. That little redhead had faced off the tall police lieutenant and held her ground. It was like a Yorkie and a bloodhound match-up. . . . No, Molina was more like a Siberian husky with her icy blue eyes and fierce competitive stance. He wished Rafi Nadir good luck with getting any concessions from Big Mama Molina.

Yet, she was vulnerable. Her daughter.

Max was alone now. No one to be vulnerable about. Just as well.

A soft scrape in the entry hall brought his lazy eyelids full open, and his nostrils too.

He sensed a shift in the air-conditioned atmosphere. The big machine cozied up against the house exterior still operated, heaving like an iron lung against the heat.

But something was moving at the edges of the house, the door, a front window, the hallway hatch into the attic.

Max looked up. Squirrels in the attic? Rats? Assassins?

He pulled back a fabric protector over the chair's broad arm, revealing a control panel.

He'd discovered it when his restless hands had detected a too, too solid bit of piping on the upholstery. His fingers did a light braille dance over the various buttons. Was it like riding a bicycle or playing the piano? Did his fingertips do the walking and rewire his brain?

He hoped so because an enemy was paying him a visit.

And still he spared a smile for Garry Randolph, Gandolph the Late Great. He remembered Garry showing him the security panel embedded in the chair arm. "You're the captain of the starship *Enterprise* in this baby. You control the security shutters, the lights, air. You can lock anyone out, or keep anyone in."

Max nodded and set his whiskey glass on the side table. It was time to fly this thing.

First, he turned off the air-conditioning.

The instant silence was deafening. A shuffle down the hall stopped a millisecond too late.

He used the control to lower the lights on rheostats all through the house. Only the highest points of the furnishings, or a face, would be visible now. Anyone moving in this house would be walking on water, an unperceived pool of darkness hiding unanticipated objects.

Max's fingertips hesitated over the unseen control panel, waiting for an intuitive action.

So far muscle memory had guided him through without a misstep. Not so for the intruder.

A careless limb banged into the living area's archway.

Max could feel the pain of a hit shin or elbow pulsing mutely in the hall.

He waited about a minute, then shut the interior metal shutters while simultaneously pushing the lights up to maximum.

His eyes were squinted and his nerves tensed against the sudden clangs and floodlights, but his visitor was not prepared.

The slight figure in ninja black from head to foot tee-tered as if on a tightrope.

Max lifted the small Walther PPK from the control compartment. It glinted like black ice on asphalt in his hand.

"You've made yourself too easy to find," she said, her voice not familiar.

"Yes," he answered with satisfaction. "I wonder who you finally followed to get here. No, don't tell me." He put up his free hand. "I love a mystery."

"I'm not carrying."

"No, not a gun in all that spandex, but a blade or blades, that's something else. Please sit down. On that chair by the archway."

"I'm my own best weapon, don't you remember that?"

He didn't answer as she pulled the ski mask off to free her hair. For a moment he flashed back. A dead face on the dark ground beside a totaled motorcycle. Dead white skin, dead black hair. Not really her.

"Your career," he pointed out, "has been hard on body doubles."

She shrugged. "Risk of the trade."

"So why have you stopped being an elusive evil ge-nius and become a confrontational one?"

"I wouldn't have been elusive if you hadn't been so hard to find for so long."

"My fault. I see. I'm told I knew you once."

"In the biblical sense."

"That's too bad," he said.

"You didn't think so at the time."

"I was young and stupid."

"And in love."

"Was I, now? A pity I don't remember the details. First love and all. But your life and my life and how and when we met doesn't need to be remembered. It's a story now, in Ireland and here in Vegas. We are legend,

Kathleen O'Connor, despite ourselves. What a hell of a thing to not remember."

"I can make you remember."

"No, you can't. That's one thing you can't force." Max thought a moment. "You've put yourself in my power. Why? And why now?"

She didn't answer, instead shifting her body on the chair. He took it for an automatically seductive move, then noticed her right arm was a bit askew on her lap. An injury?

"Aren't you going to offer me a drink?" she asked.

"No."

"You couldn't wait to swig beer in the pub in Belfast."

"I don't want to get that close to you."

"How you've changed," she whispered intensely.

"That was years ago, Kathleen. Maybe you could do with a bout of amnesia yourself. Why hang on to that misbegotten part of that day, to that act, surely only one of a painful, vengeful parade of hundreds, thousands?"

She shut her eyes. "You changed so fast. It had been me, me, me that day, and then it was Sean, Sean, Sean that night and ever after, for always."

"My cousin died in a bombing. He was a brother to me."

She hurled herself upright, on her feet. "Men! Men and your brotherhood! All the IRA men were the same. Vengeance for one of their own, and then the other side retaliates in kind, and the women are left on the sidelines as collateral damage and the cause for more retaliation, or just forgotten. I was not going to be left on the sidelines."

"That's war."

"That was you. You just left me there in the park like a piece of trash when word came of the bombing. You hadn't been like them, caught up in their games of anger and tit for tat. You were from somewhere without a history of the Troubles. You said I was the most beautiful girl in the world. We laughed. I forgot about the Troubles. You said you loved me."

"I was seventeen, Kathleen. A boy. I'd have been enamored, sure. I'd think I loved you."

She wasn't listening. "Then you left me as they always did when they were through using me. Then you had to go and find the bombers and get yourself hunted by the IRA and then become the hunted. Leaving me behind was so easy. I had always been nothing, forever and ever, amen."

"And that's why you've hated and hunted me and mine all these years?"

"No! It's because you're the only one I could have loved."

Max stared into her bitter eyes sensing past images rising like a tide over the empty beaches of his mind. He hadn't lied to her. Her beauty was extraordinary, but left him cold now. Or maybe left him with pity. Once he'd seen her with the eyes of love, and for that she'd never forgiven him.

"I think I did love you, Kathleen, as only an idealistic, randy boy can. And so I chose you over Sean that day. I didn't lose the love. It was overpowered by guilt. By letting Sean stay behind in the pub to die, I couldn't perpetuate what I then saw as my traitorous happiness. Maybe in time . . . but by then I'd heard what a . . . flirt you were. I came to believe you were toying with me and even that you knew Sean was doomed. And then, I sensed your pursuit and thought you wanted me dead too."

"So it's like all of my life, a big misunderstanding." She stepped nearer, confrontational again. "No one in charge knew what went on, and they are very, very sorry. It's been my job to make them sorrier. And you're the sorriest of the lot. You've remembered you loved me, but the feeling is gone. So sad."

"Wait. How do you know I remembered that?"

"A little birdie told me far above the atrium of the Goliath Hotel."

Max knew one feeling he had wasn't gone—a sense that something bad was in play.

He heard a bit of scuffling sound at the front door, remembering he'd never heard the intruder shut it in order to enter the house more silently.

Kathleen was armed only with her anger, but Max rose and moved to the side of the chair. He didn't want to shoot her, but might need to tackle and confine her. Who the hell would be at his front door at five in the morning?

"The irony," she said, interrupting his intense listening, "is that it was all for nothing. Your cousin Sean? He got lucky as well as you that day."

"What do you mean?"

"A barmaid."

So Sean had flirted with a barmaid at the pub after Max had left with Kathleen. Good for him. He was a good-natured guy, and hadn't been feeling angry or jealous when he'd died. . . .

"I suppose that's ironic," Max said slowly, trying to guess her point.

The front door swung fully open; he recognized the slight groan in one hinge. The house controls were no longer at his fingertips and he couldn't risk taking his eyes off Kathleen to look down and secure the door.

"What's really ironic is that her shift was up and they were on their way out when the bomb went off."

Max suddenly stood in a world without sound, or rather, with only the sound of Kathleen's soft Irish singsong lilt. "She broke a leg and had multiple lacerations, but the last she saw of Sean Kelly, fine Irish name and lad, he was staggering away with a badly bleeding, almost blinding head wound."

Thunder crashed somewhere down the hall and echoed in his head, words reverberating, not making sense. *Badly bleeding, staggering away.*

"Sean is alive?" Max saw himself mouthing from a distance, in one of those slow-moving dreams of utter shock.

"Max!" someone called.

"Kathleen, don't!" someone else called.

And then he felt a swift lightning strike of pain in his right temple.

Temple?

And faded to black.

Chapter 50

Night Stalkers

Am I slicker when I am on a running streak than wet tar!

I race through the Goliath down to the entry, happy to see Mr. Matt's very tailable blond head bypassing the main exit for the route to the big outside parking lots. After that, it is easy for me to ease unseen around the base of gaming tables and out into what is left of the night.

I am Louie-on-the-spot to eel inside the Jaguar by the last hairs on my second loftiest member and settle down for a smooth glide into my home plate, the Circle Ritz. My toot-sies have done all the walking tonight, and they are aching for a time-out.

Mr. Matt Devine is obviously disturbed by his shock-and-awe moments with Miss Kitty the Cutter. I say, sock it to her! But being a kinder, gentler soul than the average thug, he is making penitential murmurs to a higher power.

I have never found making penitential murmurs to Bast too productive. To the contrary. Being a female goddess, she likes her subjects to scrap and scratch and bring her sacrificial prey in her honor.

Anyway, I have long been out of the Great Black Hunter game and am longing to sprint up the palm tree when we arrive home for some world-class snuggling and snoozing before dawn.

In not too long, the Jaguar pulls into its home lot. I crouch behind the driver's seat to leap out at the first crack of the steel door, or whatever they are making cars out of these days, but the door remains shut. Come on! I need *some* shut-eye tonight.

I hear the automatic hiss of the driver's side window going down and pounding footsteps heading our way.

I immediately assume flat-belly posture, ears down and eyelids at half-mast to better blend with the dark carpeting. (I certainly do not want my glittering greens to betray my presence.)

"Temple!" Mr. Matt says, sounding both relieved and perturbed.

She is breathless to see him herself. "Haven't you checked your cell phone lately?" is her lovesick greeting.

Already it is down to the little things of life, even before the wedding. *Tsk tsk.*

"No," Mr. Matt says, sounding guilty.

"There's a weirdly urgent message from Max. It is like it was cut off," Miss Temple says. "We have to get to his place right away."

"I have never been there," Mr. Matt says as I hear Miss Temple running around to the passenger side in what sounds like the flap of flats.

Things must be dire if she is going out in around-the-house shoes.

"I know the route. Get to Highway 95. And floor it."

Ooof! My cheek and jowl are pinched by pain as my head

and body are slung back against the backseat base and then into the back of the driver's seat.

Belatedly, I curl my shivs into the luxury carpet and hang tough.

While Miss Temple backseat drives from the front seat, I rapidly sum up the Cat Pack situation.

Miss Midnight Louise will be on-site, since she elected to follow Mr. Max. Who took on Miss Kitty? Ma Barker. I told her that was a rough assignment for a senior citizen, but after she had slapped the starch out of my whiskers, she told me seniority meant she had the savvy and clout to slap the stuffing out of any sniveling psychopath on the planet.

I sure hope so, because I know of no way to notify the rest of the Cat Pack that something dark and dirty is going down on Mojave Way.

Chapter 51

Hit Me with Your
Best Shot

Temple read the cryptic message aloud as Matt gunned
the Jaguar away from the Circle Ritz and into the city's
residential areas.

"Hand me your phone," she ordered Matt urgently.

He dug in his pants' pocket and produced it.

"Here. Look," she said. "No, don't look. Drive. You
got the same message from Max about twenty minutes
ago. 'My place right away. End game.'"

"And you're sure it's from Kinsella?" Matt sounded
skeptical. "He's not one to call for help."

"I don't think it's help he wants. Maybe he's found
some amazing way to use the map to go right to the IRA
hoard. Get that to the authorities, and maybe all the related crimes will clear right up."

"Why didn't he call Molina?"

"Not without checking with us Round Table members." Temple frowned at the message on the screen.

"Maybe he just wanted to interfere with our sleep."

"Poor baby." She put a hand on Matt's arm and he jumped. "You've been losing too much sleep over those post-show sessions with Leticia Brown. Her Ambrosia brand will still thrive without you as a follow-up. Are you breaking in someone to replace you? A secret candidate?"

"No." Matt risked a glance away from threading through the curving residential streets. "That's over, Temple. No more nights out. I'm pulling the plug."

"Really! We can get back to normal. I'm thrilled!"

Matt spared her a quirky smile. "As a professional counselor, I can't promise *any*one can get back to normal."

She grinned. "Just think. If Max has cracked the mystery, maybe we can put Kitty the Cutter in the hands of the police for whatever crime she's been doing and we'll all be safe and happy and able to go our own ways."

"You are way too bouncy for five in the morning. This the street?"

"Yes, eighth house on the right, with the shutters."

"Nice."

"They're metal and close over the windows."

"*Hmm.* Fort Knox. I'm going to approach with caution." Matt slowed the Jaguar to a silent idle. "Let's just leave the car doors ajar, instead of slamming them. This is where Molina was attacked."

"That's silly," Temple whispered, doing as he said. "Max is in residence there now. Mr. International Agent."

Nevertheless, they both walked along the grass, not on the walkway.

Near the front door, a black cat waited.

"A stray. Five A.M. is when feral cats hunt. Way too small to be Louie," Temple whispered to Matt.

"More the type of the Crystal Phoenix mascot," he agreed.

"Midnight Louise. Face it, Matt, every black cat looks alike in the dark. Except Louie with his white whiskers."

By then, the cat was twining in and out of their ankles so persistently that they almost tripped over it. As they moved to step past, the cat arched its back, flared its fluffy fur into a dark spiky halo.

Then it stared intently behind them and darted away.

Matt was staring ahead. "The door's ajar. I don't like that."

"Max *is* expecting us."

"He's a security freak. He'd never do that."

"No, he wouldn't," Temple said. "What do we do?"

"Backtrack and call the police."

"Not Molina?"

"Regular police," Matt said. "Report a robbery. We don't want to get Max in deeper with Molina."

"Good plan."

That hadn't been Temple speaking, but a woman from inside the house. She had a faint Irish accent. She also held a gun that caught a bit of streetlight gleam.

She came out, as sleek as Louie in a black spandex catsuit, and walked around them more than once, like a human version of the curious cat on the doorstep.

"Go in. I'll follow."

Matt stepped directly between Temple and Kathleen O'Connor and her gun. They walked in like convicts, in a single row.

"Go right in, and go right," Kathleen said.

Temple led them into the main room, where Max was crumpled on the floor in front of one of two massive leather theater-style chairs. Kathleen perched her hip on the other chair's arm, swinging her free leg.

Her foot nudged Max's hip. "Had a sudden urge to nap and forgot to bring his gun along."

Temple eyed the blood streaks running down the side of Max's face.

"May be out cold," Kathleen told her. "Maybe has a concussion, poor lad. Maybe a blow to the head will revive his absent memory. Maybe it has killed him. I haven't time or inclination to look."

Temple supposed Kathleen had lured them there via Max's cell phone. But why?

"Here we are," Kathleen said. "Four sides of a romantic quadrangle." She used the gun as a pointer. "I was with Max. Then he was with Temple, then she was with Matt. Then Matt was with me."

Temple stared wildly at Matt.

"It was a platonic relationship," Matt said calmly. "That was a healthy change for her, and, of course, I was coerced into it."

"How?" Temple asked.

"The usual threats against a significant other. That's been her modus operandi from the first."

"Don't!" Kathleen yelled, spitting out each of the next words separately. "Don't speak about me as if I wasn't here." She pointed the gun at all three in turn: Max, Temple, Matt.

"You've always been here with us," Matt said gently. "Nobody's thought more about you, learned more about you, cared more about you, in a way, than anybody."

Kathleen paused, suspicious, but caught by the idea, a new way of looking at the lethal dance she'd involved them all in.

Out of the corner of her eye, Temple sensed something moving. It was the black cat from outside, padding silently into the room. It walked over to a waist-high bookcase and lofted elegantly atop it, behind Kathleen.

"Do *you* care about me?" Kathleen gibed, jerking the gun toward Temple.

Temple considered, trying not to watch the second

black cat silently entering and circling around behind Kathleen O'Connor to jump atop a desk. She adopted Matt's steady, reasonable tone.

"Max did, for a few days long ago. He remembered that only days ago. He loved you long ago in Northern Ireland. I don't know if you've knocked that out of his memory again, if he isn't dead. Matt has to love you, not personally, but because of his idiotically forgiving religious beliefs. Love the sinner, hate the sin. Me? Not so much."

Kathleen's short breathy laugh almost made Temple jump more than the gun had. "Women don't forgive. That's our advantage. Men think they control everything, including us, so they can afford to condescend."

The third black cat moved in the same stately, silent manner into the room and circled all the way around to Kathleen's left side.

Temple risked a glance at Matt. He was trying not to stare at Kathleen's gun-bearing arm. The weapon *was* pretty unnerving. In all her risky adventures, Temple had never been held at gunpoint like this. Fear had twisted her guts into a Celtic knot of anxiety.

The subtle purposeful entrance of the cats had been calming. If Kitty the Cutter had been the second Darth Vader at Neon Nightmare, she'd know how much damage a coordinated pack of angry cats could do.

But who were these cats, beyond the two she knew, Midnight Louise, the first in, and Midnight Louie, *not* present and accounted for? She recalled the eerie way she'd suddenly find Louie sitting beside her on the sofa, and notice him gone later, never suspecting he'd come or gone until he was just *there*. Or not.

Matt tried to deflect Kathleen's attention from Temple. "You haven't found another razor," he noted.

Kathleen stared daggers at him, and the gun trembled in her tighter, angry grip.

"Better you use a gun," Matt said. "You can't cut yourself with it, hurt yourself again."

That triggered some hesitancy. She licked her lips. Lifted her other palm to expose a dark slash, a long scab.

The *fourth* black cat was shambling down the hall, limping but silent. Temple glimpsed ragged fur. It circled the chair directly behind Kathleen and leaped atop the opposite arm to stare balefully at the woman. Temple held her breath.

She kept her eyes firmly away, but had an impression of a "cat from alley cat hell" expression. This was the nerviest cat present, and it was not Midnight Louie. Yet.

"Why did you really come here?" Matt was asking. "It wasn't for us. What did you want from Max, because you will never get it now, whether he's dead or alive. You can kill everyone you ever thought took something from you because they tried to have a good life, and then what will you do? You destroy your oldest enemy, you're alone."

A fifth black shadow from the hall took a hard right turn and walked right between Matt and Temple and Kitty the Cutter. Midnight Louie sat right down in front of her and stared straight up at her, as if expecting a treat.

He got it sooner than expected as a gunshot exploded in the room . . . just as Max's hand shot out from the floor and jerked Kathleen's ankle out from under her . . . as Matt pushed Temple behind him and rushed the falling woman, grabbing her flailing wrist . . . as Midnight Louie leaped for the gun-toting hand and sank his one-inch fangs into it . . . as the cat on the chair arm leaped straight for Kathleen's face with a Viking battle cry, and as the other three cats pooled on the floor around Kathleen, attacking anything black spandex or white flesh they could claim.

Matt grunted and fell back in front of Temple. She

had gone down on her knees beside him before he had completely landed.

"Matt, my God! Matt! Did she shoot you?"

Temple heard another curdling scream and looked up to see Midnight Louie leaping at the half-fallen Kathleen and leaving four deep claw marks across her ivory-white cheek.

Max was crawling across the floor, one hand slamming the gun it held down like a peg leg as he came, blood pouring down his determined face. "Where?" he demanded.

Matt had fallen back, one hand waving over his chest, searching a source for the pain. Blood blossomed when he pressed the shirt down over his left side. Temple was using her cell phone to call 911.

Max hefted himself up on his hands and leaned over Matt. "Left side."

"The heart," Temple gasped.

"Way down." Max shook his head and shed blood drops like a wet dog. "Sweet spot. Okay." He patted Matt's arm and rolled over on his back beside him.

"Max?" Temple asked through the shakes and her soundless tears.

"Too hardheaded to kill."

Sirens were already screaming in the distance.

Temple looked up. The cats were gone, and so was Kitty the Cutter, only some spots of blood on the hardwood floor showing where she'd been.

Chapter 52

Astral Protection

The sirens of the ambulances and cop cars have faded for good.

The front door is shut, the neighborhood peaceful again.

A sliver of light halos the rooftops.

Dawn is on the way but the streetlamps are still lit.

It is the magic time between dusk and dawn, night and day, hunting and resting from the hunt.

One by one, the Cat Pack reassembles on the front doorstep.

I was first to arrive, and am tending my right mitt, where several nail sheaths have been yanked out untimely. Miss Kitty the Cutter will bear my brand for life.

"Quite a right cross, Pops." Midnight Louise has sat down beside me.

"Not bad boxing," says Ma Barker, coming up on the other side, "for a domestic layabout."

"I keep telling you, Ma, I am no domestic slave, but a roommate with rights to come and go as I please."

"Your roommate is lucky to have you," adds Blackula, who has reappeared too. "But did we not do good? Pitch and I, we slip into that risky joint like Persians fresh from fancy manicure jobs at the groomer's."

"Yeah," says Pitch, "we were like pitty-pat—whatchamacallit?—ballerinas."

"Not *that* fancy," Blackula growls.

It is the usual after-rumble mumble-grumble among the guys. Ma gives me a parting cuff. Among the guys, and gals.

I amble to the curb where the Jaguar was parked. Miss Temple drove it along after the ambulances. Very gingerly.

The EMT people were swift, efficient, and talked loud enough to overhear.

Mr. Matt was all right. The bullet entered and exited side tissue. Mr. Matt will be fine. Mr. Max is going into observation to ensure he will be fine. I must hurry home to comfort Miss Temple when she finally gets back there.

I am proud that we three guys did not allow one hair on her head to be harmed through our conjoined efforts. I am also pleased that the Cat Pack under the direction of Midnight Investigations, Inc., played such a key role in the view of all concerned, especially Miss Kitty the Cutter. *Shudder.* It is ironic that she bears a nickname that falsely connects her with us of the superior breed. I am hoping if there are little gray men out there somewhere, they will abduct her to another solar system.

Maybe the humans could have handled it without us, but we added a nice note of distraction, not to mention drama.

I look back to see Ma Barker and her Cat Pack members and Miss Midnight Louise have vanished to make their secret ways home, as I should be doing.

Something strange shimmers in the fading oval of illumination the nearest streetlight casts on the pavement. I amble toward the phenomenon, hoping it is not extraterrestrial. I have had my ration of otherworldly visitors. I grow alarmed to see a familiar shape becoming clearer with every step.

"Greetings, Louie," says Karma. Her blue eyes and pale golden coat and white feet seem almost translucent in the waning light.

"What are you doing here? You are a recluse. You never leave the penthouse atop the Circle Ritz, like the snobby Sacred Cat of Burma you claim to be."

"Who do you think drew Blackula and Pitch to the scene? Who do you believe coordinated the ancient Five-Cat Surround-and-Overwhelm strategy my breed used for hundreds of years to protect the temple priests of the mountains of Burma?"

"Yeah, yeah, I heard the legend that the Birman's coat coloring went from white to golden overnight after raiders killed an old temple priest, but the toes of their feet kept the pure white of his soul, and they also got the goddess's sapphire blue eyes. It is actually quite a tale. I helped an ex-priest survive here tonight, but I do not expect to get white tippy-toes out of it, and am glad. That would be a real cleaning problem for a street cat like me."

Karma sighs. I have never heard a cat sigh like a dog so much. Her eyes grow as sharply blue as Miss Lieutenant Molina's when she is on the warpath.

"The legend ends," she intones, "'Woe to he who brings the end to one of these marvelous beasts, even if he didn't mean to. He will surely suffer the most cruel torments until the soul he upset has been appeased.'"

"That's pretty definite, but I have no intention of ending anything about you besides this conversation."

"Why do you resist the mystical side of life, Louie? Perhaps you do not realize what my breed has survived. Only two Birman cats were alive in Europe at the end of World War Two, Orloff and Xenia."

"Manx, there must be a lot of cruelly suffering souls for that. News to me, but it definitely sounds like your breed lucked out, since Xenia is obviously a foxy lady and Orloff is definitely a boy's name."

She nods graciously. "So our breed has been reborn to thrive and be prized, in the process acquiring a certain mystical cachet."

"Yeah, my people and me are all after a hidden cache ourselves."

Karma sighs and dabs a white glove over one ear, as if my words are too, too lowly to penetrate that precious orifice. "The wisdom of catkind is lost on you, Louie, but after the stresses of this night wear off, you may thank me at my customary shrine."

I would have said, "Well, la-ti-dah to you too," except that I realize Karma is fading with the lamplight into a mere hint of gold body and white toes, with the blue peepers still bold and beautiful.

"You are addressing my astral projection, poor boy, and if you wish to keep displaying your ignorance, you may do so in person when you return home."

And out the baby blues go, leaving me talking to myself on a deserted sidewalk as signs of suburban life stir all around me, from front doors opening to collect newspapers, to dogs being let out to water the grass and bark, to garage doors starting to grumble open.

Speaking of grumbling, that is how I leave the deserted scene of our mass clawdown with Kathleen O'Connor, wishing all a speedy recovery and good karma. As for Kitty the Cutdown, I hope the bedbugs get her.

Chapter 53

Two Close for Comfort

Matt dreamed he was swimming in an infinity pool that wasn't an optical illusion, but a river of water that went on and on forever, a lane of illuminated artificially turquoise water, his exact body temperature.

But his head wasn't turning from side to side to breathe, and something was biting at his side, a grim, slim fish. *Barracuda.*

He surfaced, blinking water out of his eyes, feeling the dozens of teeth still stinging, yet the sensation was blurring into an ache rather than a sharp pain.

"That was some sleeping pill," a familiar voice to his left said.

Matt turned his head in the water and saw a bizarre face. The man wore a helmet of bound gauze, like a mummy. His head was propped on one elbow. High and dry. In bed.

Matt realized his swim trunks were some sort of . . . apron? . . . wrapping him, and he was in a bed too.

"We have to stop meeting like this," Max Kinsella said. "Love the concentric circles on the gown, though. Mine has little dancing triangles on it."

Matt struggled to sit up, but stopped when the pain in his side intensified. He remembered the sound of a firecracker exploding somewhere on his torso. Oh, yeah. Shot.

"Hospital?" he asked Kinsella.

"Just for observation, but your repair job was a bit longer and rougher than mine."

"When is it?" Matt asked.

"About seven P.M. of the day after the night before."

"Temple's all right?"

Kinsella hesitated.

"She's all right?" Matt had to know right now.

"Better than us, physically. A wee bit agitated otherwise."

"You've seen her?"

"She flew by to soothe your sleeping brow and leave this." Max elevated a couple pieces of typing paper.

Matt couldn't focus for a few fuzzy seconds. Max's long, muscled freakishly bare left arm handed the paper across the chasm between the beds.

"They put us in the same room?" Matt asked, finding the fact irritating.

Kinsella nodded to a curtain on his left. "The same *ward*. We have a ruptured appendix and bleeding ulcer down the line."

Matt found himself still frowning. "What are these papers?"

"Printout of a digital story on the Vegas newspaper

site. It won't hit print until tomorrow. You'll want to study your lines."

"My lines?"

"Just read it. I predict you and Temple will set a wedding date pronto."

"What?" Matt, still woozy, realized the bandages made it look like Kinsella had an inverted white cereal bowl on his head. Ludicrous. He bit his lip to smother a grin. "And what happened to you?"

"I had a gun-butt contusion—a love tap from Kathleen—a bit bigger than a quarter on the back of my temple. They decided they had to shave off a section of hair the size of a grapefruit in order to slap a few stitches and some iodine on it."

"The Mystifying Max without half his mane? Excuse me for finding that funny."

Kinsella nodded at Matt's sheet-swaddled torso. "You now have matching scars from Kitty the Cutter, left and right. I guess we could say you're well balanced."

Matt shrugged and noticed something over Kinsella's hospital-gowned shoulder. Something as red as blood.

"Roses?"

"Wild Irish roses, thorns not removed." Kinsella made a wry face. "Many condolences to you. It looks like I've successfully diverted Kathleen's attentions back to me. The card is signed with crimson nail enamel, 'Forever.' "

"Man, I wouldn't wish that woman's attentions on a serial killer."

"Maybe you've softened her up some."

Matt shook his head, and then was sorry for jolting it. "Doubt it. I did get down to the first stratum of her psychosis. I think she hates you for getting there first."

"Figures." Kinsella had always been calm about things that would drive Matt crazy.

"How'd she get the drop on you before we arrived?" Matt wondered.

"Embarrassing. Still some cotton wool between my ears from the amnesia, I guess. Slowed my reaction time. Speaking of embarrassing, you'd better read that stuff."

Matt shifted and spotted a whole line of floral offerings on the narrow ledge of his window. "It's been too short a time for flowers—"

"Oh, word got out fast on the Temple Barr Telegraph, and Teleflora. . . . Read 'em and weep." Kinsella nodded again at the papers.

Before Matt could do either task—read or weep—a nurse in scrubs covered with colorful teddy bears whisked around the corner bearing two identical and stunning floral arrangements of purple irises and yellow tulips.

"More for you, Mr. Kinsella," she chirruped, "and for Mr. Devine."

When Matt eyed her inquiringly, she caroled out the name of the donor so the whole ward could hear. "From Tony Valentine. Lovely surname."

She was gone and Matt was scratching his head, which he could do, because it wasn't swathed with a ridiculous hat of gauze.

"That's my agent," he told Kinsella. "Why's he sending *you* flowers?"

"I told you. Read the story. Temple said it was the best she could do on instant notice."

"What would Temple have to do with it—?" His glance fell on the larger-type headline on the pages. GOSSIP-A-GO-GO. "Oh, no."

"Oh, yes. She had to explain the assault scene not only to the police but the media. She's the mistress of spin, no doubt about it. We'll have a hard time living up to her inspired improvisation."

Matt pushed himself up against the pillows, winced and sighed simultaneously, and began to read. "Oh my

God!" He glanced at Max. "That wasn't swearing; it was a religious ejaculation."

"Good thing I'm familiar with Catholic terminology, or I'd have taken your explanation for something else."

"Enough with the jokes, Kinsella. Did you *see* what this two-bit entertainment columnist is saying?"

"All too clearly."

"Good grief." Matt began reading snippets aloud in disbelief. "'Attempted robbery at semi-retired magician's house reveals an intriguing new entertainment deal in the works. Is the "hot new couple" in town Max Kinsella, aka the Mystifying Max, and syndicated radio shrink Matt Devine? What kind of act could they dream up? Magic and mind-reading? Sounds promising. These two local celebrities are a reverse Siegfried and Roy, with the brunet of the duo lean and mean and the blond warm and fuzzy.'"

"Gag," Matt said, for the first and hopefully last time in his life.

"Swearing for real is far more satisfying than sounding like a teenager," Kinsella said.

"Shut up. 'The Odd Coupling—' No!"

"Yes. It gets worse."

"'. . . could have betrayed a big secret on the showbiz front. According to well-known publicist Temple Barr, who reps both men, Matt Devine suffered a flesh wound when caught in the crossfire after a robber broke into Kinsella's Las Vegas home near dawn yesterday.'

"'The robber knocked out Kinsella before escaping without any ill-gotten goods. While police investigate, we can speculate. According to Barr, the men had been visiting backstage with local headliners into the wee hours and surprised the miscreant when they finished their tour at Kinsella's home. Let's hope this is the start of a beautiful friendship, if not a performing alliance.'"

Matt lowered the pages. "This implies a whole lot of stuff."

"I was saying, you'll want to marry Temple ASAP, just to quash the rumors about 'us.'"

"I want to marry her ASAP anyway." Matt groaned. "This is worse than getting shot."

"No, the worst thing will be telling Temple you've been dating Kathleen O'Connor for the past couple weeks."

Matt felt his stomach knot up tighter than the pain had accomplished so far. "It was the only way to keep that psycho from going after Temple."

"It's not what you did and why you did it; it's that you didn't tell her. Secrets are not a healthy foundation for a marriage."

"You're telling *me* that, Mr. Professional Prevaricator? You kept her in the dark about your counterintelligence activities for more than a year."

"And I'm not the one marrying Temple."

Matt sat up in bed and put his head in his hands.

"And," Kinsella said, "*you*'re not the one with a fresh head injury on top of a brain crash."

The guy's rueful good humor was grating on Matt. "Kathleen told Temple about our enforced 'trysts' while she held us all at gunpoint. The big shock is already over. And where is the gun anyway? You and I were hauled out of there plenty fast by the ambulances."

"Back in its safe hidey-hole in the house," Kinsella said. "I was more mobile at the time than you."

"I still can't figure how Kathleen got the gun away from you."

Kinsella shook his head, and then winced. "I'm not one hundred percent, Devine. And I never was invincible. I'm not sure how she did it, either, but I'm not worrying about it. Her next moves are worth worrying about, but I think she'll be dealing direct, now that she's finally found me."

"'She's finally found you.' Funny, that could be the title of a romantic ballad instead of a stalking song."

"Speaking of which," Kinsella said, sitting up in bed. "Temple has finally found you again."

The sound of hurrying high heels echoed in the hall. Temple appeared around the corner, a burst of color and energy.

"You can come home, Matt," she announced joyfully. "You're released. I've brought your clothes and have extra tote bags for the flowers—oh, there are more—we can hang the totes on the wheelchair that's coming. . . ."

"I'm released and I need a wheelchair?" Matt sat up, his legs dangling off the high hospital bed like a child's. "How come *he's* not getting out? I had the more serious wound."

"Hospitals kick women out a day after childbirth nowadays," Temple said, nodding at Kinsella. "Max will be released soon too. Thanks for the quick defensive motion in my behalf, Max." She aimed a smile Kinsella's way before stretching up to pull Matt's bed curtain closed.

She turned and beamed at Matt without waiting for Kinsella's acknowledgment. Her voice went low and intimate. "And now I get to undress you and dress you and undress you again."

Obviously, Matt realized with relief as she kissed him long and deep, the talk they needed to have about his devil's deal with Kathleen O'Connor was not the first thing on Temple's wish list.

Chapter 54

Cat and Mouser

Once the happy couple had wafted away in a halo of triumph and heady scent, Max sat up in bed himself. He leaned out to yank Matt's curtain back to its mooring and morosely eyed the empty bed and flower shelf.

His hands worried at the gauze head wrappings until they were a pile on the sheets. Maybe he could shape the unshaved hair and bald spot into a weird punk Mohawk.

He plucked at the dippy hospital gown and wondered where they'd hidden his clothes, although they were likely as bloody as Devine's. He didn't have a personal sprite to play wardrobe mistress and caretaker, so he'd probably have to wait until the release papers came.

Max hated being hemmed in by bureaucracy.

Measured footsteps sounded in the hall. Maybe the

hand and foot of hospital authority was heading his way with his walking papers.

Someone tall and authoritative rounded the doorjamb.

"Lieutenant," he greeted C. R. Molina. "Have you come to 'undress me and dress me and undress me again'?"

"Hell no." She frowned at his head and face, then eyed the empty bed. "I see I've been spared the mawkish departing dialogue of your likely coconspirators."

"You've got that right."

"So," she said, "we can have a private sickbed tête-à-tête. Don't tear up at a possible sympathy visit. I came to find out what really happened and consult on our mutual projects."

"What?" Max asked. "You didn't see the online digital news item? *Gossip-a-Go-Go* has the whole scoop ready to go into print."

"I don't rely on Internet little nothings. I saw the police report, and my suspicions stirred instantly."

"What tipped you off?"

"You and Matt Devine. Together at five in the morning? You taken by surprise and conked on the head like a bloody amateur? Matt taking a gunshot, possibly in your defense? Simply not believable."

"Granted that Devine and I were rushed off untimely on stretchers, but the police officers present seemed satisfied by our account of an armed robber surprising us."

"They don't know the cast list like I do. Now, I can see a certain *other* someone on the scene. I could maybe believe the two of you mixed it up over the affections of the ubiquitous Miss Temple Barr. Yet that's too melodramatic. Instead, I could see you both protecting our heroine. I smell the blood of a celebrated but elusive psycho on the scene."

By then she had paced past the foot of his bed and was at the flower shelf on Max's side, reading the accompanying cards. "Purple and red and yellow. Rather lurid. Tony Valentine, *hmm*. He's the big-time agent."

"You make that sound like an accusation," Max objected. "He *is* an agent. Mine, in fact."

"And Matt Devine's. My, my, my." She bent to sniff the roses. "From a woman, of course. The intriguing Revienne Schneider you don't trust? 'Forever.' And to think she just met you weeks ago. You certainly are the versatile Romeo."

Max shrugged helplessly.

"And you succeed better with . . . foreign females."

The name of Kathleen O'Connor seemed to be on the tip of her tongue, which her speculative expression had just exposed. Max had to admit he found her interrogation techniques stimulating, especially when unconscious.

Would she or wouldn't she bring Kathleen openly into the matter?

She put the "Forever" card down on the shelf and circled his bed again. "The crime scene techs reported an odd . . . element in your house."

Max raised his eyebrows.

"A number of paw prints were found in the dust atop several tables."

"You've broken me, Lieutenant. I admit everything. My housekeeping skills are nil. I haven't dusted the place since I returned from my sudden European sojourn, or even hired a service. Have mercy on me."

She pulled the visitor's chair from Devine's side, sat, and folded her arms over her chest. "Additionally . . ."

This was interesting. Max assumed she'd now produce news that a third blood type had been spilled besides his and Matt's. He had the common type O, but he had no idea what anyone else was.

Molina continued. "*Additionally*, three cat claw sheaths were found near the lone pattern of blood on the floor, which indicated drops of blood falling, not spatter from a weapon. Apparently you boys were neat and only sopped up your clothing. It would take quite a deep, targeted piercing to produce those lovely little blood blossoms. And there were cat hairs all over the place. Did Garry Randolph ever own a cat?"

"Not to my knowledge. And can anyone ever be said to 'own' a cat?"

"Yes. I do. Two. Both are law-abiding indoor kitties who keep their claw sheaths to themselves."

"I'm happy for you all."

"And the cat hairs present were all black. Does that suggest anything to you?"

"Just that a black cat was present."

"All from different cats."

"Really, Lieutenant. You seem to be pursuing a distracting side alley on this investigation. It isn't even in your jurisdiction. Nobody died. Next you'll be telling me that a herd of cats hauled off the gun."

"The bullet was embedded in a chair. A Walther PPK, by the way. Easy to hide."

"Excellent weapon. Too bad the intruder ran off with it."

"Fancy for a burglar. Any old Ruger would do." Molina slapped her hands on her khaki-clad knees.

She could stand a little pizzazz in her pantsuit wardrobe, Max thought, but powder blue clearly wouldn't do. Meanwhile, she was examining his outfit du jour.

"Green and blue tiny triangles. Are they to match your various eye colors or romantic life? Definitely not your style, though."

"I thought you said you wanted to consult on my assignment. Not on my wardrobe."

"I saw you dismissing my serviceable khaki," she told him. "Since you won't squeal on what happened early this morning, I have some information for you. First, did you get anywhere on finding resurfacing mob activity around town?"

"Nothing more than an organized interest in safeguarding past crime scenes, like that of the spies in the casino ceilings or Effinger's death."

"Devine outdid you there too, then."

Max noted that "too" and reserved payback for the future. "What'd he get?"

"A tip from a long-retired cop I sicced him on. Seems the old guy mistook him for a host of a radio crime show called *The Midnight Hour* and got talkative."

"That's a good ploy, but probably accidental on Devine's part. Everybody pants to be on media these days."

"Tell me about it. Mariah, especially. Anyway, Woodrow Wetherly named some old-time made men who might still be around. So I tiptoed through the mug shot archives. One of them turned out to be our Paradise Road vic, and another two were captured on the exterior videocams of the Cabana Club nightspot near the Area Fifty-four lot."

"Enough to arrest?"

"Yes. But the big news is the identity of the corpse."

"Darn! That'll knock the forthcoming Kinsella–Devine lounge act right off the chat boards."

"Giacchino Petrocelli." The satisfied glint in Molina's blue eyes made them dance like the Bellagio fountains.

Max mulled the name, pronouncing it correctly as Jackino Petrochelli. "Is that the name of an entrée or a dude?"

"Definitely a dude, a dangerous dude so hot, he dropped out of sight years ago. Never found. The Jimmy Hoffa of Las Vegas. He was known about town as Jack the Hammer."

"For his weapon of choice? Let me guess. He smashed the fingers of errant underlings or gamblers who couldn't pay up."

Molina shook her head with a smile, pleased enough to let herself look pretty. "Way off. *Jack*hammers. Construction was big then too, and he'd jackhammer his victims to death. If you saw him coming wearing overalls and a welding mask, you knew your fate."

"No wonder he had to disappear. But why kill him now and dump the body on that unlikely site?"

Molina stood up and replaced the chair. "Your job to find out. And I want you off those old casino deaths and on the Santiago situation. Why was he on that site and why was he killed?"

"That's a current crime. It's risky for you to use a civilian anywhere near that investigation."

Max needed his persuasive Irish tongue more than ever. He did *not* want to get any deeper into Santiago's death. He did not want to involve the Cloaked Conjuror until he was sure there was no other alternative.

"Why? Your head addled from the latest shaking?"

"I don't know yet."

"All your memories didn't rush back in a flood when you woke up?"

"No. Nothing."

"Forget anything new?"

"Not that I know of. Yet."

"Good." She leaned down and lowered her voice. "I did my part. I did bring you a present. Interpol gave Revienne Schneider a glowing report. Honored in her field, associated only with impeccably first-class facilities, like a certain one in the Swiss Alps, tireless campaigner for her signature charity. Happy? My advice? Marry her."

Max frowned. "Too much the Girl Scout?" Suspicion was a horrible thing to waste.

Molina's eyebrows lifted, but before she could comment, a heavenly scent wafted into the ward along with the measured click of high heels. Revienne herself appeared as if announced, her arms cradling fragrant white freesia stalks like a bride.

"Oh, sorry," Revienne said, looking more startled than sorry.

Introductions seemed in order. "Revienne," Max said, "I'd like you to meet Carmen Molina. Carmen, Revienne Schneider." He'd really want to say, *Hot blonde, meet icy brunette.* Hey, they were another *Gossip-a-Go-Go* "Odd Coupling."

"Charmed," Molina said, not sounding it. "I was just leaving. I'll ask an orderly to bring a vase for those gorgeous flowers."

"How thoughtful, yes," Revienne said, sitting on the far edge of Max's bed and letting the stalks fall to the blanket in a swooning wave of scent.

Molina vanished like Giacchino Petrocelli.

"Max!" Revienne leaned forward to touch his hair. "A head injury. I came as soon as that insane news item started being reported on the local TV news shows."

Max closed his eyes. More unwelcome publicity, he thought before surrendering to the moment. Freesias were one of the most sweetly scented flowers, and so European. Despite their overbearing odor, he could still smell Revienne's signature perfume as she leaned over him with the hovering concern of an angel.

"You're overwhelmed," she said. "It is the injury, or my flowers? The injury hasn't affected your memory?"

"It wouldn't dare forget you," he said with a smile. "Truthfully, I don't know yet. And you always overwhelm me, whether you're flower-bearing or not."

"Have they caught the criminal who did this? And is poor Mr. Devine all right?"

"I'm just dented, but he was sliced. He'll be fine but scarred."

"And you, your poor head."

"Lucky to be here to see you again."

A nurse with a clipboard and a sack of something appeared. "Good news, Mr. Kinsella. You're fine and free to go. Just sign this. Your clothes are washed and dried." She lifted an arm and eyed Revienne, reaching up for the curtain. "I'll assist you into them, and then we'll wheel you out."

Max almost expected her cheery voice to ask, *Won't that be fun?*

"Your visitor can meet you in the hall, and I'll find some more bags for the flowers." She stared at the two showy arrangements on the shelf. "Those will be difficult to transport, but we'll manage."

Max shrugged apology and gazed up at Revienne.

This was not the kind of reunion he'd envisioned.

She bent down and kissed him. "I'm so glad you'll be fine, Mr. Randolph, darling."

The nurse's brow wrinkled to hear the pseudonymous surname he'd used on the run, but Revienne didn't notice. "I'll see you home and get you settled." She turned to the nurse. "Please. Don't worry about anything. I'm a doctor. He's in good hands with me."

Revienne's car was a silver Saab. He wondered whether it was rented or borrowed.

Thinking about such things kept his mind off the humiliation of being carted out of the hospital by two women, people staring, like a helpless papoose.

His hair, not to mention his head, was a mess. Now he understood what women meant by that phrase. Humiliation.

At least his legs worked well once he'd struggled out of the wheelchair. He set the passenger seat on recline and sighed, hoping no one on the streets could see him in this position.

"Rest easy," Revienne said, amusement in her voice as

she drove the car down the driveway. "Less than twenty-four hours ago, you were facing an armed robber. Will you be safe at home alone now?"

"Yes, I'll be safe at home alone," he heard himself growl. "Damn it."

"Max. Don't pout. You're in far better condition than when we fled the Swiss clinic. I detect no greater memory deficit."

"Swell."

"Swell? The wound on your head is swelling?"

"An American expression, like 'peachy keen.'"

"Max. Go slow." A fingertip reached out to press his lips. I don't know all this American patois."

He refrained doing anything untoward with the finger. "It's called slang."

"What a crude word."

"You're right."

"I'll get you settled at your home when my GPS gets us to Mojave Way. I love GPS! One can be at home anywhere. If only we'd had it in the Alps."

She'd pronounced Mojave as it was spelled, not with an *h* for the *j*. The Spanish way.

It reminded Max she was a stranger in a strange land, as he had been on her turf recently, and he should give her the benefit of the doubt. Why did he have to be so continually on guard?

"Mo-hah-vee." He corrected her anyway. "The desert extends into Mexico, so it's a Spanish word."

She repeated the pronunciation. "The desert is like me, half one thing and another."

He smiled at her. "French and German."

"It gets dark so fast here in Las Vegas," she commented, hunching to stare through the windshield.

"That's because we're in a valley. The sky above is bright, but the shadows are creeping inexorably in from the mountains."

"We will have a desert sunset for your homecoming."
She flashed him a glance. "I can stay, if you like."

"Can you do something with this industrial haircut?"

"No. Likely no." There was a lovely foreign lilt to her
English, but it wasn't as hypnotic as Kathleen O'Connor's
Irish mist of an intonation.

Was Molina right? Did he like foreign women, or only
possibly treacherous ones? No, Max thought. There was
Temple. And there was no one like Temple.

He hadn't answered Revienne, he realized. He'd always be grateful for her aid and comfort in the darkest
moments of his life, and his ego could use some cod-
dling, but it felt dishonest.

"I'll be all right," he told her.

The car pulled up in front of his house in twilight.

Revienne made a happy sound at landing on target
and got out to circle the car and extract him.

Max squinted at his front door, now shut and not even
bearing crime scene tape, so minor the incident inside
had been to the authorities.

A cat was sitting there. No, two. Did he have double
vision? He squinted hard. Only one. It wasn't a black
cat. Its form was pale, and it seemed to be haloed by
a . . . sunset glow. He stared until his eyes watered and
he blinked.

"Max," Revienne asked, "are you all right?"

"No," he answered, "but I might be getting a long-
overdue headache."

The cat was gone.

First you see it. Then you don't. The essence of magic.
Like Kathleen O'Connor.

Max didn't view this as a reassuring omen for any of
them.

Midnight Louie Discusses Alien Species

At last! At last I get to speak of alien species in general and specifically in a literary work with which I am associated. Before I begin to strut my stuff, I must take huge exception to one of the canine breed being pictured here in *my* Tailpiece.

Even if he is unusual and cute.

Nothing personal, Rens. It is just the usual territorial dispute.

Now, I am sure all are wondering if I believe in aliens, ancient or otherwise.

I must admit all the whoop-de-do about the subject during my most recent adventure pretty much deflates the hope of anything of a genuinely alien nature showing up unannounced in Las Vegas, other than the usual cast of tourists blowing off some crazy steam and their out-of-this-world array of eye-blinding Hawaiian shirts.

I do wonder why no one besides the eccentric Silas T. Farnum ever saw that Vegas was made for an all-out alien-themed attraction. That "invisible" stunt fell as flat as Santiago on its unseen nose, though. That was a one-trick pony, and that horse has definitely come in last.

However, I do believe that Earth has been, is now, and will be visited by aliens.

After studying the piles of book covers, posters, and other alien propaganda that popped up around the Area 54 site, I admit my opinion on the subject has undergone a radical turnaround. I am no longer an unbeliever. They are out there and, even more obvious, they are us!

I would have to make many trips to ancient ruins to document my theory (accompanied by a camera crew, of course), but it is completely clear that the ancient race that visited and reshaped earthlings through the millennia are we of the feline nation.

"Little gray men," aka "Grays"? I beg to differ. Those were large gray cats.

Regard the huge, almond-shaped eyes, all dark pupils. Only cats can expand their pupils so completely.

That uniform gray color. Skin or . . . velvet-napped gray fur?

When ancient cats walked the earth, they no doubt would be a breed named *Felinus erectus* and strode upright on two rear legs. If they were not exactly the hairless breed known as a Sphinx today, their sleek gray fur made them adaptable to various climates.

Even the name "Sphinx" is a giveaway of the ancient alien lineage. For, of course, this superior breed of space travelers first descended on the ancient Egyptians when they were living in mud huts.

The sage Grays saw potential in these large, ungainly two-legs and proceeded to give them the secrets to farming and constructing weapons, chariots, and barges, working iron and gold, and the literal height of civilization then, and still a marvel today, the Pyramids.

Many were scribes who cleverly invented and clawed out the hieroglyphs.

No wonder we cats were worshipped and had our own great goddess in the mighty Egyptian pantheon, Bast.

As for the four-fingered "hands" portrayed on one of these film aliens, E.T., one digit is the opposable thumb. Alas, the instructors the ancient aliens left behind—through centuries of understandable but lamentable inbreeding with species near to themselves—lost the opposable thumb, which became the dewclaw. The three remaining "fingers" then gradually separated into four, producing the classic number of shivs I bear (and bare) proudly today.

And, as history forgot the coming of these wise creatures from far out in the galaxy, their descendents were assumed to be mute, mysterious creatures of a lower order, instead of the emperors of the universe they were and are. (Some perspicacious humans actually do treat us to this day with the proper respect and pampering.)

But I state with full confidence, if one of these so-called little gray men were found in an undecomposed state and examined, it would be proved beyond any doubt that there was a cat skeleton in that alien X-ray.

I rest my case.

Very Best Fishes,

Midnight Louie, Esq.

If you'd like information about getting Midnight Lou-ie's free *Scratching Post-Intelligencer* newsletter and/or buying his custom T-shirt, contact Carole Nelson Douglas at P.O. Box 331555, Fort Worth, TX 76163-1555 or the Web site at www.carolenelsondouglas.com. E-mail: cdouglas@catwriter.com.

Tailpiece

Carole Nelson Douglas
Goes to the Dogs

Authors often donate character names for charities. Penny and her dog Rens won their names in this book at an auction at Dragon*Con science fiction/fantasy/horror convention in Atlanta, where thousands of readers and media fans congregate every Labor Day weekend.

Rens is really a mini husky Chihuahua, and here is a photo of him. I know Louie will sniff at a dog photo in his book.

Louie's long-standing feline chauvinism has forced me to mount a defense of dogs.

Not only have they won standing as "man's best friend," but they have been a woman's best friend too. Since I wrote my first novel about fifty-nine novels back, I've wanted to be sure that animal companions were in the picture.

Of course, if you put an element into a story, it's going to spring into life and demand a real role. That's how Boru, an Irish wolfhound, became a hero at the end of my first novel, *Amberleigh*, and a King Charles spaniel stood in for the entire doomed class of English Cavaliers during their seventeenth-century Civil War in *Fair Wind, Fiery Star*.

When I switched from historical adventure to high fantasy, a crabby white cat with ninety-nine lives named Felabba showed up. And she talked too. A lot.

Rambeau, the white Samoyed dog, accompanied my second fantasy heroine, Alison Carver, into the world of Veil. And more recently, noir urban fantasy heroine Delilah Street adopted a huge wolfhound-wolf cross she named Quicksilver, a good survival strategy in a post-apocalyptic Las Vegas.

So I find a girl and her dog as natural a fiction partnership as a girl and her cat.

Louie has been no slouch in having close encounters with canine characters either. Consider Nose E., the tiny dope- and drug-sniffing Maltese. Nose E. showed up in a Midnight Louie short story and then appeared in the books. Louie must admit the little fellow has one of the most dangerous jobs in the law-and-order business. Louie, however, would never put up being toted around celebrity events by some burly linebacker. He might subject himself to playing purse pussycat for a gorgeous Hollywood starlet . . . if she was strapping enough to tote his twenty pounds around on those six-inch heels, that is.

Midnight Louie is the only one of my four-footed characters to have a narrative voice. And that's because the real and original Louie was a koi-catching stray at a fancy Palo Alto motel, destined for the pound. An out-of-towner flew him back to my home state and put an extravagantly expensive ad in the classifieds (remember them?) at the newspaper (remember *them*?) I reported for. He was on the block for a dollar bill, but only to the "right" home. When I sat down to write his saga, Louie's voice took over, and I've been Louie's collaborator ever since.

We wouldn't have it any other way.